MW00426854

the gingerbread girl

By: Wes McCloud

Copyright 2018 ©

Please visit my facebook page to learn more about me and my other novels.

www.facebook.com/wesmccloudauthor

Preface (or something like one)

Am I seriously writing another one of these preface things? This story has origins…good god, back when I was like twelve years old I think. I had this idea of a tale where a down-and-out mechanic named Jerry has this chance encounter with a rich businessman at a local truck stop. They talk and bullshit for awhile and soon they plan this high-stakes, illegal street race down route 70 in broad daylight. Jerry haphazardly signs this deal with the rich dude (that I never named, but pictured as Brad Pitt in my head) Well, "Brad Pitt" turns out to be the devil and Jerry loses the race and also his soul because Jerry was too stupid to read the fine print in the contract. Good job, Jerry. So Jerry goes to Hell and the only way he can get out is by racing the devil on this monstrous, demon-filled highway to gain his freedom. The original title was Highway Hell. I actually used that name clear up until probably half a year before releasing this book. A LOT has changed since that original idea way back in whatever year that was. The story was supposed to be a horror/action type thingamajig, but the more I wrote the more I realized it was a drama. And I was okay with that. In fact I was so okay with that that I found myself getting emotional while writing this thing on more than one occasion. I can assure you I didn't cry though because men don't do that. (don't worry, it's not all sad. Some of it is pretty funny)

I decided to keep the main story arc in the era it was conceived, the good, old mid 90's. 1996 to be exact. You remember, that awesome, grungy time between the 80's and the turn of the century? Right around the proverbial death of electronic innocence. It was a tipping point, the time that we started crawling out of the sludge that was analog and fell head first into the brave new world of the Internet, 3D video games, cell phones...all this was around years prior, but came available to the average joe. And you know, that's one thing I love about this book, there's no scenes where someone's on a cellphone or talking about the internet or Twitter or Facebook.

Among other things, this book is my homage to the American muscle car. I'm not talking just Ford, or GM, or Chrysler, or whatever brand in particular, I'm talking about ALL those gorgeous, fire-breathing beasts we keep seeing less and less of out on the streets. The cars that defined power and freedom from the 50's, 60's, and 70's. Cars that had character for god's sake…Ugh, long gone are those days. Some people are gonna throw stones at me, but about the only company keeping the American Muscle car alive now is Chrysler. Dodge Challenger, anyone? Bravo, Chrysler, my hat is off to you. Ford? GM? I love you guys, but take notes. Anyway, yeah, this book is rife with cars handpicked by yours truly to play center stage with all the human (and not so human) characters. You're welcome.

Finally I'll take a second and address the fact that my main character is a lesbian. Why? Because, why not? Quite frankly when Hutch McCray walked into my head as the lead character, I tilted my head and went, "That girl is gay." I just knew she was and, you know what, it made the story all the more interesting, heartbreaking, and utterly fantastic. I fell in love with this book. I hope you will too. So with that said, I present to you, The Gingerbread Girl, a tale of demons, gingers, and muscle cars. I'll usher you into the story with the immortal words of Cassandra McCray (you'll meet her in the book)

- "Grab onto somethin' kid, shits about to get rad."

Chapters:

A Girl Named Hutch

The smell of diesel fumes and dust danced upon the breeze . It was a breeze not born from nature, but rather the constant comings and goings of the semis screaming across one another in the unending rush to keep America running. In the backdrop of the eighteen-wheeled abstract, strode a man across a dusty, open lot. His impatient pace drilled out an orchestra of haste that could only pray to be heard 'neath the chaos of the steel giants abounding. The look upon his face displayed the obvious wrinkles of repeated disgust…he had made this journey more than once under the same circumstances. Blue eyes remained transfixed across the lot as he scratched at his red beard and mustache, occasionally fending off his own ginger locks that whipped about his face every time a rig would blow past him towards the open road. His name was Ham McCray…well, in actuality, his real name was Hamlet McCray, but he had always hated that name, so much as that he'd resorted to being called the equivalent of lunchmeat in its shortening.

Sweat began to glisten upon Ham's brow as he closed the gap between himself and his destination. The perspiration was no doubt the fault of the sun rather than the pace of the trip he was on. It hadn't rained in weeks and the days held July skies that were constantly cloud barren and sweltering. That morning was no different…it was 10 a.m. and well into the eighties.

'10 a.m…10 a.m. She had electric and an alarm clock. There was no damn excuse for it', he thought as he shook his head, now only twenty paces from a tiny camper that graced the back edge of the parking lot. With only five strides remaining, he began to hear the muffled sound of music blaring away within the alloy façade directly in front of him. *'Music?...She was definitely up…no damn excuse.'* He stopped himself just a pace before the shade of the camper's awning. His eyes searched the curtain-shrouded windows for signs of movement as he nervously scratched the back of his head. He stepped back a moment, taking in the sight of the ramshackle camper in front of him. It was a 1970-something single axle, dwarf of a pull-behind, covered in umpteen shades of paint and twice as many dents. The thing barely housed a bed, stove, and a toilet that had to be emptied weekly. *'How did she live like this?'* It was a quandary that passed through his mind ever since she took up residence in that retired tin-can over two years prior. But given the recent circumstances, she really had no choice.

Ham finally gathered himself and stepped forward into the shade, his feet finding the thin layer of green, indoor-outdoor carpet that was laid out as a makeshift patio. He rapped the door a few times with his fist and stepped back, scratching at his nose in annoyance with the task. A brief moment showed no lessening of the music inside…nor a click of the door latch in front of him. Nothing. Ham was quick to step it up a notch. *'BOOM! BOOM! BOOM!'* his hand blasted the door so hard it sent a shock wave through the outer shell.

"Hutch?!" he yelled out her name to match another round of violent knocking. "Hutch, I know you're in there…I can hear that shit you call music playin'." Two steps backwards came quick after he spoke. He could see the wheeled-dwelling begin to shift ever so slightly back and forth, a sure sign she was up and about. Ham fully expected her to throw the door open any moment…but ten seconds rained down like ten minutes, once again leading into no latch jiggling, no halt to the music, not even a muffled round of her cussing him through the curtain and window pane. Ham's patience was as good as gone. With a fist drawn high and away ready to drop like a twelve pound sledge, he lurched forwards with a smirk of anger…he never found his mark. A sudden blast of air slapped his face as the paper-thin door came whirling open. Ham juked backwards, recoiling his hand as the threshold nearly blasted his knuckles, flying onwards till it cracked against the side of the camper and shuddered. Fully expecting to see his sister standing there in a groggy rage, he peered into the darkness…a complete stranger stared back at him. A short brunette, with a bob hair cut and a half a dozen facial piercings, plopped down onto the first step. She smiled at Ham as she adjusted her wrinkled mini-skirt and plaid top, then jumped to the ground in front of him.

"Hi," the young woman simply retorted as she walked on by, headed towards the truck-stop behind.

"Hell…o?" Ham's head cocked in confusion. He watched her for some time with an almost smitten daze till her perfect apple bottom, and the petite figure it was attached to, was swallowed up by the steel wall of a passing semi….the music in the camper cut off.

"What ya want?" a voice cracked. Ham winced inside and spun round to see her standing in the doorway. Hutch McCray…the youngest of the McCray clan. The baby…the twenty-six year old was far from such. At 6'1" her thin frame towered over most men she met. Her head was only inches from hitting the top of the entry she now occupied. Straight, red locks whipped across her ivory-freckled face in the breeze of the passing trucks as she lit up the morning's first cigarette. She waited for a response from her dumbfounded brother. Ham shook his head a bit and replayed her snide inquiry out in his head once more before answering.

"What do I want?..."

"That's what I said," she exhaled a quick plume of smoke and flicked the excess ash.
Ham's irritation returned full force.

"What I *want* is a dependable sister. One that I don't hafta be the personal alarm clock for three out of five damn workin' days a week. I'm gettin' sicka stickin' up for your ass…" Hutch stood there, mocking him the entire time with her free hand, working it like a mouth at his words. "Oh, oh, this shit is funny to you?" Ham spoke. Hutch smiled a bit, blowing smoke out her nose. Ham's face was getting redder by the second. He quickly glared in the direction of where the mystery girl had disappeared, then whipped his gaze back as he wetted his lips. "Glad it's funny, Hutch...You know what else I want besides a reliable sister? I want said-sister to tell me that pretty thing that vanished over yonder was sellin' her Tupperware and not...ya know...?"

"Oh...we were 'ya knowin'...probably half the night," she confirmed his suspicions.

"And there it is....Christ almighty, how the hell is it that my sister, my baby sister, can score hotter pieces of tail than me?" Before she could even think to answer, Ham's voice raised even higher "And holy shit, would you cover yourself?!" He placed a hand up to block his view at the sudden realization that she was wearing nothing but a shirt and underwear. "Goddamn, Hutch, I ain't even had my coffee this mornin'. Last thing I need is the image of my sister in her skivvies burned into my retinas."

Hutch just took another puff and shook her head. She flicked the cigarette to the gravel beyond and reached just inside the camper. Her hand unfurled a disheveled pair of purple underwear.

"Speakin' of skivvies...she forgot somethin'," Hutch smirked as she dangled the underwear on one finger.

"Oh, for god sake..." Ham lowered his hand finally, shaking his head.

"I'll sell em' to ya...four bucks," she joked without a smile as she looked them over. Ham went to speak but was shut down as she quickly pulled the panties tight on her fingers and released them like a sling-shot into his face. A round of cussing was muffled by cotton as he frantically yanked them off his mouth and nose.

"Goddamn you! Seriously?!" Ham spat out, throwing the panties to the ground. It was all overshadowed by Hutch laughing hysterically. She wiped a small tear from her eye as she spoke, "Shit, I don't think I'd ever laugh if it weren't for you."

"Yeah...well you're not exactly ever laughin' *with* me though, are ya?"

As Hutch's laughter wound down, she pointed a finger at him.

"And that's why."

"That's why, what?"

"What you said earlier…Why does my sister get hotter pussy than me?"

"That *ain't* what I said."

"Tail. Pussy. Whatever. And my point is proven again with that sentence, you dear brother, are a prude. That's why you don't get tail."

"Me? A prude. Shiiiiit," he protested.

"Shit, nothin'."

"Examples," he demanded as he crossed his arms.

"Examples? How much time you got?" Hutch scoffed, "I can write you a damn brochure on this shit. Let's start with back when we were kids and you ratted out Hayden for havin' nudie mags. Twice! And high school, when you were datin' that Lucy girl…"

"Linda," Ham corrected her.

"Whatever. That girl clearly wanted dick but ya just kept writin' her poetry instead. And then last week that girl with the low-cut top came into the shop and half her nipple was hangin' out and *you* were like '*Ummm, ma'am. Umm, uh. You're showin'*, instead of enjoyin' the show like the rest of us were."

"Oh seriously, Hutch?! It's called being a gentleman. It's called being nice."

"There's that word, *nice*. You're too nice. You're a prude and a hopeless romantic. You're ready to marry these poor girls on the first date…we've talked about this…" she ended in an almost playful disappointment. Ham was silent as he stood there staring off, hands now on his hips.

"I don't know…just be nice to score now and again with somethin' like what walked out your door this mornin' is all I'm sayin'." His words made Hutch's eyes widen a bit. He sounded so damned defeated. Had she broken him running her mouth off like that?

"Ahhh, she wasn't all that," she tossed her hand down in dismissal, staring off towards the endlessly passing rigs.

"No?" Ham looked up at her.

"Naw…she was kinda gross."

"Gross?...gross like how?"

"Well…she had this spot on her…"

"You know what, Hutch, I don't wanna know," Ham threw his hand up, stopping her words. "Just promise me you'll get your ass into the shop within ten minutes of me turnin' round." With that, he quickly spun and began to walk away, hoping his final words would sink into her hard head. Hutch had nothing more to say as she watched her brother take several paces away...but it was short-lived. He suddenly stopped as if he had been kicked and put up a hand with a pointed finger. Ham spun round with a look of odd suspicion written all over his face as he lumbered on back to within feet of his sister once more. A peculiar look of irritation brushed Hutch's face as she stared down at him, wondering just what in the hell he was about to bitch about this time.

"Yes?" She posed the obvious. Ham said nothing at first, he just kept the pointed finger elevated as he began sniffing the air like some hound dog about to hunt. His hand dropped.

"Are you shittin' me?"

"What?" she snapped.

"Tell me I'm not smellin' what I think I'm smellin'," he spoke out with a disappointed tongue.

"What?...What?!" Hutch said in agitation looking inside, then back at her brother. "I got candles burnin' in here." She started fiddling nervously with her hair.

"Candles? You got candles burnin'? I didn't know there was a hard market for reefer scented candles nowadays...Jesus Christ, Hutch you been tokin' up?!" The words were more of a statement than a question. He knew the answer. He didn't even let her speak as he ripped into her hard. "You were in jail for thirty days. You are court ordered to go to AA now and you are damn mighty likely to get sued for that shit you did, I would think you'd be a lil' goddamn smarter about bein' around illegal shit right now."

"I know! Okay?! I fuckin' know! You think you're tellin' me anythin' I don't know right now?!" She blew up back in his face, throwing her hands around in a tizzy. "It wasn't me, okay? I didn't touch it...It was her."

"Her?" Ham raised an eyebrow. She pointed to the parking lot where her one-night-stand had flown off.

"Yeah, HER ...Lacy...Becky...Shit, Tracy?"

"Dear lord, you threw down with this girl and you can't even remember her name? You really are baked right now."

"I'm not high!!"

"Okay, okay. Let's say for argument's sake you ain't high, it doesn't take away from the fact that you're hangin' out with someone who IS and who's bringin' it into your camper." Ham shook his head as he went on in a growing ire, "I don't think you even mildly grasp the gravity of the shit you're in! YOU hit someone and drove off, drunk, no less. You don't think the local cops are watchin' you like hawks right now? They're just waitin' for you to walk, shit, or sneeze the wrong way so they can haul your ass right back to jail and keep you there for a looong time, and here you are, arguin' with me about who smoked what in YOUR trailer!" He ended his rant with a crackly loss of breath and red face to match. Hutch just stood there, staring at him for a moment, then just simply said,

"I'm not high."

"Jesus…you didn't hear a damn word I said… How the hell you get hooked up with that girl, anyway?"

"Met her at Stacy's last night."

"Stacy's? As in the bar? How the hell you get there?"

"Some guy gave me a ride."

"Some guy?"

"Yeah some dude over at the truck stop."

"Jesus, Hutch…"

"What?! I gave em' some cigarettes for the trouble."

"No, not that. Ya got inta some random guy's car at night. You're lucky ya ain't in a ditch somewhere."

"Oh, pffft! Anyway, it was karaoke night, right? And I got shit-face hammered and sung Amarillo by Morning, and…"

"Goddamn it, I'm gonna pretend I didn't hear that."

"What?! That's a good song. That's classic Strait right there!"

"Hutch, holy shit! Not the song, the drinkin'! Ya ain't supposed ta be doin' that! Was I even talkin' a minute ago?"

She sighed and shook her head.

"Ya wanna hear the end of this story or not?"

"No," Ham put his arms out.

"So she must be a mad country fan cuz she's nothin' but hands and lips all over me after I get done singin'. She drives us back here…"

"Wait," Ham put a hand up, "She drove? Was she hammered too?"

Hutch was taken off guard.

"Ummmmm…no?"

"Holy hell…"

"Yeah, but anyway, she was drivin'…a…"

"A what? What was she drivin'?"

Hutch looked a bit ashamed as she spoke, "A Geo…she owned a Geo. I'm not gonna lie, that dried me up a little. But I wasn't gonna be picky in my position, cuz fingers, well they ain't much for conversation…"

"Okay stop. Just Stop. Hutch…just get to work. Hank's losin' his shit and I'm sicka hearin' it," Ham ended in disgust.

"When isn't Hank losin' his shit?" She mumbled to herself as she watched her brother stomp off in anger. The more she watched him fade off across the dusty lot, the more she fought back a single tear dancing on the edge of her eye. If it had been anyone else chewing into her about her stupidity, she would've told them where to go, but not Ham. He was about the only damn person left in her crumbling life that she knew actually cared about her. And why? She had not a clue. He was right, she WAS always late to work, always making the dumbest of decisions…but he was still there for her. It was in that instant her lip curled in the thought that that man cared about her more than she cared for him, otherwise she would listen to his scolding instead of forgetting it minutes later.

Hutch sniffed back the verge of her unfound tears and spun round, back into the dankness she called home. She quickly went to getting dressed, throwing on a pair of unwashed jeans, her battered boots, and a thin plaid button up to conceal the stains on her undershirt. She was about as "put together" as a thousand piece puzzle in a windstorm, but that's just how she was and always had been. Lipstick, blush, eyeliner, they were unspoken words in the land of Hutch. About the only thing she owned in the way of cosmetics was a bottle of black nail polish that she used to conceal her permanently grease-stained nails and when she'd run out of that, a permanent marker always did the trick. Simply put, to her, getting "dolled up" was brushing her hair and putting pants on. Maybe it was the fault of being raised by mostly men, growing up with five brothers probably was not the most "lady-like" environment. Regardless, Hutch never dwelled on it much, and if you had a problem with it, she had no qualms with telling you which pier to jump off.

If her lack of shit-giving was not obvious in her appearance, then her wheeled abode would definitely set one straight. Just like her, it was often a disheveled mess. Her counter and table tops were blanketed by dozens of empty soda cans, candy wrappers, receipts, and what looked like $200 in loose change scattered between it all. Some of the aforementioned had even found its way to the floor. She kicked through it as she dug into nearby drawers and seat cushions with a growing impatience, looking for her only hairbrush.

"C'mon…c'mon…where are you bast –ah HA!" She finally spotted it sitting there beside a giant laundry basket full of crumpled clothing, otherwise known as her wardrobe. She opened her curtains, quickly plopped down and stared out the window, her face wrinkling and writhing as she tamed the rats from her ginger locks. Through the dust and growing heat, she eyed a large building looming in the distance, the very same place where her brother had disappeared only moments before. That structure was slowly beginning to feel like a prison to her, even more so than the actual jail cell she had occupied for an entire month not a few weeks prior. Her hair combing slowed as she began to reflect upon the events that led her there…Ham told no lies in his recitation of the things she had done. Nearly two months to the day, she had been drinking, speeding down route 8 like a bat out of hell. She side-swiped a car along the road. The owner of the car was broken down, in the process of changing a flat when the impact came. It spun his car round, breaking his wrist…it could've been worse, but it was bad enough. To add to it, his seven year old daughter was in the vehicle. She was tossed around but nothing was broken, a few stitches fixed her up. The gravity of the situation may have been lessened if Hutch had just stopped and waited for the cops, but no, she was a McCray, they were not exactly known for their good decision making skills. She dropped the gas even harder in a panic and sped home, passing out on her couch-bed. The next thing she knew, she was being dragged out by two local sheriffs and force fed a breathalyzer. She was two times the legal limit. One police car ride and an impounded vehicle later, she was being held for arraignment at the local county court. It was her second DUI. The judge instantly ordered a thirty day sentence, $1000 fine, and mandatory visits to local AA meetings. Her license was stripped for an entire year as well….and that was just the punishment for the DUI. She was now free, but was she really? She had no car, and even if she did, she had no driver's license. She was essentially a prisoner outside of prison, free to roam the seedy lot of the truck stop, her camper, and her place of employment. And the damage was all far from over. She now waited with bated breath on the next court arraignment, the one where they would begin to decide her fate in the hit and run. No date had yet been set for the case, but it was there. Always there, looming like the reaper at her door. It all deposited a permanent lump in her throat, one she couldn't drink away even if she tried. Still, there was the biggest part of her that just didn't care anymore. There were often times she lie there in bed at night, recalling the events of what she had done and wondered if she were truly sorry for what she had caused or merely sorry that she'd gotten caught. All she knew was, when she went to face her victims in court, the apology she was going to cough up was more than likely going to be faked for the sake of saving her own sorry ass. Hopefully it would be genuine enough to free her from a lawsuit that she could not possibly pay. A sigh escaped her lips as she slammed down her hair brush on the tiny table in front of her, trying to shake off the aforementioned demons that clawed at the back of her brain. She arose, keeping her eyes fixed out the window in some sober moment of reflection while she put on an old and tattered, green trucker hat and looked in the mirror,

"Hutch, you hag…let's go make some money," with that, she trotted outside, leaving the camper door haphazardly slapping shut behind her.

"Jesus Christ, was it seriously this hot already?" She thought in disgust as she fished a cigarette out of her front shirt pocket. The sun blasted into her freckled face as she squinted into the sky in the chagrin of the weather. The four seasons in this godforsaken state were as follows - Hot, Cold, Snow, and Rain. If you got lucky, about a dozen days were seventy degree, partly sunny perfection, but as a bead of sweat rolled down Hutch's forehead, it was obviously NOT one of the those days. Her smoke dangled loosely

in her lips as she lit the tip and walked slower than a turtle in quicksand across the expanse of the gravel lot. She was in no rush, nor mood, to get yelled at, but it was coming. She kept her eyes fixed on the front door of the large building she called work, knowing full well there were cross words about to be spoken to her from behind it. But there were few things to be said that she hadn't already heard "Hutch you're worthless! Hutch, you're a fuck up! Hutch, you're losing us money!" And on and on. Yep, she had heard them all, and they were probably not lies, she just didn't care one single, solitary bit.

With a quick halt, she paused in her tracks about forty feet from the block façade in front of her, flicking her smoke by her side. She was going to enjoy this damn cigarette before getting that tongue lashing that she so readily deserved…at least in Hank's eyes anyway. With a long, drawn out inhale, she took in the sight of the huge sign posted upon the roof. "McCray Engine and Machine" The words danced in a whimsical, Gaelic styled font upon the weathered billboard and matched the white embroidered letters upon her hat. Though at this point, it should've been renamed "The Gingerbread House". That's what everyone local called it. Especially the drag racers. Even their family called it that. Everyone that worked there had the signature McCray red hair. So people starting referring to it as a "house full of gingers." Which quickly led to the aforementioned nickname." It was a rather enormous edifice, spanning some one-hundred fifty plus feet across. Several large overhead garage doors graced the front, dwarfing a smaller window and front entry door for patron use. The entire complex was awash in the McCray clan signature green, a color picked out by her grandfather, Hess McCray, who started the business some forty-five years prior. He was a machinist by trade and started the company as a regular machine and welding shop. Over the years his undying love for the American muscle car drove him to change the dynamic of his business model. In the 60's McCray Machine and Welding was changed to McCray Engine and Machine, a one stop shop for custom, high performance engines, parts, and machine work. By the mid 70s the shop had made quite the name for itself. If you were local, and you were a drag racer, you had a McCray spec'd engine under your hood…anything else was second rate. The business had quickly become a family affair early on with Hutch's father, Harvey McCray, and Aunt, Cassandra McCray, working under their father as soon as they were old enough to drive. And drive they could, the McCray legacy not only grew from their proficiency of building unstoppable race machines, but also stretched onto the tracks of where those very same machines screamed to life. The McCray name became synonymous with speed and victory year after year at the local drag strips and circle tracks.

Hutch's grandfather passed away in 78', leaving ownership of the shop to Harvey. Fourteen years later the same history nearly repeated itself with Harvey falling ill but not passing. He left his eldest son in charge of everything until the inevitable came calling for him, but from there it was anyone's guess who Harvey had named in his will to take over the McCray empire. Though everyone assumed it would be the same son that was now temporarily in charge...Hank. Hank, the man that was about to do his daily duty of chewing into Hutch for her short-comings. Hutch took one final exhale of her smoke and threw it to the gravel, snuffing it out with her boot as she strode for the front entrance of the shop. A dangling brass bell chimed out a clichéd tune above her head as she made her overdue entrance inside. As the door glided shut behind her, the sounds of the thundering semis were replaced with the tunes of grinding metal, McCray cussing, and the Allman Brothers blaring away on an old stereo beyond the front counter.

"Home, sweet home," she mumbled to herself in disgust as she took it all in. Her nose was instantly introduced to the shop's familiar aroma of burnt alloys, inerasable grease, and coffee-stained paperwork. The amalgamation of the smells soon deposited a semi-permanent metallic tang upon the back of her tongue as she trod from the floor mat to the concrete floor beyond. She was instantly met by the gaze of Ham who was flipping through paperwork at the counter. His side-eyed stare and headshake was an obvious indicator that he was far from happy, but whether it was from their prior conversation or the mountain of work orders and receipts in front of him, Hutch hadn't a clue.

"Welcome back to responsibility, Hutch," Ham mouthed off with a sigh as he began pecking away furiously on an adding machine. Okay, that answered that. Ham was the shop's resident hack-accountant / counter boy. Hack accounting indeed, the McCray paperwork system went as follows - Write work order down. Collect money and write receipt. Roll said papers into a crumpled mass and throw in boxes for mice to make nests in. Come tax day they would sort of just thumb through a quarter of the papers and times that number by two, leading to some random figure they would cough up to the IRS. How the hell they had never gotten audited was beyond Hutch's understanding. And if they ever did, she was certain the best protocol would be to burn the building to the ground with everyone inside it, herself included. That sorry mess aside, Ham was responsible for the work orders. No head, block, or manifold came through that door without passing through him first. After everything was okayed, said engine part was sent to the one of three resident machinists - Hutch (you've already met her) or her older brothers, Hayden or Heath. Okay, wait a second, let's stop right there and get some minor formalities out of the way. Hutch has five older siblings, all brothers (I mentioned that earlier. Or were you paying attention?) Going from youngest to oldest there was Hamlet, Heath, Hayden, Henry, and Hank. Yes, they all began with "H", it seemed to be some unwritten and nauseatingly 'sweet' tradition starting back when her grandfather Hess, named his son Harvey. But I digress…Where was I? Oh yeah, Ham was frustrated at the counter…

"Bullshit!" Ham spouted off in anger, never taking his eyes from the adding machine.

"Now, now. It'll be alright little guy," a patronizing voice emerged from behind, along with a pat on Ham's back. Heath, came round the counter holding a coffee cup. He handed it off to Hutch saying, "There ya go princess. Pinch of sugar in there, just how you like it." He smiled wide under thick eye-glasses as she reluctantly and almost involuntarily snatched the steaming cup from his hand.

"Yes, please reward her for bad behavior," Ham threw in.

"Sandwich, you stay outta this," Heath pointed at his younger brother, calling him a nickname that he hated worse than his actual one.

"Reward, my ass. What you do to this?" Hutch said with suspicious irritation as she looked into murk of the black tea in her mug. It was her favorite, but what was he up to?

"Oh hell, why you always gotta be assumin' I'm up ta shit? Can't I be nice to my sister?"

"No, you can't. It ain't in your DNA. That set of $100 wrenches of mine that you welded together last week proves it," Hutch mouthed off as she sniffed at the tea for any signs of foul play.

"Hutch, just drink the damn shit or don't. I really don't care," Heath finally let out as he began backing away. Hutch looked over at Ham as if she were hoping for some guidance in whether or not one of their most capricious brothers could be trusted. Hutch finally forced a smile,

"Fine…I'll drink the *damn shit* but if I feel like shittin' myself within the next thirty minutes or I start pissin' rainbow colors or somethin' weird like that, I WILL kill you. I don't mean that figuratively. I'm not afraid to go back to jail." Heath just smiled his signature crooked smile and held two thumbs up as he spun round, headed back for the main work area. Hutch began sipping at the hot tea with every belief that is was dirty washtub water or laced with some illegally-hot pepper juice…but nothing. It was actually pretty damn good. A fact that only raised her suspicions even further. She turned her attention back to Ham who was number crunching again.

"What's got you riled this mornin'?" Hutch spoke dryly as she watched on at his growing impatience. He stopped his adding and slammed down a handful of papers.

"Ya mean, aside from our earlier conversation?"

"Yeah…that aside," she tried not to roll her eyes as she took another drink.

"Well, this place is an unorganized shit-hole that's gonna be the death of me. I keep runnin' numbers over and over and there's forty goddamn dollars missin from yesterday's take-in."

"Well…maybe you're not addin' it right," Hutch was quick to suggest her brother was being incompetent.

"Hutch, I've went over this shit twenty times this morning. Forty dollars. Every. Single. Time," he annunciated the syllables with a hand pounding on the counter. Hutch just shook her head as she took a huge gulp of tea.

"Well, better luck addin' it up on the next round, I guess," with that, she started to walk off quickly.

"Hold it," Ham spouted off, stopping his sister dead. She turned round. He pointed to the register with squinting eyes. "You take forty dollars out of this till yesterday?"

"What?!...No...fuck no!" She was instantly agitated at the notion. It was that same agitation that drove Ham into just staring her down like he was ripping the truth right out of her. "I was gonna put it back Friday. Okay?" she cracked almost instantly. The statement was typical Hutch. No apologetic music rang through her speech, just matter-of-fact arrogance. Ham's face turned red as he spoke as composed as he could.

"Are you fuckin' kiddin' me right now?"

"No," she simply spouted.

"Why would you do that?!"

"Cuz, I needed forty dollars. I went ta the bar last night, remember? Beer don't buy itself," Hutch kept her same tone of speech. It was only adding fuel to Ham's fire.

"Hutch, ya can't just take money from the goddamn register like that," he pointed to the till beside him.

"Well, I did."

"Yeah, I KNOW. I'm the asshole who's been countin' the money from yesterday thinkin' I have the addin' skills of a four-year-old, when in actuality my sister is just bein' a goddamn thief."

"I didn't steal shit! I borrowed it," she went on the defensive.

"Oh ya, borrowed it? This is OUR company money. Lemme ask ya this, if I hadn't have caught ya, would you've slipped it back in there?" He posed a loaded question.

"I...well if it's OUR company money why is there a problem if I borrow some?" Hutch tried her best to twist her brother's words back on him.

"Because, Hutch, it fucks up the runnin' balances, not to mention makes the hack accountant, ME, a nervous wreck. And good job avoidin' my question by the way," Ham ended his sentence with a sigh and a shuffle of paperwork. He was growing beyond tired of the conversation. As with most arguments with Hutch, it was going nowhere at a bullet's pace. Hutch took a final swig of her tea and threw it hard into the trash.

"You know what? You're startin' ta remind me of Hank," she threw out. Ham looked up wide-eyed from the desk.

"Watch it."

"Watch nothin'…" she pointed a waving finger at him, "Yeah…I'm gonna start callin' you Lil' Hank. Lil' Hank the royal lackey and rule-enforcer for his royal highness, King Hank, the ruler of The Gingerbread House."

"That's enough!" Ham slammed his fist so hard on the counter everything trembled upon it. Hutch just looked at him with widened eyes. A crooked smiled crept across her face.

"See, the shoe's fittin' even better with every move you make." Ham grabbed the side of the countertop and squeezed as hard as he could, trying to resist the urge to give Hutch the slap across the face that she was begging for. He nodded towards her as he spoke.

"You know, with every day that passes, I'm startin' to see why he treats you the way he does."

Hutch's wrinkling smile ironed itself into a straight line.

"Now who needs to watch it?" She stared him down with a palpable ire stagnating in her ice-blue eyes. Ham shook his head and broke the stare-down.

"Fuck you, Hutch," he spoke coldly as he returned his attention to the counter. The words sent a pang through her heart. He never spoke to her that way. Especially in that sincere of a tone. She had let things go too far again…but what was new? All of a sudden, her nerves jumped as a voice cut in right beside her.

"Jesus Christ…you two," the voice spoke in an almost playful scolding. The type of tone that would suggest they should keep fighting. It was Hayden, the third eldest of the McCray clan, and second favorite brother of Hutch, or better said, second least hated of Hutch. He had obviously been standing there through the whole argument without notice from either of them. An ever-growing smile overlapped a bulge of chewing tobacco tucked behind his lip. He stroked at his bushy, red beard, all the while his bald head reflected the shop lights on high as he shook it in a faked discontent of what he had witnessed. "Five minutes in the door and one of us is ready ta kill you already. Typical day at the office," he smiled at his sister.

"Yep," she spoke short. An uncomfortable silence crept in quickly as Hayden just kept standing there, smiling as if he were up to something. "You just gonna stand there fidgeting around like an asshole all day? Seriously, you need somethin'?"

"Yeah, I do. I need your opinion on somethin'," Hayden said.

"That so?"

"Yep," Hayden leaned in and shoved a cup right under his sister's nose. "This coffee smell like shit to you?" He laughed out the sentence as the smell of feces blasted her in the nose. She jumped back at the sight and aroma of a pile of scat in the bottom of the cup.

"You asshole!" Hutch blasted out, throwing a hand up to cover her nose. Hayden walked by her laughing like a mad man. "What the hell is that?!" She further blurted out.

"It's shit," he laughed out the obvious answer as he headed for the front door.

"Yeah I know it's shit. That ain't your shit is it?! Tell me that ain't your shit!"

"No! Good, god!"

"Well, what kinda shit is it?"

"Do I look like a poopographer to you? I don't know. Raccoon? Cat? Sandwich?" He pointed at Ham as a suspect. Ham just shook his head, not even cracking a grin. "Well we know it's not Heath's. Smells too good," Hayden said.

"Fuck you," the muffled voice of Heath came from back in the shop.

"Jesus...the hearing of a three-eared dog, that boy," Hayden smiled in disbelief. "Seriously though, this place is some kinda goddamn zoo. Everybody is always leavin' doors open. Hard to tell what the hell's creepin' round in here."

"Oh, bullshit," Hutch dismissed his claims.

"Naw, I think he might be right. Somethins' been takin' part of my lunch for the past week or so," Ham said.

"HA! Ham, that's been me you dumbass!" Hayden confessed.

"What? You been eatin' my lunches?!" Ham raised his eyebrow in disbelief.

"Ha! Hell no! I've been throwin em' in the trash," Hayden laughed.

"What the hell would ya do that for?!"

"Because I'm an asshole. You haven't figured that out yet?"

Hutch wanted badly to laugh but held it in. She quickly went on the defensive for her closest sibling, even if it was insincere.

"Damn Hayden, that's cold."

"Oh please. That's just like you to come to his defense. Look, all I been doin' is throwin' away his PB&J sandwiches," Hayden went fast to justify his actions. Hutch raised an eyebrow and looked towards Ham. "Yeah you heard that right, Hutch. Peanut butter and jelly sandwiches. He's almost thirty. No self-respecting man of that age eats that shit."

"Just quit throwin' away my goddamn sandwiches," Ham said coldly with crossed arms and an equally cold leer towards his brother."

Hayden pointed at him,

"Hey, all you gotta do is just start packin' roast beef…or turkey…or hell even bologna and you'll start seein' a few less of them in the trash. Just a few. I'm still gonna throw some away. Like I said, I'm an asshole and I hate you just a little bit more than I love you." He then opened the front door, giving the coffee mug he still held a snap. The mystery poo went hurling several feet out into the gravel lot in front of the shop.

"Oh yeah, throw it out the front door right where customers can walk in it," Ham scolded his brother's stupidity.

"Sandwich, you will speak when spoken to!" Hayden pointed at his youngest brother with a grin; he pulled the door shut. "Besides, what else am I sposed to do with it?"

"Umm, flush it down the toilet where shit belongs. Or do you make it a habit of crappin' in coffee mugs and flingin' it on your front lawn at home?"

"Oh, you're just a bowl full of common sense this mornin' ain't ya?" Hayden mouthed off as he walked a few steps forwards, still staring down into the cup.

"Shit…someone has to be around here…" Ham mumbled.

"Well since you're bein' all common sensed and mature and shit, I guess you can be the one who cleans that up then," Hayden said as he tossed the mug up on the counter in front of his youngest brother and walked on by Hutch.

"Ain't no one cleanin' nothin'! Throw that thing away, that's gross as hell," Hutch wrinkled her nose at her brother's suggestion.

"I'll second that," Ham madly slid the mug to the far end of the counter where Hayden had stopped. He quickly grabbed it up before it could fly off the edge, saving it from shattering upon the floor.

"Y'all sure bout that?" He held the mug up for Hutch and Ham to read.

"#1 Dad" - It was one of Hanks favorite coffee mugs.

"Well, hell. Why didn't ya say somethin' before? Should've just left the crap in there," Hutch mouthed away.

"HA! Yeah I guess I should've." He looked down inside the ceramic vessel once more. "Oh well there's some cocoa scraps still stickin down in there for him." Hayden laughed and slammed the mug down on a workbench behind the front desk. He then plodded into the machine work area beyond, leaving Hutch and Ham staring at the desecrated cup of their oldest, most pain-in-the-ass sibling. Their eyes soon drifted away and met each other's with a questioning stare.

"Someone's cleanin' that shit. I ain't even gonna listen to the hellfire that comes down when he finds that thing with dingle-berries in the bottom of it," Ham spoke in irritation, hoping Hutch would volunteer. No such luck would follow in the dead silence of her staring over at the mug once more. She soon shrugged her shoulders and walked off where Hayden had gone, leaving Ham with three words falling from his bothered lips, "God damn it..."

The aromatic rampage of heavy alloys intensified as she strode into the main work area. It was an enormous room filled with a myriad of machines painted in blues, grays, and greens, embossed with permanent stains, echoing decades worth of use. Borers, planners, grinders, aligners, honers, balancers, presses, tumblers, and blasters ranging in size from modest to grand, all came together in solemn rapport. This is where the McCray magic happened. It's where Hutch truly did feel alive despite the fact that she hated being there on so many levels. It was a place where a mere mortal could become the literal Dr. Frankenstein and play maestro to the clamoring orchestra of precision machines that quite literally brought dead engines back to life. As she stood there in the midst of it all, her mind went off wandering as it often did, but only for a moment. Perhaps it was the smell of the place. She had always heard that smell was the closest sense tied to memory.

When the aroma of hydraulic fluids and aluminum pierced through her third-eye she was always taken back. She could see a young version of herself, six years old, red hair bouncing across excited shoulders as she ran about the place, irritating the living hell out of her father and grandfather. She could see her wide smile matching Ham's as they played amongst the machines without a care in the world…but unlike the machines, people didn't stay the same. Smiles faded. Hopes died off like embers to ash. What the hell ever happened to them? To the life and the light behind their blue eyes? Hutch sighed under her breath as the memory faded off 'neath the sounds of Heath firing up the cylinder bore. The whirling sound was only another reminder to her that she had to get back to reality and actually get something done today.

Hutch walked a steady beeline over to the far wall where a large machine sat, just waiting to be opened. It was the shotblaster. A large, tub-like device that cleaned an engine block to the gleam of new via the constant blasting of tiny steel shot. She had left it run it's cycle right before departing the night before and was now in the process of unlocking the bin cover to retrieve its contents. With a quick motion, Hutch tied her hair back, slapped on two heavy canvas gloves from the work bench, and then grabbed the lip of the machine.

"Let's see what baby looks like. Come ta mama," she whispered in slight excitement as she threw the bin door open wide. It was empty…nothing but the arms of the lonely rotisserie inside stared back at her. As she leaned against the machine, she resisted the urge to scream out in the chagrin of what she was now seeing, or rather, what she wasn't seeing. With one hand still on the lid, she began darting her head around the shop, back and forth, in search of the missing block.

"Hayden?!" She soon yelled out across the shop, trying to best the noises of grinding metal. Hayden was off somewhere else, his concentration buried firmly on a set of cylinder heads he was checking for warps. "Hey, Hayden?! Hey!" Her voice began to boom as her irritation grew. She soon picked up a small wrench and flung it in his direction. It tinked across the floor and bounced off her brother's boot.

"What the hell?" He let out as he dropped the feeler gauges in his hand. His attention shot straight to Hutch who was eyeballing him down with a glare that could cut glass. *What the hell was she pissed about now? It was always something.*

"Where the hell is it?" She pointed into the wide-open mouth of the machine. Hayden could barely hear her. He paced forward and threw off his shop gloves, approaching her with a questioning leer as she spoke again.

"The 454. Where is it?" Her voice became clearer.

"What?"

"Don't *what* me. The goddamn big block! I left it in here last night right before I left."

"What?! I don't know!" Hayden went on the defensive. Hutch's hands went right to her hips and her head began to cock right along with her words.

"Oh, I believe that! You are one of three people that even work in this area and you're gonna hand me that shit?!" Hayden was in fact lying. He knew what had happened, he just didn't want to be the one to tell her, especially when he was within swinging distance.

"Well, did ya look around for it?" He patronized.

"Yeah, I looked left and then I looked right," she smarted off, "It's a goddamn two-hundred pound chunk of metal. I don't think someone just slid it a drawer!"

"Look, Hutch…" Hayden started in but his words instantly became a muffled blur to her as her gaze locked onto Heath across the way.

"Mother…fucker…" her tongue sliced under her breath. She tore her work gloves off and threw them to the concrete with a smack, quickening her pace in a menacing stride right towards her other brother.

"Hutch…Hutch? Stop!" Hayden pleaded behind her.

"Shut up. I'll deal with you in a minute," she pointed a finger behind her as she closed the gap across the shop. The noise of the cylinder bore became louder and louder, muffling each step she took until…BLAM! Heath's unsuspecting head jarred sideways as Hutch landed a half closed fist across his ear. His glasses went flying off his face.

"You asshole!" Hutch bleated out with the blow. Her brother stumbled back and away, dumbfounded, catching his balance just in time to see her turn the machine off with a wicked fire brewing behind her eyes.

"You crazy, fuckin' dike!" Was all he could get out. Hutch went ballistic. Before Heath even knew what happened, a blur of hands had landed one slap and a hooked fist across his chin. He put his own hands up fast, trying to deflect anything that came beyond that, but Hayden had since grabbed her from behind, throwing his arms under hers, and pinning his hands behind her neck. He pulled her away from Heath, but that didn't dissuade her from trying to land a kick or two as her legs went crazy, flailing in all directions while she screamed a phalanx of indiscernible cursing.

"Calm down! Calm the hell down, I said!" Hayden yelled out, trying to tame her rampant thrashing. From out in the lobby, Ham just stared through the shop doors, shaking his head. He wasn't even getting in the middle of this one, it was just another day at The Gingerbread House.

A flavor of iron, not fault of the shop, crept upon Heath's tongue and he wiped at his lip. His eyes widened at the sight of blood on the tips of his fingers.

"You dumb whore. I'm bleedin!" He yelled out at her, the whites of his eyes now completely haloing his pupils.

"Oh suck it up, ya pussy! Hutch! Stop!" Hayden shamed his brother as he further tried to get his sister under control.

"Yeah, hold her down. I'm gonna bust her lip open so we're even!" Heath hollered out, taking a few steps towards her kicks.

"Back off, or I'll give ya another reason ta bleed," Hayden threatened. Heath stopped his advances. He knew his brother would make good on his threats. He'd done it multiple times in the past without fail. Hutch soon started to lose her steam.

"You gonna calm down?" Hayden talked right into her ear.

"Fuck you," Hutch spoke. He hardened his hold on her, pulling her shoulders back. "Owwww-goddamn it!" She bellowed out.

"Well?!" Hayden asked again. She said nothing to him, she just stared coldly at Heath in front of her and got a smirk on her face.

"Oh, you asshole. Now I get why ya were bein' nice ta me earlier, with the tea shit. You're stealin' ma work!"

"Hutch, it ain't like that!" Heath went on the defensive as he picked up his glasses from the floor.

"Hell it ain't! Did ya at least blow that block off in the tumbler before ya started borin' it?!"

"Seriously? Ya think I'm stupid?"

"Yeah, I do! AND lazy!"

"Well if that ain't the pot callin' the kettle black."

"Fuck you."

"No, Hutch, FUCK you," Heath pointed right at her.

"Hey, hey, hey! Enough...this is gettin' stupid at this point. Hutch, I'm gonna let go of ya, and ya best behave. That goes for you too, Heath," Hayden chided them both and released his grip upon her. She jerked away from him with a lingering agitation, quickly spinning round to face him.

"You can kiss my ass too," she pointed right in Hayden's face.

"What the hell did I do?!"

"You knew what was goin' on before I even walked in here, Heath stealin' this engine build, and ya didn't even tell me about it," she quickly looked out towards Ham, "As a matter of fact, NO ONE, bothered tellin' me about it."

Heath opened up immediately, "I done told you once, I didn't steal shit from ya. Hank said..."

"Oh Hank said?! Hank, this! Hank, that!" Hutch started going off in irritation. "Hank is just GOD around here ain't he?!" She flung her hands up high in the air, shaking them about like she was at a church revival.

"You're goddamn right I am!" An angry voice thundered into the shop area, sending the finer metals into a singing resonance that died as Hutch dropped her hands down. She shuddered a bit as she turned round to face the source of the booming affirmation. And there he stood, in all his foreboding glory. Hank Ulysses McCray, big brother, the boss of The Gingerbread House. The eldest of all the McCray siblings and seemingly self-appointed patriarch of the same. He was a mountain of a man. Most locals knew him as Hank the Tank, a moniker that he had acquired in his younger days. When he wasn't racing the tracks, he picked up his fists at local, bare-knuckle boxing bouts, laying to waste men whose egos were far larger than their brains. He racked up an undefeated winning streak that would've made the toughest of men raise a brow until the day he finally met his match...himself. One night he was driving drunk and wrapped himself around a tree. To this day his face still displayed the subtle scars of his foolish choices, along with a small limp in his stride that was a constant reminder of the pains of the past. Needless to say, he was one angry son of a bitch, and a decade after the accident, he was still far from being a tranquil soul.

Hank's 6'10" frame towered high above all his present kin…all of whom just stared back at him with nary a word gracing their lips. Amongst the awkward silence, his green eyes peered round the room as his fingers tapped out a beat on the backside of his clipboard. Oh, his beloved clipboard. He was rarely seen without it, and it seemed to be becoming more of a physical appendage than an actual stationary need. Hutch often wondered if there was anything even written on the papers clipped to it half the time. After all, if Hank's constantly disheveled hair was any indicator of his organizational skills, there was a good chance that nothing more than candy wrappers and coloring books were strapped down to it.

Without warning, Hank barked out, "Heath, bandage that shit! Hayden, those heads ain't gonna straighten themselves! Hutch?!" He snapped his fingers and motioned with them, "Get the hell over here, now." Hutch began reluctantly making her way over, irritated with the way she had been called upon, beckoned like a dog. Hank went on in disgust as she came closer. "Never seen such unprofessional bullshit in ma life," he further mumbled as he turned round to the lobby, "And you're in here lettin' it happen," Hank pointed at Ham with wide eyes.

"What?" Ham spoke in irritation, looking up from the desk.

"*What?...What?*" Hank mocked him, "I'm bein' too nice here, but I'd venture to guess you gotta about seven more brain cells up in your head than all three of these other dipshits combined, but you're over there pretendin' shit ain't happenin'. Man the fuck up now and again, Ham. And you…" he spun back around to address Hutch who was now only inches from his face, looking up at him. Hank paused for a minute, then spoke with a smile, "How are ya today, sister of mine?" Hutch tried her best not to roll her eyes. She could just smell the impending sarcasm permeating from his grizzly beard.

"Can I get ya anythin' Hutch?…. An alarm clock? A responsible conscious? A hot, steamin' cup of '*get your shit together*' coffee?"

"You done?" She spoke coldly, crossing her arms.

"Oh, I'm not done. I have a book of one liners written just for you, sis. I sit on the shitter every night and come up with more, cuz god knows I'm gonna need em….not that they do any good," he walked away and turned the coffee pot on the back counter to give it a warm up. Hutch said nothing. She just stood there watching his actions as he returned to her. "Not that I really give a damn, but I'm gonna indulge ya, what's got ya stirrin' the shit pot this mornin'?" Hutch could feel her blood boiling. She wanted to swing at him but knew better, he sure as hell wasn't Heath. She darted her tongue around the inside of her mouth and faked an angry smile as she rocked in her current position.

"Are ya fuckin' kiddin' me?"

"Oh, I'm not a funny guy," he retorted.

Hutch's face went cold.

"The engine. The 454. Hillman's custom ordered build for the Chevelle. That was my build," she stated her case.

"Yeah, it WAS your build. Now it's Heath's build," he spoke matter-of-fact as he pointed to where Heath was re-firing the borer.

"But YOU, gave it to ME," she pointed at her chest.

"Right…And now I gave it to Heath. Holy shit, this conversation is already boring me, Hutch," Hank confessed.

"But…it was important to me," she let out in a disappointment she failed to disguise.

"Ha! It was important to ya? Well if it was SO goddamn important to ya, can ya tell me why everyday you're comin in one hour late, leavin' one hour early, and takin two hour lunches? Hillman is a pretty patient guy but he ain't that patient." Hutch went silent and stared off at the wall. "I'm sorry…I can't hear you," Hank put a hand to his ear. Still nothing came from her, angry or otherwise. Hank slapped her playfully on the side of the arm. "Sis, I'm gonna tell ya what…I'm gonna give ya a new job that'll cheer ya right up." Hutch was already not liking the sound of his tone. She watched as he walked over to the front desk and pushed their brother to the side. "Piss off, Sandwich." Ham stumbled back in irritation then looked over at Hutch who just mirrored his look of confused dread. "You, young lady, are gonna be our new receptionist," he patted the front counter with a smile. A look of absolute horror came over her.

"What? No!" She protested in disgust.

"Hell, its official, ya finally lost your mind," Ham spouted off at Hank.

"I'll second that. You are shittin, right? Hutch? At the front counter, talkin' to actual payin' customers?" Hayden's voice startled the other three as he poured a hot cup of coffee from the pot that Hank had re-fired. Hank immediately drew an ill-eye down on him.

"Hey?! Get back to planin' that head or I'm gonna bust yours in," he barked at him. Hayden shook his head and walked off, back to his duties as Hank's stare rounded the room back to the disgruntled face of his sister. "Get to it," he pointed at the counter area.

"No…" Hutch spoke.

"No?...I'll tell ya what, Hutch, I'll make a proposition for ya, if you don't march the fuck over here and man this desk, your ass is fired. How bout that?" Hutch's eyes narrowed into an angry leer. Hank went on, "But I'm sure bein' fired ain't no issue for ya. You probably got all kinds of job prospects just lined right up bein' that ya don't have a car, you're fresh out of jail, and you live in a camper. If that don't have 'employable' written all over it I don't know what does." Hutch could feel herself starting to shake. She clenched her fist tighter, trying to find words that weren't plucked from the deepest depths of a sailor's throat. But she said nothing. Her eyes just drifted to Ham's and they met for a brief moment of helplessness. Hank sighed in his own boredom with the silence at hand.

"Hutch, tell ya what I'm gonna do, a further proposal, if ya can work this desk forrrrr…four hours without pissin' a customer off, I'll give you the Hillman build back, cuz I'm THAT nice of a guy." Hutch's eyes widened back up ever so slightly.

"Four hours?" She asked for confirmation.

"Four little, teeny-tiny hours," Hank held up four fingers, "That's all that stands between you and your oh-so-precious and 'important' 454 Hillman build."

"Okay…I'll do it," Hutch finally breathed out.

"Oh, you will! That's awesome!" Hank spouted in fake excitement as he slapped her on the shoulder so hard she winced. "Not that you had any choice in the matter!" He further laughed.

His face soon went dead serious and he slapped a giant open palm on the counter. "Get to gettin," he commanded to Hutch. He then spun round. "Sandwich?! I said piss off. Go make yourself useful for god sake." Ham gave him a raised eyebrow as he watched him walk to the other end of the counter and Hutch took up her newly appointed position with the reluctance of a deaf mule. All of a sudden, Hutch and Ham jumped at Hank's booming voice.

"Heeeeyyyy!" He yelled in excitement as he thrust something up from the counter. "My favorite coffee mug! Wondered where the hell it got off to." Blissfully unaware of the fact that the urn had been used for this morning's mystery-shit disposal, Hank lumbered quickly to the still-hot coffee station and filled it to the brim as Ham and Hutch watched on with wide eyes.

"Ummm, Hank?" Ham went to speak a word of warning as his eldest brother rose the cup to his lips.

"What, shit-brick?!" Hank stopped, leering at him in irritation. Ham just gave his sister a small look and then said,

"Never mind." Hutch could barely keep a smile off her face as she watched Hank tip back the mug and take three large gulps of what had to be a sixteen-to-one turgid ratio of Columbia's best, and some raccoon's worst. No sooner did Hank lower his cup, his voice thunder out,

"Goddamn it!!" Hutch and Ham cringed a little inside at his outburst, fully expecting some rampage to ensue but, "That is some damn good coffee," was all that followed. Hutch bit her lip as she stared at Ham, trying to keep her composure while Hayden re-entered the lobby and said,

"Really, Hank?...I thought that coffee kinda tasted like shit." Hutch's stare quickly went to the ceiling as she prayed for probably the sixth time in her life that she wouldn't burst into a fit of laughter...it was going to be a looooong day.

Minutes trickled into one full hour as things returned to normal in The Gingerbread House...well as normal as they could get. The familiar tinking, clinking, and clanking of metal serenaded Hutch from the work area as she stood there at the desk, her fingers tapping out a beat written in bitter angst of her current job position. Hutch hated a lot of things, but if there was one thing near the peak of her mountain of loath, it was dealing with people. She just didn't like people in general, well…most people. Hell she barely liked herself and she had to put up with that lanky bitch every time she looked in the mirror. Simply put, she had no interpersonal skills when it came to dealing with the general public. Hank was well aware of this, so why he had decided to put her in this position was far beyond anyone's comprehension. Yes, she hated it, so in that regard it was a stiff punishment, but on the other hand, she was very likely to piss off customers, it was almost as if Hank was cutting off his nose to spite his own face. Luckily for all parties involved, not one customer had yet to step through the door. Even the phone lay silent in the entire wake of that grueling first hour.

"One down…three more to go…you got this…youuuu got this," Hutch sighed to herself as she counted the hours till the Hillman build was once again hers. She soon found herself fidgeting…fiddling with her hair, clapping her hands together, obsessively clicking the button of a ballpoint pen she held. Ham observed this as he swept the lobby for what seemed like the eighteenth time since Hank had left them to their new duties.

"Holy shit, Ham is your job always this boring? No wonder you're the way you are," Hutch let out.

"Hey, what the hells that supposed to mean?" He stopped his sweeping to protest.

"Nothin'…" she slipped out as she began messing with stacks of papers on the far side of the desk.

"Whoa, whoa. Leave that shit be. It's all in order. I gotta enough trouble with you messin' my numbers up by thievin' out of the register."

"Borrowed…" she corrected her brother's choice of words.

"Hutch, I ain't even restartin' that conversation with you right now," Ham sighed as he went back to his pointless sweeping. A moment of silence passed.

"You think he'll get sick?" She suddenly threw out. Ham looked up, stopping his cleaning again.

"Who?"

"Who? Seriously? Hank. The one who just drank liquid cat shit," she reminded him with irritation.

"I thought it was raccoon…"

"Oh, can we not split hairs this mornin'? It was shit. The man drank shit from a cup that our nephew made in art class."

"What? You feel bad about it or somethin'?" Ham asked.

"No!...I just...its poop, Ham!" She gagged a little as she thought about it again.

"Oh barely. Way more coffee than shit. The hot water probably killed off anythin' anyhow...Wow, talk about role reversal."

"What?"

"Role reversal. This conversation we're havin'. It's like I'm you and you're me. I'm usually the one concerned about people, not you. Looks like this new job position is changin' ya faster than I thought."

"Whatever..." she mumbled. Not one second later, she jumped at the sound of the phone blasting out a ring that could wake the dead. "Damn, is it always that loud?" She spoke in annoyance. Ham just stared at her, not even bothering to answer the question. Ring after ring passed down into an awkward scenario of Hutch just glaring with disgust at the machine as if it were a snake covered in more snakes.

"Ya gonna get that?" Ham finally asked as the noise persisted past eight rings. But she didn't. She just kept looking up at Ham, expecting him to do something, anything to save her from the hell that was speaking to another person.

"Jesus Christ, Hutch..." he finally mumbled. He sighed as he leaned over the counter and ripped the phone up. "McCray Engine, Ham speakin'?...What's that? No Ham...HAM. No, Yeah that's my name, sir...Yep, like the lunchmeat," Ham rolled his eyes at Hutch as she listened to the indiscernible chatter coming through the other end. "Sir, sir, I'm just gonna stop ya right there. I'm just a lowly broom-pusher here, let me, let me hand you over to our receptionist real quick." Hutch's eyes got huge as she mouthed the words "*No. No.*" over and over. "Yeah, sir. She'll take good care of you, okay," Ham spoke on as he tried handing the phone to his sister. Hutch crossed her arms, she was beyond pissed. Her tongue poked the inside of her cheek as she eye-balled her brother down with the iciest stare she could muster. "Take it. Now," he silently mouthed in annoyance. She quickly yanked the phone from his hand and mouthed back "Asshole," as she threw the phone to her ear.

"Ma-Engine, er, McCray Engine. This, this is Hutch," she stuttered like the fool she instantly felt she was. She absolutely HATED talking on the phone and her nervousness showed in her actions. Her anxiety was palpable as she began to pace the floor waiting for the customer to respond.

"Hutch? Say you're name is Hutch?" An overtly redneck tone came through the line.

"Ummm, yeah."

"Hutch?...Like a cabinet?"

"Sure...like a cabinet," she agreed for the sake of getting the conversation over with as quickly as possible.

"Damn...that sure is a weird name for a gal. You're a woman, right?"

"Uh, yeah," she answered sternly.

"Oh damn, well since I gotta woman on the phone, I need yur opinionation on somethin', I'm lookin ta build a mean-ass engine, ya know? I mean ta tell ya somethin' that makes a rumblin' that won't leave a dry paira panties within earshot." Hutch pulled the phone away for a second, dumbfounded with what she was hearing. Her eyebrow raised and her lip curled in disbelief.

"What?" Was all she managed to get out to the man.

"Oh, come on honey, ya know, an engine that will make a pussy purr!! A build that'll getta cooter screamin' louder than a baby caught in a beartrap!" The man yelled into the phone with a disturbing amount of excitement. Hutch's mouth was permanently gaped at this point. She just stared off at the wall, searching for words.

"You still, there?" He finally spoke.

"Barely..." she answered.

"Barely? Now you ain't gonna tell me you ain't never heard an engine at that shop that could get a girl goin'? One that would get a paira undies wetter than a cucumber salad in a thunderstorm?!"

"What the fuck?!" Hutch finally blurted out, losing her composure. Right at that second, a howling laughter erupted from behind her. She spun round to see Hayden leaning out of the back office with a phone in his hand.

"Biiiiiiitch!" He yelled out, pointing a finger triumphantly at her.

"Oh, are ya serious?! You ass!" She bellowed as she slammed the phone down. By this point Heath and Ham were laughing right along with Hayden who was now walking out through the lobby, strutting and smiling like he had just bested the devil himself.

"Damn, you held out longer than I thought you would!" Hayden laughed on at his sister's expense.

"Don't even talk to me…Wetter than a cucumber salad in a thunderstorm?! What the hell?! That's gross…even for you, that's just gross…Who says that to their sister?! You nasty bastard," she spoke in disgust, crossing her arms. Hayden just burst into a new round of laughter. "Seriously, this shits gettin' out of control…Yeah! Yeah! Laugh it up, y'all! It's hilarious!" She spoke out as agitated as could be, drawing most of her attention to Ham. "Yeah, Ham it up, Ham! You were in on this? You knew that was him on the line?"

"Knew it was me? Hell he came up with the idea!" Hayden jumped in before Ham could answer.

"Oh, now that IS bullshit!" Ham pointed at his brother, trying to calm his laughing before Hutch killed them all. "I didn't know that was you, but I knew somethin' wasn't right. Specially with those faces she started makin'."

"Jesus Christ…" was all Hutch could say as she shook her head. Right at that moment, the laughter was chased away from the sound of the front door chime. In strode an older gentleman, donned in bib overalls, his eyes searching the lobby as if he'd never been there before.

"Shit, it's one of them customer people. Try not to run em' off, huh?" Hayden whispered as he made himself scarce, slipping back into the workshop.

"Assholes," Hutch muttered under her breath as her brothers all seemed to disappear into thin air, leaving her there alone and still pissed, having to now deal with an actual customer.

"Howdy," the man nodded at Hutch as he approached the desk.

"What do you want?" She expelled without even thinking. The man looked at her strangely for a moment and she backtracked, "I mean…can I help you?"

"Well…I'm hopin' so. You in charge here, missy?" He spoke as he bellied up to the counter. Hutch was already doing an internal eye-roll. She could smell the reluctance all over this guy and could almost physically see his thoughts - "*What is this woman working at a machine shop for? There's clothes to be folded and meals to be cooked at home where she belongs.*"

"I'm not in charge, but I can be," Hutch spoke as she rose up to a full standing position behind the counter. The man's demeanor changed ever so slightly as he had to look up into Hutch's eyes, a thing he obviously wasn't all that used to.

"Right…well…Yeah, I gotta 300 straight block I need work done to."

"Ford 4.9. Good engine. Harder ta kill than a cockroach," Hutch said.

"That's right," the man's eyes widened a bit at her words of affirmation.

"And?" Hutch asked.

"And what?"

"What work do you want done to it?"

"Oh…right. Need it thermal cleaned n' shot blasted. You know what I'm talkin' bout right, darlin'?" The man instantly went back to speaking down to her. She felt as if she was playing some psychological chess game with him. She moved her pieces forward.

"Do I know what you're talkin' about? Let's see, thermal cleanin', I think that's where I stick that block of yours in an oven and bake it at about 500 degrees for seven to eight hours to remove dirt and grease from it. Then shot blast it….? Hmmmm? Is that where you run it through a machine with a rotisserie that throws those tiny steel beads at it, removin' any remainin' paint, rust, and carbon that the thermal cleanin' missed?" She threw out her words as descriptive and patronizing as possible.

"That's right," the man agreed, trying his best not to let his irritation show.

"Well, we can do that," Hutch smiled.

"Great. When you're done with that, I need them cylinders bored 60 over," the man went on.

"No," Hutch's smile erased.

"No?" The man raised an eyebrow at her.

"No."

"Well, why the hell not?"

"Well, I'm gonna tell ya why the hell not. Gets your cylinder walls paper-thin and cracks your block like a clay pot. Remember how I said they're harder ta kill than a cockroach? That's how ya kill that cockroach," she firmly explained as she crossed her arms.

"Well, I think you can just bore that thing over 60 and let me worry about any 'issues' that come down the pipeline, alright?" He cocked his head with a forced grin. It was obvious the man wasn't taking her seriously.

"No," was all she said once again. The man sighed and fidgeted. He began biting at his lip as he spoke up again.

"Now, honey, I want you to explain to me why the hell they'd make 60 over pistons if borin' over 60 would be an issue?"

"Just cuz they make an over 60 piston don't mean you should use em'. But I guess at the end of the day it's sort of a dick showin' contest for all you guys ain't it. You just wanna say to your hot rod buddies, *"Mines bored over sixty, bet yours ain't that big!"*

"Hutch!" A voice boomed in her ear, followed by the sharp pain of a huge hand wrapping round her arm. She was forcibly spun round right into the angry gaze of Hank who had obviously been listening to the whole conversation.

"Ham?!" Hank called out. Ham quickly appeared from the shop area. "Take over," Hank nodded to the man who was two seconds shy of walking out the door.

"Got it," Ham sped over to the counter, quickly enacting damage control as the eldest of the McCrays all but dragged the youngest down the hall by the arm.

"What the?!..Get off me!...UHH!" Hutch grunted and growled as she stumbled along trying to pry Hank's iron hand off of her arm. Soon they were in one of the back hall areas, out from anyone's sight. "Let go of my arm, asshole!" She yelled out. Right at that moment, Hank obliged her request. He released and shoved her hard against a block wall covered in poster-board. A small deluge of pictures and newspaper clippings came raining down around her as she tried to catch her breath from the brutal impact.

"What the fuck was that?! What ya think you're doin' out there?!" Hank laid into her, a finger only inches from her face as she straightened up, back against the wall. Hutch just glared at him for a moment.

"There goes that vein in your neck again," Hutch smarted off to him. Before she could even blink, she felt the stinging pain of her brother's open hand across her face. She grabbed her cheek, reeling from the surprise of the slap. Tears were fought back with near unshakable odds as she leered at him, still holding the side of her burning face.

"Oh, don't even give me that look…that was a love tap and you know it. Otherwise you wouldn't be conscious to question it…I'll ask you again, what the FUCK were ya doin' out there?"

"What the fuck, was I doin' out there?! My job! I'm keepin' some dumb asshole from blowin' his engine up!"

"Well that's where you're wrong, Hutch. That AIN'T your job. You're, job is to stand there, look stupid, which you're very good at, and take the customer's fuckin' orders. And if a customer wants a block bored over 60, you nod and say *"yes, we will bore that over 60, sir!"* Hank went off. Hutch just sneered at the diatribe.

"Oh, is that how we're doin shit now? All half-assed and sloppy? Just get em in, an' get em out, an' get paid! Is that it?!"

"Don't you even come at me with that pious bullshit. You're startin' ta sound like granddad, and lemme tell ya, you AIN'T granddad. You ain't got no idea what its like ta run a business, Hutch. Ya come in here late everyday, prance around and then leave at five o'clock. Meanwhile I'm doin' paperwork, makin' phone calls, and placin' orders till fucks-end while you're out drinkin' yourself stupid without a care on your shoulders. Have you even looked at this place lately? I mean really looked at it. We ain't exactly rollin' in customers as of late, and we're still tryin' to recover from mom's bullshit buyout. So we need to be takin' every thermal, shot blast, and over 60 we can get," Hank spouted off, nearly losing his breath at the end. Hutch just began shaking her head.

"That out there was your fault," she said.

"My fault?" Hank scoffed and pointed at his chest. He couldn't wait to hear this tsunami of bullshit.

"Yeah! You put me out there knowin' damn well I hate dealin' with people. Specially' guys like that," she pointed towards the front.

"Guys like that?" Hank raised a brow.

"You know exactly what I'm talkin' bout, cuz you're one of em'. He was eyeballin' me from jump wonderin' why the hell I wasn't nursin' a baby and bakin' banana bread."

"What?" Hank said in confusion.

"They think I'm a goddamn receptionist! Like I ain't gotta brain cell up in ma head that bleeds anythin' more than cooking, cleanin, and caretakin'....funny how a pair of tits immediately makes ya mechanically declined in some peoples eyes."

"Hutch, I ain't got time to sit here an' listen to ya cry bout your feelins of inferiority cuz you ain't got no dick between your legs. Grow a fuckin' pair, would ya? I feel like I've been caterin' to your feelins ma whole life, cuz *"you're the baby"*, cuz *"you're a girl"*. Get outta here with that shit…You need to start learnin' how to let people's bullshit roll off ya instead of on ya," Hank went on, his anger quickly boiling up again.

"Ha! Let people's bullshit roll off me? That's real cute comin' from the man who once knocked his wife's teeth in cuz she made tuna casserole instead of lasagna."

"Hey?! You're gonna get the same if you keep bringin' up my personal life ta feed your goddamn arguments…Ya think yur better than me? Hell maybe at one point in our lives ya were, but what ya got now? A suspended license, no car, a fresh drunken hit n' run, and you're basically livin' in a tin can in the back lot of a truck stop. If that ain't rock bottom I don't know what the fuck is," Hank spouted off without mercy. A tiny hint of a tear welled in the corner of Hutch's eye as his words dug deep into her flesh.

"You know what? If my life is such an eyesore to you, I'll just fuckin' leave."

"You'll leave?" Hank's eye widened as he tried to conceal a laugh. "Oh no, sister of mine…You ain't goin' anywhere. I own you." Hutch's eyes went dark as thunder clouds. She pointed right into his face. "You…DON'T…fuckin' own me. You got that? I'm no one's property," her words were laced heavy with a venomous whisper.

"Oh, I don't own you? I don't? You gotta record now, Hutch. Ain't no one gonna hire you, and even if they did, who's gonna drive your sorry ass to work? And if you think you're gonna get a glowin' job recommendation from your previous employer, ME, you got another thing comin. Let's not forget that before-mentioned tin can you're livin' in? That technically belongs ta me, so I hope you gotta tent ta pitch on your rebellious voyage to join the circus....Now ya see? I sorta DO own you on some level," Hank spoke the entire breadth of his dialogue with a snide smile that he could barely conceal. As he stood there looking into his sister's eyes, he could see the turgid storm of anger and sadness welling within them, and for a moment, if only a mere second, Hank the Tank felt a heartstring tear. He backed off of her to let her breathe better. It was obvious she had nothing to say, but he was far from finished. "Hutch," he began shaking his head once more, "Sometimes, most times, I don't want ya here as much as ya don't wanna be here. I have wanted to fire you more times than I can count...but I don't. Ya wanna know why?" Hutch had no answer for him. Her eyes had since left his gaze and were drilling into the brick wall beside them. Hank went on without her speculations. "It ain't because you're ma sister and it ain't because I just enjoy your smilin' face and sunny disposition...Look at me," he demanded her attention before he went on. Her glassy eyes returned to his...deep loathing ran through them. "I don't fire ya because you're a damn good machinist. Customer One has not came back and complained about any engine you touched. Hayden? Yes. Heath? I could write a book with that four-eyed fuck's mistakes, but not you. You and those engines...you and them machines back there...y'all got some kinda connection. A connection I'm not even gonna try ta understand but it's there, ain't no denyin' it. I still can't believe the day dad let you check and plane those 351 heads at 14 years old, by yourself. And you got em perfect...Hell I don't even think he could've done that at that age. You know he wanted you ta fuck that up. He wanted a reason to tell ya you couldn't be a machinist. He didn't want you workin' the engines...no one here did. But you proved him wrong...you proved me wrong..." Hank's words got tamer as he reflected upon the events of the past. He stood there awaiting a response from his sister, but nothing more than stagnant silence came as she kept her resentful stare transfixed into his eyes. "So this is what you're gonna do? Stare at me like ya wanna rip ma head off? Give me the silent treatment?" Hank spoke in irritation. Hutch sighed and crossed her arms, letting herself fall back against the wall with a thump as she decided whether or not the man in front of her even deserved the sound of her voice in his ears. The tiny impact of her relax dislodged a piece of paper from the poster board behind. It fluttered down and grazed her shoulder on its graceful descent to the haggard and darkened concrete below. Both sister and brother watched as the white note landed face up and slid to a stop. Hutch's heart softened a bit as she read the words in silent reflection. Words that she had read what seemed like a million times over. *"Missing: Have You Seen This Woman? Cassandra E. McCray. Age: 38 Height: 5'8" Weight: 120lbs – Last seen driving a red, early model Mustang in the Danbridge area."* Hutch broke no stride in her sober stare as she slowly bent down and fetched the paper from the grasp of the cold floor beneath.

"Two more days…" she spoke gingerly, never taking her eyes from the picture of the woman who gazed back at her.

"What?" Was all Hank released.

"Aunt Cass…Two more days…," she rose back to a stand and carefully pinned the missing poster back to the corkboard beside her.

"Two more days till what, Hutch? The anniversary of her 'kidnappin'?" Hank patronized. "Ya know, you're probably the only one of us that still believes that shit. Not to mention the only one that still pays attention ta the date that it happened."

"You're really gonna stand there and try an' make me believe you don't remember the exact day it happened?" Hutch almost mumbled as she stared at the face of her aunt, recalling the events of the days surrounding her disappearance.

"No Hutch, I don't. But I sure as hell remember the month. July…"

"**McCray McCurse Month**," they spoke at the same time, referring to the pet name they'd dubbed the month of inevitable shit for the family.

"You're damn right," Hank said, "Henry dyin', Grandad dyin', Grandma dyin, mom leavin, dad's diagnoses, your diagnoses, and Cass disappearin', ALL in July…Hell I'd suggest the entire family should hide under rocks till the month passes over every year, but one of us would probably get crushed to death by said rocks." Hutch stood quiet for a moment, thinking of every event Hank named off. Each flash of his syllables drawing up another stinging memory of loss and defeat. She knew she would never understand why one of the hottest months of the year decided to use the McCrays' faces for toilets, but she still puzzled over it just the same.

"You think she's still out there?" Hutch returned her attention back to their aunt's disappearance.

"Hope not…" Hank answered coldly.

Hutch spun round to look at him in disbelief, her face half-broken in the wake of his response. "I'm serious. She's been out there for over half a decade without as much as a postcard, phone call, or smoke signal to her family. She might as well be dead…I know she is to me," Hank furthered his all too obvious disdain with their aunt. Hutch's gaze left the face of her brother and floated downwards and away as she fought the urge to cuss him out. Hell maybe he was right…Maybe she did desert them. She was always the flighty type. Maybe she had had enough of everyone and everything that walked, talked, and resounded through her life…and there was a part of Hutch that couldn't blame her. If she had a dollar for every time she, herself, thought about crawling into her car and driving towards the setting sun till the rays burned her blind, she'd be rich enough to tell Hank where to go.

Amidst a solid minute of awkward silence between the siblings, Hutch's face grew more and more emotionless until, finally, she walked away from her brother without a word. Hank put his hands on his hips as he watched her walk off in silence…nothing good ever came from a McCray walking away like that. It led straight into things being destroyed or alcohol being consumed…or both.

"Hey…Hutch?" Hank spoke out. But as if he had said nothing at all, her steps remained the same as she opened a door that led into the back garage areas. "Where you goin?" He made another attempt, but the cold pace of her steps was all that continued to answer him back. "Christ…," he let out a sigh of aggravation as he walked quickly to catch up to her. He paced through the open pedestrian door to see her standing there amongst the shadows of the large area, staring at an object of his chagrin. A quick flip of his fingers awakened a switch that set the room alight with a glowing overhead symphony of buzzing fluorescents. The enormous back garage area was awash with empty work benches and backstocks of boxes and parts, and in the center of it all was a car covered in a pale green canvas drop cloth. Hutch stood not far from this landmark, gazing like a woman possessed at yet another canvas concealed fixture. She reached out and threw off the cover to reveal a gorgeous engine bolted to a wheeled-stand. The chrome and deep blue paint gleamed the likes of a holy sword being unsheathed to the eyes of the non-believing. The deathly gloom that seemed to flood her stare, whisked away ever the slightest as Hutch just gazed upon the chunk of metal with a trace of hunger tugging at her heart. The disturbing silence was cut over and over by the slow pace of Hank's heavy boots approaching his sister from behind. He stared at the mighty engine with not the same wandering desire as his sibling, but more the pang of contempt and aberration. His lumbering tread stopped coldly, a few paces behind, as he took the sight of the beast in. She was a 351 Windsor, spec'd, tweaked, and molded to the desire of gods and admiration of kings. The ford-blue block was bejeweled with chrome headers, valve covers, oil pan, and a menagerie of winding lines and beautiful bits and bolts that lay praise to a towering supercharger crowned by dual-four barrel carburetors, 'neath a trinity of red butterflies. The very presence of that engine was as foreboding as it was breathtaking…it was a monster dressed in the gleam of an angel's embrace. Heaven graced its metallic flesh whilst hell longed to burn within its virgin chambers…and yet here it sat, seemingly doomed to be a permanent fixture in the loneliness of the back room, forever dreaming of a hood to reside beneath and road to burn into oblivion. The sight of it was like art…every piece, right down to the lowly bolts, were anodized, chromed, and torqued with love, with purpose. This was no normal engine.

"You need to sell that damn thing, it's takin' up room…world's most expensive paperweight," Hank let his thoughts come pouring out. Hutch's trance slowly faded as his words reprised. "And that car you two were gonna put that thing in…" His gaze drew to the enshrouded auto in the center of the room. "A Maverick…A Maverick? Why not a Mustang or…or a Falcon. Who the hell drops a supercharged 351 in a damn 73' Maverick?"

"Exactly…" was all Hutch responded with a whisper. And that was just it, she and her aunt loved Mustangs, hell they were

Cassandra's car of choice…but hadn't enough of them been turned into raging beasts? Was it not time to let an underdog feel the surge of power incarnate? A Maverick…It was different, it was unpredictable, and with any luck, it would be unnerving to the one who dare step up to the starting block against it.

"I want it gone," Hank's grizzly voice sunk into her ears. She remained silent as she walked over and grabbed a long wrench from the nearby workbench. "You hear me, Hutch? I said I want it gone. Sell it. Part it out. Or Throw it in that goddamn POS under the tarp there and push it out the door while you're at it."

"Yep…" was all she spoke as she placed the socket-end of the tool into the engine's crank bolt. She began slowly turning the beast over and over as she always did a few times a week for the last five-plus years, keeping the insides from freezing up, hopelessly waiting on her aunt to return so they could finish what they had started….but as the days trudged into what was now nearly six years without her around, hope seemed a forgotten word in that frigid back garage. Hank just watched his sister and grinned the slightest, shaking his head in the ridiculousness of her ritual task.

'Hutch, if you plan on turnin' that damn thing weekly till she comes back, you might as well make it your full time job with no retirement benefits." She looked over at him with a distant sadness she could barely hide. "She's gone Hutch. Never comin' back. Accept it…the rest of us sure as hell have," with that, Hank marched away, back into the hall. As he walked on by the posterboard, he violently ripped their aunt's missing poster off the wall, crumpled it, and threw it to the floor below. Hutch didn't witness the act, but the noise was telling enough. She stopped her cranking and leaned against the engine, resting her head against the street scoop with a newfound breath of despair. Perhaps everyone had accepted it, that Cassandra McCray, the sole wild-child daughter of Hess McCray, and notorious drag car queen of Highland Strip, had in fact disappeared into the ether, never to return. Or worse, she was dead. The family never held a funeral, and probably never would. It was all so strange, that hot July night in 1990 she drove off in her Mustang and that was the last anyone had ever seen or heard of her. Some say she owed money to the wrong people and was at the bottom of a lake somewhere. And it wasn't a stretch to believe. Cass McCray was no stranger to gambling, mostly on car races of her own design. She raced the strip for years building a local notoriety as being the fiery-haired, super stock siren that the boys couldn't beat. She had a loud mouth and a lead foot to back it up, but years upon years of racing in a straight line left her bored and beaten. She longed for something new…so she soon turned her back on the drag strip and immersed herself deep into the dark underbelly of illegal street racing. This is where she finally felt alive once again. Setting up routes that traversed the local, twisting back roads. Routes that relied not only on straight speed, but maneuverability and all out gall…it was a life that was soon to suck in a young Hutch McCray who looked up to her as the mother she always wanted. As all the memories of engine building, pedal mashing, and pitch black nights of racing shady characters came flooding back to her, a single tear trickled down Hutch's face. She looked off with a stare of grim reflection and the words left her lips in a saddened whisper, "Where are you?"

Pretty Little Golden Eyes

The baleful sting of the pre-noon sun was quickly kissing Hutch's ivory flesh as she walked a line across the lot, wandering through the never-ending herd of 18-wheeled beasts that grazed upon the gravel abounding. She had fled the solidarity of the back room not long after Hank had left her to stew in her own melancholy. Without a care, or a permission asked, she walked right through the shop and out the front door on a mission to drown her sorrows in a plate of good old American grease. Now she wasn't quite sure if bacon and pancakes were FDA registered anti-depressants, but they sure as hell couldn't hurt at that point. She lit up a cigarette and was soon zig-zagging her way amongst the maze of idling semis that peppered the path between her and the truck stop. Diesel fumes stung at her eyes and her senses became numb from the rumbling symphony of galloping valves and steel exhaust flappers. It was a melody she was all too used to…she heard it in her sleep, and she felt it echo through the bones of her ears long after she would depart from it. She had traversed this lot ever since she was old enough to walk, looking up with awe at the towering giants, wondering what was inside them, where they were going, and what wonders they had seen. But such curious thoughts faded, as they often did, into the monotony and numbness of adulthood. She no longer saw them much more than the simple machines they were, idle obstacles that lay between her and her breakfast…oh how things had changed.

Smoke wisped around her face as she withdrew her cigarette, blowing a plume of marbled-white to join the dirty diesel clouds above. She rounded the last truck in the line and stopped to finish the last half of her smoke, staring at the front façade of a place she called a third home. And there she was in all of her middle-America glory, Piper Jean's Pig N' Rig, a moniker so campy you would expect it to be plastered on the side of beer coozies, bumper stickers, buttons, and t-shirts….and it was. If you went on inside you could get them at the front at rock-bottom prices. They even had key chains too. Their logo was a cheesing cartoon face of a Chihuahua wearing a trucker's hat. Supposedly it was the owner's dog, but Hutch had never seen this mythical creature in person to confirm it. It all seemed like marketing BS to her. Of course the place wasn't always like that, Hutch recalled the days when it was more of a true trucker and local's destination than a borderline tourist trap. When it was originally built, it was simply called Charlie's. The place had only seen one remodeling in the late 70's so, in a way, it was trapped in that era, and looked no different than what Hutch remembered from when she was just a kid. But times were changing and changing fast. A few big chain truck stops were starting to pepper the Big Bird and business for Piper Jeans was going downhill. It would be a miracle if the place made it another decade if they didn't update their look and reputation.

As Hutch exhaled the last draw of smoke and flicked her butt to the concrete below, her nose became introduced to another smell amongst the chaos. That sweet, smoky scent that Piper Jean's was known for almost as well as being a respite for truckers. The aromatic pang of charring meats that had been cooking since the night before. Round about noon everyday they would start serving the best damn BBQ the state had to offer…or at least that's what every local seemed to think. Hutch always had thought the place was overrated. The brisket was dry and their house sauces were mediocre at best, and she always judged a place on the quality of their brisket even above the quality of the sauce. But they did have amazing burgers on the menu, and served breakfast all the live long day, the latter of those two facts tugged on the gal's heartstrings who firmly believed morning didn't start till 10 a.m.

"Food," Hutch simply mumbled to herself, walking a beeline for the door. She cut in front of a group of older ladies making their way onto the sidewalk. With a quickness, she rounded the women that eyed her up like the giant they surely thought her to be, and she walked right through the entrance, not even bothering to hold the door open for them. Food first, manners later, she thought to herself as the smell of BBQ and stale cigarettes took up full residence in her nose. The main store and truckers' areas were off to the right, and the restaurant made up most of the left side. The interior of Piper Jean's was nothing short of lackluster for the day and age. She was, after all, still stuck in the era of bell bottoms, 8-Tracks, and pet rocks. Needless to say, the whole place was awash with wood grain paneling, crazy patterned carpet, and colors so inane that Hutch was convinced only ten percent of the population could see them accurately. Still in all, it was always welcoming to her...even though she was in there everyday. Every time she laid eyes upon the place, it drummed up memories...lots of them. She remembered shoplifting booze and magazines with Hayden. Reading comics and never buying them. Playing games till her eyes glassed over in the little arcade room that they had...god she had spent countless hours in that dank room. She would never forget the Sundays the family would meet her grandparents there to eat and she would spend the entire time running back and forth between the table and the game room begging for quarters from anyone who'd dare give them up. Often times, it was her grandfather that would be feeding her change behind his chair as if he was spreading bread out for a rabid duck. Hutch would smile, her hand gobbling them up as her grandmother would admonish her grandfather for the act, "She NEEDS to eat, Hess!" But food could wait, there were gremlins to run over, invaders to be eradicated, and stuffed animals to be fished out with steel claws. Did her grandmother not understand the importance of all this?

49

And Oh, the crane machine, she would return with prize after prize she had skillfully plucked from the depths of it, eagerly awaiting her grandfather's doting on how talented she was with that claw. Then she would return home with those stuffed trophies in hand, and together her and Ham would set them on fire or shove M80s inside of them…Ahhh those were the days.

"Excuse us," a crippled, old voice crept up into Hutch's ear. She apparently had been daydreaming a bit too much as the group of older ladies had caught up with her and were now ditching her into the restaurant. She said nothing back as she watched them get seated, she was still too caught up in her own mind to even care about much at that moment, but her memories took a back seat as her eyes fell dead upon the local bulletin board. She walked up to it in anger as she realized the copy of her aunt's missing poster was covered up by three layers of garage sale flyers and a hand-written ad looking for lawns to mow. A quick grab of a thumb tack sent the papers tumbling to the floor as she uncovered the poster for everyone to see once again. As she went to walk away, she nearly knocked over a stand beside the wall. She quickly grabbed the edge of it before the daily papers it held went cascading down to join the flyers. Her eyes read the front page as she plucked the top paper from the stack "The Carnation Killer: Looking Back on an Unsolved Decade of Death" It was an article highlighting the cold cases of murders that happened in the area. Eight women were found murdered over the course of ten years, from 1961 to 1971. All of them had been murdered and left naked with a single carnation flower placed somewhere on their bodies, hence the press dubbing the name "Carnation Killer". It wasn't exactly a moniker that would evoke fear in most folks, but to a small, rural community it was the name of the devil himself. Hutch was still a baby when the last body was found so she had no idea of just how crazy the community had gotten, but she heard the stories from her dad and grandfather. Some people were setting curfews and were afraid to go out after dark. No one trusted anyone. The first body was bad enough, but then when others began to show up just like it, the words "Serial Killer" were dropped like a bomb on the tri-county area. It was a dark period of time for most. The FBI even got involved, but what made matters worse was the killer was never found. The paper was apparently dredging up the 25th anniversary of the death of the last victim, Melissa Gellar. She was found at night on the river by two men cat-fishing. Her body was carefully placed on a natural outcropping the locals often referred to as Rock Dam. She was a gorgeous twenty-two year old brunette that worked the night shift at a local diner. The daughter of a mill worker and homemaker. Just a normal gal, as were most of the victims. And that's what made the whole thing all the more terrifying to the women of the area, the knowledge that it could be you or anyone you loved.

Hutch shook her head and tossed the paper back into place. To her, the story of the Carnation Killer was just a folktale of sorts, a parable that ended in 71', long before she had any emotional awareness of the tragedies. But to the victim's families, it was undoubtedly as real as the day it happened.

Hutch soon walked into the restaurant, right on by the "Please Wait to be Seated" marquee, a sign she continually ignored ever since she was old enough to read. It was a known fact that most people ignored that thing…Well the locals anyway. The locals seemed to be the bread and butter of the place. Most came everyday if not multiple times a day. Everyone knew everyone else, if not by name, by face at the very least. Along with that came the usual sitting spots and the same damn food ordered over and over. Hutch was no exception. After all, humans were nothing but creatures of habit. Her spot was in the farthest booth back, on the front side windows…Good, no one was currently sitting there. And her meal was…

"2X4, Hutch?" A voice spoke out as she plopped down in the booth with her back against the wall. Hutch looked up to a face that epitomized tired and cheerful in a glorious union, haloed in short, graying hair.

"Always, …" Hutch responded with a little smile. As if she really was going to answer any differently? The 2X4 was the ingenious brain child of the head manager back when the place was still called Charlie's. The concept and basic equation of this farm fresh concoction was simple – 2 eggs, 2 slices of toast, 2 strips of bacon, and 2 pancakes = 2X4. Why there was anything else on the breakfast menu, she couldn't rightly figure. Carol just shook her head with a smile, not even bothering to jot down the order.

"How you want those eggs?" She asked.

"Well, preferably in my stomach," Hutch jested, "C'mon, Carol, lets not do this. You know how I want them eggs." Carol just rolled her eyes.

"I know, but I just keep hopin' you'll change that order up, just a tick. Same ol' thing for almost twenty years…live a little, Hutch!" She smiled and slapped the order tablet off Hutch's shoulder, walking off with a laugh.

"I AM livin'.." Hutch said, "… a little….very little," as her words faded under her own numbing stare, she began scanning the room as she often did. She saw the normal faces, the late to breakfast / lunch crowd…if you wanted to call them a crowd. There was red hat guy, a man who, without fail, would tell the story of the .22 rifle he found in the creek behind his dad's place at least two times per week, often to the same folks. Sharon or Karen, or whatever her name was, the retired school teacher that was always talking about her 'perfect' grandson and her obsessive basket collecting habits. And who could forget Burt "What's-His-Face" the sports obsessed old fella that would never stop talking about "Them Buckeyes", mainly to people that couldn't have cared less. Now it was rare, if ever, that Hutch actually talked to any of these people on a level more than just "hey" or a head nod. She simply knew them through observation and eavesdropping. There was no TV hanging in Piper Jeans so the patrons were always the entertainment…or perhaps lack thereof. Of course, there were the inventible shades in the room of the non-locals…of the passersbys…the beards and/or hats painted on weary and unfamiliar faces. They were the thankless, the forgotten, the road-ridden and downtrodden. The truckers. The men and women, who truly did keep America running, though no one took a damn minute out of their day to thank them for it. But I guess in their own minds they didn't need the thanks. A gallon of coffee, a hot shower, and a spouse who wouldn't cheat on them was all they really asked for. As she had as a child with the trucks they piloted, Hutch wondered where each of the drivers were going, what their eyes had seen, and what burdens lay behind the heaviness in their eyes…Their eyes…Their cold, red eyes…Was that man's eyes red? She thought as her eyes locked with a fellow across the restaurant. He stared at her almost menacingly with what seemed like a small smile cracking through his black beard. Hutch rarely felt intimated by any living thing, let alone a stranger, but her breath slowly began leaving her as the game of "don't blink" trudged on for what seemed like five whole minutes. Who was he? Did she know him? Red…Christ his eyes WERE red, Weren't they? Soon, her own eyes regained enough guile to pull themselves up to read the tattered hat that crowned the trucker's head "Redgrace Logistics"

The spell of the stare-down was shattered by a sound of ceramic kissing the hard surface of the table in front of Hutch. She twitched inside and jerked her head up to look into the eyes of Carol who had returned with her drink.

"Thanks…" she spoke soft and wide-eyed. Carol looked at her oddly.

"Yep…You okay?" She spoke in concern.

"Umm, yeah…no, I'm fine," she looked back over to the direction of the trucker who had now seemingly disappeared into thin air. "Oh shit…Well I think I'm okay," she said as she placed her shaking fingers up to her temples.

"Okay…" Carol was admittedly at a loss for words, she had never seen Hutch behave this way. The redhead was often hard to read, but she was obviously riled by something. She quickly changed gears. "Well get some of that in ya. You'll feel better," Carol pointed at the hot tea she had brought.

"Yeah…" Hutch nodded in agreement, pulling the saucer close to her.

"Yeah…" Carol echoed her words. She cautiously walked off, taking a bit of time before she took her eyes completely off of Hutch to attend to other patrons. Hutch looked up from the drink, back to the place where the driver had been once again…and once again, there was nothing but an empty seat. She quickly shook her head of it, as hard as that was, and took her hat off, placing it on the seat beside her. Soon, she found herself trapped in her own dead-eyed stare into space, pondering over any damn thing she could think of besides the ghost trucker. The voice of Waylon droned into her ear from the jukebox as she bobbed the tea bag into the hot water below her gaping mouth, all while stroking her own hair in some odd, self-calming ritual. It was a state of semi-zen that soon dropped away the second her eyes met that cheesy, needlepoint sign that hung on the wall down the way. "Life is not measured by the breaths you take, but by the moments that take your breath away" She read that sign every time she was there, and every time she cringed from the pain of her own internal eye-roll. It was the rhetorical cheeriness of the whole thing. The numbing reciprocity. She just pictured some older lady completely enamored with her own cleverness the moment she had came up with it. *"This needs to be immortalized in yarn for the whole world to smile upon."* Hutch stopped her hair stroking and her lip curled in disgust right before she raised her hot cup to her mouth. Damn she really was a cynical creature. But on the bright side, her concern with the red-eyed trucker had left and was now firmly replaced with good old-fashioned McCray pessimism. Her angry, blue eyes just kept staring at that sign overtop the steaming ceramic vessel that steered burning English breakfast into her gullet over and over. If her unwavering stare could've set that thing on fire, it would've been done reduced to ash and vaporized by now. The sudden screech of a plate sliding across the table filled her ears and curtailed her gaze below for a moment to see the sight of her breakfast's arrival.

"Oh ma god, Carol, y'all need to take that thing down..." Hutch seethed out a voice just above a whisper, her eyes reglued to the object of her dismay. Carol joined her for a moment in staring at the sign. She shook her head.

"Well, whatever had you wound up a minute ago is obviously gone. The old Hutch is back....You need anything else?"

"Yeah, a wood chipper to toss that thing into," Hutch said. Carol rolled her eyes and sighed. "Enjoy your breakfast, Hutch."

"...Not likely," she whispered, finally regaining the strength to peel her eyes away from the wall for good. Her attention fell to the spread laid before her. An unhealthy dose of middle America fried to perfection. No sooner had Hutch found her fingers around the toast did the blazing blast of trumpets come bellowing through the jukebox, belting out the famous intro to 'Ring of Fire'...and, as if on cue, there she was. Hutch froze as her eyes drank in the sight of a young woman sashaying right in past the same sign the locals all ignored. As Johnny's baritone voice began echoing across the old speakers, time seemed to slow down inside of Piper Jean's as the mystery woman walked down the main aisle, her dark locks

bouncing off her confident shoulders. She commanded the room
and heads began to turn in her presence as she tapped a
tumultuous, hip-swaying beat upon the floor courtesy of a pair of
black high heels she seemed to be born in. She was gorgeous. She
was well dressed…to put it simple, she was out of place…and she
knew it, she relished it, and the tiniest crooked little smile seemed
to grace her face as she passed by every trucker that took their eyes
away from their coal-black coffees to look at her. Hutch was
beyond mesmerized by her presence…the toast she held began to
crumble in her ever tightening grip as the woman made her way
closer and closer to where she sat in awe. Her perfectly pressed
pantsuit had to be an indication that she was here on business,
nothing more. Was she a traveling saleswoman? The new manager
of Piper Jean's? Probably not, she didn't look a day over nineteen.
A hundred questions bounced around the room and seemed to
come alive in some surreal mumbling that no one could hear
except Hutch herself. And then it happened. The beautiful stranger
could walk no further, she was right beside Hutch's booth, and
with that, she plopped herself down right across from the
spellbound redhead. Hutch recoiled inside as the brunette reached
across the table with the utmost confidence and plucked a piece of
bacon right off of her plate.

"Tea? I figured you for a black coffee kinda girl," she spoke as
she took a bite from the stolen meat. She chewed with a smile that
seemed to span ear to ear, waiting patiently for Hutch to say
something, anything. But Hutch could say nothing. She remained
there, toast still in hand, eyes locked deep with the young
woman's…a turgid mixture of emotion powder-kegging behind
them. Did she know her? Was she someone she had met in a
drunken stooper and had completely forgotten about? No, she
wouldn't have forgotten her…not this one. She was short and
brunette and young…Hutch's kryptonite.

"Well?…I didn't figure you for the quiet type either," the girl
spoke, taking the rest of the bacon into her mouth. She then
reached for the other piece on Hutch's plate.

"Touch that bacon again and you're gonna draw back a bloody
stump," Hutch's words fell out with an involuntary roll that
surprised even her.

"There's a girl!" The young woman laughed heartily, recoiling her hand to the safety of her side of the table. Her eyes danced with her chuckling. They were an unnatural shade of golden amber and were perfectly accented by the equally unnatural vibrancy of a green carnation lapel pinned to her striped suit. The sound of her adorable laughter rung through Hutch's ears like sweet music that drowned out the 'Ring of Fire' abounding. Her cute little upturned nose…her alabaster skin…her dainty hands…This girl was driving Hutch insane inside. She wanted to rip off her face as much as she wanted to rip off her clothes. She had to get her shit together, and fast. In the next split second the only words Hutch could find came spewing out.

"What the hell do ya want from me?"

The girl's chuckling wound down, but only slightly.

"What do I want? Well I want you, silly," her eyebrow raised as she pointed, "You're a hard girl to track down, you know that?"

"I am?" Hutch spoke without emotion.

"Um, no. You live in a camper in the back of a truck stop parking lot. That was a little joke, there." Suddenly both women looked to the side to see Carol standing there with a pot of coffee and an odd look on her face. It was anyone's guess how long she'd been there.

"Oh, coffee! Yes, please!" The mystery girl spoke ecstatically, flipping over the extra cup that sat upon the table. Carol reluctantly filled the mug, all the while staring at Hutch. Hutch just glared back with the same look on her face. The awkwardness was palpable. Her duty done, Carol cast one last look at the brunette in the suit and walked off.

"Thanks, Carol. You're a doll….Now where were we?" The girl slapped the table as she spoke.

"We were at the part where I lost my appetite and was about to leave," Hutch mumbled as she put her hat back on and began to shuffle out of the booth.

"Oh, don't be like that. Sit down. Don't you wanna even know who I am?" The girl pleaded a tad. Hutch found her backside firmly placed right back down in her seat. Why was she doing this to herself? She had better things to do than trade words with this girl. She sighed.

"Fine…who are ya and why are ya eatin' ma food?" Hutch indulged her.

"Okay, let's answer that second one first, I'm eating your food because it's delicious. Duh. And my name is Regina," the girl extended her hand for a shake or a kiss…hell Hutch wasn't sure what she wanted. So she just sat there staring at it until Regina recoiled it with a smirk on her face.

"Regina?" Hutch said.

"Yep."

"Is it just Regina or you gotta last name?"

"Right, where are my manners? It's Redgrace. Regina Redgrace."

"Regina Redgrace?"

"Seems like there's a bit of an echo in here," Regina smiled at the repetition. The surname cut right through Hutch's chest and sent a chill up her spine. She sat quiet for a moment, recalling the not so distant past and the red-eyed trucker donning the hat with the name that now seemed branded onto the side of her brain.

"Regina Redgrace."

"Oh! There's that echo again. You hear it?"

"Regina…Fucking…Redgrace," Hutch drew out.

"Oh, well my middle name is actually Maud but I like '*Fucking*' waaay better," Regina smiled, biting her lip at the end of her words. This girl new exactly how to work Hutch. But still, the redhead pushed her carnal side down and out of sight as she brought the name up once again.

"Redgrace? As is in Redgrace Logistics? The truckin' company?" Hutch slowly belted out a triangle of redundancy.

"Guilty," Regina took a swig of her coffee and then went on, "So you've heard of us then?" Hutch paused before she answered with a shrug. "I guess…seen your trucks…and your red-eyed drivers around."

"Oh…well I don't think we push our drivers hard enough to make them red-eyed. They get rest," Regina put her coffee to her mouth again.

Hutch sighed, "Yeah…that's not what I meant…never mind…Look, we've established you're part of an at least mildly successful truckin' company, and I don't really care. So I'm gonna ask ya again, what the hell do ya want from me besides my bacon?" Regina hovered her mug just below her mouth as she thought deeply for a moment. Her eyes narrowed and she smirked.

"Red, do you know what I like in life?" She asked.

"No, but I'm just reelin' with anticipation."

"I like the three F's…Fucking, Food, and Fast Cars," she counted them off on her fingers as she grinned, "Now, I know you like all those too, but I think that last one you may have just a teensy bit more love for."

"So what you want? You came to me knowin' we make some of the best race engines around? The little, rich girl wants the rush of a bigger engine from McCray Machine dropped in her pink 95' Camaro that daddy bought her?"

"Okay two things, first I'm not little, I'm vertically challenged. Second, my ride is a white, 68' Mercury Cougar and I can assure you, my daddy didn't buy it for me." Hutch was officially in love. She had always loved old cars. She would take one over a brand new ride any day. There was just something about older cars. They'd been places, seen things. People had cried in them, laughed in them, reminisced about the past and hoped for the future. They smelled of life, and grief, and cigarettes past. You could hear them breathing, there was no computer telling them what to do or how to feel.

Hutch just sat there staring into Regina's golden eyes, her heart thumping. She tried to keep it under control as she asked about the 68' Cougar,

"What's under the hood?"

"Ohhh, you love to know what's under my hood wouldn't you?" She threw out yet another obvious tease. Hutch wetted her lips, but was cut short, "But I don't need an engine from you…What I need, is a challenge. Are you a challenge, Red?"

"I can be…"

"So I hear…and what I hear is you're quite the racer. You and fast cars?...Well, you two are like that," Regina crossed her fingers tightly together and winked.

"Maybe…once upon a time…." Hutch trailed off. Regina raised a brow. "What? So I won a few races on the drag strip. Hurt some macho egos…Got into some fights…Pissed some guys off and got blackballed out of there," the redhead explained.

"I'm not talking about THAT. You know what I'm talking about...You have quite the reputation for not-so-legal racing."

Hutch's eyes squinted in distrust," I don't do that anymore..."

"Ha! Listen to you," Regina laughed, "*I don't do that anymore,*" she mocked as she took a drink and looked to the ceiling with an eye roll. "You sound like a cliché from an action movie, Red....Well unlike you, I do DO that."

Hutch smirked into a short laugh. "You race? You street race? Can ya even reach the pedals?" She could hardly put away her smile.

"Well don't be mean...Is it really that hard to believe?"

"Yeah, it is."

"Well, it's the truth...annnnnd I'm pretty damn good at it."

"Right...Of course. Tell me though, if you're such a damn good racer why the hell've I never heard of you...EVER."

"Well that's cuz I've always been outside of your league, Red...till now."

"Oh shit, this is gettin' too good....I need some names."

"Excuse me?"

"Names. I need names of people you've raced."

"Oh, okay that's what you need to believe me? Well, let's start with a name you should know pretty well. Cassandra McCray." The name of her aunt being spoken by Regina screeched Hutch's heart to a stop. The room seemed to go cold for a moment. "Well that wiped the smile from your face...You need anymore names?"

"Cassandra McCray?"

"You repeat people a lot, you know that?"

"My aunt was one of the best..."

"Yes, Cassandra McCray, Queen of the Highland strip, Baroness of the back roads, and Duchess of the street scene...a local legend. Damn near unbeatable in your eyes...But she finally met her match."

"Who?" Hutch asked. Regina raised an eyebrow and smiled. "You? HA! Oh shit, you know what? I can't do this anymore. You have yourself a nice day, Regina, or whoever the fuck you really are." Hutch began to become flustered as she once again tried to take flight from the booth. She had no sooner stood up when Regina tossed something onto the table.

"Sit down, Red," she spoke bluntly. Hutch froze as the tiny object came to a sliding stop at the edge of her plate. It was a very familiar key attached to an even more familiar keychain. An unbreakable gaze was cast upon the trinket as Hutch squatted and slinked back into her seat…The gears were turning in her head. Anger, curiosity, dread, they all abounded her as she scooped the keychain up and let it dangle in front of her face. She read the words scribed in gold upon the red plastic, "The Scarlet Harlot"

"Where the FUCK did you get this?" Hutch hissed out slowly as her fingers wrapped into a fist around the ring.

"Oh, Red lets not play this game…You know damn well where I got that," Regina spoke without a smile to be found.

"You really did know my aunt…" was all Hutch could let out.

"Oh, I really DO know your aunt…present tense."

Hutch's eyes squinted with a fiery suspicion.

"My aunt is dead."

"Ha! C'mon, a lot of people believe that Red, but you aren't one of them. In fact, you might be the only one." Hutch could feel her heart racing once more. But this time it was far from the fault of lust and desire. It was the chilling pulse of rage and fear she could barely do anything to conceal as it squeaked out in her voice.

"What did ya do to her?"

"What did I do to her? No, more like what did she do to herself. You're sweet Aunt Cass made a high stakes bet with me. She raced me and she lost. Now she's reaping the consequences of that loss because she's deeply in debt to me. I took her Mustang, and she's been working off that debt to this day," Regina coldly explained. Hutch just began shaking her head at the odd realization of something right in front of her face.

"My aunt disappeared almost six damn years ago. What were you when you set up this high stakes bullshit, thirteen? How old are you?"

"Oh Red, I'm legal. If you wanna ask me on a date, just go ahead," she batted her eyes in jest. The mugs and plates jumped as Hutch's fist slammed onto the tabletop in anger. She pointed at the brunette with a seething whisper.

"Where is my aunt, you little cunt?"

"Redddd? You are so goddamn cute when you're mad, which is all the time from what I hear," Regina smiled.

"Where IS she?" Hutch began to shake. The brunette shook her head as she sipped another drink of coffee.

"Nuh-uh. It doesn't work that way. If you ain't already noticed, you and I, we're in the middle of a negotiation."

"Who are you? WHAT are you? Christ…are you a gangster or somethin'?" Hutch began to let her anger turn back into despair.

"Oh Red, I don't like labels like that. I'm just…I'm a business woman with an insatiable fetish. And that fetish just isn't quite getting me off like it used to. I race, I win. I race, I win. I win. I win, and I WIN…every time waaay too easily. I told you I needed a real challenge…and what better place to find a challenge than the prodigy of Cassandra McCray herself?"

"I told you I don't…"

"Yes, yes, you don't do that anymore…goddamn. It's been sooooo long since you've raced. Luckily for you those cops bought that story the night you were inches away from killing a father and his daughter. That poor guy was too occupied with changing that tire to see the car neck and neck with you in the other lane. But did you let hitting a bystander stop you? No, no, you're a true racer, Red. You stayed the course and you beat that shit talker in the 76' Nova. Then you blasted home and funneled as much booze as you could down your throat before the cops got there because a DUI with fake remorse was better than getting caught stone sober and racing with zero regrets." Hutch's mind replayed the true events that Regina somehow knew. Her brain spun into the chill of the not-so-distant past and the shame that came with it.

"You think ya know me? You don't fuckin' know me…" Hutch spoke with sorrow on her breath.

"Mmmm, maybe I do and maybe I don't, Red. But what I do know is you want your aunt back, don't you?" Regina dipped her finger and stirred what was left of her now luke-warm coffee. Hutch just stared off, wishing this were all some sort of dream. No answer fell from her lips. "I'll tell you what, Red. You race me, and you win, I'll not only tell you where your aunt is, I'll let her come home and consider her debts paid in full." Hutch's dead stare found new life as it veered back into the brunette's golden eyes.

"And what if I lose? I'm livin' in a camper, I ain't got jack shit to put up for collateral. Not to mention my ride is in the impound for probably the rest of eternity."

"How bout the Maverick."

"What?"

"That bucket of bolts you and Cassandra were working on together."

"It's still in pieces."

"Well put the pieces back together and race me in it. And if you lose, I'll take the car as payment. See, Red, we're solving problems left and right." Hutch began shaking her head in short little bursts as she fought back a tear. The memories of her aunt came flooding back like a deluge. The dam that had held them so firmly in place this entire time had burst apart, and now they were saturating every ounce of her. "Well? What do you say, Red?" Regina spoke up again. Hutch simply rose up from her seat and tossed the keychain of her aunt's back over to Regina.

"My aunt's dead…Goodbye, Regina." She threw a handful of crumpled bills to the table top and quickly walked off, leaving the brunette to stew as she stared at the tackiness of the wallpaper in front of her. Soon a little smile crept onto her face as she realized someone was hovering over her.

"There's that smiling face!" Regina belted out at the presence of Carol standing there with the coldest look. The brunette slid her mug over to the edge of the table. "Warm me up, doll. I'm gonna need it"

Absalom

"Enjoy your unscheduled breakfast break?" Hanks irritated voice rattled the second Hutch reentered the shop in an obvious state of duress. She just stopped and glared at him for a moment.

"As matter of fact I didn't," she replied.

"Good to hear."

"Where's Ham, I need to talk to him."

"Ham went home for the day, Hutch." Hank said coldly from where he stood behind the counter, arms crossed. Hutch smirked and her eyebrow rose.

"What? Why does he get ta go when he wants and I get yelled at for eatin' breakfast." Hank took a few steps and rounded the front desk, stopping and resting his hip against the edge of it as he spoke,

"Oh, Ham didn't leave for the day voluntarily to go pick daisies or cruise for dick or whatever the hell he does when he's not here…No me and Ham, we had ourselves a little argument. You wanna guess what it was about?" Hutch just stared at him with a twitching frown. "No I suppose you wouldn't wanna guess, so I'll just tell ya. We were arguin' over why in the hell there's forty bucks missin' from the shop money the other day. Now, he finally breaks and confesses to me that HE took it, so I told him to go the fuck home before I smashed his face in. Now he ain't fired er nothin', just on temporary leave until I cool down for the benefit of his health. But, ya know, this little voice just keeps gnawing away at me sayin' I sent the wrong person home. Yeah, I thought to myself, Ham stole money from his own family? Little Hamlet McCray, my baby brother, the same kid that ended up pissin' his pants as a teenager while tryin' to steal one pack of cigarettes, not for himself, but for you. So with all that bein' said, I have to ask YOU one burnin' question...Are you the one who actually stole that forty dollars from the till?"

Hutch wetted her lips as she glared unblinking into the brimstone stare of her towering brother.

"No. Ham told me this mornin' he took money from the till and didn't know how to tell you about it. Said he was gonna put it back Friday when he got paid," Hutch out and out lied without skipping a beat or batting an eyelash. Hank nodded his head and bit his lips together.

"Okay...That's all I wanted to know. Now get back to work."

"I'm not workin' this counter no more."

"No, Hutch you're right, you ain't. And since Ham is gone for the day I'm gonna be the one doin' this job since no one round here seems to be competent enough to handle it."

"So I can go back to the 454?"

"Ha! Fuck no. What you can do is pick up a broom, dust, scrub toilets, or any other demeaning thing you can find to do round here." Hutch bit at her lip hard and crossed her arms as Hayden walked in from the shop. "You hear that Hayden?" Hank asked.

"What's that?" He said as he grabbed a soda from the mini-fridge.

"Hutch has officially been demoted to a gopher now. So if ya need anything, your tools cleaned, your shop area organized, your bald head waxed, just tell your sister to get on it. She's gonna be the literal shop bitch for an undetermined amount of time, till I figure out when she's fit to return to machinin'."

"Nice! Now that ya mention it, my entire tool chest could use a cleanin'."

"Fuck you, I ain't cleanin' your tools," Hutch sneered.

"Hutch, you heard em'. Get to cleanin'," Hank pointed to the shop area. Hutch looked back and forth between her siblings, the one smiling, the other stone-faced.

"You are shittin' me with this?"

"Maybe you don't recall our mornin' conversations? Get a rag and get to it, or get the fuck out," Hank said, returning to the counter where he re-immersed himself in paperwork.

"Bullshit…" Hutch whispered angrily as she walked by Hayden, on into the shop area.

For the next hour, there Hutch sat, a broken woman, spraying down the chrome of tools that weren't even her own and polishing them to a gleam. Scrubbing Hayden's filthy-ass wrenches? Could she sink to any lower of a position? As she kept catching glimpses of her brothers' smirk-smiles over her shoulder, she began to miss that jail cell she called home for four weeks.

Hutch finished with a crescent wrench and chucked it with a thud back into the drawer.

"Hey now, be careful with those," Hayden mouthed off.

"Oh, you're just eatin' this shit up ain't ya?" Hutch snarled.

"With a silver spoon. Hell, I didn't even know shit could taste so good till I saw you scrubbin' my tools against your will. There better not be one speck of dirt on them things either." Hutch sighed and shook her head as she plucked another wrench from the mess that was her brother's disorganized excuse for a tool box. The more she scrubbed, the more evident it became that he hadn't cleaned a tool since the day he had bought them.

A silence of dialogue paved the way for several more minutes amongst a symphony of turning wrenches and clinking metals. Hutch couldn't help but look over her shoulder now and again to catch fleeting glimpses of Heath working on her engine build. It was the proverbial cherry on top of the banana shit-sundae she was now being forced to eat with a smile. What the hell was Hank thinking giving that job to him? That engine was not going to last.

"Hey, what you guys think about that new Metallica album out?" Heath suddenly broke in from nowhere.

"Oh, that Load, or whatever the hell?" Hayden said.

"Yeah."

"Yeah it's a LOAD of shit," he threw his opinion out.

"It's growin' on me," Hutch spoke from behind. Hayden tilted his head in disgust.

"What?! Growin' on ya? That album sucks AND they cut their hair. Stick a fork in em', they're done."

"Oh yeah, God forbid they actually play their instruments for once and try somethin' new," Hutch mouthed as she threw another wrench back, "I like it."

"Yeah, you would Hutch. All that shitty music you listen to has finally fried your sense of good taste. Queen and Gordon Gayfoot or whatever the hell his name is," Hayden mouthed off as he grabbed his feeler gauge back up. Hutch just shook her head and didn't say a word. It wasn't worth it.

"You know, I think I like that album too," Heath finally confessed. Hayden dropped his feeler gauge with a clank.

"What the fuck is wrong with everyone in this shop? I think someone packed both your earholes full of dogshit overnight or somethin'. How could you like that album?...Jesus H Christ. I waited five damn years for them to put somethin new out and they hand me that steamin' pile of elephant shit."

"Oh, my god. Dog shit. Elephant shit. Raccoon shit in a cup this morning. What is it with you and animal shit today?" Hutch mouthed off in annoyance.

"Oh, shut up, Hutch," Hayden grumbled then went on, "And another thing, I gotta say it cuz it needs said, Metallica's last album was the start of their downfall."

"Oh, Jesus, here we go again, '*The Black Album wasn't heavy enough. It was their sell-out album. Their best shit was in the eighties. Blah. Blah, Blah,'*" Hutch readily mocked her brother before he could even spit it out.

"Yeah, go ahead and mock! You know it's true, Hutch."

"No I don't, actually. It was their best sellin' album. Hell I never listened to metal before that album. You could say that album introduced me ta heavy metal."

"Well, that's just sad."

"No, what's sad is the state of these tools, you bald-headed fuck," Hutch started polishing another wrench. Hayden just shook his head and stayed silent. He was through arguing.

Several minutes of silence soon led into more small talk.

"Where we eatin' lunch," Heath asked.

"PJ's," Hutch smirked.

"Jesus, Hutch it's always PJ's with you. I just get so damn sick of that place. How you stand eatin' there everyday?" Hayden grumbled.

"Well, I kinda don't have a choice lately."

"I get sick of there too. But they do have the best cold slaw," Heath spoke.

Hutch froze her cleaning and perked up. She leered over at her brother.

"What?"

"Cold slaw, Hutch. I said they had the best cold slaw," he reaffirmed.

She tilted her head with annoyed confusion.

"Are you sayin' cold slaw?

"Yeah, cold slaw."

"Heath, its *cole* slaw."

"What? No it ain't. It's cold slaw. Cuz its cold."

"Dumbass, its coleslaw."

"What like coal?"

"Yes, cole."

"Like you mine out of the ground?"

"What?"

"The black stuff."

"Holy shit. There's not enough alcohol in the world for this conversation right now."

Suddenly, the conversation was cut short by Hank's thundering voice.

"Customer pick-up! Name - Clemens! 351 block! Needs loaded in his truck. Someone get on it. Now," Hank said as he opened one of the front garage doors. Both Heath and Hayden just eyeballed Hutch, waiting for her to hop to it amidst the growl of the rising overhead door.

"Sonuvabitch..." Hutch slammed down a wrench she was currently cleaning and walked to the back of the shop. Her eyes jumped through the shelves and stands till they fell square upon a shiny engine block with a yellow tag dangling from it.

"Windsor..." Hutch said quietly as she threw on a pair of leather gloves. She then rolled a flat dolly over and carefully slid the beast onto it. Her stare soon squinted under the sting of the afternoon sun as she wheeled the cart and its precious cargo out to the edge of the concrete where an older gentlemen stood patiently beside the open tailgate of a Ford pick-up.

"Howdy," Hutch simply spoke.

"Well howdy to you," he happily returned the sentiment. It was a genuine welcome, nothing more, nothing less and Hutch could sense it. She never considered herself a real prize, but after being around almost nothing but men for twenty-six years of her life she always could sense that tiny tinge of suggestiveness. A man could say "Hey there." But what she heard was, "Nice ass." And most times they meant nothing by it, it was simply in their nature. But not this stranger. No, there was a placidity to him that Hutch could feel. His soft eyes and voice told her there was no mischief in him, not one lick. She could almost feel the stresses of the day melt from her as he spoke.

"Nice day ain't it?"

"If it weren't 95 degrees out I guess I could be on the same page with ya there," she answered then read the work order, albeit indirect.

"Windsor. Thermaled, shot, and bored 40 over," she said. She removed the tag attached to the block then took a bear hug around it as she squatted down.

"Whoa, now. Hold on. I'll help ya…" the man couldn't even finish his insistence of help when Hutch lifted the block all by herself and placed it carefully onto the tailgate. All he could do was nod his head slightly, wide-eyed and as impressed as he was shocked.

"You look like you've done that before."

"Yeah," Hutch started in as she slid the block on back into the truck bed, "Noticed the older I get the lighter they get. Comes with the territory."

"I bet. So how long you been workin' here?" The man asked as he began strapping the engine block down.

"Oh, bout ma whole life if ya wanna get technical," Hutch spoke as she helped him with the straps.

"So you're a McCray then?"

"Unfortunately."

"Ahh, okay," the man pointed in revelation, "You used to race at Highland, I remember you now. You were good. Real good."
Hutch smiled and shook her head

"You're probably thinkin' of my aunt. People always mistook us for sisters."

"Naw, I don't think I'm mistaken. I...I think I know who your aunt was. Cassandra? Harvey's sister right?" Hutch's eyes widened with slight surprise.

"That's right."

"Yeah she was a pistol, that one. I don't recall ever seein' that woman lose. Boy last time I ever saw her race probably been the better part of ten-twelve years ago. She retire?" Hutch thought about the question for a moment. "Yeah...yeah she retired." She felt it best to avoid a lengthy explanation of her disappearance.

"Oh well...that's too bad. So what about you? You don't race anymore then?"

"Naw. Ain't for me."

"Why?"

"Lost a few times. Don't like the feelin' of it. Guess I'm just lookin' for somethin' else in life is all."

"Hmm, shame."

"Is it?"

"Well...Yeah I think it is. I tell ya, it was refreshin' to see ladies coming out to the track and actually being behind the wheel instead of waving flags in skimpy outfits. Now whether you win or lose is irrelevant. My granddaughter loves the strip, she loves cars. She's ten." Hutch smiled as her mind took her back to that age, starry eyed and awestruck by the sounds of the thundering engines and the smells of fuel burning into the summer night. The man continued, "Now there's a place for everybody, some gals like to show off what god gave em', but I know my granddaughter would rather look up to the girl behind the wheel than the one posing topless on the hood. I guess what I'm sayin is, the world needs more Cassandra McCrays. Just ma two cents," with that he closed the tailgate and climbed into the truck. "Hope you find what you're lookin' for, Hutch," He ended as he looked back then fired the engine. They both exchanged a little wave as he left behind a cloud of dust that blotted out the passing trucks creeping in the foreground. *Hope you find what you're lookin' for, Hutch.* His words resounded again in her mind. He knew her name. She never even told him her name. He'd remembered it from the track…

    And so the day of gopher duties trudged on like a hung-over snail sliding through cold molasses. All day it was "*Hutch do this. Hutch clean that. Hutch take out the trash.*" She was beginning to know what Cinderella had actually felt like in that Disney movie she had watched wide-eyed as a kid. Only she didn't have any talking mice to keep her company nor a fairy godmother to whip up a chariot from a pumpkin. Though if a fairy godmother did show up she would've settled for a lifetime supply of smokes and the Maverick put together so she could race Regina. Oh, Regina…Don't worry, she hadn't forgotten about sweet, adorable Regina. Ms. Redgrace had been stuck in her head like a splinter since the moment they locked eyes. Rage and happiness tore one another apart at the thought that Regina was telling the truth about her aunt. Was she really still out there, working in some godforsaken speak-easy or running drugs for this teenaged gangster till she paid off this supposed massive debt she owed? It wasn't true…it couldn't be. But the key to the Mustang…Regina's intimate knowledge of things…Hutch could barely stomach any of it. It rolled and rolled over her like the inescapable tides of the ocean, blasting her mental wounds back open and setting her mind adrift as she swept, scrubbed, and polished her way to the end of that godforsaken day. The only thing that seemed to keep her sane was the fresh memories of the kind old customer and his 351 block…it made the minutes seem less like hours.

    The clock had just passed the 3 pm mark when she found herself sweeping the back hall for what seemed like the nineteenth time that day. It reminded her of when she had detention with the shop teacher in high school and she was made to keep sweeping the floor for two hours straight even though every atom had been removed from it ten times over. What the hell was Hank trying to prove with all this? He was bitching about the business being low on money and he was placing a broom in the hands of their best machinist…Idiot.

    Hutch stopped her sweeping and began staring at the wall. It was covered in a collage of never-ending newspaper clippings, Polaroid's, and award plaques. It was a proverbial paper sea of memories of the McCray clan, mostly of racing origin. All starting with the peppered black and whites of her grandfather's older cars up to the full color 6X9's of Hutch's short lived stints at the strip. It seemed nearly every one of them had been behind the wheel at one time or another. Some of them, like Cassandra and Harvey, were made for the track, but most of the rest of them simply weren't. Ham raced once, speed was simply not in his DNA. Hayden ran his mouth more than he ran a car. Hank raced for years but was mediocre at best. Heath, well he couldn't drive in a straight line to save his life, he totaled one of their super stock drag cars and he never went behind the wheel again. Hutch had promise, but much like most McCray's she couldn't hold her tongue or temper. She got behind the wheel at eighteen and destroyed the competition almost every weekend much to the chagrin of the male dominated sport. After countless verbal altercations and a final humiliating loss that led her into a literal fist fight with the other driver, she was banned from the track. It was probably for the best…At least that's what she told herself. It seemed all the McCray's siblings were a disappointment in the wake of their father and aunt's accomplishments…that was, all except for one. As Hutch's eyes slowly panned through the abstract, they began falling upon picture after picture of her other sibling, Henry. Henry was the second eldest of the family but was the first at the finish line. While almost every picture of Hutch's brother's showed somber faces standing next to drag cars and drunken women, Henry was always donning a smile and trophy or plaque of some size was raised far above his head. He was the striking image of his father Harvey, inheriting both his good looks and his skills behind the steering wheel. Like father, like son, he decimated the competition over and over, undoubtedly winning the favorite son award from Harvey, though Harvey would never admit to such a thing. But just when it seemed he was on top of the world, tragedy struck. At the same age that Hutch was now, he died in a car accident just outside of town. No alcohol was found in his system, but he had been going so fast that the car literally ripped into pieces upon impact…it was a closed casket, there was nothing left to show of him. Hutch and Henry were close but nothing like she and Ham had been and still were. She was thirteen at the time and it crushed her as it did everyone in the family….but life went on, time healed wounds for everyone, except Harvey. He was never the same after that…a different man altogether, broken at the loss of his prodigious son. And for some reason, he seemed to take out his remorse and frustration on Hutch more than anyone. It was a thing she never could quite wrap her head around. Her father and her had butted heads before, but times became bleak after that cursed day and their relationship turned to shades of rust ands ruin. Hutch let out a sigh at the brackish memories. She unpinned and held up a photo of Henry with his arm around her. They were beside the McCray Racing 64' Falcon super stock, a car painted in the same green as the building. It was taken a few months before he had died. Things looked so light and full of life then and, just like that, the thoughts of McCray McCurse month returned. She couldn't help but wonder if this July held another hidden tragedy just waiting to be sprung upon one of them.

"Sicka sweepin' yet?" A voice resounded behind her in the doorway. Hutch jerked, re-pinned the photo back to the board, and turned to see Hank standing there with that typical stone-sour look upon his face.

"Nope," she answered with spite.

"Too bad. Got a new job for ya," he spoke as he slammed down a box full of file folders that were a bird's nest of a mess.

"Now what? I suppose ya want me ta put all them right side up?" She was sure she was in for another pointless task.

"No sister of mine, I want ya ta take the truck and drop these off ta the accountant."

Hutch's lip curled.

"The accountant?" She scoffed, "I didn't know we had one. Thought Ham did all that shit?"

"Well Ham ain't too good at handlin' money no more is he?" Hank said as he tossed a set of keys to Hutch. She dropped the broom and caught them in midair. With a wayward stare she looked at the box of files and back to the key she held.

"Yep. Sounds great. Might've overlooked one teeny, tiny detail though. I ain't got no license. Ya do remember that, right?"

"Hutch, I don't give a shit about your problems. You're takin' a company truck to do business for the company. You're allowed to do that." She stood there and stared at him for a moment.

"Actually, I don't think that's right. They're supposed to tell me when and where I can drive after my next court hearin'.""

"Hutch, since when the hell did you start havin' a problem with doin' somethin' potentially illegal? Now quit draggin' your goddamn feet, would ya?" Hank said as he plucked the file box up and shoved it into her hands. "Get this thing outta here NOW. I want ya back before five so ya can mop the floors before we close."

Hutch just sighed.

"Jesus Christ...so where am I takin' this to?"

"Address is 161 Cranberry Dr." Hutch suddenly stopped in her tracks and her face went dark. She dropped the file box to the floor with a thud.

"Accountant, my ass. Take it your damn self," she protested at the realization of where she was headed.

"You gonna stand there and tell me ya can't just drop these off ta him? Just see him for two damn seconds?"

"Two damn seconds is too damn long," she walked over and retrieved the broom.

"Drop that shit!" Hank smacked the cleaning utensil from her hands. Hutch just crossed her arms as she watched her brother's nostrils begin to flare with anger. He quickly dropped it down a notch.

"He's dying, Hutch..."

"Good."

She could see the anger welling back up in Hank's eyes. She almost expected an encore to the slap she had received from him earlier that day. But it never came. In fact, that very same ire seemed to melt down to an expression Hutch had never seen from him before, sadness.

"....Look, I know you've had your fair share of his bullshit, hell we all have, but he ain't got much time left. All I keep thinkin' about is this damn month and what it means for our family in the past. If he lives to see August, I won't know what to think. He needs these files. Might as well kill two birds with one stone."

"I'm not goin."

"Okay....Okay," he nodded. And by the look on his face it was obviously NOT okay. With a growing sense of dread, Hutch watched him walk away on a steady beeline towards the front. He disappeared for a moment only to reappear with a five gallon gas can in tow.

"What?...What are you doin?" Hutch leered with suspicion. Hank muscled on past her, headed for the back of the building.

"Somethin' I shoulda done a long time ago," he responded cryptically.

"Hey?...Hey?! Where are you goin'?!" Hutch craned her neck around the corner, watching him disappear into the back garage area. Her panic intensified. She bolted down the hall and flung open the door to see her brother dousing the canvas shroud of the Maverick with gasoline.

"What the fuck?! Stop it?! I said stop it?!" She began screeching. She pushed Hank as he continued his insanity. It barely budged him.

"Back off of me, Hutch! I mean it!" He glared at her with a pause in his pouring, but instantly started dousing the car once again, walking around it with an evil stare branded into his eyes.

"Are you fuckin' insane?!" She screamed so loud her voice cracked. Right at that second, Hank shook the last bit of gas from the container and gave it a mad hurl across the room. He quickly yanked out his lighter and fired it up, standing there staring at her like he was about to set the whole world ablaze with a song in his heart.

"Don't...Don't. Please don't," her screams had receded to a whimper as her eyes began to glass over.

"You gonna take them papers to dad?" He took a few steps closer to the car.

"Yes..." she whispered.

"I'm sorry, what was that?" He stepped even closer.

"Yes!! Yes!! I said Yes!! Goddamn it!!" She screamed. She was terrified that the fumes alone were about to ignite at this point. "Click" the sound of Hank's lighter shutting, echoed through the room.

"Well that wasn't hard, was it?" Hank smiled slightly. He walked fast past the Maverick and threw the lighter at Hutch. It bounced hard off of her shoulder and tinked across the floor as his footsteps disappeared behind her...the door slammed shut and she was all alone. Now whether it was the odor of the gasoline fumes or the thought of the last thing that tied her to her aunt potentially going up in flames that started the crying, she'll never know. She felt herself collapse to her knees and she let loose every last tear she had held in since the day Cassandra disappeared. If her aunt truly was still out there, she needed her now more than she ever had.

Words were in short supply as Hutch gathered the file box and took flight from the Gingerbread House in the company truck. Her eyes and tear-stained cheeks burned in the wind that whipped through the open window as she made a steady run out into the countryside beyond. She kept sniffling and wiping at the corners of her eyes for what seemed like ten whole minutes, trying to rid herself of the remaining tears that plagued her…but then she realized something…this was the first time she had been behind the wheel of anything since the night of the hit and run. To that end, she nodded her head in some kind of self-reflection, an acknowledgment that she was driving again, and it wasn't the horror she'd expected it to be. No, it was quite the contrary. It was as beautiful and as freeing as she had ever remembered it. With a wayward sigh, she let the smells of the farm fields beyond fill her lungs with a scent that no courtroom or jail cell could replicate…A peace fell upon her and she felt the sadness inside her eyes ebb back into the unstable shelves of her mind. She was never going to be truly rid of sadness…no one ever was. So she took the time to remember the little things that made her happy - A gas pedal below her foot and a steering wheel in her hands. What more did a girl need?

Mile upon country mile was traversed. Twists and turns and curves like the backs of intrepid snakes fell under the tires of the pick-up she helmed ever closer to a place she was slowly dreading to be. She was only a mile away now…the gorgeous calm that had filled her heart only moments before, began to melt away at the thoughts of the unknown ahead. She hadn't seen her father in almost two years, let alone talked to him. The thoughts of the last time they had spoken still resounded in her mind as if it were yesterday. The hate. The venom they spewed at one another. It was all too vivid and she wanted desperately to bury it before she knocked on that front door, but there was just no way of erasing such malevolence. And soon, there it was "Shady Oaks

Community" It was a fancy name for nothing more than a trailer court. It was also false advertisement considering Shady Oaks had neither one oak tree nor any shade to speak off. It was nestled between two vast corn fields and seemed to be the final resting place for the man she'd rather not see that day…or any other day. Her anxious grip tightened on the wheel as the tires met the first main gravel road that sliced between the tightly knit rows of mobile homes. She began counting down the addresses while porch-sitters and playing kids eyeballed the truck with suspicious gazes. Hutch had only been there a handful of times at best. She could barely remember what the trailer even looked like, in fact, they all looked the same to her. But before she could even prepare herself, there it was "161" in the form of old steel number plates, tacked to the corner of the white mobile home that now stared her down like the unwanted stranger she felt she was. The truck rolled to a stop in the road, and that's where she sat for what seemed like five whole minutes. She kept staring at the beaten exterior of the trailer and looking in the rearview to the road some dozen driveways back, the same road that would lead her the hell out of there if she so chose. But she couldn't take that path. She couldn't go back and lie to Hank. He had been two seconds away from setting a car on fire, inside the family's own business no less, she didn't even want to imagine what would go down if she chose not to follow through with this. With grave reluctance, she finally spun the wheel and rolled into the drive, stopping right beside her father's truck. As the engine sputtered to a stop with the twist of a key, she sighed heavy and quick. Her eyes began panning the smoke-yellowed curtains in the windows, looking for a sign of her father's prying eyes, peering out to see who had pulled in. But there was nothing…only a cold, ghostly silence seemed to linger in the air. A creaking of metal was eaten whole by the slam of the truck door as she climbed out into the blistering sun once more. She paced as slowly as possible around the vehicle, opening the other door and retrieving the file box she was entrusted to deliver. Her pulse quickened as she slammed the door with her foot and spun round to face the literal music…the tiny sounds of Lynard Skynard crept out a partially-open window that lay beside the front door. If there was one thing that man did love besides racing, and their dearly departed Henry, it was Skynard. The sound of the music took Hutch back a tick in time....well more than a tick...Her and Ham playing in the dirt piles with Tonka trucks at the old McCray homestead while the sounds of Skynard resounded amongst the cursing of her father as he worked on the cars in their garage. You see, this banged up abode that lay in front of her wasn't the place they all grew up in...no, that was miles to the east. It was an old two-story nestled back in the pines with a giant garage built in the back. That was a time when things, at the very least, seemed normal...whatever normal was. But as life often does, it changes, and often times more for the bad than the good. Even though her father had stake in a successful machining business, that didn't mean they were rolling in money. Raising six kids and having a wife that stayed at home wasn't cheap. Couple that with a racing habit that was more expensive than a drug habit and you hadn't much left. But then there was that summer...Hutch was nine. She remembered not feeling well, getting sick often, and missing the first few weeks of school. She was finally taken to the doctor for tests...she was diagnosed with leukemia. It was a dark time for the family. Hutch well remembered being so sick, but perhaps she was simply too young to understand the gravity of it all until she was older. The family pooled their money for her treatments...but things got worse and within months the doctors told her parents to pick out a cemetery plot. But then, one day, Hutch woke up and felt different...she felt better. In fact, she felt completely normal. To the doctor's surprise her tests all came back negative...her cancer was gone. Seemingly whisked away within the scope a few days...she was cured. It was nothing short of a miracle...but the damage had already been done to them financially. They eventually had to downsize into a smaller home and the close quarters proved to be living hell on the larger family. They were all at each others throats more often than not. But time marched on, the kids all moved out. Regardless of the final peace and quiet her mother had had enough. She finally filed for divorce right about the time her father became ill. She took a large buy out of McCray Engine and hit the road with no regrets and not one goodbye to any of them. They barely heard from her to that very day. All of that compounded into her father having to move into the decrepit thing that still lay before her. The great Harvey

McCray, from local champion racer, to forgotten trailer park hermit…Oh, how the mighty had fallen. But hadn't they all…

"Knock. Knock. Knock." Hutch finally got the gall up to tap away at the flimsy front door. For what seemed like an eternity, she stood there, eyes glued to the door with her brain reminiscing in the muddy thoughts of the fights she and her father had engaged in…The last one being the absolute worst. What was he going to do? What was he going to say? Hell, what was she going to say? But as the moment after her knocking trudged on into a solid minute, she was beginning to wonder if she needed to say anything at all. Thoughts started swirling around her, ill in nature *"My god, was he dead?"* Was he rolled up in a ball, passing away, listening to his favorite band…I guess that wasn't the worst way to go. Jesus Christ, she was being morbid…but there was that tiny tinge in her that hoped it was true and she could never have to worry about the awkward scenario that still might be playing out if she knocked again. *"Bam!Bam!Bam!"* She walloped the door hard as the irritation of the heavy load of files began to drag her down.

"For shit's sake. Let's just get this over with…" she mumbled to herself. Right at that moment, her heart skipped and then hardened at the sound of the latch being turned. The door swung open with a sickly creak, revealing the outline of a sickly man behind it. Her eyes stared unblinking as they adjusted through the door onto the skeleton of a man that used to be her strapping father. Did she have the wrong house? Was this zombie that wavered in front of her truly the man that, not but a couple years ago, was still at least recognizable to her?

"Pooj? Whatchu want, girl?" Her father's voice crackled out to her. If there was any doubts of the identity of the corpse that stood before her it was resolved with that name…Pooj. Her dad called her that more than he called her anything. To this day Hutch had no idea where he had pulled it from. She fought the nearly unshakable urge to cuss him out as the thoughts of their arguments came full circle again…but she couldn't. He looked so…so defeated…so done. Her words started as a stutter.

"Uh-uh…Umm…Hank, wanted me ta drop this off to you?" She nudged forward the box of papers that were becoming heavier with every breath. Harvey's graying mustache just twitched a bit below his glasses.

"Whaaa?' He spoke in confusion as he pushed the door open and started rummaging through the box. "I don't know what the hell this stuff is. Looks like tax shit. I don't handle any of that stuff anymore." Hutch was confused for a second, but only a second. Her anger began to rise as the words,

"That fucker..." whispered in a tone so low even she could barely hear. Hank had obviously tricked her into getting her over there. With the demented persuasion he had thrown at her, it only added insult to injury. It was soon apparent that she wasn't the only one getting duped. Her father chuckled a bit.

"Your brother...told me he was bringin' me a late lunch. So instead I get you and a pile of worthless papers...looks like we both been duped, Pooj." Hutch sighed and rolled her tongue around on the inside of her cheek as she relaxed the box down past her hips...an uncomfortable silence quickly crept in. For an awkward span of time, father and daughter just stared at each other, not knowing what to say as the same dark memories wisped through their minds. With a ragged breath, Harvey finally broke the hush between them,

"Well? Don't just stand there. Ya might as well come in for a minute." Those were the last words Hutch had expected him to say. With a nod and an almost breathless whisper she responded,

"Okay." And so Hutch pushed round the screen door into the darkened trailer. Her nose was immediately greeted with a trifecta of stale cigarettes, garbage, and urine. It was almost unbearable.

"Don't mind the mess..." her father spoke as he limped over to the recliner against the far wall. And a mess it was indeed. Mountains of newspapers, food wrappers, and inches of dust laid upon nearly every surface she could lay her eyes upon through the grimness of the gloom. She felt her heart began to sink at the sight of it all...it sunk even further when she realized her father was wheeling an oxygen tank in front of himself on his journey across the living room.

"Just set them files on the table..." Harvey said as he plopped down, out of breath in his chair. Hutch looked towards the kitchen table, it was piled with a disheveled pyramid of mail that nearly peaked one foot tall in the center. She looked back at him "Well, hell if you can find room...Well just throw em' on the floor there. Wait? Should you leave em' here? Hell with it, leave em' here.

Hank can come get the damn things if they're so important. He owes me a sandwich anyway. Little lyin' bastard," her father wheezed out as he rummaged through his end table. Hutch dropped the box to the floor and returned her attention to her father who was now putting a cigarette up to his lips and lighting it.

"Dad…should you be doin that?" Hutch let out as she made her way over to the couch.

"Should I be doin' what, Pooj? Oh, just shove that stuff on the floor so you can sit." Hutch eyeballed the mounds of papers and god knows what beneath, that completely covered his couch. She did as she was told, heavy-heartedly pushing the mass onto the floor till she cleared enough space to sit.

"Now, I should be doin' what?" Harvey asked as she sunk into her seat.

"What?" Hutch said.

"You said I should be doin' somethin'?"

"No, I said should you be doin' *that*?" She pointed towards his smoke. Harvey cocked his head in confusion, not catching her words.

"Dad, the cigarette. Your cigarette. Should you be smokin' while on that oxygen?"

"Oh hell, Pooj, ya go n' get your medical degree since last time I saw ya? Don't bust ma damn chops alright? I was just startin' to like you again." Hutch went quiet for a moment as Harvey took a few labored breaths and then inhaled deep the smoke that had got him into the position in which he currently resided. She finally went to speak but was cut short,

"Pooj, this here oxygen tanks keeping me alive long enough to enjoy every last cigarette I can," he smiled as he slapped the side of the steel cylinder.

"Right…Well I was a tad more worried about you blowin' up this place with us in it."

"Ahh, hell," he scoffed, "Things turned off right now. I'm not a complete idiot."

"Okay," was all she could seem to muster. She just sat there for a brief tick, watching her dad sort of stare off into space, smiling and puffing away like the world was his oyster. Like that cigarette was his first and last, all rolled into one. It had been years since she had seen him crack anything that even resembled a grin. For a crumbling second she couldn't help but wonder, was being on the edge of death what made him happy? Knowing he was going die…Did it make him rejoice? Yes...it did. And why wouldn't it? All those years of anger and sadness were going away with the last breath he took. Which seemed to be direly soon. A sick part of her almost envied him.

"Here…" Harvey said, leaning towards Hutch, cigarette sticking out from the pack he still clasped. She eyeballed the protruding cylinder that beckoned unto her, she hadn't had one in hours. Before she could even reach up to snag it, her thoughts went steadily drifting to the mass of darkness eating her father's lungs from the inside out and, to that end, did a thing she never had done in her life when offered a smoke…she hesitated. Harvey took immediate notice.

"Well...gonna take one er' not? I know they ain't them fancy smokes you're used to, but beggars can't be choosers."

"I just…I…" Hutch stuttered. Harvey looked at her oddly. He then looked at his oxygen tank and then stared off before returning his stare to her.

"Oh hell, Pooj. I know what you got up in your head. Don't go quittin' on account me. Christ one smoke ain't gonna kill ya. Ya wanna quit, quit after you smoke one last one with your old man for shit's sake. Now, go on," he beckoned the pack to her once more. She nodded and plucked one loose. "Thata girl." Harvey smiled as he put away the pack and watched her light up. "Cancer…" he whispered with a laugh.

"What?" Hutch said.

"On nothin', just thinkin' out loud, I guess. Your great aunt, that woman smoked since she was twelve…TWELVE, Pooj. Two packs a day. She died at eighty-five. And you remember what she died from?"

"She choked, didn't she?"

"She choked…She choked to death on a goddamn chicken bone. Well technically she had a heart attack caused by the panic set in from chokin' on the chicken bone, but ma point is, after seventy-three years of smokin' 2 packs a day, that's 14 packs a week, 60 a month, 730 a year, with a grand total of 53,290 during the course or her life, give or take on all those numbers, she had a clean bill of health…Well, beside the chicken wing lodged in her throat. Now all that said, you know what the moral of this story is, Pooj?"

"Life is stupid. Smoke all you want?" She responded as she blew out a plume of smoke to join his. Her father nodded.

"And stay away from bone-in chicken." They both smiled. "Now see there, a smile looks good on ya."

"Ditto," she spoke.

"Yeah…Ya know you're lookin' more like your mom everyday," Harvey said.

"I am?" She spoke in confusion.

"Ha! Naw…You look like your aunt…" The words silenced them both. The thought of Cass's disappearance came full circle, haunting their minds as they sat there in some heart-sobering stupor, waiting for the other to speak on the matter. In the end, neither of them did. There was simply nothing to say.

"So how've you been," her father switched gears.

"Um…well…Okay. I guess."

"How was jail?" Hutch flicked her cigarette in the nearby ashtray, looking at him with a surprised shame behind her eyes. "C'mon, Pooj. You think I wouldn't find out about that?" Harvey said. She took another inhale and sighed forcibly out.

"It was…jail. It was…I don't know, I didn't like it." Hutch felt put on the spot. She hadn't the slightest idea where to go with the conversation.

"Yeah, jail ain't fun…" Harvey spoke soberly, "And…and the people you hit? They…they gonna press charges or anythin'. File a suit or?" Hutch felt her blood begin to boil. Why was he doing this to her?

"Umm, I…they…can we…can we just talk about somethin' else?" She stuttered out, trying desperately to keep calm.

"Yeah…yeah, we can talk bout somethin' else. Well…how's the shop?" The question instantly hit another sore nerve. An annoyed smile came across her face.

"I don't wanna talk about that either," Hutch glared towards the other wall.

"Well shit, Pooj. You tell me what you wanna talk about then. I'm runnin' out of ideas, and quick." Hutch just hovered her cigarette inches from her mouth as she peeled away the layers of potential things to converse over…she quickly realized something, her life sucked. There was little to talk over that didn't want to make her put her fist through the wall. She lived in a camper, she had no car, and her current job title was toilet cleaner/ broom pusher. There was nothing she wanted more than to tell her dad about everything going on at the shop. How Hank was ruling it like a dictator. How the business was horrible, and how she was being made to do the janitorial work when she was the best machinist there. Nothing good would come of it. In the unlikely event that her dad would even give a shit, she would catch hell from Hank when their father admonished him for everything.

"Let's talk about..." she started in, trying desperately to think of something. Her father eyed her strangely waiting with bated breath. As Hutch's eyes drifted around the room she began seeing the pictures and dust covered trophies scattered among the ruins of this once legendary racer's abode. And then it hit her...

"Let's talk about cars, dad."

"Cars?"

"Yep. Cars n' racin'," Hutch's smile returned. And so they did...For a good hour the two reminisced about victories and losses. Horsepower and roaring crowds. The taste of exhaust left burning in your throat as you drifted off to bed drowning in the ring of your own ears. They talked about the racers that could and the races that couldn't...the sixteen flips old John Baker took in his super street Grand National and how he walked right off the track unscathed. They talked about Johnny "The Troll" McGee's fuel line breaking and his AMC Javelin going up in flames. The poor guy wasn't even on the track yet, it went up like a pyre in the pit area while the National Anthem played and old Johnny just put a hand over his heart and cried for car and country. And then of course there was the night that Ray Nash's Trans Am engine blew up right at the start line. And by "blew up" it went nuclear. Thing threw a piston so hard it ricocheted of the track and soared into the audience, hitting a kid right in the head. It didn't kill him, but it didn't make him any smarter either. Some poor war vet thought the whole strip was under fire when it happened. It took a solid hour to talk him out from under the bleachers. In the mist of all these memories, part of Hutch's consciousness drifted out to sea where it found an unknown harbor...it was a port of confusion. Who was this man that sat beside her? She couldn't recall a time before she was fifteen where they conversed this long without hatred being spat out. He had said some of the most disgusting and hurtful things last time they were in the same room together and it wasn't easy for her to forget them, even amongst the cheerful banter they now resided within. But even so, she pushed them away…and she didn't do it for him, she did it for herself. Life was far too short to have that venom coursing through your heart.

"….And remember that old 70's Pinto that old what's-his-face used ta bring out there? Ahhh hell I can't remember that guy's name ta save ma life. He owned a roofin' business," Harvey tried to recall.

"Owned a roofin' business? Well that narrows it down to about half the people in this county," Hutch said as she lit another smoke.

"Ah, hell forget his name…You remember the car? Wood paneled thing, baby shit green. Rustin' out a little round the fenders. He ripped all the seats n' everything out of it. Everyone used ta laugh at that thing but goddamn if he didn't run solid elevens in it."

"I think I do recall that car now that ya mention it."

"Sure ya do, Pooj. How could ya forget. Fuckin beast Pinto wagon…who the hell crams a 429 Boss down in a damn Pinto?"

"Ma future husband," Hutch jested.

"Ha!" Harvey let out. Right after those words left her lips she shuddered a bit. She didn't want to get that conversation started, about how she still wasn't married. How she had no kids. After all, the main reason they fought the last decade was over her sexual "preferences". As she sat there puffing anxiously, she waited for the words to roll from his lips…but instead…

"You ever get behind the wheel anymore, Pooj?" The question confused Hutch. Maybe her dad was going senile. It would explain a lot.

"Now, dad you know I'm banned from Highland."

Harvey sat up in his chair a tad and turned towards her.

"You know that ain't what I'm talkin' about. Talkin' bout all that nonsense you and Cass used ta get into. You still at that?" Hutch just stared at him for a moment, his eyes glared back over his glasses in the typical scolding father flame.

"Naw, dad. I don't do that no more."

Harvey just sighed and pushed himself back in his chair.

"That's good…That's real good. Keep it that way… Nothin'
good ever comes out of that, Pooj…nothin' good." Hutch couldn't
find the words to respond. She sat there biting at her lip watching
her father leer at the far wall as the curtains whipped in the breeze.
Thoughts of Regina came flooding back to her, the proposal she
had made and the supposed survival of her aunt. And to that end,
the words just fell from her lips with almost a whisper.

"Dad?" Harvey turned his head her way.

"Yes, Pooj?"

"Does the name Redgrace mean anything to you?" And it was as
if a light switch had been flipped directly into the off position.
Something went dark in her father's eyes. She could see it. The
name *did* mean something to him and judging by his elevated
breathing it meant nothing good.

"What did you just say?"

"I…I…I said…"

"I heard what you said!" He barked and turned away, staring
off. Hutch began to tremble the slightest.

"Does…well, so you know her?"

"You need to leave," her father said coldly. It cut through her
like a knife. Was he serious?

"Dad?"

"I said, get out," he pointed towards the door without a look
cast her way. Hutch quickly stamped out her smoke in the ashtray
and just glared at her father who seemed to now refuse to even
look at her. She was fearful but angry, she wanted answers.

"Dad, what happened to Aunt Cass?" But Harvey just played
silent fiddle. He sat there stewing, not even acknowledging her.
"Dad?...Dad?!" She tugged the side of his robe. Like lightning, his
baneful stare shot over at her and the poison fell out.

"You still beddin' women?" Hutch felt her heart drop.

"What?" She fought back a tear.

"You heard me. You still munchin' carpets? I told you no
daughter of mine was gonna be a dike! Now, get the fuck out!"
Tears began to well up in Hutch's eyes as she jumped to a stand
and stared hatefully down into the eyes of the father she thought
had changed. Why was he doing this?

"Fuck you," was all she could whisper.

"Yeah, fuck me…Why don't you go fuck a man, might do ya some good!" He began to rant as she made her way to the door. She spun round at the words as she threw the door open. Her cheeks began to glisten with the warm hurt Harvey had dredged forth.

"I…I thought you changed," was all she could squeak out.

"None of us change, Hutch. Specially you…now get out," he spoke one last line of cruelty. With that, she slammed the door. Several plaques and pictures rained to the cluttered floor below as Harvey began to shake where he sat. He listened as the angry engine fired up loudly right outside his door and peeling gravel went peppering against metal and wood alike. Soon, the roar of the truck faded away to the sound of nothingness in the lonely trailer. That same absence of sound was soon replaced by Harvey McCray weeping like a child. He felt his open hands fill up with the warm essence of the regrets and anger that had held him captive for so many years…This was all for the best. Within a minute, he began to try and calm himself. He rose up and limped across the room to the kitchen table, pulling his oxygen tank behind him, sniffling and wiping at his face the entire trip. As soon as he reached the windows, he glared out into the settling dust that his only daughter had left behind for him. It was the only thing that proved she was ever there at all, that and the dozens of items that had tumbled from the walls and shelves upon her angry exit. He looked down to see one such picture amongst the pile of mail that was cascading onto the floor below. It was memory of him and Hutch, not too long after she had gotten well again. Harvey bent down and retrieved it, holding it in his shaking hands. It was him, squatted down next to her in front of an old Fairlane he'd been tinkering with, his arm wrapped round her. They were both covered in grease, donning smiles of happy times….her hair was so short. It was just growing back from the treatments she had undergone. Before he could even think to control it, his tears were falling once more onto the shattered glass of the photograph.

"I'm sorry, Pooj. You'll always be my baby." As Harvey stood there trying to decide if he had done the right thing, a darkness suddenly crept in the room. It was a chilling aura that swept around him and went right down his throat…he shuddered. Someone was standing behind him.

"Oh, Harvey…Sweet, Sweet Harvey. I see what you tried to do there. It won't work. I have my claws too deep in her," a voice spoke into his ear. He trembled as a pair of tiny arms wrapped round his waist, embracing him with a gentle hug from behind.

"Why can't you just leave me alone?" He spoke in despair.

"Oh, but why would I want to do that? I wuv you!" The voice squeaked as it hugged him harder. Suddenly, the head of the person rested lightly against his shoulder. He craned his neck to look down into her golden eyes and the hell that burned beautifully within them.

Hutch was a mile away within what seemed like an eye's blink, wiping at her face, trying to quell the torrent her father had started. She hadn't cried in years and somehow managed to fall apart twice in one day, all the fault of her own family no less. She was speeding and well aware of it, but she simply paid it no mind. Getting herself as far away as she could from that man was all she really cared about, and if she got pulled over and thrown back in the pen, so be it. It was a risk she was willing to take.

Mile after mile screamed below her tires in her rampant race to get back to the shop and put this disaster of a day behind her…but something loomed. Through the dizzying abstract of her whipping clementine locks she saw it there in the review…A pin-prick breaching the horizon. A vehicle…But how, Jesus, she was going over 85 mph. Never the less, the pin-prick grew into a blotch. *"That can't be dad….it just can't be. Christ he could barely walk,"* she dwelled in an uneasy thought. But even so, the idea chilled her. Was he seriously running her down to further give her hell? Apologize? No…it wasn't Harvey. Through the slithering daze of the heat, appeared the image of a broad, bird-like beak trailed by a tail that towered into the sky. Hutch recognized that model of car anywhere…1970 Plymouth Superbird. Within seconds, the muscle car was at her backside, riding the truck bed so close that she could barely see the hood of it. The vehicle quickly began honking, swerving to and fro in a tell-tale sign of impatience and aggression. Hutch's feelings were mutual.

"What the hell, asshole?!" She caterwauled through the deafening sound of engines and the road beneath. And then it happened. Hutch felt her body blast forwards as the driver punched the pedal and kissed the nose of the Superbird right into her bumper. "Are you shittin me?!!" She bellowed in surprise. With a growl she buried the gas pedal as far as it would go. The old Chevy lurched and came to life, blasting past the 90 mph mark, instantly creating a gap between her and the insane driver behind. Before she could even look in the rearview again, the thundering sound of the Plymouth consumed her senses as it slid right around her and came neck and neck with the exhausted truck. The vehicle had seen much better days. It was awash in a multicolored patchwork of rusted panels. "What do ya want, ya crazy fucker?! What?!" She began spouting over and over, looking back and forth between the straight away and the car that now was feet away from her door. And as if time suddenly stood still, her eyes came full-focused down on the driver to see the crazy person that was forcing her to dance with the reaper. But it was the face of no person, no man, but insect…Through the dusty window of the Plymouth she beheld the horrific sight of the head of a cricket where a man's should've been. Hutch's eyes widened and her mouth fell agape as she lost all touch with reality. Was this happening? Everything seemed to cease to exist…the bellow of the engines, the rampage of the road, the wind that whistled through her ears, it all became nothing while the creature stared her down through gloss-black eyes, its mandibles sawing back and forth as if were trying to speak to her. Hutch couldn't speak, she couldn't even breathe as the cricket-man punched the gas hard and sped right out in front of her. His bumper was so close she could read the rusted personalized plate as clear as day. "ABSALOM". She didn't have time to process that word when the Plymouth tapped its brakes, causing the truck to slam into its bumper hard enough to rattle Hutch's teeth. "This is bullshit! You wanna play this game! We'll play, asshole!" Hutch screamed as she took her turn bashing into the car's bumper. "Yeah, how'd ya like that?! Can't make that piece of shit look any worse!" She rammed him again and again, smiling like a maniac. Suddenly the tables turned. The Superbird took a sudden swerve, blasted its brakes and slammed its rear quarter right into the truck's front end, instantly causing Hutch to lose control of the high speed she was topping into. Tires screeched and burned upon the pavement as she grit her teeth hard, trying to keep from spinning out or rolling the truck over. She

feathered and braked and violently caressed the wheel but, in the end, still lost the road beneath her. The machine-gun blast of corn smacking the front end of the truck chaotically erupted as she veered right into a nearby field. Panicked breath and breaking stalks consumed her senses as she plowed the pedal till she finally came to a rest amongst the maize. The engine cut out and was replaced with the sounds of the Superbird echoing like drumfire off in the distance as it left her there, staring at her own white knuckles. Soon, the silence crept in…her breath was all she could hear. Her breath and the wind whistling through the stalks that surrounded the truck, whispering to her like the lips of wandering ghosts. As her heart rate began to wane to something that resembled panicked instead of terrified, her mind played backwards. One word slithered cross her quivering lips…
"Absalom"

Sex and Brimstone

Night had fallen, it was after 10 p.m. to be more specific, and there Hutch sat in a tattered lawn chair outside her camper. Gordon Lightfoot belted out from a radio perched in the window, showering down a mellow tune that mingled well with the rainbow array of plastic lights strung overhead. Hutch tapped her foot and quietly sung along in between sips of a beer she told herself she deserved after putting up with that day. As she stared into the ceiling of her cloth awning she could do nothing more than recall the thoughts of the day, especially the last bits. Being chased down by the Superbird, then having to limp the truck back to the shop. She was lucky it even started back up, let alone was roadworthy enough to make it the rest of the trip. Fortunately, Hank had been away over at Piper Jean's when she got back. She parked it round the backside of the building and he never even went to check on it. But all it did was buy her time. She had no idea what she was going to face when he saw it the next day. The Chevy wasn't exactly the best looking truck to begin with, but there were definitely quite a few new and noticeable marks from the game of bumper cars she had been playing, not to mention the 70 mph deluge of corn. Still in all, she tried blocking it all out, but the name still hung there between her ears "Absalom" What the hell did that even mean? Was it a name? She hadn't the slightest. What she also didn't have the slightest about was her grasp with reality. The driver had a cricket head...didn't he? With that thought, she took the biggest swig of the night and just shook her head in the strangeness of it all.

The day had been hot...unfortunately the night was no different. Beads of sweat still ran down her forehead in the midst of the seventy-eight degrees and rising humidity. She wiped at her forehead and continued to sing as she watched the trucks in the lot afar. Most of them idling as they waited for the dawn to take them on their way. And soon it happened...beyond the dizzying thoughts of the car chase, she began to think of her father. She knew she couldn't block it out. The awful things he had said to her...And why? What the hell had happened? All she did was mention Redgrace and he went ballistic. It all seemed beyond odd. As the words he spoke rang again through her ears and mind, she began to think of all the fights they'd had in the past...The tears returned. Within seconds, her shoulders were bouncing in the throes of her sobbing. God damn it, she was so sick of crying. Between the chattering of diesel valves, the music, and her own sorrowful breathing she didn't hear the footsteps that approached her in the gravel beyond.

"You cryin'?" A familiar voice called through the night. Hutch scowled and straightened up as fast as she could to see Ham approaching her.

"Hell no," she clearly lied to him.

"Right..." he said as he leaned against another chair she had set up. "This seat taken?" He asked.

"Does it look like it?" She mouthed off. Ham just sighed and sat down. He stared up at the cheesy owl-shaped lights that dangled from the awning above.

"So you finally went and saw him, huh?" Ham said. Hutch looked up in slight surprise.

"What?"

"Dad. You went and saw him?"

"You talk ta Hank?"

"Hutch, I ain't talked ta Hank since he told me to fuck off earlier. I just know ya don't cry much, but when ya do, there's a ninety percent chance it was because of dad."

Hutch just took another swig and sulked.

"Told ya I wasn't cryin'."

"Yeah he's a funny creature ta figure out." Ham spoke of their father.

"He's an asshole."

"You see Hutch you're right and wrong about that." She looked at him oddly. "Now lemme explain, What dad is is a 'nasshole' He's a nice-asshole. And I don't mean the nice asshole you see at the Fox's Den at 1 a.m. after you gave the girl fifty extra bucks, I mean he's nice at times, but mostly he's an asshole. And to me that's the worst thing you can be. You see, there's three different types of people, Nice People, Assholes, and then there's dad, the Nassholes, the people that fall in that gray area in between. Dad thinks he's a nice person, and he tries to act like one. But after he makes nice with you and you think he actually is a nice person, he turns around and treats you like a piece of shit for next to no reason, thusly he becomes a Nasshole. If you're nice, great. If you're an asshole and wear it like a badge, awesome, I respect ya. If you're an asshole that tried to pretend to be nice and ya cause me mixed emotions, go fuck yourself." Ham wrapped up his sage theory.

"Nasshole...makes sense," Hutch spoke.

"Of course it does," Ham smiled, "Now, that doesn't make it any better to deal with."

"Suuuure doesn't," Hutch agreed, as she peeled at the label of her beer.

"How'd he look?" Ham asked.

"Bad...real bad," she answered. Ham just nodded. The next few moments were broken with Hutch's lips curling down uncontrollably. She began to sob.

"Hey...Hey. What's wrong?"

"Oh just..." she sniffled back her tears, "...just, how the fuck can ya hate someone and love them so much at the same time? It's like I hate him, but I don't want him to die."

Ham just shook his head and looked down.

"Great mysteries of life, Hutch," was all he could say. She wiped at her face and regained control of herself the best she could as she let out a fake laugh,

"Life…Jesus Christ what a joke. And death? Even funnier…No one cares. I mean does anybody really care? From the outside lookin' in…at the end of the day, when you're not the one who is dead, and there's always that part of you that looks in the coffin and says, '*better them than me. At least I'm not dead.*' I mean, you never say it, but you know it's there. And then they shove you in a box and toss dirt over you. A preacher you didn't even know says some bullshit, and then everybody goes to a buildin' and stuffs their face with shitty potato salad and baked beans while they exchange stories about ya. And then they all say to one another, '*We really need to start hanging out more as a family instead of only coming together at funerals*'…and then everyone nods, but no one ever does it. And what's left of you when you go? A pile of shit you leave behind. Clothes…tools…" Hutch paused a second and tossed her bottle, "…empty beer bottles. You're just gone. You're nothin' but the words on people's lips…and soon that fades…Two generations later ya ain't even a ghost. Someone points to a photo and says '*That there tall gal was your great, great, aunt…*' and the kid goes '*Wow…*' and that's it. No one alive really knows who you were…and no one cares. No one."

"Wow, Hutch…that was…"

"The truth?" She interrupted Ham as she cracked open another beer.

"Well, I think the word I was lookin for was depressin', but we'll go with that for now." Hutch just stared at him as she took her first swig on the new bottle. She wiped her mouth,

"Why the fuck are ya here, by the way?"

"Well, it's nice to see you too," Ham laughed in annoyance.

"Shit, I saw ya this mornin'. It's after ten, shouldn't ya be in bed or somethin?" She said as she lit up a cigarette.

"Or somethin, I guess…Wait, how the hell you go see dad anyways?" Ham suddenly thought about that fact. She sighed some smoke into the air.

"Ain't important. I saw dad. End of story."

"No, *not* end of story. I know sure as shit no one drove ya there."

"I took the damn work truck okay?!"

"Hutch, what the hell are ya thinkin'? Or are ya even thinkin'?"

"Look! I don't wanna talk about how or why I got there! I'm back, I didn't get caught." Hutch's angry words all but split the air down the middle. Ham just sat there, staring at her in a leer of disappointment.

"Well that would explain the condition of the work truck then."

"What?"

"Oh, don't *what* me, Hutch. The work truck. I saw it pulled round back. It didn't look like that this morning. Hank see that yet?"

"As a matter of fact, he didn't, and we're gonna keep it that way."

"Oh yeah? How ya gonna do that? And what the hell is this *we* stuff? Don't you drag me into this bullshit. I already got dragged into this forty dollar short-till business. I ain't gonna keep takin' falls for you the rest of ma damn life."

"No one's asking you too!"

"No, Hutch, but you sure as hell never step up and keep me from takin' the blame, do you?" Ham said. She went silent and stared at her feet. He let out a sigh.

"So how the hell did the truck get that way?" He feared to ask.

"I was all pissed off at dad. Swung too wide and hit a pole when I was screamin' out of his drive..." Hutch explained, never making eye contact.

"Oh you hit a pole, huh?...One of the best drivers I've met, got flustered and hit a pole backing out of a driveway...You wanna tell me what really happened?"

"I *said*, I hit a pole."

"Okay how many poles did you hit exactly?"

"Huh?"

"Looks ta me like ya hit about sixteen poles. Front, rear, and one driver side."

Things went silent for a moment. "Were you racin' someone?"

"What?! No!"

"Hutch?"

"Ham, you fuckin' seriously think I'd be racin' someone in that clunker truck?"

"Hey, I've seen you race in worse shit than that. I seen you race kids on your big wheel for Little Debbie's. You're addicted to that shit like cocaine. You always have been. Now…were you racin'?"

"Someone ran me off the road, alright?!" She finally let it out.

"What the hell? Seriously?"

"Yep."

"Seems like somethin' ya might wanna tell someone. You just decided ya were gonna keep that locked up?"

"And who the hell am I gonna tell, the cops? '*Yes officer I got ran off the road today. Oh, by the way, I ain't supposed to be drivin' cuz I got a suspended license.*"

"Well, who was it?"

"How the hell should I know. Happened too fast."

"You owe money to someone?"

"Why the hell does everyone immediately go that route? Every time some bullshit happens to me everyone assumes I owe people money or I'm out doin' ill shit." Another pass of silence crept through.

"So no plate number? No make or model of the car, nothin?"

"Oh my fuckin' god, you need to just back off me now…," her unlit cigarette danced on her lips as she shook her head in discontent.

"I'm not backing off of shit till I get some straight answers out of you."

"It was a rusted up Plymouth Superbird and the driver had a cricket's head!" The words took a minute to settle into Ham's ears, especially the last bit. It kept echoing inside his mind as he floundered for the next question to ask.

"Uh…uh what?"

"A Plymouth Superbird. Ya know, the one with the big wing on the back?" She patronized him.

"Hutch, I know what a damn Superbird is, I need you to skip ahead one for me. A cricket's head? What the hell does that even mean?"

"Yeah a cricket, Ham. His head, not a human's, it was a goddamn cricket's. Or grasshopper…or some shit. It was a fuckin' bug's head, okay?" Hutch started shaking as her words flooded

into the open air. Ham became slightly unnerved. She was telling
the truth. He knew it. He quickly began to try and make reason of
what she saw, other than the obvious thing he wanted to spit out,
that she was high. He knew that wouldn't go over well.

"Well...guy was probably wearing a mask, right?"
Hutch stopped shaking for a second and stared at the side of her
camper. Maybe Ham was onto something. Maybe she hadn't been
hallucinating. She felt stupid for a moment, but obvious questions
still abounded.

"What, like a Halloween mask?"

"Yeah, like a Halloween mask."

"In the middle of summer?" She looked right over into his eyes
with doubt.

"Hutch, you don't know what some of these damn tweakers do
around here for fun."
Hutch just shook her head and took a drink followed by a deep
drag of her smoke.

"Ya say he was drivin' a Superbird? You sure?" Ham brought
the car make back to the conversation.

"Yup. I'd recognize one of them cars anywhere. Henry hated
those goddamn things."

"Yeah, he sure did," Ham half smiled.

"I still remember the day I was making eyes at one in a
magazine and he slapped the thing out of my hand. Said they were
the ugliest damn cars he'd ever seen."

"I could see him doin' that."

"Hell, I don't know...," she trailed off. Her eyes began darting
around as she replayed the traumatizing ordeal with the battered
car and it's cricket driver. "There was somethin' else..."

"What was that?"

"The car's plate number. It was a vanity tag...I remember it."

"Well, that's good. What was it?" Ham asked with bated breath.

"Absalom," the strange word rolled from her tongue. Ham's
brow rose.

"Absalom? Like the son of David? The most handsome man in
all of Israel?" Ham spouted off three questions that only got her
reeling all the more.

"What the hell?" She said in surprise.

"From the bible, Hutch. I guess I was the only one of us listenin' in church when we were kids."

"Absalom…So what then, this guy ran me off the road is some bible thumpin' nut who gets his jollies off terrifyin' people by wearin' a Halloween mask?"

"Hutch…I don't know. What I do know is we probably oughta report it."

She began shaking her head 'no' as she stared at the side of the camper. "Yeah, I think it's best. I'll get up super early and tell Hank I borrowed the truck to run an errand. Tell him someone ran me off the road. Hell, we got the car description and plate. I'll just report it to the cops in the A.M. They can find the crazy sunovabitch and get em' off the road."

"No," Hutch simply spoke.

"No? You don't want the bastard off the streets?"

"No, I don't want you to do that. To lie like that. I'm done. I'll just tell Hank the fuckin' truth for once. If he believes me, fine, if not…well I just don't give a shit anymore."

"You sure about that. Think that might be the alcohol talkin'."

"What is with you? Ya just told me not too long ago that you're always takin' the fall for me, so I decide to finally end the streak and you're actin' like I'm doin' the wrong damn thing!" She yelled as she put her cigarette out in the gravel beside her.

"It's just…I don't know…" Ham stuttered.

"Well? What?!" Hutch begged for clarification. Ham went silent. She peered right at him with a suspicious leer, "You know, maybe I'm not the entire problem here. Maybe you want to take the fall for me cuz it makes you feel like some kinda goddamn hero or somethin'. Hell I don't know, maybe you get off on that, bein' the good guy. You just use every opportunity I screw up to play the saint and clean it up for me, only it's really not for my benefit but for your ego. Yeah, maybe you're a Nasshole, Ham. You ever think about that?"

"Okay, enough!" He jumped out of his chair and stared down at her. "I'm not gonna sit here and let you berate the shit out of me…You wanna know why I came out here tonight? It wasn't to check on the shop, it was to check on you. To make sure you're okay. I'll repeat that if it didn't sink into your thick head, to see if YOU are okay. I didn't come here to make myself feel better that's for damn sure, and, for your information, I rarely ever feel 'good' when I help you out."

"Then stop doin' it."

"You know what, Hutch? I'm gonna stop. Startin' tonight…cuz I'm sicka this shit. You can forget me coverin' for your ass, gettin' ya up in the mornins', and ya can especially count me out of drivin' you to these fuckin' AA meetings you're required to be at, which by the way, you're already taking so seriously from the pile of bottles round your feet."

"Oh fuck you, Ham. I'm not an alcoholic, okay?"

"That's exactly what alcoholics say. Speakin' of which, you know who you're reminding me of right now, Hutch? Dad."
Hutch's eyes went cold and dark.

"You better get the fuck out of here before I break this bottle over your head," she snarled as her body began to quiver with rage. Ham shook his head and started in,

"Hutch…"
She cut him short,

"Before you say one more word to me, I want you to ask yourself one question, 'Is it worth me shittin' out my own broken teeth tomorrow for?'…Well, is it? Get the fuck out of my face."

Ham let out a short laugh. His anger was building as he paced a bit where he stood.

"Yeah you're a tough bird, ain't ya Hutch," He put his hands on his hips then quickly threw them in the air. "Fine, I'm leavin'. Tired of this shit. Tired of your shit." He spoke as he walked away toward the shop. He hadn't gotten twenty feet when Hutch jumped up in a rage and kicked the chair he had been sitting, into the gravel lot beyond.

"That's right get the fuck out of here! I'm not dad! You hear me, Ham?! I ain't dad! You're the Nasshole!" She pointed at him, never losing grip of her beer in the other hand. Ham simply gave her the finger over his shoulder and never looked back. Hutch let out a growl so loud it shook her teeth. She barely contained the urge to run after him and jump right onto his back, fists flying…but in the end, she let it go. With a grit-toothed scowl she watched him get into his car and rip out of the lot, disappearing behind the rumbling big rigs. She just continued to stand there, fists clenched so hard she almost broke the bottle in her hand. Her anger just wouldn't wane, it was still there building like a pressure cooker. And so she did the only thing she could, she screamed and chucked her beer against the side of the camper. It shattered into pieces, making yet another dent in the aluminum façade. Her butt hit hard, back into her lawn chair as she fought the returning tears amongst a growling groan she emitted.

"Fucker...can't believe he said that to me...Shit," a repetition of cursing whispers fell from her mouth. She was almost physically trying to push the tears back in her head at that point. With a crack of another beer, she took a deep breath and let it all out, successfully turning off the tap of emotions that escaped through her eyes.

"There ya go, Hutch...There ya go. No more cryin'," she chanted to herself and took a giant swig. The bitter liquid spun round her tongue, burned her throat, and warmed her chest. She sighed in the blissful feeling it gave her...She was gonna forget this day, and if it took every beer in Piper Jean's coolers to do it, so be it.

The clock ticked on past the midnight hour with Hutch singing along to every song she put on the radio. She was getting lit and fast, and she absolutely loved it. Soon enough, her singing had turned into some kind of slurring moan that strung together, becoming more sounds than words. It was now an almost whale-like symphony of drunken harmonics that hummed across the air. But through her blurring syllables, a new sound emerged to her ears. Footsteps. She spun round to see a young woman standing there, almost timidly, donning a coy smile. It was her one night stand from last night.

"Hey," the girl spoke.

"What the fuck are you doin' here?" Hutch involuntarily blurted out. For a moment she wondered if she thought it instead of saying it. But as soon as the girl's smile turned to a scowl, Hutch knew she had most definitely said it out loud.

"Well, I thought I was surprisin' you. Thought you'd be happy to see me?" This girl was getting too clinging already and Hutch wasn't having it. Dear god, they only were together one night.

"Oh Becky, you know I'm happy to see you," Hutch slurred out.

"My names, Anna," The girl placed her hands on her hips and began fidgeting in annoyance.

"Jesus, I wasn't even in the ballpark…," Hutch mumbled to herself, trying not to laugh, "Anna…right. That's it."

"Yeah, Anna. And who the hell is Becky?" Anna crossed her arms and scowled. Hutch took a swig of beer and scowled right back. This girl was not only clingy she was the insanely jealous type. She had to get rid of her, and fast.

"Becky's another girl I let go down on me. You got a problem with that?" Hutch lied. Anna was visibly shaken, but seemed to play it off as she walked close to Hutch and put her hands on her shoulders.

"Well, that's cool I guess. I can share. I bet Becky don't do it as good as me though," she spoke seductively, running her hands through Hutch's hair. Hutch wasn't quite sure what it was, maybe it was the shittiness of that particular day, but the more the girl rubbed up on her, the more disgusted she became.

"Stop. Just stop." Hutch jumped up out of her chair, pushing her away.

"What's wrong, baby?"

"I just…stop, okay?" Hutch was getting soberer by the second. She didn't like it one bit. Anna grabbed her hand.

"Chill. Come on. Let's just go on inside and smoke up. Let's fuck."
Hutch violently stripped her hand away from the young woman's. They both leered at one another.

"Anna, I kinda had a rough day so, why don't you go fuck yourself, okay?"
Anna's lips curled in disgust.

"Wow…you're a bitch."

"Took you almost twenty-four hours ta figure that out? Ha! You really are as stupid as you look."

"Oh my god! Fuck you! You know what? I'm outta here," Anna threw her hands up and began walking off.

"Oh no, please don't go. Come back and smoke all my weed up for free while you talk bout how were meant for each other," Hutch smarted off, waving her hands about, never losing her grasp on the beer she held. Anna simply threw the finger over her shoulder. "Oh that's original! Afraid I already seen that one tonight. Get some new material…and get that spot checked out near your cooch, that things lookin ripe." Hutch yelled a barrage of insults as Anna's fast footfall was swallowed by the hum of the rigs. She started in again, "And wash your butt for god sake. It's called soap..." her words faded down to a whisper, "Gross bitch...goddamn..." She took one final swig on her beer and let it drop with a clang to the pile by her chair. The noise sent a shockwave through her head and the earth around her started to spin...she knew right then she was lit...like another world kind of lit. The multicolored owl lights above her head started to become a blur as she fought the urge to fall over right then and there. "Oh shit...blurgh...bedtiiiiime..." she mumbled to herself as she fell against the side of the camper, her hands slithering along, feeling for the door handle. Soon enough, she found her footing on the metal steps and pulled herself up through the open screen door. With a quick step, she loosened her boots and kicked them to the corner, pulled her couch out into a bed, and fell face first onto it. She closed her eyes and began to moan as the entire room spun round her, hellbent on bringing every last drop of beer right back up. "I'm never drinkin again, god. I'll change ma ways...Just don't let me die..." she mumbled. Wow, if she had a dollar for every time that came from her mouth she wouldn't have been living in that camper. "*Tap. Tap. Tap.*" A knock at the door resounded. Hutch's eyes popped wide, staring right down into the blurry flannel pattern of her couch-bed.

"What the fuuuu...?" she groaned. Surely she was hearing shit? Was Anna seriously back?

"*Tap. Tap. Tap.*" The knocking returned. Hutch peeled her face a few inches off the couch. "Fuck off, Anna..." she spoke loud.

"*Tap.Tap. Tap. Tap. Tap.*"

"Damn it! I said go wash your dirty butt and smoke someone else's weed!"

"*Tap. Tap. Tap. Tap. Tap. Tap. Tap. Tap. Tap. Tap!*"

"Oh, fuck no," Hutch pushed herself up off the couch in a rage, "I am too goddamn drunk for this shit." With that, she stumbled forwards and threw the screen door open, nearly hitting the person who stood there, "Anna I said...!" but she cut her words short. Her whole demeanor changed in one blink as she saw Regina standing there, wide beaming smile on her face. "Oh...it's you," Hutch quickly tried to erase the look of desire on her face.

"It's meeeeee," the tiny brunette drew out in her squeaky, cutie-pie voice. Hutch melted a little inside, but tried keeping her cool. "Well?" Regina said.

"Well what?" Hutch spoke back.

"Aren't you gonna invite me in this...whatever this thing is you live in?" She looked around with a playful frown at the dents and damage abounding the siding.

"No. Fuck off," Hutch said coldly.

"Okay then," Regina smiled as she pulled herself right up into the camper and squeezed by Hutch. The brunette looked around, nodding her head. "Nice digs. Oh, you have a little TV and everything," she pointed at the tiny television up on the shelf with a grin. She then focused right in on Hutch. "Oh Red, honey you look like hell." Hutch just leaned forwards and opened the screen door, leering at Regina. "I said, fuck off. Now get out," she pointed to the noise of the lot beyond. The brunette just smiled even bigger. She pushed herself right up against Hutch and looked into her eyes...Hutch could feel her warm breath tickling her neck.

"You look like you've had a few too many. Hmmm, maybe I should just take advantage of you," Regina let out in a seductive whisper that tingled the back of Hutch's neck. Before the redhead could even think to respond, Regina's hand slid right down the front of her jeans and she locked her lips around hers. My god, her lips were so soft, how was it even possible to have lips that soft? Hutch's mind reeled back to a blue velvet blanket she had as a kid. After a wash, her mother would dry it in the glory of the mid-day sun and Hutch would pluck it down, press it to her flesh, and smile... it sent a wave of sensuous electricity through her...and these lips, they did just the same. It was like the very first time she had ever kissed a woman, only times infinity. The feelings of joy, of dread, of everything and nothing, coming together to erase time, life, death, and all things that surrounded them except for that kiss. The kiss was all she could feel. She wanted nothing more than to rip this girl's clothes right off...But no, she couldn't. This was the same woman that held her aunt captive. With a jolt, she pushed Regina away and slapped her hard across the face. The brunette stumbled back and grabbed the side of her cheek. Hutch could barely believe what she had just done. She fully expected Regina to raise her head up with a leer of anger and storm off, joining

Anna and her brother in the "We Hate Hutch Club". But no...With
a steady rise, the brunette's head came up. A tiny stream of blood
seeped from a small spot Hutch had opened up on those soft
lips...She cringed at what she had caused, but Regina didn't. She
just smiled wide and licked at the blood, pulling it into her mouth
and savoring it as if were top shelf liquor. Her golden eyes were
aflame with an unbridled excitement brought on by the violence
that Hutch had dished out on her. And Hutch herself couldn't help
but feel the same...What was happening? Before the redhead could
even think to make any rational move, the two of them collided
into each others arms. Playful teeth found lips and flesh alike while
torn clothes began to rain down in the deluge brought forth from
impatient hands and ripping fists. There was nothing left now, no
thoughts, no fears, just the electricity of the sex that consumed
them as their naked bodies hit the bed below. And so the two of
them writhed like the carefree serpents that they had become,
coiling and intertwining one another, all inhibitions tossed to the
four winds, cold-blooded instinct was all that remained. It felt so
right as it did so wrong, but wasn't that the beauty of it all? To
bury the anxieties of the human condition and let the animal out to
play? To let sex simply just be sex and not a game of guilt and
overthinking?...Yes...Yes... "Yes", Hutch cooed as she felt
Regina's velvet-soft lips go from her breasts, to her stomach, and
below; her ivory skin being tickled by those gorgeous, shadowy
locks through the entire journey. The redhead's mouth fell agape.
Fists clenched and toes curled as she let the sensation swallow her
whole in scarlet shades of ecstasy....And so she just let herself go,
allowing the powers of passion and fornication ferry them both
deep into the belly of that hot summer night. Hutch had never felt
quite so alive...

For what seemed like hours, the brunette and the redhead
ravaged one another until they both felt the pull of fatigue tugging
at them. They rolled off one another and laid there side by side,
staring at the ceiling of the camper, perspiration beading from their
brows. Hutch had since become quite sober, though she was now
drunk on something else entirely, the tiny brunette next to her. For
what seemed like ten solid minutes, they remained there in silence,
their sweat matted locks sticking to their faces and necks as they
glared skyward, seemingly waiting for the other to speak. But how

did one break the ice after such an ordeal. Hutch, herself, had not the slightest idea of what to even say while she laid there. She started playing with her hair, twisting it around her finger in a state of growing anxiety, just begging that Regina would speak first so she didn't have to. The redhead let one hand down, and crept it over towards Regina's about to take hold of it. She stopped herself. Jesus, what was she doing? Was she seriously about to hold this girl's hand? And she was the one going off in her own mind about Anna being "Too clingy". But before she could pull it away in second thought, Regina grabbed onto it, squeezing it hard. My god, she had a grip for such a tiny, little thing. Hutch felt her heart melt a tad…that was not good. What was this girl doing to her?

"What're you thinking bout, Red?" Regina suddenly broke the silence. Hutch's eyes grew large. She surely didn't want to say the things she was currently thinking. She clawed for something else...and this came out…

"Do you believe in God?" She squinted in her own stupidity. What the hell was that?

Regina giggled a little.

"Of course I do…I met him once, you know."

Hutch smiled.

"Wwwwhat?"

The brunette turned and looked at her.

"Yeah, I met God, I said."

Hutch just started laughing a bit.

"Wow, okay. What were you smokin' at the time? I need some of that."

"Oh…little bit of life, little bit of death, and the jagged crimson bits in between," Regina answered cryptically. Hutch started staring at the ceiling again, almost afraid to divulge what was now on her mind. She let it fly.

"An angel came ta me once."

"A what? An angel?" Regina asked.

"Somethin' like it. I never told anyone that. When I was little, I got cancer. I was so sick…like ready to die, sick. I remember one day I was lyin' in the hospital bed, I was just out of it, and this…this woman stood over me and she was surrounded by this halo of light that was so bright it blinded me. All I could see was these gorgeous sky-blue eyes, nothin' else. She leaned in, grabbed

my hand, and whispered. '*Everything is gonna be okay,
toots*'…And it was. There was all this pain, like radiating through
me, but then it went away and I passed out. My cancer was
just…gone…It's stupid. Probably a damn dream er' somethin. But
it stuck with me all these years."

"Oh, Red, I don't think that's stupid…you know, the
supernatural is something that isn't supposed to happen, but it does
happen."

Hutch's eyes widened over a grin.

"Aw, I love that movie," she proclaimed. Regina looked at her
oddly.

"What movie?"

"The one you just quoted…You know?...The Haunting?…Never
mind," the redhead just let it go. Regina then released her hold on
Hutch's hand and rolled over on her side. From the edge of the bed
she began rummaging through her clothes on the floor while Hutch
beheld a beautifully disturbing sight across the brunette's back.
From the top of her shoulders all the way down to the small of her
back, was a tattooed patchwork of keys, all pieced together and
intertwined like the endless depths of some otherworldly jigsaw
puzzle. Hutch reached out and ran her fingers down the flesh of
Regina's back, tracing along the lines of the fathomless lock
engagers.

"Awww, you like that, Red? You have any ink that I failed to
notice while I was devouring you?" Hutch's face twisted a bit. She
actually didn't. Funny, she had always thought about getting
tattoos but never did.

"Nope," she responded.

"Yeah, well, if you ever decide to, make sure it means
something," Regina's spoke as she continued to dig through the
mess on the floor.

"What's yours mean?" Hutch was beyond curious.

"Glad, you asked, Red. Every time I beat someone in a race, I
have their key tattooed on my back. Every single one is a picture
perfect replica of the one that started the loser's car. It's a collage
of trophies, I guess you could say." A bit of a chill ran up the bare
flesh of Hutch's back. There were hundreds of keys on the
brunette's back, if not more. They were too intermeshed to even
count at this point. How many years would it have taken to amass

such an organic wall-of-fame? Not to mention the skill that came with it. It all got the redhead back to wondering just how old Regina was despite her youthful, late-teen appearance. As Hutch kept herself entranced by the abstract of ink, her eyes soon led her to a tattoo quite unlike the rest. It was a name. "Marnie" it simply said, scrawled in a graceful font on the back of her neck, right beneath her hairline. She almost found herself doing an internal scowl. Who was Marnie? Jesus, was she getting jealous?

"Ahh, there you are," Regina's voice slightly startled Hutch. She recoiled her hand from her flesh as the brunette laid flat on her back once more. In her hand she now held what Hutch thought to be a homemade cigarette. It was coal black from tip to butt, she had never quite seen anything like it. An animalistic hunger abounded as she watched Regina strike a lighter and ignite the tip of the mystery stick.

"What ya got there?" The redhead spoke, trying desperately to not seem overly eager. Regina took a deep inhale and exhale, releasing a plume of what almost appeared to be purple smoke. "Is that...is that H?" Hutch stuttered out before she received an answer to her first inquiry.

"What? No," Regina laughed.

"Weed?" Hutch cocked her head. Surely it wasn't.

"Oh, no."

"Crack?"

"What the fuck?! Now you're just insulting me."

"DMT?"

"Ha!Ha! Listen to you! You just can't stand not knowing. You're like a little puppy dog waiting on the promise of a treat," Regina laughed, "It's adorable." Then the aroma of the smoke wafted into Hutch's nostrils. It was like nothing she'd ever smelled. It was sulfurous, metallic, and almost floral all at the same time. Mother of God, what was that? She gave up.

"Well? What is it?" the redhead playfully shoved Regina. The brunette giggled.

"I'm never gonna tell you. It's getting me hot watching you just sitting there, on the brink of explosion, wanting that first hit sooooo badly."

"Stop, you tease," Hutch pleaded with a smile.

"Oh, Red, you're being so damn cute right now. Kiss me."
Without a thought Hutch obliged her, pressing her lips hard upon
that perfect satin mouth. Several seconds of slow, sultry smacking
instantly sent the redhead's temperature back through the roof. Her
kissing intensified, speeding up to a level she could do little to
control. All of a sudden, she felt a pain at the back of her head as
Regina grabbed her by the hair and pulled her off. The brunette
smiled as she took another hit of her enigmatic drug of choice, the
one Hutch would all but kill for at this point, even though she still
had no clue what it actually was.

"Now suck on my tit like a good girl...annnnd I'll give you a
taste," Regina shoved Hutch's head down to her bare breast.
Again, Hutch was more than happy to give her what she wanted.

"Oh yeah...Yes, yes, yes," the brunette cooed amidst the sounds
of the redhead's eager lips and flicking tongue.

"That's right, baby. Harder."

Hutch sped up the tempo.

"No. Harder." Regina spoke.

Hutch pressed her face in deeper.

"Harder! Get those teeth in there," the brunette commanded. The
redhead obeyed, and began nibbling at the tender flesh inside her
mouth. She could feel Regina's nipple engorge all the more with
every moan she expelled.

"Harder! Harder!" The brunette yelled her demands. Hutch was
beginning to panic. How much harder could she go? And then...

"Bite it, Hutch! Make it bleed!" Was she serious? "I said make
it bleed, you bitch!" She screamed right into the redhead's ear. The
fear exploded inside her as she bit down hard and felt the flesh pop
between her teeth. A steady stream of warm life poured into her
mouth and covered her teeth in a film of metallic essence. The
brunette howled in pleasure, grabbing a fistful of red hair. Both
horror and ecstasy danced between Hutch's ears as she kept
gnawing and sucking, the blood filling up her mouth from the
nipple she dared not neglect till Regina commanded it so. The
more the red liquid filled her mouth the more she felt vampiric, on
the fringe and alive, but also sick to her stomach all in that same
moment in time. What was she doing? What was she becoming?

"Red?...Red?!" Regina repeated for several moments before
Hutch finally came to her senses. The animalistic fever lifted from

her heart and she released the breast from the grasp of her rabid mouth. She raised her head, wide-eyed, blood smeared across her lips and beyond. Blue eyes met a golden stare...

"Huh?" Was all Hutch could expel in the wake of her returning sobriety.

"I said you can stop, silly...Here," Regina smiled, handing the black drag over to the grasp of the still dazed McCray. Hutch rolled over onto her back and propped herself up onto her elbows. Her mind was still astray, a mess within a mess, disgusted and pleased at the act she had just committed. She felt numb.

"Well, just don't lie there and stare at it," Regina spoke. The brunette tenderly wiped the excess blood away from the redhead's lips and then from her own breast. Hutch's eyes slowly drifted to Regina then back to the obsidian stick that lay between her fingers, its cobalt smoke gently drifting into the air. She went to put it to her lips but paused.

"Wait...W-w-what is it?" She hesitated slightly. The brunette grinned.

"Don't you remember? Life...death...and the jagged crimson in between," she paraphrased her own bizarre line from earlier. "Take it in, Red. Take it allll in." And so she did. She drew in the foreign smoke with a deep inhale. It tasted just like it smelled, a garden of roses and lavender, sprouting forth from a bedrock of sulfurous coal. Turgidly, it mixed with the iron tinge of blood that still coated the inside of her mouth and fell down through her throat to the depths of her lungs where it sat like a fog laced with lead.

"How's that feeling, Red," Regina grinned. Hutch just sat there feeling unable to release the smoke that seemed anchored to the bottom of her chest. Soon, she began to panic. Horror set in...She couldn't breath. Hutch shot up to a sit and began lurching and gasping, feeling as if she were on the brink of unconsciousness.

"Uh-Oh," Regina simply said. She leaned over and blasted the redhead in the chest with her clenched fist. A sickening exhale exploded from Hutch's lungs, discharging a purple cloud into the air above her. Regina patted Hutch on the back while she went into a maelstrom of wet and violent coughing.

"Yep, let it out. Let it out. It's okay. Sometimes that stuff stops your heart on the first go. Should've warned you about that." The redhead's surprised eyes shot to Regina's as she continued to cough her last few hacks. *'Are ya fuckin' kiddin me?!'* She thought but couldn't speak the words. Within another moment, her coughs had waned down to a heavy breath, one that was haloed by eyes of distrust. She leered at the black drag in her hand, teetering on the thought of flicking it to the floor or out the window, but then it hit her…That feeling…It was tiny at first, but then grew steadily into something unexplainable. Soon, it was like nothing she had ever felt in her life. No drug she had ever taken felt the way that this did…The heavy weight that had resided in her chest receded and spread throughout her body, manifesting into a tingling aura that crept through every reach of her circulatory system…she could feel every vein, artery, and capillary inside herself expanding and filling with the sensation….Was it life? Was it death? She felt like everything and nothing and, indeed, all of the crimson shards that patched it together. She was floating yet she was sinking at the same time, her dark half separating from her light half, two version of the same soul perfectly pulling themselves apart to make the perfect version of each. And when they were halfway detached they stopped, floating there in some enigmatic limbo, like yin and yang, hovering amongst an outline of where her body still sat in the soiled and blessed mouth of the "real" world. One reality had divided into three…the shell, the soul, and the anti-soul. And there she remained, like a flower of every color and no color, blooming into petals patterned in the triplicity of everything that ever was and ever would be. And just like that, she knew what she was made from…She was star dust. She was angel's tears. She was demon's blood…She was God's daughter. Earth's sister. Satan's lover, and the Astral's Wife…And in the realization of it all, every piece of her wept. But amongst the sadness and joy, crept a shadow….there was something more…a swirling dread…Darkness overtook. Everything around her faded… The camper. Regina. The earth. Her very breath. It was all gone. It was all swallowed so deeply that she began to wonder if it had all been a dream, every tiny shard of it. Was she dead? Or was she ever born at all? And it was right then and there that she felt earthly sensation once again as her feet touched lightly down on the bitter coldness of a ground she couldn't see. Her mind's eye peeled back to see a desolate landscape. It was like a beautiful sunset turned inside out, the colors inverted into a horizon tempered in shades of indigo nightmare frosted in flame…nothing but black above and black below. And it was endless…The smell of sulfur was all that remained. She had no clue of where she was, nor the path to take back home. No matter where she looked, every stitch of the horizon remained the same as if she were in the very epicenter of a purple ring of fire with walls that were an unfathomable distance away. She felt her breath return…her numbness ebbed and she began to run as her muscles reconnected….but no matter how far she ran or how hard she breathed and wished, nothing changed. It was as if she were running in place within this void. Forever stuck and too far out to sea. And then she heard it…

"Hutch?" It was a soft cooing tone coming from the beyond that surrounded her. Hutch's horror elevated. It was the voice of her aunt.

"Aunt Cass…?" the redhead found her voice.

"Hutch, I'm here," the ghostly voice slithered again.

"Where?! Where, Aunt Cass?!" She began running around the ebony field once more, getting nowhere.

"I'm down in the depths. Help me, Hutch…Find me…Bring me home…"

"But how?! Hutch began screaming out in helplessness. Soon thereafter, her aunt's voice faded and nothing but the numbness of the air stung her ears. Tears began pouring down her burning cheeks as exhaustion overtook…With nothing left within and without her, she collapsed to her knees and then fell to her side, curling up into the fetal position until she felt like a babe in the womb ready to be reborn into anything but the place she now called hell…And even though it seemed impossible, unconsciousness took her…she went to sleep…dreaming within a dream swallowed by a nightmare…

Meaty Graffiti

With a jolt, frightened blue eyes burst open to the glorious sight
of something other than the propane flames of a prison not long
forgotten. The mist of consciousness stung Hutch's squinting stare
as she realized she had awoken into reality…she had found her
way back from the abyss. A fiery blaze of gorgeous sunshine
poured forth from her windows and her ears were reintroduced to

the sounds she had always known…the rigs rumbling in the foreground.

"Whaaa…what the…?" was all she could squeak as she moved her jaws about. God, her mouth was sore, so was her neck…hell, everything was sore. She felt as if she had been hit by the proverbial truck that all older folks talk about. With all she could muster, she thrust herself from her face-down position on the bed; a string of drool tethered from her pillow to her mouth. She began wiping at her face as she remained there, bent over upon hands and knees amongst her disheveled bed, trying to regather what the hell had happened the night before, aside from the nightmare she had just awoken from. Her distant memory recalled drinks…cigs…her brother…Regina…REGINA! Hutch sat straight up in a panicked breath, looking around the camper for signs of the brunette…but nothing was there. No trace of her seemed to abound…Not even a shred of the clothes that she had all but torn off her body. Hutch's head began to spin even harder as she elevated herself to a stand…She peered through the windows on all sides and then began fishing through her own clothes upon the floor, desperately digging for anything that Regina may have left behind…but again, nothing was there. Soon, the feelings of delusion began to set into Hutch's cloudy brain…Had it all been a dream? The sex? The drugs? Just a fabrication of something she must have secretly hoped would happen…perhaps…With a sigh to end all sighs, she sat down hard upon the bed, but then instantly jumped back up from a stinging pain. She grit her teeth and winced, grabbing her backside, only to have the pain come back two-fold.

"Ow! What the?!" She bemoaned. With a grave worriment, she paced over to her bathroom door and stood there examining her naked flesh in the long mirror that hung there. Within seconds, she realized that the previous night may have not been the lie she had just made it out to be. Her fingers slid down her ivory body, accentuating things that were not there the day before. Scratch marks on her shoulders. A bruise on her inner thigh. Countless scrapes and marks peppered her skin beneath her gaping mouth and disbelieving stare. Once again, her hands slid round to her rear and the same pain panged away. She jumped ever so slightly then spun herself round to see exactly what the hell was going on back there. Given the other sexual battle wounds upon her flesh, she almost dared not to look, but there it was staring back at her, a halo of red…A bite mark right on her left ass cheek. Hutch twisted her neck hard, displaying a look of shock at the tooth tattoo that little Ms. Redgrace had left behind.

"What the? What the fuuuck – OW!" She screamed out as she touched it once more. She grit her teeth as she grabbed a nearby towel and started dabbing at the wound. "Jesus Christ…" she whispered through a clenched frown. All of a sudden, she dropped the towel as the thoughts of the real world came flooding back to her. What time was it? She jumped across the room and began digging through the strewn bed covers, looking for the alarm clock she never used. Soon she pulled it from the deaths of the bed crease. "10:06"

"Shit!" In a whirlwind, she began gathering up clothes and throwing them on, not caring what they looked or smelled like. Hank was already making her life hell, now she was late once again and had the job of trying to explain what the hell had happened to the work truck on top of that…She started wondering if she should be packing all her clothes rather than throwing them on herself.

A mad explosion erupted into the metallic air of The Ginger Bread House as Hutch came barreling through the front door, wide eyed and breathless from the run across the gravel lot. Ham was standing there, back at his usual duties behind the front desk. He looked up from his calculator pecking to see her still adjusting her clothes.

"Hey," Hutch spoke meekly to him, suddenly recalling the events from the night before. He just shook his head and went back to pushing buttons.

"Wow, you got up on your own for once…looks like ya don't need me anymore. Too bad you're an hour late though," he spoke in the gravest irritation. She put her head down a bit and walked slowly over to him, saying something she rarely said,

"I'm sorry…"

"What was that?" Ham still didn't bother looking at her.

"I said, I'm sorry."

"Bout what?"

"You know what…last night."

"Ohhh, yeah. Last night. Right…," he started in with sarcasm, "So what then, Hutch? You gonna tell me it was just the beer talkin'? You were havin' a bad day?"

"I *was* havin a bad day."

"Fuck off."

Hutch just sank her head further at her brother's words of dismissal. She then went to breathe and speak again. Ham cut her short.

"I said, fuck off."

Hutch just scowled and went to walk off, but then quickly turned back round.

"Ham?"

Ham just threw down his pencil and slid the calculator away, leering at her, waiting to dismiss whatever bullshit was about to fall from her mouth.

"What are we gonna tell Hank about the truck?"

Ham just forced a smile and rubbed at his chin.

"Are you fuckin' serious right now?"

"What?"

"What?! I can't believe after all that shit you said to me last night you'd have the gall to come in here and ask me what WE are gonna do about the truck YOU fucked up. Actually, you know what? I do believe it, coming from you," Ham unloaded, pointing right at her the entire time. She just stood there, numb looking, searching for words.

"I said I was sorry."

"Hutch I don't think you know what that means. I think it's somethin' people like you just say because they see other people with actual feelings say it. Now fuck off so I can get some work done." For the second time in less than two days she felt that pang of heartbreak go through her from her brother. She was walking right on the knife's edge, about to fall off into a pit where no one trusted her, and even fewer people wanted to be around her. With regret, she stood there and stared at the only man that actually cared about her stewing over his paperwork, praying for the moment she would walk off and leave him alone. And so she did….but she didn't get far.

"Hutch?!!!" A roar blasted through the front room. She shuddered as she turned around and met the fiery eyes of Hank standing there at the back hallway. Words were impossible to find at that moment, it was all too obvious that the eldest McCray had seen the damage done to the work truck…this was the beginning of the end for her. With a red face and heavy breath, Hank extended a hand and beckoned with one finger,

"Come here…" he said coldly. She did as she was told, slowly walking over towards him, all the while staring at Ham, hoping that he would do something, anything…but he remained silent. She was on her own.

"What?" Was all she could expel as she stopped only a pace from her towering sibling. She could all but feel the rage radiating off of him as his nostrils flared with every angry breath he took.

"Follow me," he spoke as he turned about-face and headed down the hall. Hutch quickly took pace behind him, trailing him through the side pedestrian door back out into the blaze of the mid-morning sun. The absolute anger in his body language was palpable. The way he walked, arms out to his sides, fists clenching now and again in some nervous dance between plain mad and apocalyptically pissed…He was going to kill her. He was going to beat her to death behind this building, stuff her in the dumpster, wipe his hands together, and go back to work like nothing happened…or at least that's what Hutch was picturing inside her nervous imagination. Still, she kept behind him, and did the only thing that seemed right at the time, she fished out a cigarette and her lighter. If she was going to die in this back lot, she was going to enjoy a smoke beforehand. They rounded the corner as she lit up and took her first puff.

"Look at this shit!!!" Hank roared out, stopping dead and pointing. Hutch went to speak, about to explain away the damage she assumed he was rampaging about.

"I…I…What the fuck?!" She let out in surprise, her cigarette fell right from her gaping mouth, dying in the gravel below. The truck was not as she had left it. In fact it was a whole galaxy away from that. The corn stalk scrapes and Superbird-blasted panels were the least of the carnage. The truck was an abstract of sledgehammer dents, broken windows, and slashed tires. It was all obviously intentional and malicious. And the icing on the cake? A black spray-paint collage of dicks, some complete with balls, all surrounded by the numbers '666".

"Can you believe this shit?!" Hank screamed out.

"I….I…" Hutch stuttered, still engrossed in the mayhem.

"Fuckin' kids!!"

"Huh?" Hutch questioned.

"Kids, Hutch!" He repeated, then started walking around the truck, "Would ya just look at this?! Goddamn it…Lil' pieces of shit, can't they go snort coke and get their girlfriends knocked up like normal teenagers?!"

And it was at that exact moment that it hit Hutch…She was off the hook. Hank thought it was vandalism. Jesus Christ, maybe Regina hadn't been lying about meeting god, apparently he did exist. She immediately pandered to Hank's presumptions.

"Wow…Ya, know I have been seein' lots of high school kids hangin' round the lot lately. Little fuckers…" she shook her head and lied, trying to catch up with her brother's irritation.

"Well, were there any hangin' out last night? What cars were they drivin?" Hank stopped his pacing and asked. Hutch crossed her arms.

"Ya know I don't remember seein' any last night. I went ta bed kinda early though. Probably showed up after that…Goddamn lucky I didn't catch em'. They wouldn't have been walkin' outta here alive I can tell ya that. Fuck!" She ended with a theatrical kick to one of the flat tires to drive home her performance. Hank started rubbing the back of his head and wetting his lips.

"Well hell…get some thinner and some rags. At least try and get most of this damn artwork off here before a customer pulls round and sees it. I'm gonna call the insurance company…Christ," he ordered out to Hutch as he walked back towards the front of the building. She watched him till he disappeared into the side door. Her eyes then drifted back to the totaled truck beside of her…a huge and uncontrollable smile crept across her face, followed by the only piece of dialogue she could muster at that moment,

"God bless the children…."

The jingle-jangle of the front entry being breached shoved a wave of hot air into the lobby. It slightly jolted Ham from his calculations, but he stayed the course for a moment,

"Be with you in a second…" he spoke to the customer whom he'd yet to even gaze upon.

"Take your time," a tiny voice talked above the patter of tiny footfall. The pecking of his fingers upon the calculator were akin to the pecking of a hundred rabid hen's at feeding time as he tried to ignore the approaching patron just enough to not seem like an ass. The footsteps ceased as did Ham's fingers.

"Sorry bout that, I just had to wrap that up or I'd be lost when I went back to it. How can I..." Ham looked up, "...help...Hello." He felt himself go slightly stupid as his stare met the most gorgeous pair of eyes he'd ever seen...Golden as the setting sun. Regina smiled.

"Well, hello to you...you big hunk of ginger." Ham went from slightly stupid, to just plain dumb at the remark.

"Ummm...uh...," he began to stutter.

"I think this is the part where you ask me what I need?"

Ham shook his head, feeling like an idiot. He smiled.

"Right. Sorry. What can I do for you?"

"Well, actually, I'm looking for someone who works here?"

Suddenly it hit Ham like a freight train. A perfectly dressed, gorgeous young girl walking into a machine shop that wasn't here to sell him something. It all made better sense now.

"Ahhhh...you're lookin for Hutch."

"Now how'd you know that?" Regina tilted her head and grinned.

"Well let's just say she's a magnet for pretty things...Wait, that's not to say you're a *thing*, or anything...or that you're pretty, I mean you ARE pretty...I just...What I mean is, Hutch tends to...You know what? I'll just go get her for ya," Ham put a finger up, trying to hide a frown that was the result of his own idiotic blubbering.

"*That* would be awesome," the brunette smiled.

"Right. One sec..." Ham turned round and began shaking his head. He rounded the corner to see Hayden gnawing away at a donut. His brother began to chuckle quietly.

"What?"

"Oh nothin, that was just goddamn smooth, Ham. How your dick remains dry all the time boggles the mind," Hayden spoke through a mouth haloed in white sugar. He had obviously overheard the whole conversation, if you wanted to call it that.

"Fuck off. She's here for Hutch anyway," he whispered. Hayden's face drew into a scowl as he chewed. He peeked around the corner to see Regina fiddling around in her purse. He looked back to Ham and swallowed.

"*That* is here for Hutch?"

"That's what I said. Hell and that ain't the one she was with the other night."

"Ah, that was probably a lot lizard she had the other night."

"Naw, that girl wud'nt no lot lizard, and that one out there sure as hell ain't one."

Hayden peeked one more time.

"Yeah, naw she ain't. Dressed too damn good. Probably a damn creditor or banker that Hutch owes money to."

"Nope," Ham shook his head in defeat, "Make no mistake, that beautiful young thing and our sister are goin' at it."

"Well I think it's pretty obvious what's goin on here then?" Hayden said as if he was just hit with an epiphany

"What's that?"

"There is no God," he said matter of factly and walked off leaving Ham to wonder if there was any truth to the joke.

"Huh…" was all he could muster as he pulled at his beard. Soon he went back to the task of retrieving his sister.

Outside, amongst the heat and rolling dust of the lot, he found her there within the next minute, scrubbing away fruitlessly at the vandalism covering the tattered work truck.

"Hutch, there's…What the fuck?" Ham's eyes widened as he rounded the corner to see the condition of the vehicle.

"What'd you do?" Ham held his hand out.

"What the hell ya mean, what'd I do?" she said as she soaked the rag even more with thinner.

"Well it wasn't like that when you brought it back. You go nuts in the middle of the night or what?"

"What? Why you keep insinuatin' I had somethin' ta do with this?" Hutch's irritation grew even further. Ham took a few steps forward, really getting a good look at the damage.

"Well…didn't you?"

Hutch stood up from where she had been scrubbing.

"Yeah sure! I got up in the middle of the night with a hankering to draw dongs, balls, and satanic bullshit on the side of a truck I was already gonna get murdered for damaging in the first place!"

"So who did it?"

"I DON'T KNOW," Hutch drew it out, arms out to her sides. Ham was at a loss for words. Hutch spoke again, "To be honest with ya, I thought maybe you did it."

"What? Why the hell would I do that?" Ham asked in annoyance.

"Well, now that Hank thinks it's vandalism and I'm off the hook, it got me wonderin' maybe you did it to cover up the damage from yesterday," she threw out a theory that had plagued her since she saw the truck.

"Hutch, not to down my own intelligence, but I ain't that fuckin' smart. And even if I was, I wouldn't use it to help you. Told ya I'm done with that shit."

Hutch just shook her head and squatted back down, rubbing away at the black paint.

Ham suddenly remembered why he had come back there.

"Reason I came lookin for ya in the first place is there's someone up front ta see ya."

"Huh? Who?" Hutch said in disbelief.

"Pretty, young thing. Bout yay-tall," Ham put his hand out, "And I do mean young. Like she's about to move out of her parent's young. You check her I.D. before ya threw down with her?"

"Jesus Christ..." she mumbled. She stopped a moment, bit her lip, and closed her eyes. Her head rested against the truck door with a thud.

"I'm serious, Hutch. I'm just lookin out for ya. I mean if she's legal, she's legal, but..."

"Tell her ta fuck off," she resumed her scrubbing once more.

Ham made a face.

"Tell her ta fuck off?"

"Yep."

"I think you're gettin' more paint thinner up your nose than you are on that truck...So you want me to march back up there and tell that gorgeous creature with whom no man I ever have met could get as much as look from, ta fuck off?"

"Nowww you're gettin' it," she smarted off.

"Okay, Hutch. Will do."

(45 seconds later….)

"She said ta come on back," Ham said, back at the desk, donning a smile towards the young brunette.

"Yaaaaay," Regina playfully drew out.

"Come on round here, I'll show ya the way," he motioned for her to follow.

"So you're her co-worker then, huh?" Regina said as she rounded the counter.

"Yeeaaah, that and, unfortunately, her brother. Fact, so are the three others that work here."

"Niiiiice. So you're sayin if things fall through with me and Red, I got four other strapping young McCrays to choose from?"

"Red?" Ham questioned.

"Yeah, that's my pet name for her."

"Ahhh, okay then," Ham chuckled.

"What?"

"Oh nothin. She's…she's just hates bein' called that, is all. Once saw her blacken two-eyes with one punch on a girl that smarted off and called her that…Guess what I'm gettin' at is, she must like you." As they walked deeper into the back hall, Hank came walking past. Ham just nodded at his brother, but got nothing in return. Hank the Tank was busy staring down at the tiny thing trailing his baby brother. But it wasn't the type of look you'd expect. No daze of infatuation or creepy stare grazed his face. Instead, he looked at her oddly as she gave him a playful wink and smile, passing him right on by. Hank stopped dead in his tracks, his mind working a hundred and ten plus, puzzled and befuddled in some bizarre thought process that displayed a look that he never let show to anyone…uneasiness.

"Right through here," Ham opened the side door, letting Regina walk out on past him into the gravel lot. "Just follow the edge of the building to the back there. She's right around the corner."

"Thank you so much, sweetie," Regina said as she put on a huge pair of sunglasses.

"Yep," Ham said, sneaking a look at the brunette's butt as it swayed on down the way.

"Mother of god…" he whispered as he shut the door.

"There's my sweet thaaaaang. My naval orange. My Georgia Peach. My Scottish snowflake. Mmm, mm! I wanna just drink you up like Ginger Ale!" Regina threw out a slew of cutesy nicknames as she smiled away at Hutch, who was far from amused. The redhead once again stopped her scrubbing, thinking about how hard she was going to punch Ham next time she saw him.

"What do ya want?" Hutch spoke lowly, never even bothering to look away from the truck.

"Oh, you know, just checking on you after last night. Making sure you were still alive and all."

"Last night. Hmm, doesn't ring a bell," Hutch tried playing it off.

"Ha! Yeaaaah, that happened. You certainly didn't think you bit your own ass? And no phone call, Red?…I guess chivalry is dead." Hutch looked up from the rag she held with a sneer. Regina smiled. "Look, I'm gonna cut right to the chase…" she grabbed her stomach, "I'm pregnant." It was all followed by a round of jovial laughter. Hutch's patience was wearing thin.

"What the fuck do you want from me?" She once again began rubbing away at the truck door.

"Oh, you know what I want, Red. I want you to race me. I mean fucking you was fun, but racing you, that will *really* get my pussy wet."

"What reason do I have to race you?"

"You don't want Cass back in your life?"

"I told you, my aunt is dead."

"Oh, you don't believe that. Not even for one second."

"Yeah, you know me so well, right?"

"Well I do know about every square inch of you now, and I know you heard her last night in your dreams…She called out to you. You know she's out there."

A chill ran up Hutch's spine. She tried her best not to look visibly shaken by Regina's words.

"I don't know what the hell you're talkin' about."

"Offff, course you don't…You talk in your sleep, ya know."

"It was just a fuckin' dream, okay?...A nightmare more like."

"I'd think of it more as a vision, Red. After all you inhaled preeeeetty deep." .

Hutch just shook her head . Her rising anger became evident as she scrubbed even harder and grit her teeth. Regina just sighed as she looked around the gravel lot.

"Look…I didn't want it to come to this but, I'm gonna up the ante on this whole thing. You race me, and you win, not only will I let your Aunt come home, I'll give you one-hundred thousand dollars."

Hutch let out a short laugh. She looked up at the brunette from where she was squatted down.

"Shut the fuck up."

"C'mon Red. That's a lot of money."

"Sure is. And with a bigger purse comes a bigger risk. What the hells the catch on my end?"

"Same as before, I take that car from you. That's it."

"I'll think about it."

Red, all you got to lose is that piece of shit Maverick in there," Regina pointed to the garage.

Hutch glared up at her for a moment.

"That piece of shit in there means a lot to me."

"I know, Red. It's the last piece of anything that still makes you feel close to your aunt. That's why it's the perfect collateral. Just like racing, the thought of taking something from somebody that means that much, ALSO gets my pussy wet."

"I said I'll think about it."

"Oh, Jesus Christ, Red, think about what? Think of what you could do with that money. I mean, is this what you really want out of life? Sitting there in the dirt rubbing cartoon dicks off the side of a truck that needs set on fire? You could take that dough, tell your brothers to get fucked. Upgrade to a dual axle camper. Maybe open up your own machine shop down the road."

"Uhhh, yeah, sounds great but one-hundred K ain't gonna cut openin' up a machine shop," Hutch pointed out, "Three-hundred K would be a start though."

Regina darted her tongue hard into the inside of her cheek.

"Oh that's cute. I see what you're doing there, Red. I could just offer you *zero* dollars like before," the brunette smiled.

"Nuh-uh. It doesn't work that way. If you ain't already noticed, you and I, we're in the middle of a negotiation," Hutch spat out one of Regina's lines from yesterday, verbatim.

Regina began to bite at her lip, trying to hold back a smile.

"Fine...Three-hundred thousand dollars. But I plot the race course, the time, the date, everything," she became stern.

"Deal."

"Deal?" The brunette questioned in disbelief.

"That's what I said," Hutch confirmed.

"Well that wasn't so hard...No, actually it was. You're kind of a stubborn twat." Hutch just grinned. "Now there's a smile for me," Regina bubbled happily.

"Enjoy it. I don't do it often."

"You certainly did it plenty last night," Regina stepped forward and removed Hutch's hat. She started running her fingers through her red locks. Hutch wanted to tell her to knock it right off, but she couldn't. Instead she scrubbed the graffiti harder, trying to ignore the fact that it was the greatest feeling at that moment in time. Regina soon placed the tattered green hat back atop her head.

"I'll come by later...We'll talk terms on this little race. Okay?" Hutch sighed. It came from her heart more than her mouth.

"Okay..." was all she let out as Regina walked off and left her to her demeaning duties.

"Oh and, Red?...." Regina turned round and began digging through her purse. Hutch put down her rag for a moment and watched as the brunette retrieved something from the bowels of her oversized handbag.

"Figure it might be a little easier just covering that shit up rather than scrubbing it. Here.." she tossed something right at the redhead. Quickly, she stopped the object in mid air and realized she was now holding a can of black spray paint...

"It's the perfect matching shade, I think," Regina laughed. Hutch looked at the graffiti in front of her and then back at the can, speechless. She gazed back at Regina. "Yeah, that's right, bitch. You owe me one. Buuuut, I won't count it against you. See you later on, Red," with that, she blew the dumbfounded redhead a kiss and walked off into the swirling dust clouds kicking from the rolling rigs beyond.

The repetitive click-click of a ball-point pen sang a steady and monotonous song below the thumb of Ham as he stood there alone at the counter. He kept pressing it in and out, in and out, with his mind adrift in the previous events of the day. Suddenly, his daze was interrupted by footsteps coming from the hallway. He eyeballed Hutch as she returned from her outdoor duties, prepping hot water at the back counter for some tea. All Ham could do was just start shaking his head over and over in some odd show of disbelief as Hutch tried her best not to acknowledge that he was even standing there. She could see her brother's head just waving back and forth like some broken bird sticking out of a coo-coo clock. Finally she turned his way in irritation.

"Your head broke or somethin'?"

Ham just continued to shake it back and forth slowly, casting her a stare of disappointment. He clicked his pen one last time and dropped it to the counter below. Turning towards her, he finally spoke,

"You got all that graffiti off already?"

Hutch went back to her tea making.

"I took care of it."

"Well that sounds like a 'no'."

"I said, it's taken care of."

There was a pause of dialogue amongst the tiny sounds of George Strait playing on the radio.

"Who is she?"

Hutch began dipping her tea bag in the hot water of her cup.

"Who?"

"Jesus Christ, Hutch, can we not dance around like this? The golden-eyed angel that fell from the sky? You remember, don't ya? Bout yay-tall? Ass looks like it farts rainbows and shits skittles?"

"Yeah. That rings a little bit of a bell, I guess."

"Oh, does it now?...Well, who is she? With the fancy suit and all. High dollar handbag...you go and get yourself a sugar momma?"

"It's complicated..."

"Yeah, well everythin' you're ever involved with is."

"Speakin' of all that, I gotta bone to pick with you."

"Oh, you gotta bone to pick with me?" He pointed at himself, trying not to laugh. "That's rich. I got about four dozen to pick with you, but, by all means, let's hear yours."

"I told you to tell her to go away."

"No, I believe your exact words were to tell her to fuck off. You really think I was gonna do that?"

"Yeah! Yeah, I did."

Ham sighed and crossed his arms.

"You wanna know what I think?"

"Not really."

"I think you're afraid of commitment, Hutch. You just can't stand the thought of being with someone for more than one night. I think you're afraid of being happy. You wanna be miserable so someone somewhere will always pity your ass."

"Hey, I ain't afraid and I sure as hell don't need anyone's goddamn pity!"

"So you're just gonna tell that girl to fuck right off then? Or did ya already do that a little bit ago?

"Told ya its complicated."

"She seemed like a decent girl. Like she has her shit together."

"You talked to her for three minutes, what the hell would you know? You don't know her. Hell, I don't think I even know her."

"I don't know, Hutch…Just got the vibe she actually liked you is all. Likes you for more than just pussy or drugs."

"Whatever…" she dismissed, pulling her cup off the counter.

"You know, I've seen so many people that care about you come and go out of your life. And when they get too close to ya, you just put these goddamn walls up and tell them to fuck off. You want that girl gone too? Do it yourself, like you did all the rest. I ain't gonna be responsible for any of that shit."

Hutch had nothing to say. She was beyond irritated as she sat there, cup in hand, shaking her head and staring at the floor. The tea she had just finished making would help, or at least that's what she told herself. If only for one fleeting second that hot liquid would make the world go away long enough to regather some shred of her sanity. With nothing left to ponder, she took a huge swig of it…but something was wrong. With a lurch, she violently spit it across the room while Ham watched in surprised disgust. Hutch's eyes became wide as she spit a few more times and wriggled her tongue round her lips. She looked into the cup and sniffed it.

"Mother fucker!!!" She screamed. Ham went to speak but was cut short by her flaring up again. "I'm gonna kill em'…I'm gonna fuckin' kill em'!"

"What? Who?!" Ham let out as he watched his sister run over and throw the shop door open. She pointed across the way to where her other brothers were toiling away.

"You, mutherfuckers!" She bellowed out. Heath and Hayden soon caught sight of her flailing hand pointing over and over again at them. Hayden made a face and lifted one side of his ear muffs.

"What?!" He yelled back.

"Which one of ya did this shit?!" Hutch pointed with ire at her cup of tea. Hayden just smiled away and sat down his grinder. He walked over with a proud strut as Hutch backed out of the doorway, letting him into the lobby.

"Ya like that?" He grinned, shutting the door behind him.

"What did you do?" She snarled.

"Oh, you know, just made you a special brew of homemade tea, that's all."

Hutch glared at him as she walked over to the back counter and grabbed her box of tea bags. She started thumbing through them. She instantly noticed the odd coloring inside their mesh housings.

"Jesus Christ you did it to all of them?! What the fuck is wrong with you? What is this shit?!" She threw the box of tea into the trash.

"Oh, little bit of tea, some old coffee grounds, some dust out of the pan, cigarette ashes, and just a pinch of Heath's armpit hair," he grinned as he counted off the ingredients on his fingers. But he didn't even get the chance to laugh…With a jolt, Hutch heaved her cup up, throwing the tea right into her brother's face. He didn't even have the chance to yell out when she punched him right in the gut, knocking the wind clean from his lungs. She wrapped her arm round his neck as he doubled over in pain and began trying to take him on down to the floor but Hayden's anger went bright red. Within seconds, the pair became a blur of cussing, punching, and kicking as they scuffled round the room, knocking pictures off the wall and papers off the desk. Ham threw himself into the mess, getting clocked in the jaw as he began trying to pry them apart. Hutch quickly locked onto Hayden.

"You bitch!!" Hayden bellowed. "Ham, get her off of me, she bitin' me! She's fuckin' bitin' me!"

"Hutch, goddamnit!!" Ham yelled as he began trying to help his brother pry her away. Suddenly, Hutch felt herself being grabbed and tossed like a ragdoll across the room. Her back slammed hard into the front wall and she fell to her knees, only to look up to see Hank throwing Hayden in the opposite direction.

"Idiots!! The lot of ya! What the fuck now?!" Hank roared as his face turned redder than his beard.

"He…" Hutch went to speak but Hank cut her off,

"Shut up, Hutch! You!!" He pointed at Hayden, "Get the fuck back to work, NOW." Hayden did as he was told while Hank spun round to Ham. "And you!..."

"Me?! What the fuck did I do?!"

"You didn't get these two broken up fast enough! I had to do it for ya! Get back over ta that counter!" Ham did as he was told. Hank bent down and picked up Hutch's crumpled hat from the floor as he grumbled, "This is bullshit…re-fuckin-diculous…Hutch?!" He looked over at her and snapped his fingers. "You! Me! Office! Now!"

Within moments, the two of them were in the back office, a space once occupied by their father and their grandfather before him. Apparently this was King Hank's dominion now.

"Sit," Hank simply spoke as he slammed the door and tossed Hutch's hat to the desk in the middle of the room. He plopped down in the big chair and began rocking in it, trying to calm himself while Hutch slipped her hat back upon her disheveled head of hair. She fought back and wiped at the tears that reclaimed her face, not tears of sadness but ones of pure, unadulterated rage.

"I said, sit," Hank let out more sternly than before. Slowly, Hutch grabbed the chair back and slid down into it. As she sat there, she couldn't help but recall all of the times she had been called in the principal's office as a teenager. Back then it seemed like a weekly occurrence. She was always fighting, skipping classes, and any number of other ill-willed shit. She recalled the time she spat onto Assistant Principle Vicker's desk and gave him the middle finger right to his face before being promptly expelled for wiping the floor with Teddy Logan's ass when he called her a Bag-Piping Dike-A-Saurus.

A moment of grave silence passed as the two stared each other down while being serenaded by the abrasive tapping of Hank's fingers upon the wooden top in front of him. Hutch was waiting for the worst to come gunning from his mouth. What the hell was taking him so long? She quickly decided to start without him.

"Well? What are ya waitin' for? Go ahead, tell me I'm a fuck up. Tell me I'm worthless and you're gonna burn my camper down with me in it! Set the Maverick on fire and make me watch! Take every damn thing I love and throw it in the trash, cuz I'm sicka this shit and I'm sicka you!" She went off while pointing right at him. The words nearly hadn't the time to echo back in her mind when she realized what she had done. She was fully expecting Hank to give her a closed fist across the lip but instead he just folded his hands and leaned up in his chair.

"Ya done?" Was all he spoke.

"Maybe…"

"I think you're done…Hutch, I didn't bring ya in here ta talk about that fuckin' spat ya had out there. We're McCray's, fightin's kinda our thing."

Hutch lowered her defenses a tad.

"So what the hell are we in here for?"

"That girl that was here earlier. She here ta see you?"

She was instantly on edge once again.

"Yeah. Why?"

"Thought so…What is she to you?"

Hutch looked off for a moment, thinking long and hard about how to answer that question without getting into some theological debate with her eldest brother on the "sinfulness" of her "lifestyle choices". She answered the only way she saw fit.

"Just a friend."

"She have a mom?" Hank questioned. Hutch smirked slightly.

"Well I assume so. I don't think a stork shit her out of a tree."

Hank became riled. He slammed his fist on the table.

"Hutch, you know damn well what I mean!…Her mom look like her much?"

"I never met her mom, okay? I don't really know that much about her…Jesus Christ, can I go now?" Hutch began to rise up from her chair.

"Sit the fuck down!" Hank roared. She dropped right back on her bottom. He was angry, what was new, but there was something else slithering across his face. Something Hutch rarely saw in her brother's eyes. Worry.

"Why do you wanna know about her mom?" Hutch became sternly curious.

Hank licked his lips and scratched at his nose.

"It's…it's nothin'…fuck it."

"No. What, Hank? What is it?"

"Look…You may not know this…in fact, I think I'm the only one who does. Dad was havin' an affair back in the day. Right about 69' if I recall correctly."

"What?" Hutch wasn't all that surprised. But never had solid confirmation till now. The man was constantly leaving on weekends for "shop business".

"Yeah, fact I caught em' at it. I was like eleven at the time. He had me in here one night after hours. Gave me sweepin' duties and took off and told me he'd be back and to not come lookin' for him. We had Henry with us, and hell he was eight then and he was just whining to beat all that he wanted ta go home. So finally I went lookin for dad and he was in the back lot neckin' with this young thing on the hood of the Firebird. And he wud'nt too damn happy when I caught him. But…I told em I'd keep it between him and me. Weird part of it is…the girl he was fuckin?…Spittin' image of that one you got comin' round. And by spittin' image I mean identical twin…Only saw her the one time, but I remember that face, and I remember them golden eyes."

A chill filled the room as Hutch's ears tried to make sense of the whole story. But soon enough, the silence was pushed aside by her chuckling. Hank raised a brow.

"What the fuck you laughin' at?"

Hutch tried to stop her giggling but it seeped right into her dialogue.

"Well, I think it's pretty obvious what's goin' on here."

"And what's that, dare I ask?"

She put her hands out to the side with wide eyes.

"She's a vampire. Duh! Explains everythin'," Hutch went into a hardier laugh.

Hank was quickly losing his patience.

"Yeah sit there and yuck it up, bitch. I know what I saw."

"Oh come on, Hank. You said yourself you were eleven years old! I thought I saw Santa Claus out the window one night when I was that age."

"You tryin' ta piss me off?"

"Oh, when aren't you pissed off? You're always pissed off."

Hank shook his head and cracked his knuckles.

"You wanna take a guess on what month that little tryst between golden eyes and dad took place?"

"Lemme guess, July?" The answer was quite rhetorical. Hank pointed at her,

"Exactly. McCray fuckin McCurse month. Hell that may have been when it all started for all I know."

"Oh Christ…So what are ya sayin'? She's a bad omen or somethin'? Is this where we're gettin' with this curse shit? Just plain paranoid and psychotic?"

Hank sighed and pushed himself to a stand. He walked over to the door and opened it as he spoke.

"I don't know, sister of mine. Maybe I'm nuts, maybe you're nuts. All I know is what I saw with my own two eyes. You even said yourself you really don't know that much about her."

"Well I think I know enough ta know she ain't pushin' fifty goddamn years old."

"Hutch, I don't care what you know…What I know is this, when I start smellin' shit, I get ma shovel ready…and so should you." He pointed towards the open door, "Now get the fuck out." She quickly jumped up and fled into the hall with those words ringing between her ears. Hank was clearly delusional. Wasn't he? Still and all, it had Hutch wondering once again, Who the hell was Regina Redgrace?

Dresses and Dilemmas

"Miss, do you know how fast you were goin'?" A sheriff's stern voice cut through the open window of an ivory white Mercury Cougar. He stood there, beyond frustrated with the young woman that did nothing but smile back at him.

"Seventy-five?" The girl coyly spoke.

"Guess again."

"Ummmm, ninety?" Her voice squeaked with a doubtful smile and wrinkling nose.

"I clocked you at one fifty-five…"

"Ewwwww," she grit her teeth with a frown.

"Tell me, miss…" he looked at her license once again, "…Redgrace. Just where exactly were you headed in such a rush?" She brushed her hair back and went to speak but was instantly interrupted. "I'm sorry, could you please remove your sunglasses for me," he all but demanded. She cast an annoyed smile and pulled the huge, dark lenses from her eyes, up on top of her head.

"Happy?" She asked.

"Very…Now explain to me why I shouldn't throw you in the cruiser and impound your car for goin' almost three times the posted speed limit?"

"You know that's a funny story actually," she began with a huge smile. She was once again interrupted.

"Hold on…" the sheriff looked over his sunglasses at the brunette, studying her like an instruction manual, "I know you."

"Oh yeah?'

"Yeah…Yeah, you're that girl who…." but his words were cut short with an explosion of crimson. Regina felt her breath sucked away in the percussion as a semi sped by only inches away from her mirror, plastering the sheriff across its grill. His body detonated into a mist that painted her in the deepest shades of red. Within seconds, the truck was slamming its brakes up ahead, leaving Regina dumbfounded, mouth agape, in the throes of some bitter disgust. She opened her eyes through the thick crimson that coated her face and held up her hands in a frozen state of absolute shock as she heard the backup alarm of the truck resound. Slowly, it reversed until the cab was parallel with her Cougar. The side door flung open and a familiar trucker stared down at her with glowing red eyes, seemingly waiting for her approval…he got the opposite.

"What the FUCK was that?!!!" She screamed out. She began spitting the dripping blood out from her mouth in disgust and wiping at her face and neck, flinging the crimson off of her finger tips as she growled.

"You were supposed to wing him not pulverize him!" Regina roared as she kicked open her car door. She jumped out and slammed it behind her, still wiping away at the mess that coated her.

"Look at him! You turned him into soup!" She pointed to the mess all over the road ahead. "How is anyone gonna wear this?!!" She yelled as she grabbed up the sheriff's severed arm from the hood of the Cougar and began flailing it around in absolute rage. "He's in a million goddamn pieces now! He's worthless to us!" She tossed the arm to the ground beside the rumbling Redgrace rig. The red-eyed trucker's face had since gone from pleased to timid, like some admonished dog cowering in the street.

"Well?!! Don't just sit there, clean this mess up!!" No sooner had her words rang out, the back doors of the semi trailer exploded open. Several other men, quickly jumped to the ground below and began scattering across the road, picking up body parts and sweeping blood into the soil of the berm and beyond.

"Would you look at this…Worthless shits can't even take simple directions…Fuck!…" Regina mumbled over and over as she ran a finger through the blood on her hood. Her ramblings were overshadowed by the sudden blast of a powerful engine winding down on the road. She jerked her head to see a beaten Plymouth Superbird braking to a stop in front of the semi. The dying engine gave way to a creaking door being flung open, out of which rose a towering figure dressed in a dark trench coat. The man lumbered over towards Regina, staring at her the whole trip through the black eyes of a cricket head. She pointed right at him.

"And where the fuck were you?!"
The man-creature stopped right in front of her, looking down some two and half feet to the tiny woman whose every word seemed to make him shiver. The mandibles of his cricket head writhed about, expelling some symphony of indiscernible clicking and whistling. Regina shook her head in disgust.

"Oh, don't give me your bullshit excuses! Just get that damn car in the truck now!" She pointed back at the cruiser the dead sheriff had left behind. The cricket man did as he was told, lumbering off towards the direction of the still flashing lights.

"And make sure there are rigs blocking both sides of this road! All we need is someone to see this shit before it's all cleaned up," Regina yelled over her shoulder to the departing creature. For the next moment, she just stood there, shaking her head as she watched all the men gathering up what was left of the tattered sheriff's body. They spoke not a word as they scuffled about with the most inhuman movements, cleaning, picking, and sweeping the roadway clean of every last drop of the officer. Regina crossed her arms and sighed.

"Crims…bout as worthless as they are ugly," she scoffed to herself. She then yelled out, "And would someone bring me a towel and coffee for fuck sake?!….Goddamn it's gonna be a long day…"

Five o' clock had rolled round fast, but not fast enough in Hutch's mind. She sat there in her lawn chair, pensively staring out through the lot at the passing rigs as she lit up the first cigarette of the evening. Her mind was astir with the obvious things…it was a maelstrom of confusion, raining down drops of doubt, fear, and outright insecurities. Of course, every bit of this metaphorical storm was pouring from the dark cloud called Regina…

"Regina…" Hutch's lips mouthed the name while her smoke danced in the corner. Who was she? Who was she really? It was a question that passed across her mind every second since the day she'd came into her life. She had slept with her, smiled with her, gotten high with her…Still, she really knew nothing other than the claim of her owning Redgrace Logistics and the obvious elephant in the room…She had her aunt held as some sort of slave. That very fact alone should've made Hutch ashamed of the things she had done with the brunette, but oddly enough, it didn't. And that brought her to the next problem she had brewing in her head and heart…She was feeling bizarre around Regina. Butterflies had danced in her stomach the very moment she had first laid eyes upon that golden-eyed girl…and now those same butterflies were swarming with an aggression she could do little to quell. Every time that girl smiled, laughed, frowned, or simply breathed around Hutch, she felt feelings she hadn't felt in years. And she didn't like it one damn bit. How could she let her guard down like this? How could she let this happen to her again? But it seemed there was simply nothing that could be done about it. Even now, she waited impatiently for the brunette to arrive, and honestly she cared little about the race terms they were to discuss that evening, and more so about being able to see her again.

Hour upon hour pressed on with no sign of Ms. Redgrace. Hutch began popping bottle after bottle and soon enough she lost herself in the haze of the setting sun. Sleep took her.

Hutch felt herself jolt back into the land of the living as someone poked at her ribs.

"Midge?!" She yelled out involuntarily, taking a verbal piece of a dream back with her. A cackling melody of empty beer bottles danced across the ground as she kicked her feet out and grabbed onto the sides of her lawn chair, trying to make sense of what was real and what wasn't. Her eyes began to adjust to a now dark parking lot peppered with running lights from the idle semis beyond, their orchestration belting out that same numbing tune that covered up the tiny noises from the tiny woman who now sat beside her.

"Hey, cutie," a voice fell in Hutch's ear.

"Jesus!" She hissed as she jerked to see Regina sitting there as calm as could be.

"Well now, looks like someone's having a rough night," the brunette grinned. She watched Hutch rub at her eyes and groan like the day itself had sat right on her chest.

"Every night is a rough night…" the redhead said. She perked up a tad at the realization of just one of the words that she'd spoke…Night. She grew agitated "Speakin' of which…What the hell happened to you bein' here in the afternoon? Fuck…What time is it anyway?"

"Oh, turn it down a notch, Red. I had other business to take care of."

"That a fact? Business more important than discussin' terms of a race that'll get my aunt back in my life?"

"If you win…Yes."

"*When*, I win," she corrected. Regina sighed.

"Oh, you McCrays…Always so sure of yourselves. Trust me Red, I don't need your shit. I spent the better part of the afternoon getting blood cleaned off my car and having a new suit tailored."

Hutch raised a brow.

"Blood?"

Regina looked back and forth between the parking lot and Hutch. She quickly backpedaled from her stupid slip.

"Oh, I hit a deer."

"A deer?"

"Yep. Big bastard."

"Well…your car okay?"

"My car is fine. That deer though…not so much. I'm fine by the way!" She ended on an obvious annoyance with the redhead's concerns for the car and not her. Hutch just smirked and shook her head, turning her attention back to the rigs beyond. There was a short stint of silence between them. Regina crossed her legs and spoke,

"So this is what you do every night, Red? Just sit here and watch these trucks?"

"That a problem?"

"No…I suppose not," Regina leaned back in her chair, "I kinda get it, you know? Sitting here wondering where they're going. Where they been…Who they're missing. Who's missing them…"

Hutch just sat there in silence, trying not to show that her heart fluttered at the words. Regina really did get it. But she wasn't about to let her know that.

"Oh…I got you something…" the brunette spoke as she leaned over and grabbed an item up from the ground beside her.

"What?" Hutch replied with confusion. She watched as Regina handed over a large bag with looping handles. The brunette placed it in her lap. Odd feelings from the past were beginning to tug at the redhead…She didn't like this one goddamn bit. She eyeballed Regina, who simply sat there with that signature, gorgeous grin on her face.

"What did you do?" They were the only words that Hutch seemed to be able to find at that moment.

"Just open it, Red."

Hutch's heart elevated as she began to dig through the top layer of tissue paper until her hands felt the soft touch of satin beneath. Her breath left her. She soon enough brought a white garment into the rainbow glow of the lanterns above. With a quick swirl she unfurled and revealed what she'd dreaded it to be. What the hell was happening? Was she still dreaming?

"What the fuck is this?"

"It's a dress."

"I know it's a fuckin' dress…I don't want it," Hutch hissed as she stuffed it back into the bag and threw the whole lot onto Regina's lap.

"Wow…I just thought…"

"Well you probably shouldn't," Hutch cut her off. She quickly brought out a cigarette and lit it. Her leg began bouncing in an obvious fit of nervousness as Regina scowled at her actions.

"What's wrong, Red? You don't like dresses?"

"I don't like surprises."

"Noooo...that's not it. It's something else," Regina pried with her own suspicions. She laid the bag back to the ground waiting for a confession from the anxious redhead. None came. Regina folded her hands across her lap,

"Is it that you just don't think you'll look good in a dress?...Or maybe it's that whole tough-girl persona you're always putting on. Yeah, a dress wouldn't look good on that, would it?"

"Would ya just shut up..." Hutch sneered.

"No. Not until you tell me why a tiny little thing like a dress has you so riled," Regina said as she reached out and rubbed Hutch's shoulder. The redhead flinched a tad and exhaled hard on her smoke.

"I'm not your fuckin' doll, okay? I'm not your doll ta dress up and play with!"

Regina withdrew her hand and sighed.

"Would you at least try it on?"

"I said I don't want it, Midge!" Hutch's eyes instantly widened at her slip up.

"Midge?" The brunette raised a brow.

"I...I...I meant Regina."

"Obviously...Who's Midge, Red," the brunette crossed her arms.

"No one."

"No one? You've said that name twice since I got here. That's anything but no one."

"Someone I used to know, okay? And why the hell are ya drillin' me about that? Who's Midge...? Who's Marnie?! That's what I'd like to know. Why don't we talk about that?" Hutch growled.

"What?" Regina scowled.

"Marnie. Her name is tattooed on the back of your neck? I saw it last night. Who is she?" The redhead grumbled.

Regina's eyes seemed to go soft, yet there was a strange hint of rage inside them. Hutch had hit a nerve and she knew it. She expected the brunette to start yelling at any second.

"Marnie...Marnie was...That's none of your fucking business," her voice had become sad and cold. It was a tone that made Hutch feel bad for even bringing it up, though she tried desperately not to show it. The redhead spoke, "Whatever...Now, can we just get on with these goddamn race terms already?"

"Sure..."

Regina uncrossed her arms and sighed as she dug out a manila envelope and tossed it into Hutch's lap. The redhead reared back and looked down at it.

"What's this?

"Oh, don't worry, Red, it's not another present. No jewelry or anything like that cause god forbid you own anything girly for once. And since you don't like surprises, I'm gonna go ahead and tell you what it is, it's the race route. Detailed map on where we start and where we finish. About ten miles in total. Now, like I said before, you have a little over two weeks, that's the third Saturday from now, to get that bag-of-bolts running in the garage over there. If you fail to get that done you forfeit the race. Unless of course you want to try and race me on foot," Regina smiled and batted her eyelashes. Hutch scowled and folded the envelope over twice, shoving it in her pocket for later use.

"I need more time," the redhead muttered.

"I'm sorry what was that?"

"I said I need more time!"

"Hmmm, I think being around all these trucks has muffled your hearing, Red. I said you have a little over two weeks and then, no dice."

"I'm one fuckin' person, for god sake. There's...there's so much that needs done, parts I might not have, problems with the body and chassis, it's been sitting there for years...Hell it probably needs tires. There's an engine break in period, fine tuning, diagnostics. Christ, and the most important thing of all, the bonding..."

"The bonding?" Regina questioned.

"Yeah, the bonding...Car and driver. Driver and car...How the wheel feels in your hands, how the pedals feather under your foot. The way she shifts and explodes. The way she grabs the pavement, caresses the corners, deals with the backhands and uppercuts of gravity. How she breathes and talks, tells you what she needs from you...A car is like a person...they're all different, but one thing is for sure, you got to get to know them a little before you take them to the next level."

"Very poetic, Red...Buuuut, you still got a little over two weeks. Better make that bonding experience a one night stand with that car of yours. So buy it a drink, take it out to a movie, smack its bumper, do whatever it takes because time is ticking."

"Whatever..." Hutch sighed as she leaned forwards, placing her head in her hands.

"Other rules," Regina raised a finger, "And these should be pretty textbook considering most of them were laid out by your aunt. Carbureted engines only. Blowers are allowed but no nitrous oxide and don't try hiding that shit because I will inspect your car before we race. Car interiors have to be as close to stock as possible, i.e. no roll cages, no tearing out the seats, door panels, headliners, or whatever other tiny weight-saving shit you can dream up. No wingmen, no hiring someone to sabotage the race and drive the other guy off the road. And last but not least, no helmets and no five point harnesses, because if you're gonna die, then baby, you better do it in style. You got all that?"

"Yes..." Hutch answered, raising back up in her seat.

"Good. The race starts at twelve."

"Twelve? We usually would race after 1 a.m. but I guess that's okay."

"Oh, no-no, my peach, twelve as in noon."

Hutch jumped out of her chair.

"Are you out of your fuckin' mind?!"

"Oh, I think you already know the answer to that."

"Noon?! Broad fuckin' daylight?! They'll be shit tons of people outside. Cops will be swarmin' us! No! No! Fuck that! I'm out!" She went off, ripping her smoke from her mouth. She violently stomped it out while Regina rebutted.

"Relax, Red!"

"Relax?! Fuckin' relax?! I'm gonna venture to guess I got way more to lose than you do if the cops snag me."

"Not gonna happen."

"And how's that?"

"Let's just say I have the cop situation under control. They won't be bothering us."

"I don't know what that means, and I don't wanna know what that means. But I told ya, I ain't racin' at noon."

"Okay, Red, you don't race me at noon, you don't race me at all, how bout that? No race, no Aunt Cass. No money."

Hutch just stood there seething. She wanted so badly to smack that little smirk right off her little face, but she didn't. She breathed deep and put her hands on her hips.

"C'mon, Red, you always wanted to be just like your aunt so be like your aunt. Live a little! Dance on that edge and race in the daylight. Cass certainly never had the balls to do that one. One-up the bitch for old time's sake."

The redhead sighed and flopped back into her chair.

"Is that a yes?"

"Ain't like I gotta choice now, do I?"

"No you don't!" Regina smiled and squeaked out with a grin, pinching at Hutch's cheek. The redhead smacked her hand away.

"Uh-oh, someone needs a nap."

Hutch just shook her head in disgust.

"Well, on that note..." Regina grabbed up her things and rose up, "I'm getting' the hell outta here. You study up good with that map and maybe you'll get a passing grade, Red."

"You're leavin'?"

"Uhhh, yeah. This whole situation has my pussy suuuper dry. It's like the Sahara down there."

"Well...where ya goin?"

"Got stuff to do. People to see. That a problem?"

"No..."

"Awww, Reddddd? You gonna miss me or something? Look at you leaning on your chair with them little puppy-dog eyes. It's adorable."

"No! I'm not gonna miss ya. Get the fuck out of here," Hutch quickly shook her feelings away.

"See ya around, Red," Regina winked and laughed as she walked off towards Piper Jean's. Hutch just sat there, sinking down into her chair as she went to the task of battling the conflicting emotions that raged within her chest.

One hour later, Hutch found herself lying in her bed, staring at the dim-lit ceiling of her camper. Of course, she was lying there just stewing about Regina. Not even about the fact that she had only given her two weeks to get ready for this race, or the fact that she had made it take place at noon, but the fact that she hadn't stayed the night…That she was out there possibly seeing other women…Jesus…She was jealous, she was actually jealous. It was a feeling she hadn't experienced in years and it only made her shudder all the more. She had to get that girl out of her head toot-sweet. For the next hour or more, she rolled, tossed and turned, even laid on her stomach, which she hated, but sleep wouldn't come. Jealousy soon turned to anxiety and anxiety into depression. She was losing herself within the thoughts of that girl being by her side. Holding her. Talking to her. Just being with her. It was going beyond sex, beyond passion, back to a feeling she had only felt but once before in her life.

With a flop, she rolled herself to the edge of the bed and dug through a drawer nearby. She soon pulled out a tattered Polaroid. It was a much younger version of herself with an arm wrapped round another girl, playfully putting her into a headlock. Hutch wanted to smile but the ghosts of the past were too cold and calloused to let her do such a thing. With a sigh, the redhead rolled over on her back and tipped the bill of her hat down, trying to use it as some metaphorical umbrella to keep the bad memories from drowning her. It did little to help…She laid the picture face down on her chest as her brain flipped through the stupidity of her youth clear back to the chapter ten, age ten to be exact, the time in her life she began to realize she wasn't like most of the other girls. Soon, another name overtook Regina's in the misty hallways of Hutch's wandering mind…

Red and Midge

"Midge" It was name she hadn't whispered for almost a decade. It was the name of her best friend...well, once upon a time. Until it fell into a million unfixable pieces. The two of them had become friends right about the time Hutch had gotten over her cancer. Up until that point she had seemed content being friends with no one but boys...perhaps it was simply all she knew given the fact that she was raised around five brothers. She simply hadn't the time nor desire for girly conversation or girly companions...but that was all to change. Her hair was still in the process of growing back in from the chemo treatments. It was barely two inches long and she was beyond self-conscious about it. She wore a hat everywhere she went...maybe that's what started the hat wearing, she couldn't be sure. Her mother never bought her dresses or anything of the like. Having a 5 to 1 boy to girl ratio in the house called for simplicity, so Hutch always adorned the hand me downs from her older brothers - jeans, flannels, t-shirts and such. Between the short hair, baseball caps, and overall garb she wore round the town, she was always getting mistaken for a boy. Despite her tomboyish ways, it was something she always took offense to, especially when she was called names from people who knew better. Some of the local kids would take fun in calling her boy names on purpose knowing damn well she was a girl. Of course her actual name wasn't exactly feminine, but it got her fuming just the same. Back then Hutch wasn't much of a scrapper. She would let things roll off her shoulders more often. Yes, she had choice words to yell back at naysayers, but for the most part, fists were never raised. Though perhaps if they had been, more kids would've shut their mouths about it. Still in all, she was feeling one-hundred percent better and was happy to be alive after the ordeal she had gone through. She spent most days of that summer pedaling round the area on a

Schwinn Stingray 3 Speed her grandfather had bought for her for her seventh birthday. God she loved that bike. The blue paint, the white banana seat, 3 speed hub transmission and high handlebars with streamers blowing in the breeze…it was the open road, it was freedom, it was a car before she had even driven one. Every Saturday she would pedal it down to LC Market to get herself a Coke and bag of Swedish fish, and every now and again shove a comic book or two down the front of her shirt and pants and walk out as cool as could be. Of course, there was the main reason she'd go down there in the first place, to take turns bike racing the Gentry brothers, Bobby and Clay, for antes such as said Swedish fish and stolen comic books. They seemed to be the only ones around that were still stupid enough to keep racing her and losing their proverbial asses in the process. This particular day was different. After about an hour of reading and re-reading about the X-men dealing with Dark Phoenix round the back of the building, she stared at her empty coke bottle and realized those Gentry boys weren't showing up. Maybe they'd finally grown half a brain after all. Well at least one of them, here came Clay…

"Where's Bobby at? You gonna race me one at a time or take me on at once?" Hutch yelled out.

"Ain't nobody racin' nobody no more, McCray. Bobby ain't comin'," Clay spoke out as he circled around on his bike.

"Well…why not?"

"He's sicka losin his shit to you."

"You race me then."

"Ain't happenin'."

"Why not?"

"I'm sicka losin' my shit to you. Find some other suckers, McCray," with that he made one more circle and left her behind with a scowl on her face.

"Oh yeah?! Maybe I will! Maybe I'll find someone with some actual balls in their pants!" She yelled out as she watched him disappear round the corner. "Hell…" she muttered as she threw her hat on the ground and pouted. She began running her fingers through her short hair and that's when she heard it. A voice from behind…

"I like your hair."

Hutch spun round to see the source of the unlikely compliment, and there she was. Sarah. She was a tiny thing for her age. Brunette locks blowing in the breeze round a smile that could tear the sun from the sky and make it her own. And with that inerasable grin she continued to stand there, straddling her pink cruiser bike, waiting for a simple "thank you" in return. Hutch was so dumbfounded by her that she forgot to speak, She just stood there, eyeing her down with her mouth agape.

"Can you not talk or somethin'? I said I like your hair," the girl spoke up again.

Hutch finally shook herself free from her entrancement and said, "I…I like yours too."

The girl smiled even wider, if that was even possible, and blushed the slightest.

"Got a name?" She asked.

"Yeah. Hutch."

"Ha! What's your real name?"

"That IS my real name," the redhead became slightly agitated.

"Hutch? Isn't that a piece of furniture or somethin'?" The brunette scratched her head in confusion. Hutch frowned a bit at the question and retrieved the hat she had thrown to the ground. She put it back on her head as she spoke,

"Yeah I guess…but my daddy named me after Kenneth Hutchinson from Starsky and Hutch," she threw out a fabrication. She really hadn't the slightest idea where her name had come from.

"He named you after a boy?" The girl spoke as her lip curled with disbelief. As enchanted as she was with this mystery girl, Hutch was losing patience with her, and fast.

"Maybe! What's it to ya?"

"I don't know…I don't like Hutch too much. I'm gonna call you Red."

"Look, what ya want with me? I got stuff to do." Hutch started gathering up her comics and candy.

"Well, I really don't want anythin' with you. Just like your hair is all. You're the one gettin' your panties in a bunch."

Hutch went from five to ten in one second.

"Piss off."

The girl just started laughing.

"Piss off, before I kick your ass!" Hutch clarified as she glared at the girl. The brunette just continued to chuckle. "What's so damn funny?!"

"Oh...nothin. You just think you're tough is all."

"I AM tough." Hutch corrected her.

"Yeah, maybe a little...I think you got most people fooled. I think you gotta soft heart and don't want no one to know it."

"You don't know me," Hutch growled as she walked up to the girl whom she towered over. She pointed right at her, "I ain't soft. Not one bit. Best remember that..." she then walked back to gather her bike.

"Then prove it," the girl mouthed.

"What did ya say ta me?"

"I said prove it, Red. Why don't you race me like you were gonna race them boys."

The redhead's anger went straight to amusement. She chuckled in disbelief.

"And how you gonna race me? You're barefoot and wearin' a dress?"

The girl looked down at her white sundress.

"So?"

"So? SO? That dress is gonna be in your way. It's gonna cause drag. It's gonna..."

"Put me at a disadvantage?" The girl finished Hutch's words.

"...Yeah."

"Well, I guess you ain't gotta worry about losin' then."

Hutch just scratched the back of her head, a bit at a loss for words. Soon she found them,

"Well, what's the ante then?"

"Ante?"

"Yeah. What we racin' for.? We gotta race for somethin'.."

"I don't have nothin'," the girl shrugged her shoulders. Hutch started eyeing her up as she shook her head. She pointed to her bike,

"Well, how bout that fancy basket on your bike there? I'd like ta have that," Hutch spoke as she walked back and bent down, "and if you win you get all these," with wide eyes, the redhead raised back up, holding high her bag of Swedish fish as if it were the trophy to end all trophies.

"Uck. I don't like Swedish fish."

"Who the hell don't like Swedish fish? They're like a delicacy in Sweden."

"Pretty sure that ain't true, Red. Besides, think I'd be gettin' shorted, your lanky butt done ate half of those."

Hutch just eyeballed her in annoyance.

"Well what you want if you win then? Not that that's gonna happen."

"Ummm, how bout your hat?"

Hutch pulled her cap down off her head once more and looked at it with a raised brow. It was an old Pennzoil trucker hat she'd confiscated from one of her father's dirty garage shelves. It was full of holes and covered in greasy fingered graffiti.

"My hat? This old tattered hat? You're gonna put that nice basket on the line for this thing?"

"Sure, why not? It'll look good on my dresser as a trophy."

Wow, this girl was a shit-talker. Hutch was starting to like her even more, though she did her best not to show it.

"Fine. Line em' up!" The red head yelled.

"What?"

"Your tires. Line em' up. Right here, on the edge of the sidewalk. That'll be the startin' line," Hutch explained as she lined her own bike up on the crumbling edge of the concrete. The little brunette did the same. Hutch just sat on her bike watching the girl as she went through some odd ritual of cracking her knuckles and stretching her arms and such, as if she were about to race in the Olympics. The redhead just began shaking her head and asked,

"How old are you?

"I'm eight...goin on nine"

"Good god, you look like you're six goin' on four. Your mom not feed you or what? What's your name anyways?"

"Sarah."

"Sarah? I don't like that much. I'm callin' you Midge."

"Midge?"

"Yeah, short for midget....Jesus, two years younger than me, barefoot, and wearin' a dress. Feel like I should give you a head start or somethin'."

"Oh, I wouldn't do that if I were you."

There was that shit talking again. Now, Hutch was only ten but she was already starting to see a huge correlation between people's height and the size of their mouths. The shorter they were the bigger their words.

For what seemed like another whole minute, the brunette continued on with her routine, which now had switched emphasis to her legs.

"Are you gonna be done with whatever it is you're doin' there soon?"

"It's called stretchin', Red. You might wanna try it sometime."

"Yeah naw, I'm good. Let's just get this show on the road for god sake."

"Suit yourself. Where we goin' to?"

"We'll do a block race. Down the hill here, left on Garfield, then up Cedar, then Pinecrest, right back to that there dumpster behind us. Whoever touches that first wins. Questions?"

"Yeah, just one. What's that over there?!!" Sarah yelled out. Hutch jerked fast to look but instantly felt a smack as the brunette slapped her hat right off her head and took down the hill laughing in the biggest fake-out of all time. The redhead frantically grabbed up her hat and threw it backwards on her head as she watched Sarah flying down the hill without her.

"Cheatin' little shit!" She snarled as she blasted off down the decline. Within seconds, she throttled her legs down hard and passed up the brunette right on the first turn at the bottom of the hill. Her tires squealed out under a fast brake and then she accelerated hard once more with a smile growing on her face as she quickly approached Cedar Ave. Hutch went to look behind her, but Midge wasn't there. Damn, she must've really passed her up!

"Hey!" A voice drilled into her ear. The redhead jerked to see her "unworthy" opponent right next to her, neck and neck. This girl was either fast or she could teleport, Hutch's ego was desperately hoping for the latter.

Tires screeched in unison as the two made the second turn and battled side by side up the incline to Pine Crest. It wasn't but ten seconds that Midge was leaving her behind. She had that damn lightweight advantage cranking up this hill. Hutch hadn't thought this route through too well. With all she could muster, the redhead mashed down hard, getting a good rhythm as her bike snaked side to side from the torque she threw down. Lungs and legs burned, but soon it paid off as she cut the brunette off at the top of the hill and headed down the homestretch. With the beautiful checkered flag of a dumpster now in sight, she thought she had it all in the bag…she was wrong. With one hard crank down, she felt it, that all too familiar feeling, the dreaded Charlie Horse. The cramp to end all cramps. She screamed out, and wrecked over the curb into the grass of LC Market's back lot, holding her leg and clenching her teeth as she went. Hutch rolled into a pile, writhing in pain, but she tried pushing through it. She looked back to see Midge gaining fast. Hutch was off her bike, but the race wasn't over, no not yet. With all she could muster, she crawled like a pathetic dying crab, one hand leading while the other clenched her aching thigh muscle. And soon she was there, within three feet, she could just taste the sweet, burning hot metal of the side of that gorgeous dumpster. That bike basket was as good as hers, leg cramps be damned! But that's when she heard it…Footsteps beside her. She looked over to see Midge grinning down at her. Her bare feet confidently loosed from her pedals now propelling her across the pavement in some smart-assed, slow walk to the finish line. The little brunette reached the dumpster and stuck one finger out, hovering an inch away from the steel that was victory. Hutch was now half a foot away, groaning and moaning as she too stretched out her finger tips. Right then their eyes met. As if time stood still, Hutch could see that look in Midge's eyes, she knew she had won, but she was now toying with her, making her feel as if she had a chance. Just as the redhead heaved for that last inch, Midge's finger touched it ever so lightly and she smiled like the devil. The redhead sighed in defeat and just rolled on to her back as the brunette's words cut right through her.

"That stretchings soundin' like a good idea now, ain't it?"

Hutch couldn't even find the breath to shoot her mouth off back to her. She just laid there and continued to hold her leg while Midge bent down and took her hat right off her head. With a grin, she placed that dirty old Pennzoil hat atop her head as if she were donning a crown of jewels.

"Wow, you don't look so good, Red. Lemme help you out," Midge bent down and stretched her hand out. Hutch went to grab it but the brunette passed it on by and dove into her pocket, retrieving the bag of Swedish fish. She quickly pulled one out and ate it. "Mmmmm, the sweet taste of victory." With that, she turned round and hook-shot the whole bag of candy right into the dumpster. "See ya around, Red." She smiled big as she picked up her bike and pedaled off, leaving Hutch lying there in a literal, painful defeat.

As the real world sank back in, Hutch found herself back outside. She sucked her cigarette down right to the butt and flicked it into the gravel beyond. She stared off, reminiscing in the memory, which at the time seemed like a bad one, but she soon learned to love it, only to later hate it once more. It was the start of a beautiful friendship, or at least Hutch thought. It wasn't long that the two of them became inseparable. They spent the summer pedaling round town and getting into more mischief than most of the neighborhood boys combined. Knocking over trashcans, stealing soda and candy, shooting out car windows with BB guns. Midge was bad for her, and she knew it. That's what she liked about her.

Summers passed and their friendship grew along with the hair on Hutch's head. Things were changing...There were strange feelings fluttering inside of the redhead for her friend. They weren't the typical feel-goods you got from having a best friend that would do anything for you...no, these were quite different. And try as she may, she couldn't fight them off. She recalled quite vividly at least one occasion where she tried peeking in on Midge when she changed clothes...What was happening to her? She knew she had to get these thoughts cleared from her head...but then again, what if Midge felt the same? After all, they had grown so close. Midge had even told her she loved her once...of course, love came in different forms and different meanings altogether. She was so confused, scared, and frustrated, and the worst part of it all was she had to keep it hidden from everyone she knew....And once again the memories came flooding back. The memory of that day that things changed forever...Hutch was thirteen now and Midge was eleven. She recalled them catching crawdads while they smoked cigarettes Midge had stolen from her dad on that breezy day in July. After hours of trudging around in the creek, they sat there in a field by the edge of the water, soaking in rays of sun that fluttered down between the dancing limbs of two giant birch trees.

"What we gonna do with all these ugly little guys?" Midge said as she tipped the old bucket towards her.

"I don't know. Let em go?" Hutch answered, puffing on her smoke.

"Let em go? What the hells the point of catchin' em?"

"For lookin at."

"For lookin' at?" Midge scoffed in annoyance, "Red, this was your idea. You had me sloshin' through this creek, messin up my dress, just to turn round and let em' all go? I don't understand you sometimes."

"Yeah, well, I don't understand me either, sometimes…" Hutch sighed.

"I thought you were gonna eat these things or somethin'?" Midge said.

"What? Eww, no. Why would ya think that?"

"Well, you eat Swedish Fish."

"Those aren't real fish ya know."

"It was a joke, Red."

Hutch said nothing back. She just stared off as if she were somewhere else. And, in some sense, she was. She was lost in Midge's tiny, upturned nose, the way it wrinkled with every annoyed word she expelled. Lost in the dip of that little crooked smile that now and again would adorably plunge down at the corner when she talked. Lost in the vibrant blue of her eyes that seemed like tiny windows on her face in the backdrop of the perfectly matching blue skies behind….God she was losing it…She had to get it together.

"Red?...Red?...RED?!" Midge called out.

"Whuu?" Hutch suddenly snapped out of her trance.

"Lord, where were you just now? I said, you sure ya want me to dump these guys?"

"I done told ya they're for lookin' at," Hutch said in slight annoyance.

Midge raised a brow and grabbed the bucket,

"Well, okay then. Be free, tiny lobsters," she spoke as she tipped the bucket down the bank. A deluge of brackish water gave way to dozens of writhing crayfish that all tussled cross one another in their panicked descent to go back to the rocky bed they called home. With the task done, Midge pulled the cigarette from her mouth and coughed a bit. She chucked it into the empty bucket and let it fall over on its side with a clattering thud.

"Well, what ya wanna do now?"

"We could go shoot some car windows out at Riverside," she referred to the junkyard nearby.

"Hmmm, nah. We did that last week."

Hutch scratched at her chin.

"We coooould, go ta Pizza Shack and play Galaga."

"Ya mean, *you* could play Galaga while I watch? Cuz that's what always happens."

"Oh, nuh-uh."

"Red, last time we went I got so bored I ended up leavin' and you didn't even notice for an hour after I left. You hog that damn game."

"Hey, I can't help that I kick ass at it."

Midge just rolled her eyes and shook her head. Hutch suddenly perked up and pointed.

"Hey, let's go skinny dippin'," she uttered with an over-excitement that made Midge raise a brow.

"Whaaat? No."

"Why not?"

"I just dumped a hundred mudbugs back in that crick. I ain't goin' butt-neked in there with all them things look for a crack to crawl back in."

"Well, I'm runnin out of ideas. You think of somethin'," Hutch crossed her arms, clearly getting annoyed with the brunette's dismissals.

Midge bit at her lip for a moment and then spoke completely off subject,

"Hey, I got somethin' for ya," the brunette stared over coyly. Hutch was almost afraid to ask.

"For me?"

"Yep." With that she walked over to her bike leaning against the tree and dug something out of the big basket on the front. It was a crumpled paper bag that she soon transported over to where Hutch sat in the grass. She presented it to her with a straight face.

"Here."

Hutch just continued to sit there, staring at the brown paper in front of her wondering beyond wonder at just what the hell Midge was up to. She had never gotten her a gift like this before. The brunette sighed.

"Well? Take it already…It won't bite. Fact it might be dead. I forgot to poke holes in the bag so it could breathe."

Hutch's eyes grew large.

"That was another joke, Red."

The redhead scowled the slightest and grabbed the bag from her friend. She took a moment to untie a bit of string holding the mess altogether and then peeled back the paper to reveal a white material inside. With a confused look, she pulled the fabric out and held it idle, letting it dangle in her lap. She bit at her lip and carefully turned it over and over with a growing confusion.

"What is it?"

"It's a dress, dummy."

"A…a dress?" She stuttered the slightest from the surprise as she rolled it over and saw the sleeveless straps. With misty eyes she quickly back-pedaled in the realization that she was getting far too soft. "Why would you think I'd want a dress?" She tried to protest. Midge was having none of it.

"Oh please. Don't you go givin' me that line. You're always talkin' about how your mom doesn't buy you dresses. And every time we pass Maybold's front window I catch you staring in at the mannequins. Now it ain't no Maybold's dress, but I hope you like it. Bought it at the thrift store. I just hope it fits your tall ass." As Midge spoke Hutch seemed to be in some daze as she stood up and held the garment to the front of her, letting in dangle down past her knees. And that's when the smile came. The brunette had never seen her fawn over something so much. It was almost comical to see the stoic Hutch McCray grinning so goofily over something that would seem so trivial to most.

"Well? Try it on," Midge mostly joked, but by god Hutch went right to it. Throwing the gown right over her sleeveless shirt and jeans as if the fate of the entire world rested on how fast she could achieve it.

"How do I look?" She spun round, showing it off.

"Well…probably a lot better if you didn't have clothes on underneath, but it's a start," Midge spoke the truth, eyeballing the obvious bulges from her normal clothing through the thin cotton of the dress.

"Midge, I love it!" She bubbled forth. Trying to iron out the bulges of her clothes as she passed her hands down her sides to her hips.

"I knew ya would…" the brunette smiled. All of a sudden, Hutch ran over, dropped, to her knees and wrapped her long arms around the tiny brunette.

"Thank you so much! Thank you! Thank you!" Hutch chanted happily while Midge struggled for air.

"Oh, okay! Okay! Ha! You're welcome, Red!" She smiled, almost feeling the slightest bit overwhelmed from her friend's reaction. "Okay, c'mon, you're gonna muck up the knees on that dress." Hutch released her embrace the slightest and drew herself back. Right at that instance, their eyes met for a moment that seemed to stop time dead in its tracks. Blinking, breathing, everything seemed to cease between them as Hutch's mind went a million miles an hour in that awkward tick in time. Then the redhead quickly did the only thing she thought she could…she leaned in and kissed Midge right on the lips. For a split second it seemed as though the kiss was being reciprocated, or perhaps that was just Hutch's wishful imagination running wild as she finally let go of all that emotion that had been brewing inside of her over the past two years.

"Red. Red?! Red, what are ya doin'?" Midge pushed her away the slightest.

"I…I…Uh. I thought…" Hutch stuttered as her heart began to sink to the pit of her stomach.

"Red…I…Red are you?…do you like girls?"

"No…NO! I just…I love you…"

"Red, I love you too…but…but…"

All of a sudden, both their heads jerked in the direction of a horn blaring away over and over from the road that lay not but two stones throws away. It was a twenty-something year old Hank McCray hanging halfway out the window of his Ford truck screaming over and over. Hutch suddenly realized she was still lying on top of Midge in a half-hugged embrace. She instantly became terrified and jumped to her feet, letting Midge fall gently to the grass below.

"Red? Red?!" The brunette began saying as she watched her friend speedily gather her bike and run with it to the waiting pick-up truck.

"I gotta go!" Hutch yelled back.

"Wait, but…" Midge shook her head, not knowing what to say.

"Get your ass over here!" Hank's thundering voice became deafening as Hutch made her way to the roadside. "How fuckin hard is it for ya to keep track of time?! You done missed supper, no one knows where ya are, and who the hell gets appointed with the task of runnin' your ass down? Me! Christ I don't even live at that house anymore, but yet here I am!" As he finished his diatribe, he lumbered out of the truck and eyeballed his sister down as she stopped and cowered in his presence.

"What the fuck are you wearin'?! Take that shit off!" Hutch could do no more than shake her head no. "Give me that!" He yelled as he ripped her bike from her hands. She cringed as she watched him chuck the Schwinn with one hand into the back of the pick-up bed. It rattled around with a sickening symphony of metallic scrapes and clangs.

"I said take that shit off!" He bellowed once more about the dress. Again Hutch shook her head no as she fought back a tear. "Fine! Keep the thing on. Just tryin ta save you some embarrassment. You look stupid…And what were you doin' when I pulled up just now?!"

"Wha-What?" Hutch muttered.

"*Wha-wha-wha?*," He mocked her, "I'm talkin' about your girlfriend over there. You two makin' out?"

"Ha! Your sister's a carpet muncher, McCray!" A voice laughed from the passenger side of the truck.

"Shut the fuck up, Randy!" He warned his friend. He whipped his attention right back to his sister. "You didn't answer me, were you lovin' up on your friend over there?" A tear rolled down Hutch's face and her lips quivered.

"Don't-Don't tell dad…"

"My fuckin' god…you have got to be shittin' me, Hutch!" He spoke with a disgust he did little to cover up. "Oh, I'm tellin' dad, alright. Everyone's gonna hear about this shit."
Hutch shook her head violently; her tears began to blind her.

"No…no…please," she whimpered as she grabbed his arm.

"Get your hands off me! Wipe your face and get in the goddamn bed fore' I throw you in there like I did that piece of shit bike," he grumbled as he climbed back in the cab and slammed the door. Quickly, she jumped on the bumper and clamored in the back just as Hank punched the gas. She flipped over and rolled, trying to regain herself as he sped down the roadway like a madman. With a quick thud, she sat down on her butt and walked herself backwards on hands and feet till her back was pressed firmly against the back of the cab. Her eyes led her to the interior where she saw Hank shaking his head and then to his buddy, Randy, who sat in the passenger side, trying not to laugh at the events that had just unfolded in front of him.

The wind angrily whipped through Hutch's hair while she stared back down the road through tear-swollen eyes at the sight of Midge standing by the edge of the field with a sober look on her face. As she watched the brunette disappear on the horizon amongst a fury of kicking dust, that is when she realized it. She knew it to be true. She was only thirteen but she knew…She liked women…and she despaired in it as much as she rejoiced.

The Keys to the Kingdom

Despite the storm of emotions that saturated her soul during the night, Hutch still managed to find sleep. She awoke in a fright as the alarm clock screamed right into the back of her head, belting out the stinging tune of reality remembered. With a groan, she sat up and ran her fingers through her ratted hair, placing her hat back atop her head while she stared down at the floor beneath her. And there it was, the Polaroid she had tucked against her chest when she had finally fallen asleep. She picked it up with a numb look upon her face and tossed it back into the drawer from whence it came…This day was already off to a bad start, and she hadn't even put her boots on yet.

The first half of the day went according to King Hank's new reigning rules. Sweep the floor. Take out the trash. Sweep the floor. Clean the toilets. Sweep the goddamn floor AGAIN. It was all mind-numbing and enough to make her want to just throw that damn broom to the floor, walk off and never come back. She barely spoke a word to anyone that day, and it didn't go unnoticed. Even Hayden and Heath's practical jokes and smart-assed comments barely got a rise out of her. And they soon realized that this zombie walking round the shop just wasn't their sister anymore, but a broken shell of something that once was.

Around 2 o'clock she found herself sweeping the back hall for what seemed like the tenth time. She soon began passing the open door to the office where the King himself sat, gnawing away like a Viking on a late-lunch sandwich. Hutch knocked on the side of the door and stepped right in. Hank's eyes drew over to the attention of his sister, he ceased his biting and dropped the sub he ate to the desktop with a smack.

"What the fuck do you want?" He spoke as he chewed, "Get out of here before I lose my appetite."

"I cleaned the toilets," she simply said.

"And? You want a fuckin' toilet cleanin' medal or somethin'?"

"I cleaned the toilets. I took out the trash. And I'm done sweeping the floors. What else can I do?"

Hank looked at her strangely, "Oh you're done sweepin' the floors? I don't think ya are." He no sooner ended that sentence when he slammed a fist down on a bag of chips that sat beside him. He then emptied the open bag of crumbs all over the floor in front of Hutch.

"Ya missed a spot," he said as he pointed and sat back down.

"Okay," she sighed, moving the broom without protest.

"And I'll tell ya somethin else. Bout soon as I finish this sub, got me a good feelin' them toilets are gonna need your attention again."

Hutch said nothing in return, but instead quickly cleaned up the mess and dumped it into the trash can.

"Well, that's done. You need anything else?"

"Wait, why you bein' all prim and proper right now?" He asked with suspicion. Suddenly his eyes widened, "The answer is *no*."

"What the hell, I ain't even asked you anythin' yet."

"A-ha! I knew you were wantin' somethin'. Fuck off."

"Whatever.." she went to turn around and leave.

"Wait…what the hell is it? What you want? And DON'T make me regret askin' that."

Hutch hesitated for a moment but then she just came out with it.

"I want a key to the shop."

"Ha!Ha! Oh fuck, you're out of your goddamn mind, I said DON'T make me regret askin'."

"Fuck this…" she started to walk out again.

"No, no, no. Now wait…Humor me a minute. I need a good laugh this afternoon. Why you need a key?"

"Well, I was thinkin'…"

"There ya go doin' that thinkin' shit again," Hank interrupted.

"I was thinkin' I could work after hours…"

"I ain't payin' ya overtime."

"Would ya let me finish for shits sake? I don't want overtime, I was hoping I could use the shop after hours to finish the Maverick and sell it off. I could use part of the money to pay you all the back rent and buy the camper off of ya. And hopefully buy Ruby back when she comes up for auction."

"Hmmm…Go get me a rope."

"What? Why?"

"So you can toss it to me and help pull me out of this pit of bullshit I'm drownin' in over here."

"I'm not lyin," her agitation grew.

"I don't know, Hutch, something stinks round here, and it ain't this shitty sandwich which is now cold because of this conversation," he threw what was left of the sub into the trash and wiped his hands. "You wanna know what I think? I think you're gonna put that thing together and start racin' again for money. Let's face it, that's what you and Cass were buildin' that damn thing for in the first place."

"No. I'm done with all that," she tried to keep her calm. How the hell did he always know what was going on? If this man wasn't the bane of her entire existence, nothing was.

"Okay. Sooo, lemme get this straight now, you're gonna put that thing together? You're droppin' a very high dollar engine, in a very undesirable car."

"In your opinion."

"No, in my fact. What you need to do is scrap that damn Maverick and just sell the engine outta here. I could have that thing sold within days to one of these droolin' gear-heads we get in here. Seriously, Hutch, who the hell ya thinks gonna buy that thing when you're done with it?"

"I am," a voice entered the room along with a tiny brunette. Hutch's eyes widened as Regina barely ducked right under her arm to get around her in the doorway of the office. She stopped just short of Hank's desk and stared at him.

"You again?" Hank spoke with a snide look on his face.

"Me again," Regina smiled, "She's selling the Maverick to me. That's why I was in here yesterday...Ain't it, Red?"

Hutch was still dumbfounded by Regina's entrance. She stood there trying to find her words. "I said, ain't it Red?" The brunette repeated as she looked back at her.

"Uh, yeah. Yes."

Hank leaned forwards, elbows on desk and hands folded, his thumbs twiddled atop them. His eyes darted suspiciously between the confident stare of the short girl in front of him and the side-swiped look of his sister behind.

"Uh-Huh...And what price did you agree on with our sawed-off friend here, Hutch?"

Hutch went to speak but Regina cut her off,

"Sixteen."

"Sixteen hundred?" Hank spoke with a tone of disgusted disbelief at the tiny number.

"Uh, no. Add another zero behind that," Regina traced the shape of an "O" in the air in front of her.

"HA! Sixteen thousand?!" Hank laughed as he leaned back in his chair. Hutch couldn't tell if he was pissed or pleased. Probably a bit of both. He spoke again, "Wow, lady, you got looks but no brains apparently."

"That makes two of us," Regina retorted without an emotion to be found on her face. Hank grew deathly quiet for a moment, not knowing how to respond. His face started to display that same shaken look Hutch had seen yesterday when he was talking about Regina looking familiar. Soon, he cleared his throat and brushed it all off,

"Well...Yeah...Ummm," he muttered as he dug through the desk drawers in front of him. The distinct jingle of a key came full circle from the metallic depths. With a quick flick of the wrist, he tossed the key to the desk and it slid to the corner.

"Shop key, Hutch," he uttered. He then looked at Regina as he stroked his beard. "I guess ya got yourself a car then."

"Another one of many," she spoke back, never once blinking those golden eyes. Amidst the awkward silence, Hutch grabbed up the key and walked out of the room, leaving the brunette and the King of the Gingerbread House staring each other down.

"You need somethin else?" Hank finally spoke as he glared all the more. Regina placed her hands on the desk and leaned in towards him. She whispered...

"Yeah, I need to know how a boy, who used to sweep these floors like a good son, would grow up to be such an asshole..." with her final word, she smiled wide and slinked off, leaving Hank to deal with the emotional repercussions of what he had just heard. Chills ran up his spine, and his eyes watered in the wake of them. He was right all along...Who was she? What was she?

Hutch stood there at the corner of the hallway in silence, arms crossed as Regina suddenly emerged and walked right on by her without as much as a look in her direction. As she watched her walk on around the front desk making a beeline for the door, her anger kicked in. She couldn't let it go. With a jolt, Hutch found herself at a near run, pushing the front entry open with a clang as she followed the brunette out into the searing heat of the afternoon sun.

"What was that shit? The fuck are you doin' here?" She hissed in a whisper.

"Oh please," Regina rolled her eyes, "Don't even pretend you're not happy to see me after that look you gave me when I left last night.

"I don't need your help. I had it under control."

"Ha! No you didn't. I was saving your ass by the sound of things in there. What's that make, two times I've come to your rescue now?"

"I can handle shit myself. I don't need anyone's help," she spat forth, still following the brunette across the parking lot.

"Yeah, keeeeeep telling yourself that, Red. Maybe you'll believe it one day," she spoke as she turned and started walking backwards, facing Hutch, "Now, do us both a favor and stop following me. You gotta car to build. I'll see you in two weeks, Red...You'd better be ready." With that, Regina dropped her huge sunglasses across her tiny face and turned round, sauntering away with a newfound sway in her hips. She left Hutch behind, dumbfounded with the dust of the lot whipping round her face from the gusts of the passing rigs. The redhead squinted and pulled her untamed locks over her ears, staring through the glare of the sun as the little brunette seemed to disappear like some mirage amongst the waving heat and diesel exhaust. A one note song of sorts sung out below her along with the cackling valves of the engines beyond. She stared at the source of the jingling, it was the key that still dangled there between her fingers. Hutch raised her hand and stared at it as it spun on the end of a plastic tag ring that displayed the words, "Shop Spare" scrawled in black magic marker. It was there…It was actually real and she had it to use whenever she pleased. She soon made it disappear in her closed fist while she nodded to herself in an understanding that only she seemed to grasp. All those years of tirelessly waiting around for her aunt to return to help her finish the car seemed all for naught. Now she had to finish the project all by herself to save the very woman she vowed she would never leave out of the build…It all seemed poetic.

…It was time.

The rest of that day came and went with nothing more than the thoughts of the Maverick filling Hutch's head to a dizzying capacity. Even Regina fell by the wayside inside her mind as she mentally pieced the project together. What parts would she still need? Was it all going to work? Could she possibly do this all in two weeks time? It consumed her, digested her, and regurgitated her, only to devour her once again. Every task she performed for the rest of that day felt more robotic and automated than they ever had. There were times she was quite sure she had forgotten to blink for minutes on end as the project grew and grew inside of her, transforming her into some glass-eyed doll that knew next to nothing of her surroundings. Oh, if thoughts had accomplished real world duties that car would've been together and running before she'd pushed the last bit of dirt into the dustpan that day. Hutch's mind wasn't the only one roaming the Gingerbread House in a daze for the remainder of that day. Hank stayed nearly fastened to the office chair he had been in since Regina had left him. Behind his green eyes stirred a numbness and calloused fear of the unknown…A fear of his own memories toying away at him. The words that had slithered from that girl's mouth kept repeating a haunting echo between his ears, stirring up the remembrances of his eleven year old self. He knew what he saw…He was right? Wasn't he? Amidst his unblinking stare, he reached into the bottom drawer below him and removed a bottle of whiskey. He clinked it down upon the desktop in front of him, popping the top off as his eyes met the soft gaze of his dead brother Henry looking back at him from a photograph on the far wall.

"You believe me, right?" Hank spoke to the picture as if his sibling were standing right there. With nothing more to mull over, he picked up the bottle and let the warm burn wash down his throat. He clenched his teeth and sighed as he dug into the front pocket of his work shirt, bringing to light a token he carried nearly everywhere he went. It was a sobriety coin from AA. With a dead glare he spun it around a few times and then flipped it over the side of the desk, letting it fall into the trash amongst the crumbs of the chips he had forced his sister to clean up. And just like that, ten years of being sober died along with the emptying of that bottle in front of him. He didn't know what was real anymore…And he didn't care. Life was becoming numb, meaningless. Just one mundane day placed in front of the next. Like blank pages being flipped on a slow, wordless read to the grave that was the back cover. Soon, he began thinking about the last time whiskey had touched his lips. It was right before his accident. Slowly, he reached in his pant pocket and withdrew a butterfly knife. He pulled it up and flipped it around to the open position, only to reverse the process and close it once more. He turned it over and looked at the name inscribed upon the alloy - *"Caldwell"* - No one knew the truth behind that night. No one alive, anyway.

Closing time had finally crept over the shop. Just like everyday, Heath and Hayden all but ran out the door, throwing a maelstrom of rocks out from under their spinning tires as they bolted for home or more likely the closest bar. Hutch drifted through the main area, closing the overhead garage doors, locking down the machines, and cleaning up the messes that her brothers had left behind for her, most of them deliberate and intentional. She was no genius, but a cold, mustard covered hotdog smashed in the bench vice didn't seem like an accident. A hard scrub and a sigh later, she found herself walking back into the office to see Ham still there stacking up receipts. Despite seeing each other dozens of times that day, they hadn't spoken one word to each other. Hell, they hadn't even as much nodded to acknowledge the other was alive. Ham broke the silence.

"What? You need to borrow some more money? Get your dirty little hands right in there and get ya some," Ham opened up the till.

"That's not funny," Hutch said as she crossed her arms and leaned against the back counter.

"Didn't say it was," Ham slammed the register shut and threw the remaining receipts he counted into a box, then followed with, "You been awful quiet today."

"Yeah well, so've you. What's up your ass?"

Ham turned round and crossed his arms as well with a sigh, "You tell me what's up your ass first. I saw Golden Ass walking through here earlier. She break up with you? Is that why you're roamin' round like a zombie on valium?"

"Golden Ass?"

"Yeah, That's what we nicknamed your girlfriend."

"Christ... She didn't break up with me. Hell, she's not my girlfriend. I told ya before it's complicated."

"Right. Right. So what then?"

"What?"

"What's up your ass?"

Hutch reluctantly went to speak but Ham cut her short, "Actually you hold that thought, what the hell are you even still doin' here? You're usually bailin' out that door right behind dumb and dumber."

"Well...I..." Hutch's words were once again cut short by the sound of a door slamming in the back hall. A trudging footfall echoed down the corridor as Hank's towering frame came from the shadows. There was a bit of stagger in his step, though it was almost hard for one to make out amidst his normal limp. He stopped briefly and glared at the two of them before he shook his head in disgust and sauntered on out and around the front counter. He put his hand on the front door and then spun back round, drilling an icy stare into his sister.

"You," he pointed right at her, "Don't fuck this up....and you lock every goddamn door when you leave. If anythin' gets stolen out of here, you ain't gonna have to worry bout findin' another place ta work n' live, cuz you'll be buried in my garden feedin' the tomatoes."

Hutch barely nodded. Hank veered his pointed finger at Ham.

"Hear that Sandwich? I just made a threat. Better call labor relations and report that shit…this is a hostile work environment." He sneered a bit, and then slinked out the door. Hutch and Ham stood together and watched him as he swayed his way out of sight towards his truck.

"You smell that when he walked through?"

"Yep," Ham sighed, "Old Jack and Hank are friends again."

"Should we stop him?" Hutch walked closer to her brother.

"After you," Ham simply waved a hand forwards, waiting for his sister to make the first move at keeping Hank from driving. After a few awkward seconds, it was evident that neither one of them was going to budge. "That's what I figured," Ham said. He lowered his hand and turned his full attention to Hutch. "Now, all I can keep thinking is, what the hell prompted him into diving back into the bottle after all these years. And I can't get that little voice out of ma head that keeps tellin' me you had somethin' to do with it."

"Me?! What the fuck?! I didn't force it down him. Hell, I didn't even know he had any at the shop."

"Okay," Ham simply said.

"Okay *what*, Ham? What do you want me to say? And how the hell you know this is the first time he's drank. We only see him eight hours a day, what about the other sixteen hours?"

"Missy ain't said a damn thing to me about him pickin' up the bottle again. But sure as shit he walks through the door like that tonight, she's gonna be callin' me."

"And what are you gonna tell her? That it's my fault?"

"I'm just sayin' the timin' is coincidental is all. With you and him fightin' more than usual, and this girl comin' round the shop, and now he's spiralin'."

"Fuckin Christ, Ham, are you on his side now? It's like you feel sorry for him or somethin'."

"Hey, I ain't on anyone's side here, but what the hell did he mean '*don't fuck this up and lock every door when you leave*' What's that all about? What aren't you supposed ta be fuckin' up,

Hutch? You wanna get me up ta speed on that, or ya just wanna tell me a pack of lies like ya always do?"

"Stop it! Just fuckin' stop, now!"

"Well...I'm listenin'," Ham said.

"Okay, look...I think I might, MIGHT, have some idea on what's goin' on with him.

That girl I've been seein'?...Hank told me dad and her...well, they were fuckin'."

"What?! Jesus Christ...dad is dying. Hell, she certainly can't be after his money he really don't have any."

"No Ham, not...not now. They're not fuckin' now. Hank said he caught dad cheatin' on mom back in like 69'. Said the woman looked just like her."

Ham placed his hand on his hips and his mouth fell agape in a show of borderline amusement.

"Wwwwhat?"

"The girl dad was cheatin' on mom with looked, according to Hank, looked exactly like Regina."

Ham stood there in silence for a moment, scratching his chin at the words that had just rolled out his sister's mouth. He could think of nothing else to ask but,

"Well...do you think it's her?"

"Has everyone in this place lost their fuckin' minds? No! No, I don't think it's her, Ham! And if it is, I need to get the number of her plastic surgeon or start takin' the same vitamins or some shit."

"How much you even know about that girl?"

"I know enough ta know she ain't nearly fifty years old."

Ham sighed.

"Maybe dad was seein' her mom or aunt or somethin?"

"See, that's what Hank wondered. But I got the feelin' he didn't really believe that...I really think HE thinks she's the same damn woman he saw twenty-some-odd years ago."

"So you ain't met her family then?"

"No, I didn't meet her family! We're not a couple! Christ, how many times do I have ta say that...We're not pickin' out curtains and buyin' furniture together and talkin' about the future."

"But you want to," Ham called her out.

"What?"

"Hutch, I saw the way you looked at that girl…You ain't foolin' me. You're in love."

"Fuck you. No," she shook her head violently, "No, that ain't true. You don't know me…You don't fuckin' know me at all." Ham crossed his arms and his eyes widened.

"Oh I don't know you? I know your favorite color, movies, songs, and foods. I know ya secretly want to punch people that chew gum around ya. I know the real reason ya won't get tattoos is because you're terrified of needles. And I also know ya hate bein' called Red. But you let that girl call you that all day long and I think you like it because she reminds you of…"

"Don't you fuckin' say her name, EVER," Hutch cut him off quick with a snarl and a pointed finger, "She ain't got nothin' ta do with this! Nothin'!"

"All I'm sayin' is you're my baby sister. So don't you ever tell me I don't know you."

Hutch hung her head down and bit at her lip. Ham quickly walked away from her and made his way round the counter. He spoke up again, "And as far as this business of you needin' to lock up after hours, I don't even wanna know what that's about. I get too little sleep as it already is cuz of your bullshit.…But whatever it is you got goin' on, I'm gonna join in with Hank when I say, Don't fuck it up," Ham said as he grabbed the front door handle. "See ya tomorrow…" with that, Ham disappeared, leaving the tiny jingle of the front door chime to serenade Hutch into a complete and bitter gray silence. She was alone, but the shop was hers.

166

Remembrance

The hum and crack of the ballasts belted out a tune as they fired up the lights high above in the back garage. Hutch stood there watching with pause as the room flickered and illuminated to her the sights of the engine and the Maverick sitting there as idle as they had been for the last half decade plus. After all these years, she never thought she would be in this situation...finishing this build without Cass here...but still in all, it had come. It was as real as the stench of the fuel that still hung in the air...The aromatic reminder of Hank's mental breakdown that forced her back into her father's life...if only temporarily.

Her steady footfall echoed as she made her way over to the Ford, stopping only a pace away from where it sat in the back. The smell of the unleaded remnants intensified as she reached out and ran her fingers across the top of the vehicle. She had since removed the gas dowsed tarp, but it hadn't done the paint job any favors in the short time it laid there. The faded blue of the Maverick had long lost its clear coat years ago and the corrosive liquid had seeped right into it in many places, leaving behind a ghostly swirling pattern of marbled indecency. She wasn't pretty to begin with, but now she looked more like an old spinster with nothing left to prove…Though Hutch was quickly reminded of a thing her father had once said to her, "*lookin good don't add horsepower.*"

The entire garage came alive with the serenade of squeaking hinges as Hutch opened up the driver side door and plopped down in the tattered vinyl seat. She slammed the door and placed her hands on the wheel, staring out the cruddy windshield at the engine across the room that would soon call this car back to life. Her mind started reeling back through her memories and landed upon the day her and Cass had procured the Maverick. It was a fresh fish coming into Riverside junkyard. Her and her Aunt had been looking for a project car for months but couldn't seem to agree on one. They both wanted the same thing though, something different, something unexpected. A car that most people would stick their nose up at until it left them in a cloud of burnt rubber and unraveling pride. Hutch remembered kicking rocks in the dirt lot, walking down the new arrival row with Cass as Lloyd waddled along beside them. Lloyd Romine. That man was a wheeler and dealer, hell he still was. Mind like a goddamn steel trap, that one. He knew every car on that thirty acre spread. What parts were in them. What ones had already been sold. He knew the colors, the years, and the exact locations. Not a shred of paperwork to help him. You told him you needed a power steering pump for an 82' Impala, he'd just look at you and say "*Four rows back, Go right. She's six cars in. I can pull it out for ya, or you can take er out and save yourself ten bucks.*" And you'd pull that pump out yourself, because god knows you needed that Hamilton for beer later when you were putting it in the car.

Cass pointed out a few usual suspects. A 74' El Camino that was some aftermarket shade of dogshit brown. A 67' Thunderbird with what appeared to be bullet holes in the front fender. Hutch had to admit that one was tempting, she always loved the hidden headlight look. But in the end, she still shrugged it off.

"What about that one there?" Hutch said, pointing to a faded blue 73' Maverick. The car sat there sad as could be with four flat tires and broken headlights.

"That piece a' shit?" Lloyd nodded towards the Ford. "It was a preacher's car outta Guernsey County. Well that was until he was caught boppin' a twenty year old from the choir inside the damn thing. Apparently his wife didn't do what Jesus would. Hence the flat tires and busted headlights. They got divorced and it went on the auction block. And now she's here with me."

"Jesus H Christ, Lloyd, we didn't need ta know the car's life story, we need to know if it's a solid ride. She got cancer under her skirt? Any frame rot?" Cass said as she walked around it with suspicion. Hutch joined her, looking in upon the interior. Several slash marks were carved across the vinyl seats, courtesy of a kitchen knife; more carnage from the woman scorned.

"Oh hell yeah, Cass. She's as solid as can be."

"That a fact?"

"Sure as shit."

"Funny, cuz about a minute ago you called this car a piece of shit," she busted him out as she kneeled, eyeballing the straight lines of the car looking for signs of filler repairs.

"Oh, hell now...You know how I just run ma mouth sometimes."

"Yeah, ya got a big mouth on ya...How much ya want for her?"

"Oh damn...I don't know," he carefully drew out as he sized up the sparkle in Hutch's eye. She wanted that car. "Bout eight hundred, I think."

Cass rose up with a raised brow from behind the Maverick.

"Eight hundred?...Dollars?"

"Yes, dollars. C'mon now don't be breakin' my balls on this, Cass. I gotta make money. Look around ya, you think this shits a hobby?"

"Who's breakin' whose balls here? Hell we gotta get four new tires, headlights, taillights, and front seats....How bout I give ya eight hundred dimes for it?"

"Eight hundred...?" He quickly added it up with a mumble, "That's eighty damn dollars? Hell that thing runs like a top still. I'll toss ya the keys right now if you don't believe me. She purrs like a bobcat."

"Oh Christ, I don't give a shit about that. That engine and tranny are comin right out of there first thing. We got plans for this car, unlike Mr. Preacher who owned it beforehand, those plans don't include spreadin' legs and the gospel at the same time."

Lloyd glared at her for a minute chewing away at his cigar.

"Four hundred."

"Hundred bucks."

"Goddamn it, Cass…" he growled, "Two fifty."

"One twenty-five, and you pull the engine and tranny out, keep them for yourself."

Lloyd squinted in the midday sun, his eyes shooting back and forth between Hutch and Cass's poker faces.

"Fine…But I ain't deliverin' that shit nowhere. Ya gotta provide your own hauler."

Cass looked at Hutch who had since opened the door and was now sitting in the driver's seat.

"What'd ya think, kid? She the one?"

Hutch gripped the wheel tight with both hands and stared through the window, imagining the day turning to darkness and the open road rushing through her hair. She looked up at Cass.

"Yeah. I think she's the one."

Cass looked over at the junkman and smiled wide, "Lloyd, looks like you just sold yourself another car."

Reality came back to Hutch, unraveling the patchwork quilt of idle cars in the distance and the sight of the junkman shaking his head in disgust. The sun transformed back into the shining fluorescents on high and her aunt's smile dissolved into nothingness. The silence crept back in as she realized she was still alone in that back garage, gripping tight the wheel of a philandering preacher's former car. She swore she could still smell the sin on the seats…

Hutch walked around and around the Maverick for what seemed like a solid hour. In the midst of all of it, she began thumbing back through the pages of her memories, trying to recall everything her and her aunt had done thus far. She circled the car, laid upon the floor, peered under it as best she could, then popped the hood to look at the sad emptiness that stared right back at her. As far she could see and remember, the undercarriage was complete. Wide tires and mag wheels had replaced the flattened and ugly stock set up along with four wheel discs and upgraded suspension components to help with cornering. A performance driveshaft mating a beefed up C4 transmission to a modified 9" rear end, had already been installed as well. Even the dual exhaust system had been laid into place waiting for the headers to be bolted up. A new sense of hope began to slowly wash over her…Hell, maybe two weeks was going to be enough after all, but then that tiny voiced whispered in her ear, the same voice every person who had ever turned a wrench more than twice knew all too well – this is a custom car build, you're going to have problems. But as with any voice of reason or reality, the inner McCray voice was quick to answer back "Kiss my freckled ass."

Hutch spent the rest of that night cleaning out the engine compartment, freeing it from the dust, debris, and cobwebs that had claimed it as their own over the years. She also spent the better part of an hour trying to locate the engine mounts they had secured to work in the car. They ended up being in an old potato carton box with the words "old piston rods" hastily written in marker. To the absolute shock of no one, the old potato box contained zero potatoes and zero piston rods, just the engine mounts for the Maverick, nearly buried by a mass of old random bolts and nuts. Jesus Christ...the back garage was as about as organized as a bucket of legos in a hurricane, and in that realization, the two week deadline was starting to look ugly once again. Still, Hutch shrugged it off and fastened the mounts down with bolts that took her nearly another half hour to find amongst the abstract of hardware in the same box. She sighed and eyeballed the clock high on the wall. "10:35" How the hell was that even possible? She had accomplished next to nothing. With a broken saunter, she paced over to the overhead garage door and opened it up, letting the cooling air of the night snake in along with the faint wisp of the diesel fumes beyond. She slammed the Maverick's hood shut and sat upon it, staring out the door into the dark horizon of farm fields beyond as she lit up a smoke and listened to the whisper of the idling trucks to the west. Her eyes were beyond heavy, she felt as if she could just nod off right then and there on the hood of that car...but she didn't. She couldn't. Her thoughts were once again churning up the past, keeping her from slipping into the dream realm. Thoughts of Cassandra dominated of course...Given the fact that she restarted the build they had worked on together, her aunt was an obvious consuming thought...but the thoughts of Midge still remained. Like tiny pieces of broken glass, they were always there, lodged into the side of her skull, occasionally breaking free and drifting where they shouldn't go. And so the two memories joined, and Hutch was instantly transported back to where her mind had left her the previous night….

She vividly remembered running straight to her room when Hank pulled in the drive. She stayed holed up in there till the evening draped down over the summer sky, blackening the outdoors into a symphony of crickets and tree frogs. Ham came in several times trying to get her to speak but she simply had nothing to say. For hours, she just stared out the window, her cheeks burning from the salt of her dried up tears. All that consumed her mind was the idiotic thing she had done to her best friend and the horrific thoughts of her oldest brother telling their father what he had seen. Her ears kept peeled to every sound that murmured through the house, trying to catch any banter of the events that had unfolded hours prior, but more importantly than that, she listened for the phone to ring…hoping and fearing at the same time that Midge would call her to say something, just anything. But the ringing never came. Why was this happening? Why was she like this? At this point, it wasn't even a matter of why she liked the same sex as much as it was the plight she had brought upon herself from choosing to fall in love with someone that may never love her back. She may not only be losing a chance at love, but losing her best friend at the same time. It was a thought that absolutely shattered her. She felt stupid, betrayed by her own foolish heart that she kept wishing would stop beating insider her chest so she could escape this hell that she knew was only just beginning. Hours passed like three long days with no nights inside that evening, until the ten o'clock hour rolled round and her bedroom door creaked open.

"Pooj?" Her father's voice quietly called through the stillness of the air.

Hutch shuddered from where she still sat with her arms folded cross the window sill. She didn't even want to breathe let alone speak. Maybe he would just go away.

"Pooj? Mom said you didn't eat any dinner."

"I ain't hungry," she squeaked out.

"Well why not?"

"I just ain't…"

There was grave silence between the two for what seemed like four eras and an eon. It was so long in fact that she thought for certain he had left her be until...

"Why don't ya get up and help me with somethin' out in the garage real quick."

The statement sent a wave of terror through her. He knew something, she could just sense it. He had never asked her to help him with anything this late at night.

"I'm pretty tired, dad. Think I might go to bed."

"Naw, this won't take too long. C'mon, get up."

With a grave reluctance, she arose and wiped at her face, trying fruitlessly to erase the rose-red stains of the not-so-distant past. She faced him with the strongest face she could.

"C'mon now," he beckoned for her to follow. The walk through backyard felt like the offspring of eternity, yet it was not nearly long enough in Hutch's mind. As she eyed the falling boots of her father through the darkness in front of her she couldn't help but wonder what things lay in wait for her. She felt as if she were walking down the hallway of death row, never to return.

The near unison footfall of father and daughter soon began to clod onto the stained concrete of the garage. She caught a glimpse of herself in a small mirror upon the wall as she walked onwards, suddenly remembering she still donned the dress she was gifted. Her father had made no mention of it, much to her surprise. In fact, he had made no mention of anything, he just kept walking until he led them to a 400 engine block firmly locked into an old stand at the back of the building. It was a personal project that he had been working on in his spare time. He had plans of dropping it into the red, 68' Firebird that sat lonely in the corner, Ruby, the same Firebird that would later become Hutch's. The same one she street raced in, made love in, and got high in. She didn't get her name from her signature red paint, but rather from Hutch's great, great grandmother, Rubella "Ruby" Siegel. Now, whether that woman was named after the disease, or the disease was named after her, was still up for debate. That car had always been the apple of Harvey McCray's eye since he bought it new off the lot. But after 1980, he seemed to retire it to the solitude of the garage, letting the cobwebs, dust, and time pepper her in shades of neglect.

Without much hesitation, Harvey grabbed up a cylinder head from the workbench and carefully slid it into place on side of the engine. He pointed to a cardboard template on the bench with bolts punched through it in a particular pattern.

"Start handin' me those. One at a time now," he said as his hand outstretched with impatient fingers. Hutch did as she was told, carefully placing each head bolt in her father's hand after the last was started in the engine. She watched his face attentively, the way his lip twitched and face fidgeted with every careful thread turned. It was all dreadfully silent aside from the moths and crane flies that continued to smack into the overhead fluorescent lights on high. It created an orchestra of pinging whose notes seemed to make more sense than the task she was now being handed. A task that she fast realized her father could do with his eyes closed. She wasn't here to help at all…something else hung stagnant in the nighttime air.

"Okay…Now take this," he handed her a socket wrench, "And start running these all down in. But don't torque em' at all. You get where the bolt heads about to make contact and you stop. Okay?"

"Okay…" Hutch acknowledged. The ratchet started clicking away as she went to it. She watched her father as he placed the other cylinder head on opposite from where she worked.

"What'd you do today, Pooj?" Harvey asked.

Hutch's lips twitched a tad as the memories flooded back.

"Nothin…"

"Nothin, huh? That don't sound like you."

He was right. It didn't sound like her. She needed to say something more, and fast.

"Hunted crawdads."

"Oh, ya did? You catch a bunch?" Harvey didn't even look her way as he threaded another bolt into the head.

"Yep."

"You keep em?"

"Nope."

Her father stopped a second and eyeballed her.

"So ya threw em' all back?"

"Yep."

"What the hell was the point of catchin' em all then?"

Hutch did her best to conceal her eye-roll.

"For lookin' at," she sighed.

"Huh. I don't understand you sometimes, girl," Harvey mildly scoffed as he started the final bolt into the engine. He took a break for a small moment and lit up a smoke. The aroma quickly snaked into Hutch's nose, arousing the memories of earlier. Memories she was now praying to god would stay hidden for the rest of her life.

Harvey exhaled and began spinning the bolts down opposite his unusually quiet daughter, their ratchets spewing out a metallic duet of clicks.

"So this crawdad huntin'…you went and did that with that little friend of yours?"

"Midge," Hutch confirmed. It wasn't her dad's fault, he really didn't know her name, or nickname rather. Hutch never brought her round the house. She didn't want her to have to deal with her brothers.

"So you and Midge went and caught crawdads and then let em' go…Then what you get up to?" Goosebumps started forming on the back of Hutch's neck. She knew at that very moment that he knew. Why wasn't he just getting to it already?

"Sat in the field for awhile. Talked," Hutch said.

"Nothin else?"

"Nope."

Harvey suddenly dropped his wrench. He looked right at Hutch. "Pooj, look at me."

Hutch stopped her ratchet turning and did as she was told. There was a grim apprehension hovering in his eyes. He pulled his cigarette from his mouth and ashed it out as he spoke once more. "Pooj, your brother told me that when he saw you in the field today you were…you were layin' on top of that girl. Said you two were neckin'. That true?"

Time seemed to stand still as the fear welled up inside Hutch. She did everything she could to keep herself from crying right then and there.

"Daddy…I…"

"Pooj! Is it true? I asked!"

She jumped a bit and held the socket wrench in towards her chest.

"Daddy…I love her," she squeaked out as she stared at the floor.

"Jesus Christ…Jesus lord, this ain't happenin'…" he wiped at his face as the dismay took over, "Hutch, you're thirteen years old, you don't know what love is!...And that...that certainly ain't love. What you're doin' there...You need ta get your head right, girl."

A tear began to run down her cheek as she stuttered out,

"Dad, please don't be mad."

"I ain't mad!...I'm...I'm upset."

And then she saw it. A tear coming from the corner of his eye. A tear. She hadn't seen that man cry a day in her life, not even on the day her grandfather died, but she was now the sole cause of the first time. Her stomach turned.

"Daddy, I..."

"Go back to the house, Hutch. Go to your room," he said coldly as he wiped at his mouth not even looking at her.

"But..."

"I said, go now, damn it!!!" He pointed with a fire blazing in his eyes. Hutch dropped her wrench and ran off as fast as she could. She remembered the path back through the yard being a blur both inside and out. Her eyes fogging over from the deluge of unshakable sadness that washed across them. She hit the bed hard, burying her face deeply to muffle the sounds of her own wailing. Whether it was the shortness of breath or the fatigue from simply crying so much that made her find sleep, she wasn't sure. But she was awakened by a sound. A flurry of sounds. She rose up in bed and listened through the dark at the noise murmuring through the walls. With apprehension, she creaked open her door and tiptoed towards the source of the clamoring. It grew louder and louder with every step she took towards her parent's bedroom. She stopped just shy of the door, watching the shadows dance across the light shining at the bottom of the threshold. A reluctance overtook her, but still, she did what she couldn't help but do, press her ear against the door.

"What are we gonna do?" She heard her mother speak.

"How the hell should I know, Lonnie. Ain't exactly somethin' I got experience in."

"Well, should we tell someone?"

"Tell someone? Tell who, what? You ain't helpin' one damn bit here, you know that? What we sposed ta tell? That...that our thirteen year old daughter likes gals. That she's a dike?"

Hutch bit her lip, trying to fight back the tears.

"Don't say that word," her mother said.

"Well I'm sorry, Lonnie but that's sort of what were dealin' with here."

There was a pause in the talking, all overshadowed by her father's pacing footsteps.

"What if that girl likes her back?" Her mother spoke.

"You need to just shut the fuck up. That ain't…that is not an issue here. I'm sure that girl was raised right, she's a good girl…and in the out-of-this-damn-world event that she *does* like Hutch, they sure as hell ain't seein' each other again….She's confused…Hutch is…she's just confused is all. You know…I blame you for all this."

"Me?!"

"Yeah you. You even notice what she was wearin' tonight?"

"What?"

"A dress, Lonnie. A white dress. Your cheapass insisted that we keep doin the hand-me-down clothes shit and never once bought that girl anythin' girly to wear! I don't know where she got that dress, but maybe if her mother had bought her one years ago she might not be actin' like this!"

"My cheapass?! Someone's gotta watch the money in this family! You're always spending without a thought on all these goddamn cars!! Ta hell with a dress, she's lucky she's got food on the table half the damn time thanks to you!"

"Bitch, you better start usin' your inside voice with me. I'm gonna say it one more time…This is your fault."

"My fault?! This is your fault! You got all those nudey pictures of girls all spread out all over the damn place in your garage. She's been seein' those since she was old enough ta walk. That couldn't have been good for her."

"Oh, give me a goddamn break!"

"No, I won't! You did this! You wanted another boy, Harvey, and by god you got yourself one!"

Hutch had heard enough. With her eyes once again set adrift in a sea of tears, she tore down the hall and ran out the front door. Barefoot and mind astray, she walked down the road with the full intention of never stopping lest her feet fell off or she sauntered right over the edge of the earth, itself. She couldn't go back…She wouldn't. Everything was broken now and all the tears in the world couldn't put it all back together again, yet she still let them fall.

A half mile out into the darkness of that back road is when she heard it. Over the hills, a roaring rumble that gave way to a beaming ray of light not unlike the son of a sunrise that blinded her upon its cresting of the hilltop. She squinted in the overwhelming rays of two beams that refracted across her tear-washed cheeks…The car came to a screeching halt beside her and her heart elevated.

"What the hell are you doin' out here, kid?" But it wasn't the voice of a stranger. As the door slammed shut, her eyes adjusted to the magnificence of a ruby-red 67' Mustang fastback shining in the dim light of that cloudless night. Her heart stepped down a beat. The idling purr of the garnet beast was accompanied by the clip-clop of boots coming cross the road towards her. The figure stopped in the headlights, her concerned face illuminated amongst half a smile in the ridiculousness of her only niece standing there on the roadside after midnight. The once-thought stranger was a thirty-one year old Cassandra McCray. The Scarlet Harlot herself…That woman was ivory and fire and everything in between back then. She liked going fast on and off the track…After all, she was a McCray, it was in her blood to bury the gas pedal and ask questions later. When her fingernails weren't digging into the steering wheel of a drag car, they were buried in the back of the first handsome man that dared to buy her a drink. And time and time again she proved she was simply too much for them to handle. Much like the car she drove, she was an untamable mare that had an undying lust for cars, sex, and trouble, and she didn't care what anyone thought about it. Even her hair complimented her lifestyle, it was set ablaze in a magnificent shade of red so true you'd believe she could light her own cigarettes with it. It waved and danced round her freckled face in a voluptuous wind-whipped abstract that was styled courtesy of race helmets and open roads. Those same carmine locks came to a rest low on the shoulders of that signature white and red leather jacket she wore every single time she was behind the wheel, or anywhere for that matter.

She just continued to stand there, shaking her head for what seemed like a solid minute as she waited for Hutch to say something, but nothing came from the teenager's mouth.

"Cat got your tongue then, huh?" Cass finally spoke up again, hoping it would evoke something, anything. Silence still hung as Hutch stood there with red, swollen eyes and a numb look upon her face. Cassandra sighed. "Well looks of ya, I'd say it had somethin' ta do with those brothers of yours…Lemme guess, it was Hank?....Sound about right?" She cocked her head as she popped the question, convinced her niece would finally open up, but she didn't. Instead, Hutch went running right towards her and threw her arms around her, squeezing her tightly.

"Whoa, okay. Okay, kid. Wow…" Cass reeled from the surprise of the hug as much as she despaired in it. Hutch didn't hug that often, especially her. In fact, she wasn't sure if they had ever really hugged until this point in time. Something was definitely wrong and it went beyond the normal antics of brotherly teasing she had seen in the past. Soon, Cass put her hands on her niece's shoulders and pushed her back until their eyes locked. Tears were reappearing as Hutch sniffled a bit. Cass once again sighed.

"Well…You gonna tell me what happened?" Hutch just lowered her stare to the ground, seemingly losing the ability to speak altogether. Cass nodded her head and removed her hands from Hutch's shoulders. "Okay. Just get in the car," she spoke as she rounded the driver's side.

"No. Don't take me home. I don't wanna go back there," Hutch spoke in a panic.

"My stars, she speaks!" Cass patronized, "Relax, kid. I'm not takin' you there." The car door slammed and Cass leaned over the passenger seat, staring at her niece through the open window.

"Where we goin'?" Hutch whimpered as she grabbed the door handle in reluctance. Cass sighed.

"If you don't get in here at the count of three I'm leavin' ya out here….one…two…" Hutch threw the door open and flopped down into the vinyl seat.

"That's what I thought…Grab onto somethin kid." She quickly warned as she slammed down the gas, leaving a symphony of squealing tires and smoke behind them.

As expected, the car ride that followed was awkward. Both of them stared off into the headlight illuminations on the road ahead, neither one of them daring to speak a word. Hutch wanted badly to just start lamenting, but the words wouldn't come. Her and her aunt had never been that close. They spoke the occasional word to one another but as far as a "normal" niece / aunt relationship went, theirs was far from sleepovers and long talks about the future. Maybe it was her fault, maybe it was Cass's fault, it didn't really matter at the end of the day to Hutch. She was busy being a kid, riding bikes, and breaking bottles and Cass, well, she was Cassandra McCray, too busy racing cars and breaking hearts.

Hutch couldn't help but notice how fast her aunt was driving. But even so, she slowly found herself mesmerized by Cass's actions. The way she clutched and shifted in perfection. How she finessed the wheel. How she took each corner at twice the speed the signs suggested. And most of all, how her face stayed sober throughout the whole thing. Nothing flinched, her lip never quivered, her eyes didn't bat, they stayed transfixed much like that of the hawk's, spying down every square inch of pavement as if it were infinite prey she consumed that would never fill her infinite appetite. She was made for this. She was born into it. This car and her, they were one and the same as she carved a path through the winding back roads of Dillon County, headed towards a destination as of yet unknown. And despite the excessive speeds and forces of gravity that pressed upon her chest, Hutch had never felt safer than she did at that very moment.

Two shakes and a half a tick later, they were sitting across from one another at a twenty-four hour dive diner outside of town. The place was rough looking to say the least, and Cass just stuck out like a fresh marigold flower in a pile of pig shit. It was the type of establishment that every sad sod would clamor into when it was time to sober up for the night and soak up that greasy Americana served hot and ready by a questionable short order cook missing one arm. Chicken fried chicken, French fries, deep fried pickles, in short, if it wasn't fried, you weren't getting it at this place. About the only thing that wasn't breaded and lowered into oil was the coffee that steamed away in front of Cass as she stared over at her niece, trying her damndest to figure out the words to speak…She just wasn't good at this.

"You sure you ain't hungry, kid? You can have anythin' you want, it's on me."

Hutch just shook her head as she stared down at the tabletop in front of her. "Okay then…you at least gonna tell me what happened? Why you were walkin' god knows where this late at night?"

Hutch didn't reply. She just sighed and sniffled a tad. Cass smirked a bit as she hovered her coffee inches from her lips. She put the cup down and followed it all with her own sigh of impatience.

"Look...this is obviously pretty deep for you to be actin' like this. I know you and me we ain't been too close, but I can tell when somethin' bad's happened. One of your brothers hit you or somethin?"

"No," Hutch snapped quietly.

"Well, what then?" Cass's eyes widened. She was finally talking at least.

"No one did anythin'...It's me."

"You...What'd you do?"

"I...I'm a freak."

"Ha! Darlin' you're a McCray. That sort of comes with the territory. I think ya need to be a little more specific."

There was grave silence for several moments. Cass could almost see the gears of utter reluctance turning inside that poor girl's head as she finally looked up at her and uttered the words...

"I like girls."

Now almost instantly Cass knew what she meant by those words, but there was that little tick of doubt that made her ask for clarification.

"You...you like girls? Like in the sense that I like boys?"

Hutch nodded in despair. It was at that moment that Cass began to chuckle a bit and Hutch's eyes drilled right into her as her heart began to break once more. How could she be laughing?

"Oh, darlin'...I thought you were gonna tell me you were bein' molested or...or you liked torturin' little animals, or somethin' just awful...You like girls? That ain't nothin' to worry your head about," Cass spoke in the most sincere tone. Still, Hutch rebuked.

"How ain't it a bad thing? Everyone hates me now. Midge hates me. Hank hates me. Mom and dad hate me."

"Now, not everyone hates you. I don't hate you, so that disproves that first point of yours. I don't know who Midge is, but Hank hates everyone, so he don't count, and Lonnie and Harvey?

Well…they'll learn ta live with it. And if they don't, then that's on them, not you."

Hutch just sat there slouching, letting her aunt's words sink into her. She asked,

"What I am I sposed ta do?"

Cass took a swallow of her coffee and replied,

"Well, darlin', you just be you. It ain't that hard."

"But I don't like bein' me…"

"Ha! Well newsflash, kid, most of us don't like bein' ourselves for the most part. Were always wishin' we were someone else, had nicer things, different circumstances…Ah hell, I just feel like you're too damn young to be worried about any of this shit…" Cass drifted off as she stared out the window. She looked back towards her niece whose eyes were glassed over with hope and despair, waiting for her to finish. She went on…"No…I…I've drifted away from friends cuz they got married, had kids, and all that, but none of em' are really all that happy with all that domesticated livin'…well, hell maybe some of em' are…the point is, you're never gonna be happy in life doin' the things that other people expect out of ya. Don't deny who you are…Don't do things just to avoid gettin' hurt…" Cass sighed as she paused a moment, "What I'm tryin' to say is, don't spend your life bein' someone else's dream. You understand?"

Hutch nodded and smiled. And she did understand. More wholly than she could've ever imagined…But it didn't make reality any less bleak and turgid to the touch. People were cruel as was the world they dwelled in.

Sleep and dream came, and consciousness returned to the scream of that goddamned alarm clock. It was a process that happened over and over for the next few days as Hutch and her brothers went about the everyday grind that came with the machine shop. During the days, she would push dust and clean grease, and in the evenings she would turn wrenches and then sit down and think…mainly she did the latter. It wasn't like she was putting a stock vehicle back together. She quickly found out more fabrication was needed. There's was no radiator, the stock one had been chucked out long ago to make way for a performance cooling system. Issue was, she still had the new radiator but it didn't mount up of course, so she had to go about making a bracket from scratch out of angle iron and flat bar from the leftover stock of welding supplies that still haunted the back garage. It took her another solid night to perform that task…That week was slipping away far too fast and the anxiety was building.

Pink Trucks and Flashing Lights

"What the hell is that thing?" Hayden's disgusted words fell out. All of the McCray siblings stood outside the shop in a neat row on that mid-week morning. Ham, Hutch, Hayden, and Heath were a mosaic of smoking cigarettes, downing coffees, and shaking heads as they beheld the sight of Hank getting out of the new shop truck and walking over to them.

"Well, there she is," Hank said as he joined them, taking a drink of his own coffee. They all stood in silence, one only a foot from the next, heads tilting a bit as each waited for the other to say something, anything.

"It's fuckin' pink," Hayden finally spoke up. He followed it with a huge spit of chewing tobacco.

"It's fuchsia," Hank corrected.

"What?" Heath squinted as he spoke.

"Fuchsia, ya dumb shit," Hutch looked over at him.

"Fuchsia? Is that French for pink, cuz that fucker is pink," Hayden jumped back in, pointing at the flamboyantly colored 89' F-150 that sat in the front of them.

"That thing have purple rims or ma glasses fogged up this mornin'?" Heath asked.

"They're purple," Hutch sighed.

"That's it. I'm out," Heath said, raising a hand as he began to walk away.

"Get the fuck back here," Hank barked. Heath stopped and rejoined them all. Hank spoke again, "Now, y'all need ta quit actin' like babies, It ain't that bad."

"Ain't that bad? Christ, you throw a red racing stripe down that thing and it'll look just like my last hemorrhoid," Hayden said.

"Only smaller," Heath muttered.

"Kiss ma ass."

"Enough already. Godddamn..." Hank belted out.

"Enough of what? We're gonna be a goddamn laughin' stock down at the track when word gets out were prancin' around in a pink truck. We start deliverin' shit in that, it's game over. No ones gonna come round here no more," Hayden threw out his grievances.

"What I wanna know is, who the hell had a pink truck with purple wheels in the first place," Ham finally spoke.

"Ross's Party Rental & Supply," Hutch said matter-of-factly.

"Now how the hell you know that?" Hank growled.

Hutch walked forwards and pointed at the side of the door, "Says it right there. You can barely see it. Paint musta faded a tad from where the vinyl letters were.

"What? Where?" Hank pushed her out of the way and rubbed at the paint, tracing the letters with his fingers. "Well shit..."

"Ha! Ha! Well hell that went from bad ta worse?" Hayden laughed.

"What the hell happened to the insurance money for the other truck?" Hutch questioned.

"There was a thousand dollar deductible," Ham sighed.

"Yeah and that damn thing wasn't worth that. This one here was only six-hundred. Only has 88k on it. Hell of a deal really," Hank spoke.

"There's a reason it was six-hundred, Hank," Hayden scoffed.

"Yeah, I'm aware, asshole. I figured we could get it painted for a couple hundred by that guy in the alley behind Steiner's. May not be tip-top grade but it'll do better than pink. Still be under a grand and have a truck with a quarter of the miles on it.

"Jesus Christ..." Hayden sighed.

"It'll be fine, alright?" Hank turned towards him, "Now...she's on E, so go fill er' up over at PJ's." He tossed Hayden the keys and started to walk off.

"Wait, what? Fuck that, I ain't drivin' that thing nowhere."

"I ain't askin' ya. I'm tellin' ya," Hank stopped and glared.

"What the fuck, that's Hutch work. Besides she's a girl. No ones gonna give her shit for drivin' a pink truck."

"Hayden, if you don't get your happy-ass in that thing and go fill it up right now, You're gonna be scrubbin' toilets and Hutch is gonna be doin ALL your work from now on...Any questions?"

"Yeah, I do have a question, should I fill it up with unleaded or fruit punch?" Everyone smiled, except for Hank.

"Get the hell out of my face...Park round back when you're done."

"Well that kinda goes without sayin'..." Hayden mumbled as he walked round the truck.

As the dust kicked up from the new shop truck, Hutch couldn't help but wish she was a fly on the gas pump over there. Especially so if there were about a dozen bikers filling up at the same time as Hayden. She smiled inside at the simple thought of it as she returned to the belly of the shop along with everyone else.

Several minutes later, Hutch found herself walking by the main office, broom in hand. She shuddered as Hank's voice drove straight into her ears.

"Hutch. Come in here."

She reluctantly stepped just inside the doorway, awaiting further word.

"What the hells goin' on?"

"With what?"

"You kiddin' me? With what? With this goddamn Maverick build of yours. I was back there before I left last night and it looks like you ain't done shit yet, but you been stayin' over every night."

"I been cleanin' it."

"Tell me those words didn't come out of your mouth just now."

"Well that and I put the engine mounts in. Checked out the chassis to make sure it was all good there. The radiator mount had to be fabricated so I been busy with that and..."

"Stop right there...Your mouth keeps doin' this," he flailed his fingers, making them talk like a silent puppet, "But all I keep hearin is '*Hank I'm fuckin up*' over and over again."

"There's a process to this shit..." Hutch tried not to growl.

"Yeah there is, and the process involves ACTUAL work and a runnin' car. How long you got ta get this done? You two agree on some sort of deadline?"

Hutch sighed, "Two weeks…Next Saturday."

"Ha! Jesus Christ. Well at this rate she's gonna have a sparkly-clean yard ornament come next weekend."

"I'll get it done," she spoke coldly.

"Yeah you better, cuz come that followin' Monday if ya ain't got this money ya promised me, I will throw you in a dog cage and sell ya to the first pervert trucker with a ginger fetish I find out on that lot… Now get the fuck out of my office," he spoke menacingly as he turned his attention to some paperwork in front of him. Hutch went to turn and leave with a look of ire upon her face, but then stopped and the words sort of just fell out of her unwillingly,

"You drinkin' again?"

Hank's head slowly rose with a storm brewing in his squinted eyes.

"You're walkin' into shark infested water right now, bitch…and you're about knee deep. Now, you're welcome ta keep on wadin' in or ya can back out now before you lose your legs…Got it?"

Hutch tried her damnedest not to start going off on him, but that look on his face…there was actual danger there. Instead she said the only thing she could,

"Well…my apologies for actually givin' a shit." And with that, she left him alone.

Despite all of the usual Hank insults and overall prickish behavior, there was still something different about him, and it went beyond the drinking. Ever since Regina last visited, he had been different. It was the slightest change, but Hutch could sense it…he was scared, riled, and some tiny part of him had broken off and fell into the liquor once again because of it. That same subtle change was enough to make Hutch even more on edge. If Regina had the ability to drive Hank the Tank McCray back to the bottle, then she was someone that you had to keep one eye on no matter what….And it was in that moment that Hutch knew she had to get the Maverick finished before the brunette's deadline, or Hank would be the least of her troubles.

Bolts turned beneath chattering ratchet songs long into the following nights…things were coming together. And before Hutch knew it, she had the beast's heart dangling from chains upon a hoist. She had since removed the hood of the car and was now lining up the engine, preparing it to be dropped into place. With great care, she feathered the jack, lowering it and pumping it, moving it millimeters from one side, then the next, until the front end of the Maverick squatted beneath the weight. And then she went to it, the agonizing and often enraging process of getting everything to mate together. Bolts were turned in quarters, hammers tapped, and the hoist was bumped up and fro, but finally the last turn of the ratchet resounded along with her sigh. A grunt emerged from Hutch as she stood up, straightening her back for the first time in what seemed like two hours. She unshackled the chains and rolled the engine hoist to the wayside, then turned round to behold a sight she wished her aunt could've been there for. It was glorious, the 351w sat there tucked in and proud as could be, a beast within the monster. Even still, much had yet to be done before the tires could set the pavement ablaze.

As usual, the night had crept upon her without her even noticing. She walked away from the Maverick to the open garage door and peered out into the darkness, a starless coal-black sky stared back with an ominous flickering on the horizon. A storm was rolling in…Hutch had overheard Heath mention something about storms tonight but took it with a grain of salt considering the weatherman was about as worthless as a one-legged man at an ass-kicking contest.

She lit up a cigarette and walked a pace out into the cooling air, her lungs filling with the stagnation of smoke and the virginity of impending rain. As she leaned against the side of the building and watched the semis idle below an obsidian sky hemmed with lightning's breath, she couldn't help but feel a calm rush into her soul. There was just something about a nighttime, summer storm…the way it glided in and romanced the landscape, creeping in like an unforgotten ghost...sending the chill across your naked flesh to brush away the absurdity of heat the day had left behind. And then there was the smell of the rain…an aroma without match. The fragrance of nature's aridity transforming and transcending back into the sweet vivacity it once knew…To become whole again…To become alive again. One could only imagine that is what the tears of God smelled of….Few of earth's perfumes were as bittersweet.

Hutch took another puff of her cigarette and watched through the smoke at movement in the lot at Piper Jeans. A truck was gearing up and going into a slow crawl across the gravel, headed towards her camper. She eyed it cautiously as most trucks didn't make swings that wide and most certainly not that close to her home. With wide eyes and mouth slightly agape, the redhead watched the rig miss her awning by inches as it swung in her direction, blinding her in the fire of its headlights. She almost fell to her knees as the horn resounded and sliced through her ears with a deafening bellow.

"What the hell...?" she mouthed as the truck made its full u-turn in the lot. As her eyes adjusted back from her temporary blindness, she made out the words written upon the rig as it rolled its way back across the lot towards the road. "Redgrace Logistics"

"Son of a bitch..." she whispered aloud. The gears began turning inside her head at a fevered pace...Her eyes widened, and an ill-conceived plan was already set in motion as her head darted about the garage. She bolted across the room as fast as her legs could take her, bursting through the back hallway door. She flung open Hank's office door and began rifling through drawers.

"Shit. Shit. Shit...Where are they?..." she snarled lowly as she threw open every door, "Damn it!" She quickly fled to the front and began laying open drawers at the front counter. As she dug away, her eyes caught something shiny to the right of her. She quickly perked and looked to the shelf. There they were, right beside the radio. The keys to the new shop truck. Without thought, she grabbed them up and blasted back the way she came, right out the open garage door and into the arms of the now falling rain. The door to the pink pick-up was thrown right open, hell Hayden hadn't even locked the damn thing...and she was always the irresponsible one. Her key-toting fingers fidgeted under her own words, "C'mon. C'mon..." as she sloppily guided the brass into the slot and turned. The engine fired up, followed by an immediate surge of the reverse gear as she tore across the gravel like a maniac. Drive was engaged and she flew through the lot, almost losing control as she hit the wet pavement headed west in the direction of the departing Redgrace semi. She flipped on the wipers to high speed and the deluge cleared from the glass in front of her, over and over. The blurry brake lights of the rig ahead shined brightly as it paused at the intersection and turned left, headed towards route 70. As the pounding of the rain intensified and drove a deafening echo through the cab, she hit her brakes and watched as the truck faded from sight. What the hell was she doing? Was she seriously going to follow this truck? The thunder rolled and shook the shop truck as she just stared into the rain at odds with her own mind. All of a sudden, a horn blared away behind her, a car had come up and was no doubt getting irritated with her sitting there behind the stop sign when no traffic was in sight. Hutch jumped a bit at the sound, but kept her cool. She pressed the gas and turned left against her better judgments.

With the greatest of caution, she slowly followed the Redgrace rig down the 70 westbound ramp. She kept what she thought to be a safe distance behind, trying not to draw attention to herself from the driver. Cars passed by, headlights blinded, and the rain danced down in a horrific downpour as the same words came rushing back into her head. "What are you doing?" What was she doing, indeed. Somewhere in her head she thought following this truck could lead her to something, anything. Answers as to what the hell kind of business Regina was running. Hutch suspected for a long time now that it was some cover-up operation, a thing to distract everyone's eyes from the seedy things she was undoubtedly up to behind closed doors. She began wondering what was even inside that truck...if anything at all. Hell her aunt might be in there for all she knew or half a dozen other poor schlubs that owed Regina something. And that was the other reason, perhaps the top one, that lead her down this stupid path she was currently taking. Maybe this truck would lead her to her aunt. Maybe, just maybe, she could find out where they were keeping her and free her.... "Goddamn, Hutch, You're so stupid." She snarled aloud to herself. Yet her own words did little to calm the force of her foot upon the gas pedal.

Miles sped by beneath the raging storm as she kept a ten car distance away from the truck ahead. The pace was slower than all get out courtesy of the relentless rain abounding...40 MPH was the top speed. It was grueling and tedious and was giving Hutch far too much time to think about the cons of this venture. When was she going to decide that enough was enough and turn around? Ten miles? Fifty miles? One-hundred? Hell this truck could be headed four states away for all she knew. Redgrace headquarters could be anywhere, if it even existed at all. And then there was the matter of her stealing the truck she now drove. Or did she commandeer it? She had no clue, all she knew was she was driving a truck she had no permission to take with a suspended license…none of this was going to end well.

Soon, the rain began to ebb and fold back into a drizzle. The lion's share of the storm appeared to be filling nothing but the rearview mirror at this point…only darkness and taillights remained through the blur of the clearing windshield in front of her. She punched the gas and bridged the large gap between her and the rig till she was within a few cars length, trying to see if there was anything written on the semi for clues to where it was heading. But there was nothing, not even a "How's my Driving" phone number was written upon it. Just the Redgrace Logistics Logo, a Red "R" with a star in the loop and an arrow pointing downward off the drop. There wasn't even a proper plate that Hutch could decipher. It was plain white and didn't reveal a state I.D. With all the missing info, she had to guess that the truck wasn't even street legal, yet nothing and no one was stopping it from trudging along.

As Hutch's eyes peered around the back of the trailer, her review mirror became engulfed by a blinding set of lights moving in fast. She jerked her head up, darting her squinted eyes around to all of the mirrors to see another semi barreling up on her rear with a quickness she wasn't prepared for. The rig stopped within half a cars length of Hutch's bumper and coasted along with her at speed, unleashing a bone chattering horn blare that cut right through the rear window glass.

"Shit!!" Hutch yelled out. She feathered the steering wheel and the pedal below as her watchful and anxious gaze shot around the cab, trying to figure out just what the hell was going on. If this asshole was in such a rush, why didn't he just go around? They weren't even in the passing lane. But as the seconds ticked on to a solid minute of the semi hovering just feet from her tailgate, the more an ominous feeling began to creep in…Something wasn't right. And in that next moment, her suspicions were realized. Out of nowhere, a third rig came flying up the passing lane, but instead of rolling on by it stopped there and hovered beside Hutch…She was now completely blocked in from all sides. Panic began to root itself deeper within the redhead as her attention stayed with the passing lane rig. She read the words on the side of the trailer "Redgrace Logistics"

"Fuck…" was all her lips could mime as the adrenaline began to pump even harder. With a jolt, the rig in front of her slammed its brakes a bit, destroying the gap between it and Hutch. The redhead gasped but dared not to brake for fear of the semi behind her crushing her flat. The forward rig stopped within feet of her front bumper…and there she sat, trapped between three semis and the guard rail, rolling at a steady 65 MPH with mere feet on all sides keeping her from meeting a certain doom. Her terrified heartbeat elevated and she began to breathe like a winded dog after a rabbit run. Eyes watered in the wake of blinding tail and headlights, and her mouth dried as she kept her feet upon the pedals, steadily pumping them back and forth, maintaining the exact pace of the rigs that were just waiting for her to make a mistake…She had to keep it together. Minutes seemed as days within the carnage of her own mind. She felt like an animal trapped in an old cage, only the walls of this cage were moving, almost breathing, seemingly waiting for her to give up and just hit the brake…But then it happened. Just like that, the semi behind her slammed its brakes, creating a sizeable gap. Hutch quickly followed suit, slamming the pedal so she could try and slip out behind the passing lane rig. No such luck. The back rig stopped right at the corner of the other, and that's when everything went from bad to worse. There was now a large space between the front and rear trucks, so large in fact a whole semi could fit in between them both…and so one did. Hutch's head whipped to the side to see the passing lane rig slowly moving towards her, filling the gap the other two trucks had created for it. She was now being slowly forced into the guard rail. Her panic kicked into overdrive as she realized she had nowhere to go while she watched the rig come closer and closer. With teeth clenched, she feathered the wheel to the right until she was inches from the speeding berm.

"Shit…Shit….Shit…." she hissed a whisper as the truck came closer. "C'mon you motherfucker! Just do it!" She suddenly snapped and smiled as the guard rail began to nibble her driver side door. A storm of sparks began to spray like mad, slowly stripping the pink paint from the truck right to the bare metal beneath. Her knuckles went white on the steering wheel as she kept the truck solid as a rock, waiting for the last few inches to be severed and the rig to mash her right against the rail. She closed her eyes and counted to three, expecting the evitable. But when three was reached, something happened...She opened her eyes to the sight of the rig beside her suddenly retreating. It jerked over to the far left and sped up, passing the front semi as it went. Right at that moment, the rear semi followed suit, flying over into the other lane and passing Hutch right on by. All three of the Redgrace rigs blasted the gas and left her behind and that's when she saw it...A flurry of blue and red lights flooded her mirrors. As she slammed on her brakes and came to a stop on the side of the road, she realized she had never been so happy to see the cops in all of her life. And yet, she had never been so terrified either. She was busted for sure. The cops may have saved her sorry ass but she was going right back to jail, and fast. At least Hank couldn't kill her in there. With defeat, she slumped in the seat and rested herself against the steering wheel, peering up ahead to see the three Redgrace rigs all stopped in a row along the berm idling ominously. For a split second she thought about blasting the truck into drive, and just whipping out of there, but where was she going to go? She was in a pink truck for shit's sake, it didn't exactly scream anonymity. A sigh fell hard from her lips and her eyes drifted from the sight of the semis to the review mirror where she beheld a figure with a hat silhouetted in the spiraling lights from behind. It had to be a Statey...She would definitely be getting no mercy.

Hutch cut the engine, reached over, and began rolling down the window. The sound of the crank was soon overtaken by the fall of wet footsteps upon rain-drenched asphalt. The officer was almost right on top of her. What the hell was she going to say? What was her excuse? God, she was so stupid. She ruined everything. But what else was new?
Right then she became blinded by the flashlight of the officer.

"License and registration, slut!" A odd, gruff voice blasted into the cab. Hutch's eyebrow rose at the demand, but before she could even speak the flashlight clicked off and her eyes adjusted to an unbelievable sight. Standing there where an officer should've been, was a tiny brunette in a pinstripe suit and a huge Highway Patrol hat.

"Oh, Red, you should see the look on your face!" Regina belted out with a round of laughter. Hutch was speechless. What the hell was happening? She wanted to punch that smile right off the bitch's face, but couldn't bring herself to do it. Instead, she sat there in a menacing silence as her ears echoed with Regina's fading laughter.

The brunette sighed and grabbed the rim of the patrol hat she wore as she spoke,

"I told you I had the cop situation under control, didn't I?"

Hutch said nothing. She just stared forwards down the road.

"Ahhh, don't tell me you're gonna give me the silent treatment. That is so not you."

"You don't fuckin' know me."

"Welllll, I know enough to feel like maybe you were snooping a little. Hmmm? Doing a little snoopery? You know, Red...you're not doing your poor, sweet aunt any favors by pulling shit like this. Kinda makes me wanna withdraw our deal and disappear from your life altogether"

Hutch drew her attention back quickly, trying to hide a look of worry.

"But I won't....You know you are fucking adorable when you're mad and scared at the same time," Regina spoke as she reached into the cab, trying to playfully pinch at Hutch's cheek. The redhead slapped it away with a sneer.

"Feisty! There's that fire I like!" The brunette grabbed a handful of Hutch's hair and jerked her head over till their faces were only inches away from one another's. Hutch could feel Regina's breath gently brushing her lips as she gripped her hair painfully tighter.

"You wanna see your aunt again, Red?"

"You know I do."

"Then stop. Pissing. Me. Off. The next time you think about sticking your nose somewhere, you need to remind yourself where it really belongs...between my legs," With that, Regina laid a passionate kiss upon the redhead. She pulled away, still nibbling a bit on Hutch's lower lip, and released her grip on her hair.

"Now get the fuck out of my face. You gotta car build to finish," Regina spoke as she took off Hutch's hat and threw it to the truck floor. She then removed the patrol hat from her own head and placed it firmly on Hutch's, giving it a gently pat as she walked away.

"You have a nice night ma'am. Drive safe," the brunette laughed as she walked back to the cruiser. All Hutch could do was sit there and shake in the fury of the situation as the patrol car behind her peeled out and went screaming by. Regina laid on the horn and killed the spinning lights, passing Hutch on her way to meet the idle semis ahead. One by one, each of the three rigs took off in a lumbering synchronization, following Regina to a destination unknown. But just when she thought it was all over, it happened…a roar from behind. A familiar screaming and burning, hell of an engine, bellowing from the bowels of the night. She winced as the truck rocked in the aftermath of a car passing at over 100 MPH. It was a Plymouth Superbird.

"Absalom…" the name leaked from Hutch's lips while she watched its dingy taillights fade along with the others of Redgrace Logistics. The redhead was left all alone amongst the darkness of the interstate, her mind racing at thrice the speed of the car that had just passed. She couldn't help but notice there hadn't been one other normal car that passed on either side ever since the semis had blocked her in. What was, by all rights, a busy stretch of road, even this late at night, seemed no more than a thoroughfare for ghosts and whispers. Even the tiny wind left in the wake of the storm had little to no voice in Hutch's ears. It was all beyond bizarre and only added to the mystique that was Regina Redgrace. And amidst it all, she couldn't help but wonder just who Absalom really was. Masked man or no, he was obviously in league with Regina…Hutch was left with more questions than answers.

With an angry leer, the redhead ripped the patrol hat from her head and tossed it out the window. She quickly retrieved her own hat from the floor and placed it back atop her head as she kept her eyes fixed into the obsidian horizon where the brunette and the rigs had disappeared. With a defeated shake of her head, she turned the key over and threw the truck into drive. She pulled a U-turn across the drenched median grass and headed back east, to the shop…Sleep would not come that night.

Black and Blue Memories

"Well would ya look at this shit? Up with the sun, rarin' to go. I love how when you're supposed ta be at work you oversleep every goddamn day, but now that you have a personal project to work on, you're up before the rooster," Ham's voice echoed through the back garage as he spied Hutch toiling away under the hood of the Maverick. It was morning, thirty minutes before shop opening time and, as usual, he was the first one there, coffee in hand, bright-eyed and bushy tailed. He wasn't human. No one should be that happy in the morning, especially on a work day. Hutch spoke nothing back to her brother's smart-assed remarks. She kept grunting and working away on the front end of the engine. Ham walked over and stopped just a pace away, looking in at what she was dabbling in.

"Shit she's coming tagether. How much more you got to do?" He spoke as he took a swig of coffee. Hutch just kept mumbling incoherencies under her breath as she tugged and pulled away, adjusting bolts and realigning brackets. A solid minute of this yielded no response to Ham's question. He was beginning to think she was so entranced she had no clue he was even there.

"Hutch?....Hutch?....Hey?!"

"What?!" She finally burst aloud, breaking away from her spell of frustration. Still she kept her head down and hands busy.

"Hey? Look at me," Ham spoke. She did as she was told. "Jesus Christ. You didn't get here early...You been here all damn night."

"And how the hell would you know that?" Hutch growled.

"How could I not? Hell ya look like a damn raccoon with two black eyes and a coke habit."

"Thanks. I needed that this mornin'."

"Well? Ya want me ta lie to ya? That's your department. You look like shit."

"Okay! I fuckin' got it, alright!" Hutch yelled. She went right back to her ratcheting as she spoke again, "What the hell ya want me to do about it?"

"Well, for starters, get some goddamn sleep and knock this shit off," Ham spoke as he plucked one of six empty beer bottles off the top of the car.

"That's my go-juice," Hutch mumbled.

"Yeah, well you need to GO to bed."

"I'll sleep when I'm dead."

"Ya keep this shit up and that's statements gonna be truer than ya think," Ham said. Hutch just kept her mouth shut. Her brother placed the empty beer bottle back atop the Maverick and sighed.

"This car build is gettin' outta hand. You ain't got enough time. Can't you ask your girlfriend ta postpone this race the two of you got planned?" Right at that moment Hutch dropped her wrench to the floor and stood straight up, glaring at him.

"Yeah that's right...ya don't think I know what the fucks goin' on here? You're just like Cass, Hutch. This is like a drug ta you, always has been. Sixteen-thousand dollars for this car? My ass. Look at the interior? Look at the paint? I don't know how ya got Hank fooled on this. What are you two racin' for? What's the purse?"

"None of your fuckin' business," Hutch spoke coldly, still leering at him.

"Yeah that's what I thought…And what if you lose, Hutch? You got the money ta pay out? I doubt that shit. Hell if ya don't end up wrapped around a telephone pole during this dumbass race, you're gonna end up with two broken legs lyin' in a ditch somewhere when ya can't dish up the money for losin'. Ya remember what happened ta Aunt Cass when she lost and didn't cough up the money?"

"I ain't gonna lose!"

"Yeah, well, maybe, maybe not.…You said yourself ya don't know much about this girl. What if she's got a mob family and you end up with a bullet in your head and cinder blocks tied to your feet?"

"Sounds like a win/win ta me!"

"You don't mean that…"

"Oh, I fuckin' mean it! I really mean it! I can finally be out of everyone's hair! Who's gonna give a shit when I'm not around?!" Hutch's voice cracked under her bellowing. She fought back the tears.

"Hey! IM gonna care! Hayden and Heath are gonna care."

"Oh, bullshit," she mumbled.

"And as much as Hank treats you like dogshit, he'll care. Believe me, he may never show it cuz his black heart won't let em', but he'll care just like the rest of us." Hutch just crossed her arms with a sneer on her face. She remained silent as Ham finished the last gulp of his coffee.

"And speakin' of his royal highness…What story you gonna spin him bout that work truck when he gets back?"

Hutch's eyes widened. She had almost completely forgotten about the guardrail damage amidst the hell on the interstate.

"Yeah, ya better start thinking of somethin, and quick. What the hell happened anyway? You get hit by another masked man? Was it Absalom? Or was it a guy wearin' a wolf mask this time named Abraham."

"No. And what's that tone supposed ta mean? Ya don't believe me?"

"Hutch I learned a long time ago ta only believe about half of what comes out of your mouth. Now, what happened?" She stood there for a moment, gathering her thoughts. The flashbacks of the traumatic events played back across her mind in vivid-black shades of horror. She couldn't tell him the truth. Hell the truth was too unbelievable.

"I took a ride ta clear my head last night...deer ran out. I swerved, kissed a guardrail."

"Kissed a guardrail? Looks like you went all the way with that thing ta me....Jesus, Hutch...You're gonna have to..."

"Good fuckin' mornin'!" A voice roared into the garage. They whipped their heads to see Hank entering through the open overhead door from the back lot. Hutch shuddered.

"Hutch ya got about ten minutes ta wrap that bullshit up. You ain't doin' that on company time. Sandwich?!" Hank pointed at Ham, "Go unlock the front door, and prep the register, and turn the open sign on, and do whatever other worthless shit you do around this place. What I'm tryin' ta say is, get the fuck out of here."

Ham shook his head and headed for the back hall door.

"And make some coffee!!" Hank yelled.

"Already done," Ham yelled back.

"Okay...already done...right," Hank mumbled to himself as he turned his attention back to Hutch. "Sister of mine, you look like hammered shit this mornin'."

"Yep," was all Hutch responded. Hank took a few ominous steps towards her as she bellied back up to the Maverick, about to gather the tools she'd been using.

"What the fuck happened to my truck?" He asked coldly. Hutch could feel a lump building in her throat. She hadn't had the time to even prepare herself for this.

"Your truck? Don't you mean the shop truck?"

"Gettin' smart with me probably ain't the best course of action right now. So specifically, the pink, Ford truck outside with the huge fuckin' scrapes down the side of it. Now I assume you were here all damn night by the look of ya and your glass buddies perched on top of this piece of shit you're workin' on, so what the fuck happened?"

Hutch's mind went into a tizzy, trying to come up with something to save her own sorry ass. She was starting to wish she had beat the shit out of the thing and spray painted dicks all over it, although lightning didn't strike twice that often. But at least it would have given her some kind of satisfaction.

"I'm fuckin' waitin'," Hank began to lose his patience. Hutch had had enough.

"I did it, okay?! I fuckin' did it! I took the thing for a midnight ride and a deer ran out in front of me. I swerved hard and blasted a guard rail. End of story. Happy?" Hank's stare went dark as he stepped towards her, bridging the gap until she could feel his whiskey flavored breath blasting out his flaring nostrils. Still she didn't back down. For ten solid seconds the two glared each other down until, suddenly, Hank's eyes started to go soft and his cheeks rose up. He began to chuckle...and that same chuckle went straight into a full-on laugh. Hutch had no clue what to make of it. She kept standing there, chest puffed out, not knowing whether to keep her mouth shut or laugh right along with his inane behavior. But upon the cusp of the exact second she decided to smile, it happened. The fist happened. With a painful blow, Hank swung up quick and blasted her right across the mouth. She hadn't the chance to even reel from the strike when he laid his left fist hard right into her gut, dropping her forwards. She could do little more than gasp as he grabbed her and spun her round, pinning her arm behind her back and slamming the side of her face right into the fender of the Maverick.

"Remember when I told you NOT to make me regret givin' you that fuckin' key? Well this is me regrettin' it," he said as he twisted her arm all the more. Hutch winced in the absolute searing pain of her tendons being stretched beyond their limits. She could feel the warm blood welling up in the side of her check and rolling down the metal below. "I should break your fuckin' arm....But I'm not gonna. A dike with a broken arm ain't no good for finishin' a car," he spoke, his voice sounding of hardened steel. He leaned down till he was inches from her ear and whispered. "You're gonna get this car runnin', get paid, and I'm gonna take all that sixteen-thousand dollars to buy a new shop truck. So you can consider your debts NOT paid, and you can forget about gettin' Ruby back. Remember, I fuckin' own you." With that, he released his grip and threw her to the side. She hit the concrete with a pitiful thud and whimper. And just like that, Hank walked away like nothing had even happened, slamming the door to the back hall behind him, leaving his own sister battered and beaten upon the floor. She shook as she pulled herself up onto her hip, spitting blood as she went.

"You don't own me," she whispered as she wiped her mouth and stood up upon trembling legs. With a groan, she opened the passenger side of the Maverick and flopped into the seat. She stared out of the open garage door and felt the sting of the impending swelling overtake her lips and jaw. A tear ran down her cheek as the pain let a memory flood in and the words of Ham resounded from the not so distant past. *"Ya remember what happened ta Aunt Cass when she lost and didn't cough up the money?"* She did remember…She was there. And that motherfucker cheated….

1986…

"You takin' a long way round or what? This ain't the way ta Grizzy's," a sixteen year old Hutch questioned as she looked over at her Aunt.

"I know that, kid," Cass spoke at her post behind the wheel, her cigarette danced on her lips as she spoke again, "I told your dad that's where we were goin'."

"And we ain't?"

"Nope."

"So where are we goin'?"

"Kid, kid, kid, ya ask too many questions sometimes, ya know that? Ya just gotta learn ta let life be. Go with the flow. Carpe diem and all that shit."

"What?" Hutch raised a brow.

"There ya go again…"

Hutch just sighed and leaned back in her seat, watching the darkness of the road being cut in half by the lights of the Mustang.

"Relax. Here, get one of those in ya," Cass rummaged around and beckoned her pack of smokes to Hutch. She looked at her Aunt oddly, trying to decide what she should do.

"Oh, Jesus, kid just grab one already. Ya think I don't know about you gettin' busted two damn times at school for this shit? Now take one for I change ma mind?" Hutch quickly drew one out and put it in her lips. Cass handed her a lighter and she went to the task at hand, sparking the tip and inhaling the relaxing devil within.

"Thata girl!" Cass cheered, "Marlboro, that's on the food pyramid, right under beer and blackberry pie."

Hutch smiled at her Aunt's words as she blew the smoke out the window into the tepid September night.

"You really wanna know where we're headed?"

"I guess…"

"Ha! You guess…Well, ya know how you're always bitchin n' belly achin' about life bein' so damn boring and there ain't nothin' ta do round here?"

"I don't know why you're bein' so damn snarky, It's fuckin' true," Hutch said.

"Hell, I know its true, kid! I was your age once."

"Yeah, tell me bout your pet mastodon again."

"Watch it. It's a long and dark walk back home. Goddamn thirty-five ain't that old…Is it?"

"The hell it ain't, you're bout halfway ta bein' dead."

"Jesus Christ I never thought about it like that…That's just downright dark….Wait, what the hell was I talkin' bout 'fore you started bein' a little asshole?"

"It's boring round here. See, you're already gettin' senile."

"Damn right. It's boring, and lemme tell ya what, it only gets worse the older ya get. Ya, see kid, folks like you and me, we bore easily. Ain't our fault, it's in our nature. We're just different. That's why we break windows, get in fist fights over nothin', smoke in school," she pointed to her cigarette in example, "We…we just expect adventure and all life gives us in return is stagnation and stale bread, over and over, and pretty soon ya find yourself drunk every other night, snuffin' cigarettes out on your own nipples just to see if you still feel anythin'…" Hutch's eyes got wide. Cass went on, "…and it's in that moment you look up and know you got to find an outlet or you're gonna just fall down and whither like the dead flower you're becomin'. It's like the drag strip, for one. Hit the gas. Straight line. Hit the gas. Straight line."

"I thought you loved racin'," Hutch looked over at her.

"I do darlin', it's just…after goin' sixteen years in a goddamn straight line over and over again, no amount of cheerin' and trophies kills the monster inside."

"The monster?"

"The beast, kid. The darkness that sits in the corner waitin' for ya ta come off cloud nine and drag you back down into the swamp that is your miserable existence. When you think you finally found happiness, he's the one that whispers in your ear, '*Not so fast.*'" Hutch couldn't think of one word to say as her aunt went on about the mundanity of life. She was quite taken aback by it. That woman had always been haloed in rays of sunshine and hope bright enough to blind the doves that flew through them. Was it because she was getting older? Having some midlife crisis? Hutch was actually beginning to feel bad about busting her chops for being in her thirties? Even though it was just a joke.

"You know, I remember the first time I strapped into a car and tore off the line. Those tires hooked up and sent my heart right into ma damn stomach. Goddamn what a feelin'…It was terror and happiness. Darkness and light. Hell and Heaven wrapped up in a neat little package with a bow and tag signed 'To: Cassandra. Love, Gravity.' And it only lasted about twelve seconds but you know what? Beat the hell out of any roller coaster I rode or orgasm I'd ever had…or ever have had, if I'm bein' honest," Cass ended her sentence with a lonely stare as she drove almost on auto-pilot, flicking her ash out the window welcoming the ghosts from the past to visit her once again.

"Then the monster came?" Hutch broke the silence.

"The monster came… the creature came callin' with his bag of boredom and monotony and dumped it all over me like a bag of old burn-barrel ash. And he does it every damn night I race. Like clockwork, he's sittin' there in the passenger seat beside me, reminding me that no matter how fast I go. How many milliseconds I shave, or how many cheers I get, it's all for nothin'," Cass paused and flicked what was left of her cigarette out into the darkness. She looked over at her niece as she spoke again, "I'm retiring Hutch. I'm done with the track. I've been done with it for years."

Hutch was at a loss for words as she sat there staring, smoke paused inches from her gaping mouth. She never thought she'd hear such words in a thousand years come out from the Scarlet Harlot's mouth. She was a local legend, a track hero, she wasn't supposed to retire, she was supposed race till she was ninety years old or until the track took her away in a flash of fire and steel.

"Well…what're ya gonna do?" Hutch finally asked.

"What've been doin the past few years now. That's where I'm takin' ya…" as Cass's words slowed, so did the tires upon the Mustang. Hutch looked up to see them descending off the road into a gravely-bottom turn-around near the river. Through the phantasmal beams of the headlights, she beheld the sight of an old, beat up pick-up truck and a 70' Chevelle blacker than the night sky above. Three men stood near the vehicles with one of them at the forefront staring forwards with his hands on hips. He began to walk towards the Mustang as Cass rolled it to a crawling stop and killed the engine. The night air came to life with the sounds of katydids, rippling rapids, and the unnerving crunch of boots across gravel. Hutch leered with suspicion at the approaching man who smoked a skinny cigar dangling from a crooked grin. He looked like a crony right out of the movie Grease, with slicked back black hair to match his leather jacket, Hutch already didn't like the feeling of all this.

"Kid, look at me," Cass snapped her fingers for her niece's attention, "Let me do all the talkin'. You just keep your mouth closed. Can you do that?"

Hutch nodded and pitched her smoke out the window as the man in the leather jacket rounded to the driver's side.

"Well, well, there she is. Thought for a minute you weren't gonna show," his voice slithered forth a tone that Hutch could only imagine a snake would speak like.

"Yeah, well I'm here now. Let's get this show started."

"Now hold on just a minute," the man took his cigar from his mouth and bent down, resting his arms on the window frame of the Mustang. He stroked his grizzled beard and glared in at Hutch who just glared right on back.

"What the fuck is this, Cass? You bring me a little midnight snack," he smiled showing all of the ten teeth he had left in his head.

"No, Sid, I didn't. THIS is my niece and she's sixteen-fuckin' years old."

"Well that's a good eatin' age. What you say sweetie? I bet you like older men, don't ya? I'll give ya mustache ride. First ones free," he spoke as he leered at Hutch all the more. The goosebumps raised on her arms as she fought the urge to cuss him out.

"Sid, if you keep talkin' shit like that, I wanna remind ya, you're about a dozen fuckin' teeth away from a set of dentures. Do ya catch ma drift?"

"Now, now Cass I'm just havin' a little fun, you know that. Lighten' the fuck up. Besides, didn't you say no passengers. Did you just break the rules before we even started?"

"Mutherfucker I made the rules. You can have passengers, what I said was no collusion. Since I know you don't know how ta read let alone own a dictionary, that word means no outside bullshit. No other people trying to sabotage the race. Besides that, who the fuck are those two yokels over there?" She pointed to the men in the shadows beside the old truck.

"Oh, those two over there? They're my insurance case you decide not to pay up when I dust your ginger ass."

"So you brought two full grown men to make sure you get your money from a one-hundred n' twenty pound woman? Is that what I'm gatherin'? You're a real fuckin class act. Let me tell ya somethin, you might as well go ahead n' tell them two fuckwads over there ta take the party on home cuz you ain't winnin' nothin' tonight."

"Cass McCray, always talkin' shit," he shook his head and drew his attention back to Hutch. "Whata 'bout you, Red, you a shit talker too?"

"Don't call me Red you toothless fuck," Hutch hissed out.

"Hutch!" Her aunt admonished her with a fierce whisper. Sid just began to laugh away.

"Finally got a rise out of her. Hell, that didn't take much actually. She's definitely your niece."

"For shit's sake, small talk is over. Can we get this goddamn show on the road or what?"

"Oh now, I guess," Sid spoke then leaned into Cass, "Lemme get a kiss before we start?"

"Jesus, your breath smells like dogshit!" Cass pushed him away.

"Well that's better than dog pussy, right? HA!! Woof! Woof! Woof! Owwoooooooo!!!!" He laughed and howled into the night, inciting a chuckle from the men by the pick-up. "Okay, McCray since you're in such a hurry, lets move out."

"Hold it! The coin toss," Cass stopped him in his tracks.

"Hell…" he spoke as he walked back, pulling a quarter from his pocket. "Heads is lefty, tails is righty." With that he gave the coin a flip, caught it, and smacked it on his wrist. "Call it!"

"Heads," Cass confirmed. Sid slowly removed his hand and sighed,

"Shit….heads"

"Righties, bitch. Your nights already startin' out shitty."

"Fuck it, I'll beat ya out the gate anyway. You won't have it for long."

"Whatever you say."

"Meet ya up the road where we talked about." With that, Sid flicked his cigar into the weeds and walked back to the obsidian Chevelle. The beast roared to life and cut a rumble through the backwoods cul-de-sac that shook the leaves abounding. Cass answered back with the turn of her key, calling the Fastback into action. She revved the engine in a show of agitation as Sid sped by and up the gravel embankment, back onto the road. Cass was slow to follow, being sure to give the cronies he had brought along with him a proper stare down as she followed the Chevelle.

"Well I don't like the looks of those shit bricks one bit," she whispered.

"What the hells happenin'?" Hutch finally spoke up.

"Oh, C'mon, kid, you're a smart girl. What's it look like? We're killin' the monster and we're doin' it together."

"What?"

"We're racin', Hutch. And I assure you this ain't in no fuckin' straight line," Cass smiled as she topped the embankment and sped up the road. She looked like a woman possessed, the proverbial kid in the candy store. She was alive again and Hutch could see it beaming across her face. As they sped up the road a piece, the brake lights of the idle Chevelle could be seen ahead. Hutch turned her attention to Cass,

"What the hell is righties and lefties?"

"Right lane or left lane, kid. You flip a coin for it. You obviously want right lane, which we got. When ya get righties, not only do you get the choice lane you get ta do the count off. That's how we always do it."

"We? You just race this guy all the time?"

"No, we, as in, well…a lot of us. And not just drug dealin', scumfucks like Sid. All walks of life. Farmers, Businessmen, Waitresses, hell there's even a teacher among us. Some of us got aliases or nicknames. Moped Dave, Cotton Jenny, Barry The Boner, Chocolate Chubs, just ta name a few. Sometimes we race for money, Sometimes just glory."

Hutch smirked, "Chocolate Chubs?"

"Yeah. He's a black fella that races with us."

"Chocolate? Cuz he's black?"

"Ha! Hell no. One night he rolled his car and shit himself mid-tumble. He was fine but the interior of his car wasn't, if you catch my drift."

"Jesus. I don't even wanna know how Barry The Boner got his name," Hutch smirked. She could barely believe what she was hearing. She was smack dab in the middle of what appeared to be an illegal racing club. And Cass was the apparent ringleader. She went to speak again but her aunt cut her off.

"I'll explain all of this ta ya later in detail. Right now, we gotta race ta win." In the next moment, the Mustang was nose to nose with the idling Chevelle. They cut their engines off simultaneously, leaving the symphony of the night to serenade them once more.

"What you think, firebush, you ready for this shit?" Sid smiled.

"Always," Cass answered.

"I was talkin' to your niece, McCray," he chuckled. Hutch leaned over, about to unleash, but her aunt cut her down.

"Don't…you keep rollin' in shit with the pigs you eventually become one," she whispered.

"What's that, Cass, I didn't catch that. Speak up," Sid put a hand to his ear.

"I said, repeat the route!"

"Oh, bullshit. We know the route."

"Repeat the shit, now."

Sid sighed, "Up Dry Fork, left on Oak Hollow, right on Grayson. Does that please the Harlot?"

"Finish line?" She said.

"Christ…the four way on Grayson where Lobdell crosses. Now can we fuckin' race or what?"

"Start em'," Cass spoke. With that, the two machines exploded back into existence, their spinning cams loping a fire-breathing song of hell and carbon flavored ash. There was a hush before the storm as the two racers eyed each other down amidst the smell of the stinging fumes surrounding.

"Grab onto something kid, shits about ta get rad," Cass spoke, never taking her gaze from Sid's.

"Count it from three, bitch!" Sid yelled out.

"One....Two..." Hutch swallowed hard in the nanosecond before the bomb dropped,
"THREE!!!"

The September air exploded with the sounds of squealing tires and internal detonation. The two blasted off the line, screaming neck and neck down the dark, backroad, fighting tooth and nail for pole position. Hutch could barely breathe. She was sucked back into her seat with her panicked heart beating inside her guts....And it was orgasmic.

"C'mon, fucker!!" She could barely hear Cass scream as she shifted hard and fast, trying like hell to get a nose out on the roaring Chevelle beside them. Hutch couldn't figure out if she was yelling at Sid or her own car, but soon, none of that mattered. She pulled away and took the lead, driving herself smack dab in the center of the road so he couldn't pass.

"Ha! Ha! Suck on that, ya gummy, bastard!" Cass cheered herself on. Hutch was thrown back and forth across her seat as her aunt began swerving left and right, continually slapping down every foolish attempt Sid made at passing. The teenager looked over her shoulder with wide eyes. The Chevelle was now only inches from their bumper. So close she couldn't even see the headlights nor the 'SS' emblem between them. She quickly jerked her head round and laid her gaze upon the gauges in front of Cass. They were topping 100 MPH...but not for long.

"Hold on!" Her aunt caterwauled as she downshifted and smashed the brake...The first shift on the race route had come. Gravity reversed itself, throwing Hutch forwards and then against the door as tires screamed and brakes burned in a maddening slide of a left hand turn. As the car violently righted itself, Hutch looked back to see Cass had created a sizable gap in the race with her maneuver. Sid had fallen far behind, nearly blasting into the fence row at the mouth of the road amidst his sloppy turn. But despite the fully lain throttle of the Mustang, the Chevelle was quickly regaining ground. The second leg of the race proved to be far more winding. Hutch grit her teeth as they slid round hairpin turns and snaked along for nearly a mile with her knuckles burning white atop gripping fists. Her aunt was now possessed. She could see it in her eyes. The way she wavered not in spirit nor body, her limbs acting as a well oiled machine, shifting, turning, gassing, braking in absolute perfection within perfection…Then the Lobdell Road sign came. The last turn was reached. Hutch tried her best not to careen into her aunt as the screeching tires paced a path onto the third and final stretch. The rear end of the car violently fishtailed and whipped as a collision was made courtesy of the Chevelle kissing the Mustang bumper.

"Fucker!!" Cass yelled out as Hutch's eyes grew wider amidst the escalating turbulence. Like the true racer she was, Cass righted her rig straight and punched the gas to leave Sid in the dust once again. The four-way stop was not even a mile away now…

"We got em', kid! We got the bastard!" Her aunt bellowed in absolute elation. But suddenly, her smile erased at the sight up the road. Two perfect glowing spheres cut through the darkness of the back road. A car was coming…

"Shit. Shit. Shit," Hutch chanted at the sight of the oncoming headlights.

"Calm down! This shit happens. I got this!" Cass hovered in the center of the road, waiting for the perfect moment to fly over into the right lane and let the oncoming car pass right on by. Hutch once again looked behind them. The Chevelle had slowed way down. So much in fact that she could barely see his lights. Something wasn't right.

"Aunt Cass.."

"Shut up, Hutch! I said I got this!" Cass cut her off fast, never averting her stare on the road in front of her.

"C'mon, C'mon…" she chanted with eyes transfixed on the blinding headlights barreling down. "Now!" A command blasted from her lips as she braked and downshifted, sliding gracefully into the legal lane. Things didn't go to plan. In what seemed like an all out intentional maneuver, the passing vehicle went left of center, headed right towards the Mustang.

"What the FUUU!!!!" Cass could barely expel. Hutch closed her eyes right as the vehicle passed, the last thing she saw was a familiar beat up truck as the wheel was jerked in evasion. They blasted into the berm hard and the Mustang violently bounced around as the passenger side wheel dipped into the ditch. A mixture of squalling tires, cussing, and shredding metal resounded as Cass tried to keep everything together. But in that instant, the Chevelle went screaming on by, taking the lead with ease.

"Goddamn it!!!" Cass screamed. She jerked the wheel hard to the left and hopped out of the grip of the ditch. The sickening sound of metal kissing pavement resounded amongst the sound of an exhaust that was now twice as loud as before. One of the mufflers had been torn off and was now dragging and bouncing beneath them as Cass made a do-or-die run for the taillights in front of her, but it was simply too late. Sid plowed right through the four-way stop with a triumphant war hoop that could be heard even over the Mustang's damaged exhaust. Three seconds later, Cass went through the four way, she slowed down to a normal speed as she got behind the Chevelle.

"Sonuvabitch!!" She screamed as she punched the steering wheel. Sid pulled over into another cul-de-sac similar to the one they had met up in before, off the road, down into the woods. Cass quickly followed and slammed on her brakes. She threw the Mustang into park and began digging under her seat as she expelled an indiscernible tirade of cussing and ranting.

"Wait here!!" She commanded to her shaken niece as she pulled out a tire iron from underneath her seat and threw the door open. With a huff, she went out to meet the supposed victor as he climbed out of his car with a smile on his face.

"WOOHOO! Where's my money, bitch?!" He took a few steps towards her then stopped as he saw the tire iron in the lights of the Mustang. "What the fucks this shit, McCray? You bein' a sore loser?"

"Remember what I said about bein' a dozen teeth away from a pair of dentures? It's game time! Who the fuck was in that truck back there?!"

Sid put his hands up and chuckled in disbelief. "What now?! Who?! Just calm your ass down a minute. Put that shit down 'fore you get hurt."

"Only one gettin' hurt round here is your coked-out ass. Now I'm gonna ask ya again, who was in that truck?! They swerved right at me!" Right at that moment, the turn around was lit even brighter by another set of headlights. The truck who had housed Sid's "insurance" had arrived. They pulled up on the far left and the two piled out, coming up behind Cass where she stood, ready to fight.

"Shit…" was all Hutch could whisper to herself as the situation went from bad to worse. She was beginning to regret all of those times she talked about her boring life to her aunt.

"Put it down," one of Sid's henchmen spoke as he spit a wad of tobacco.

"You heard the man, Cass. Put that shit down now. Pay what ya owe me and ya walk out of here stead of crawlin'," Sid's voice went from cheerful to menacing faster than he'd crossed the finish line. Cass was quiet as she looked at the headlights of the truck, the same shape of the ones that still burned into her retinas from moments before. Her gaze drew to the two men.

"You dirty motherfuckers…it was you two," she pointed the tire iron at them.

"Better calm that tone and stop pointin' stuff at me, bitch."

"Cass. Cass. We can sit here and argue all night bout who did what, but we both know who crossed that finish line first. Am I wrong? I ain't wrong…" Sid's voice turned to a patronizing tone as he crept towards her. She spun round and shoved the steel rod towards his face.

"Back the fuck off!" Sid stepped back with his hands up as she howled on, "There ain't nothin' ta argue, ya cheatin' piece of shit! There's rules to this game!"

"Yeah, YOUR, rules, Cass. Maybe it's time you stepped down off your podium as leader of this little club and let someone new take the reins. Start makin' this shit a tad more interestin'."

"Who?! You?! Ha! Go fuck yourself, Sid. I started this 'little club' you sorry piece of shit and the minute I tell the others about this, your ass is kicked out. No question."

Sid's demeanor went darker.

"Okay then, Cass. If you make all the damn rules then what's your mental rulebook say when two people reach an agreement on a purse and the one loses and don't follow through?"

Cass hesitated before she spoke.

"It says the two have to hash it out amongst themselves, but---"

"No buts, Cass, let's hash this out!" Sid yelled and nodded. Suddenly, Cass was grabbed from behind, wrapped in a bear-hug by one of the henchmen. She started screaming a storm of obscenities not even a sailor could discern as Sid stepped forwards and clocked her hard across the face.

"You fucker!" She yelled as she dropped her tire iron and spit blood in his direction. He went in again but was met with a violent kick right to the groin. He dropped like a bag of hammers while the other two started swinging in from the sides, blasting her ribs and face over and over as she desperately tried to break free. It all happened so fast that Hutch could barely even react. Her eyes went wide as she tore off her seatbelt in a wild panic, flinging the door open with a scream as Sid returned to his feet.

"Get off of her!"

Sid looked over at her and smiled as he held his crotch, nearly out of breath.

"Oh, you just sit tight now, firebush. You're next," with that said, he ran right back into the rampage of the fight. Fists flew and bones cracked amidst the sickening beatdown Cass was at the epicenter of. She got a few hits in but was simply no match for three grown men.

"Get the fuck back!" Cass's weakening voice gurgled from her bloody face, warning her niece to stand down. Hutch ran closer and stopped to see the abandoned tire iron lying in the dirt. She pounced upon it and raised up, blasting Sid right in the side of the neck. He hit his knees and grabbed his throat.

"You fu-fu-ckin, little cunt," he could barely squeak out. Hutch raised the tire iron high ready to drop the pain but she was shoved to the ground by one of the other men. Within a split second, the man was on top of her, fists raised, ready to unleash his fury when all of a sudden her ears were deafened by a bellowing horn. The man rolled off of her as a truck came to a sliding halt only yards away. With a dizzy head, Hutch laid there and watched as the men got closer to one another, still holding onto her aunt, but peering with worried eyes through the blinding lights of the intruding pick-up. Was it the sheriff?

"Well would ya look at this shit! I've seen momma possums with bigger balls than you three!" A familiar voice roared atop a slamming truck door.

It wasn't the sheriff…but they were going to wish it had been.

"Fuck off! This don't concern you!" Sid got his voice back.

"Now ya see, that's where you're wrong. That piece of hamburger meat you're hangin' onto there? That's my aunt," Hank McCray's voice sliced the air amidst his ebbing footsteps. He stopped at the front of his truck, cracking his knuckles so loudly they could be heard over everything the night had to offer.

"Ya see, this is normally the part where I would say, 'Let go of her and get in your cars and no one gets hurt'," he said while he rolled up his sleeves, "But, that ain't happenin'. Someone's definitely gettin' hurt."

"Don't just stand there, fuck em up!" Sid commanded to his buddies.

"Sid, you know who the fuck he is?! That's the Hank the Tank!"

"Who?"

"He fuckin' bare knuckle fights down at Abby's. They had em' fight a live bear one night over there," he looked right at Sid, "The bear didn't win."

"Jesus H Christ, that's a bullshit rumor," Hank shook his head, "It was TWO bears at once. Now…y'all want ma autograph or ya gonna put those fists up?" He finished, impatience growing by the second. Suddenly, the man that still held Cass threw her to the ground. She crumpled into a moaning pile as he walked a line right at Hank muttering, "I got this shit.."

"Oh you got this shit, brother?" Hank patronized him as he walked closer, putting up his dukes. The man said nothing as he eyeballed Hank down and stepped up to the plate. He swung wildly as the eldest McCray dodged and juked out of the way with ease. Then, with one seamless move, Hank blasted the henchman in the jaw, spun him round, and drove his face right into the fender of the truck. The man fell into a miserable pile. Hutch clearly remembered thinking he had killed him. Hell she wasn't convinced he hadn't and no one came to claim the body.

"Well, that was goddamn pathetic," Hank smirked in disappointment.

"Get em!" Sid shoved the remaining henchman.

"Fuck you! You get em!"

"Oh for shits sake! Why don't you two just get me together? Didn't work out too well for those bears though," Hank scoffed. And so the two of them did. They rushed in head-on to meet him thinking they had safety in numbers…Not so much. Fists flew and bones cracked amongst the melee. Hank kicked the henchman's knee in and bent it backwards. He screamed like a girl as he went to fall to the ground, but Hank silenced him with an uppercut that sent him to the dirt even faster. Sid backed off, his bloodied face had already taken two hits and he was staggering, trying to fight the dizziness overtaking him.

Hank put his fists up and started to stare overtop them but his eyes widened at the sight of a tooth stuck in his knuckle. With disgust he pulled it out and held it between his fingers as he looked at Sid.

"Jesus…is that yours?" He laughed.

Sid, reached into his pocket and whipped out a butterfly knife. He flipped it open with a menacing grace and pointed it at Hank.

"What the hell ya think you're gonna do with that?"

"I'm gonna lay you open, boy!" Sid yelled as he rushed in and started slicing. Hank went to swing but Sid ducked and stabbed. The knife buried in his hip and stuck there as the eldest McCray pushed Sid off and started blasting him in the face over and over until he could barely see out of his swelling eyes. Sid hit his knees and rolled back, slamming against the Chevelle that had gotten him into this mess in the first place. Hank slowly backed off with a smirk on his face but soon felt the warm flow of liquid down his leg. He turned to see the knife still sticking from his flesh and he chuckled a bit through the pain.

"Well goddamn…would ya look at that," he grinned as he pulled the knife from his hip with a wince and a sigh. "Nice pig-sticker…" Hank said as he looked at the weapon he now held. He read the name upon it. "Caldwell, huh? I'll make sure they carve that on your tombstone." His attention slowly drew from the bloody knife to the man he had just sent to the ground. With a heavy stride he walked over, flipping the blade around in his hand, ready to stab Sid where he laid.

"Hey! You dropped somethin'!" Hank yelled down at him as he went to plunge the steel deep.

"Stop!!" A voice cracked from behind. Hank halted the knife just inches from Sid's stomach and turned round to see Hutch rolling up on her hip in the gravel.

"Just stop…" she whined with a tear gracing her eye. She had seen enough. Hank sighed and turned round to Sid. He grabbed him by the collar and hoisted him up to a stand like a limp doll.

"You see that girl right there?" Hank snarled into Sid's face. Sid could barely see anything, he just stared in Hutch's general direction and said nothing.

"I said, do ya see her?!" Hank screamed in his face. Sid nodded in a fit of terror. "Good. That there's my baby sister. And she just saved your life. Now, you need to thank her from keepin' me from cuttin' you dick-to-ear, you sorry sack of shit." Sid just wavered there where he stood, with Hank's hand still tight to his collar. "Well?!" Hank yelled, waiting for his order to be carried out.

"I…I'm sorry," Sid whimpered.

"That's a gentlemen right there!" Hank said. He then grabbed Sid up and tossed him violently through the open window of his Chevelle. He crumpled into a moaning pile with the shifter jamming into his back. Hank brushed off the knife and placed it into his pocket, then walked over and grabbed Cass up from where she still laid. He dragged her across the gravel by the back of her jacket and dropped her right beside Hutch.

"Get her in the car and get the fuck out of here," Hank commanded.

"You're bleedin'…" Hutch looked at the growing red patch on her brother's hip.

"It's a fuckin flesh wound, Hutch. Nothin' a little duct tape won't fix. Now get the fuck outta here, I said." He began walking back to his truck.

"Wait…what…what do I do with her?" Hutch looked at her brother with terrified eyes.

"I don't give a shit. Take her to the ER, the morgue, whichever comes first. And hey? I wasn't here. YOU weren't here. Now get goin'," Hank spoke as he slammed his truck door. He tore off, leaving Hutch sitting there amongst a whirlwind of dust and the beaten body of Cass. Soon, all she heard were the sounds of the katydids and crickets once more. She had never felt so alone in her entire life.

Reality soon flooded back in, along with it the pains of her newly inflicted wounds. She felt her swollen lip and jaw, and once again played back the scenes of Hank beating those men all to a pulp that night. To this day, she couldn't help but wonder if he'd fought them because he actually cared about her and Cass, or he did it simply because he liked hurting people…Maybe it was a little bit of both. With a grunt, she pulled herself back out of the Maverick and grabbed a greasy rag to wipe away the blood from her lips. She spit crimson over and over into it as she stood there leaned against the car that had vicariously gotten her into all of this mess. The creeping pain in her jaw slowly began to slither into her neck and head amidst the thoughts of Hank's punishment. Sadly, she knew damn well that he didn't even hit her close to full force. If he had, she'd be waking up in a seedy ER with no recollection of anything that happened the past twenty-four hours…Hell, maybe that would've been the better scenario. All in all, the thoughts of handing over sixteen-thousand to him when this was all over, hurt more than the pain he had dished out…but it was a small price to pay to get him out of her life forever….That is, if she would win the race. No, she had to win. There was no other option. With nothing more to mull over but dull aches and unfinished cars, Hutch slowly walked out into the morning sun of the back lot, and left the Gingerbread House behind.

"Where's Hutch?" Ham finally let forth a inquiry that had plagued him since Hank had re-entered the building with a smirk on his face.

"Don't know, and don't fuckin' care," Hank answered as only Hank could. He walked on by the counter with his slight signature limp and disappeared into the office without another word. A chill ran up Ham's spine as a dozen scenarios, none of them good, trudged through his mind of Hutch's absence. He soon found himself walking down the back hall and throwing the door open. He hoped beyond hope that Hutch was still back there, ignoring Hank's words to get on the clock, toiling away on the Maverick, but cold silence and a tiny breeze were all that greeted his worried stare.

"Hutch?...Hutch?" Ham called out as he closed the door behind him and walked out through the garage. The sun soon stung his gaze as he panned the back lot. She wasn't back with the beaten shop truck, nor round the front smoking a cigarette. As Ham stopped at the corner of the shop, he stared out through the vast herd of idling rigs for even the slightest glimpse of his missing sister. Then his eyes turned to the camper along the edge of the lot…Surely she wasn't?

'*Knock. Knock. Knock,*' rapping fell across a flimsy aluminum door.

"Fuck off," a voice stung back from inside. At least she was alive, Ham thought.

"Hey, what're you doin' in there?" He spoke through the door.

"Hidin' from life…Now get fucked," she said.

'*Knock. Knock. Knock,*' he blasted the door harder.

"We've already established that I'm in here so why the hell ya still knockin?!"

"To annoy ya. Is it workin?" Ham spoke with equal irritation. Right then the door came flying open with Hutch leering down at him, ice pack held to the side of her face. Her left eye was already starting to blacken. Her brother could do nothing more than just stare at what he knew was the aftermath of Hank. His blood began to boil.

"What the fuck?...He do this to you?"

"Naw, I fell on my face while walkin' over here…What do ya think?"

"I'm gonna kill em'…" Ham mumbled as he turned round to walk off.

"Stop!" Hutch yelled. He spun round. "You ain't doin' shit," she added.

"What? Ya don't think I can take em?"

"No, I don't. You fuckin' go back in there and start shit you're gonna end up just like me, black eye, busted lip and….and…" she felt at her mouth with an odd look on her face. She bared her teeth a bit, something was off. "Son of a bitch! He knocked ma tooth out!" Ham watched his sister stand there wide eyed, pushing her tongue through a small gap beside her canine.

"Good god…well he obviously found out about the truck…"

"Ya fuckin' think?" Hutch smarted off.

"We can't just let him get away with shit like this," Ham said.

"Really, we can't? We've been lettin' him our whole lives. Why change now? Besides, I figured you'd be proud of me."

"What? Why?" His eyes narrowed.

"I took responsibility for my own bullshit for once. I didn't come ta you askin' for help. I didn't blame someone else. I didn't run away till it all blew over...Maybe I had this one comin'...."

"He walloped you, Hutch. You're a woman for Christ sake..."

"I'm a woman? I'm a woman?!" She became riled at the statement, "No, I'm person who made a dumbass choice and I paid the piper in the end....let's just fuckin' let it go." There was a brief silence between the both of them, one that was drowned to death by the sounds of the rigs behind.

"So...what are ya gonna do?" Ham finally asked.

"What am I gonna do?" She pulled the ice pack away from her jaw, "I'm gonna do what I need to. March right back in there, sweep the floors, empty the cans, and act like nothin' happened. God knows that's what he's gonna be doin'. He may've beat my face in, but I'm not givin' him the goddamn pleasure of me tuckin' tail and not facin' him for the rest of the day." Ham simply nodded at her plans. There wasn't much more to say. "But before I do all that, I'm gonna have a smoke," she spoke up again and she placed a cigarette in the side of her mouth. To her surprise, the Marlboro tucked up into the gap where her tooth had been and stuck there. She relaxed her lips a tad and smiled even though it hurt to do so. "Shit, would ya look at that? It's like a damn smoke holder." She pointed to the cigarette that was firmly jammed between her teeth. "Well, that's one upside of gettin' ma clocked cleaned, I guess." The flick of her lighter resounded and she exhaled a plume of smoke as she spoke again, "Every dark cloud, right?"

"If you say so, Hutch," Ham sighed, "If you say so."

The Dog's Leg

The rest of that day was cold as cold could be within the concrete walls of the Gingerbread House. The normal banter, practical jokes, and flinging insults went extinct among the siblings. Everyone knew what had happened between Hank and Hutch. Even Hayden and Heath knew, despite the fact that no one spoke one word of it to them…the evidence was written all over their sister's face. And in that wake of realization, they left her alone. They didn't throw things on the floor just for her to sweep up, they didn't gang up on her with unnecessary insults, they remained quiet for the most part, turning wrenches and grinding metal. And maybe, on some level, this is exactly what Hank had wanted, for everyone to be quiet and subservient. Or at least it was a thought that had dawned on Hutch after being amongst the wretched silence for hours on end. Perhaps he had won…Perhaps her beat down was more than just about a scraped up truck and more about returning some sick alpha-dog order to the shop. What better way to shut others up than letting one of them parade around with the scars of disobedience painted on her face in fresh shades of blacks and blues. She shook her head of it. She was giving her brother more credit than he was due…Or was she? All she knew was McCray Machine was turning into something far different than when her father ran the place. Yes, there was tough love and shit sandwiches to eat on the regular back then, but the state of it now was just…morose. In the end, she felt there was simply nothing she could do about it. So she did the only thing she could - She became a good little dog. She swept the floors, stayed silent, and she bided her time, waiting for her chance to break her chain and never return…

And so evening crept in again. Everyone parted ways in the same hollow silence that had embraced them for that entire day, everyone except for Ham. He was the last to leave, telling Hutch goodbye and not to do anything stupid as he exited the garage where she went back to task once again. She cleared away the empty shells of the glass demons from the night before. Tossing them into the bin with a solemn vow that she wouldn't crack anymore open that night…of course, she was lying to herself. One hour into the aggravation of trying to line up the pulley and belt system upon the engine led her into a beer run over at Piper Jean's. She was beginning to think there just wasn't enough alcohol in the place to ebb the frustrations of this build and the pain that seared across her face. A pain that only worsened every time she bent forwards to work on the car…a six pack would do the trick…or maybe two.

Hours passed and the pulley system finally fell into place with the proper spacers and adjustments. She stood back to look at the fruits of her labor, but instead of feeling accomplished, she felt numb to everything. Once again, the thoughts of Cass not being there to see this build made it seem all for naught. Funny how the departing of one soul from your life could change the feelings of all you did from there on out. With that thought kept close, she cracked open another beer and downed a healthy gulp, plopping herself into the front seat of the Maverick as she fished out the keys. The time had finally come. The moment of truth. Gas tank was full. Fluids topped off. Everything accounted for. She slid the key into the ignition and turned it with reluctance…nothing happened. She became instantly agitated as she held her beer in one hand and twisted the key back and forth in the other as if her anger was going to change the fact that the car just wasn't starting.

Hell it wasn't even making a sound. With a grunt, she leapt from the seat and slammed the beer down on the roof, leaving it behind as she began searching under the hood, looking through the wiring for obvious signs of disconnect. She knew damn well the battery was good and charged. A loathing of her own stupidity soon grasped her as she looked down to see that the starter wasn't even hooked up. The main wire dangled there where she had left it days before. She rolled her eyes and grabbed up a wrench, leaning deep into the mess, popping on the bolt and securing the terminal.

"Well, that should make a difference, you stupid bitch," Hutch whispered in admonishment of herself. But, just as she was about to rise back up, she saw it lying there. An ivory-yellow fragment that just didn't belong amongst the abstract of steel and aluminum. It was her tooth. It could've been mistaken for a tiny pebble had the car not seen the road for so many years. Her eyes widened in an almost disgusted manner as she reached in and retrieved it from where it laid nestled down by the engine mount. She looked it over with her drunken head spinning all the more in the thoughts of how it came to be there. Her lip curled and she shook her head while she flicked her tongue round the empty slot where the tooth laid less than a day ago. She placed the tiny piece of herself right into her pocket not knowing what the hell she was keeping it for exactly. With that, she once again retrieved her beer and flopped into the driver seat with her fingers caressing the key in a moment of hesitation. She stopped breathing for a moment.

"Hell with it…" she finally expelled and turned the key. The starter whirred and engaged, rotating the engine into an explosion that Hutch's buzzed brain was barely prepared for. The walls of the garage reverberated with the thunderous roar of the monster as it came to life, caterwauling its glorious rebirth into the ears of its maker. Hutch's heart fluttered amongst the clamoring symphony and the smell of freshly spun fire and steel. She smiled wide as she took another drink from the bottle she held, letting the shuddering lope of the beast rock her body through the vinyl seat that felt more like a throne at that moment. Every slice of pain that still throbbed through her mouth and jaw seemed to melt away in that glorious moment…She had done it. She had brought the monster to life. Her growing grin was simply inerasable now. With a spike of adrenaline, she blasted the gas pedal down with two deep pumps.

She knew she shouldn't be doing it, but she couldn't resist the urge of hearing the beast rev up and scream its song of detonation into the surrounding walls. It delightfully deafened her as she whooped her own song of victory into the air, feeling the unbridled power of the engine as it twisted the frame and rocked the Maverick to one side.

Hutch sat there and took another minute to revel in what seemed like the first positive thing that had come her way in recent memory. Soon, she calmed herself and slammed the door as she threw the beast into reverse. She backed up and then went forward, piloting the car till the front end was just outside the open garage door. Then she went to…the task of breaking in the engine. It was the last thing she wanted to do at that moment. As she looked out through the darkness, all she could imagine was her plowing the gas and riding off into the night, never to return, but alas she could not…the break-in process was important, as a machinist, she knew this. With great reluctance, she exited the Maverick, and spent the next few hours monitoring the RPMs, checking the ignition curve, and adjusting. All through the process she felt like a kid on Christmas Eve…heart aflutter, patience pushed to the max, and wide-eyes soft and shining in the wake of the excitement that was yet to come…and so it did. A falling garage door signified the end of the break-in. Hutch walked out through the door, back to where she had left the beast idling in the side lot. She was a sight for sore eyes, that car. Hutch couldn't help but take a moment to look at her in the glory of the open air as she purred away in a lope amidst the tiny, screaming whirr of the supercharger atop her. Cass would've melted at this. Hutch could just see that freckled smile lighting up the night as she spoke the words "We did it kid. We brought er' back ta life." And then she would've teared up. That woman was something else. Break her heart or slap her face, she wouldn't shed a tear, but show her a beautiful car and she'd cry like a baby. Lord, how she missed that crazy bitch…

In some involuntary maneuver, Hutch went to shut the hood of the Maverick down but suddenly realized there was none. She hadn't put it back because it still needed cut out to accommodate the blower on top of the engine. She shrugged as she lit up a cigarette. Hoods were overrated anyways. With nothing else to do, she once again fell into the driver's seat and shut the door. As she looked out through the idling lightshow that was the semi lot, she began to wonder if a break-in ride was the greatest idea given the previous night's events…She couldn't help but wonder what fresh hell awaited her out in the blackness beyond. And then there was the fact that she was slightly inebriated…That six pack-plus had gone bye-bye slowly over the course of the night, but she was still feeling it just the same. Her eyes narrowed as all the thoughts of why this was a bad idea picked away at her, but soon enough she stuck her cigarette in her tooth gap and shifted into drive. She looked over at the empty passenger seat just picturing Cass being there as the Maverick lurched forwards with an anxious breath that matched her own.

"Well…this bitch ain't gonna break herself in…" Hutch muttered as she made her way to the open road.

In the next hour, Hutch found herself snaking around the back roads and straight-aways of the county, making damn sure not to even come within eyeshot of the interstate or worse yet, a Redgrace rig. Though quite traumatic, the events from the night before seemed to disappear, replaced with the memories of what the roads beneath her tires now evoked. The comfort of the summer night's air whipping through the open windows of the Maverick brought a long forgotten peace back into her heart. Everything seemed so right yet so wrong at the same time…Memories of the ill shit her and Cass used to partake in came flooding back. The smell of the burnt rubber. The dark and humid kiss of the July air. The orchestra of frogs and crickets that serenaded alongside burning pistons and dancing cams. She remembered the races…the bad and the good. But mostly the good. Hell, the very road she was on was once a route for a race she did, and probably the same held true for Cass countless other times before her. It was real out here…raw. Nothing like the shining lights and madness of the strip. Out here it was two cars, two people, and the sweet embrace of the nighttime air.

As the 3 a.m. hour passed, she felt her drunkenness begin to wear off and become replaced with a trancelike state that she could've stayed in forever if she were allowed the pleasure…but such euphoria was not meant to last…She blasted the brakes as soon as she saw it. The smell of burning brakes and violated rubber filled her nostrils as the car came to a complete stop and angrily idled there in the blackness of the road. With grave reluctance, she looked into the rearview to see the source of her malcontent. There, illuminated in the ghostly red shades of the taillights, was a road sign that read "Banner's Ridge" It was a route that eventually lead into the backside of town, on the south side of the river, a normal road one could say, but for Hutch, and most of her family, it was often avoided. She felt her inner peace take its last breath as she kept a sideways eye upon the road sign behind her. Her stare soon drifted to the forefront…there was nothing there behind her eyes. She felt numb as she shifted the beast into reverse against her best wishes, slowly drifting back until the old road marker was ahead of her. With a sigh, she pulled her cigarette from her mouth and flicked what was left into the darkness…she had to go down that road. She owed it to herself. The smooth shift of the drive gear fell forth and before she could even breathe, all four tires were slowly moving towards a place of despair.

A mile went by at a zombie's pace. Her eyes darted through the glow of the headlights as if she were looking for the very ghosts she expected to be haunting this place. It wasn't even the road itself as much as what lie up ahead upon that road that was the harbinger of bad memories and dark times. But soon, the lights illuminated a sign "Warning 10 mph" accompanied by an arrow taking an extreme left hand turn. Hutch slowed the Maverick all the more and then made a complete stop as her widening eyes beheld the spectacle ahead. It was the Dog's Leg, or at least that's what most local people called it. But she had heard it called a plethora of other monikers – The doom pipe. The keyhole. Cass had always called it the stair step. It was essentially a tunnel going under an abandoned railroad, but the road took an extreme left turn into it with nearly no warning aside from one sign. The tunnel itself was barely wide enough to get one car through, and then, on the other side, it took another extreme turn to the right. It was everything a safe road pass shouldn't have been and as Hutch turned off the key to the Maverick and arose from the door, she wondered just why in the hell it was still here. She shuddered in the silence as she walked away from the car, leaving the door wide open and lights still on. The closer she got to the tunnel, the colder it became. The chilling, mossy breath of the opening began to chase away the humid night air that once surrounded her. She could feel her heartbeat elevate beyond her control, along with her breath…She shouldn't have been there. She needed to get the hell back in the car and turn round, go home and call it a night. But no…she kept walking, pacing herself as she followed her own apprehensive shadow that cast across the wall leading into the Dog's Leg. And there, atop that very wall was the object she searched for…an old wooden cross. With all the graffiti and signs of vandalism, she couldn't believe it was still there. She stretched up and brushed away the vines and debris, revealing a weathered name carved into it "H. McCray". Henry…It was the very spot where he took his last breath. It had been exactly thirteen years since that night. He was twenty-six years old, the same age as Hutch was now… Her heart sank as she saw another word carved into the cross vertically, "MURDERER". She would never forget waking up that next morning to the news, she became absolutely numb to it, as if it were all some nightmare. Her mother was sobbing. Her father was inconsolable…Hutch had never seen him like that. There wasn't one coherent thing coming out of that man's mouth for the next two days…her mother almost had to make funeral arrangements by herself it was so bad. There was no doubt in her mind that a piece of everyone in the family passed along with him that horrible night…but he wasn't the only one to die…You see, the Dog's Leg had a reputation other than being a headshaker of road engineering…Some people, more specifically, gear heads, had turned it into a game, trying to see how fast they could take their car through the tunnel and manage not to hit the sides of it. You had to be good to do it and any rate of speed…damn good. The walls were peppered and smeared with the remnants of paint from cars past trying to "shoot the dog" as it came to be known. It was no secret that Cass had done it many times, but apparently Henry had decided to take his skill off the track and give it a whirl that night. Unfortunately, there was another vehicle coming through the tunnel on the opposite side. A husband and wife and their son and daughter, coming home from a late night softball game down in River Park. As they went through the tunnel and rounded the turn, Henry hit their car going in excess of 80 mph. Hutch couldn't even imagine what the sound would've been like. She once overheard a medic that was at the scene say he had never seen an accident that horrific…it took them quite some time to figure out what body parts belonged to whom. But that wasn't even the most horrific thing about the whole tragedy…The son in the other car was apparently still alive amongst the mess when first responders arrived. A chunk of the car had smashed into his abdomen so hard that he was internally cut in half…and aware of it for ten whole minutes. Rumor spread from first responders that the boy kept saying nothing but the words, "Chirp-Chirp," over and over again as they tried to make him comfortable. Speculations abounded about what that meant. Though most accepted it was the simply the absurdities coming from a dying brain, others said that maybe he thought he was a bird, flying to heaven. That was something you could hardly stand to hear, let alone witness first hand. Hutch remembered the county sheriff quitting the very next day. Then rumors began to fly almost immediately. Henry was on drugs. He had been drunk. He committed suicide. Sadly, the latter of the three almost seemed plausible. After all, he was going incredibly fast, far too fast to take that tunnel, and there were no signs of braking. No skid marks from his tires to show that he was even thinking about slowing for a shot at that deadly corner. Even still, Hutch and everyone in the family refused to accept such a claim or possibility…Henry was happy…Wasn't he? Then there came another shot to the gut, before any toxicology reports were even given, the local paper had the audacity to print the first page headline "Local Drag Car Champ Kills Family of Four and Himself in Drunken Wreck". Unfortunately, Harvey was one of the first ones to see the paper outside of Piper Jean's that day. Hank and Hayden had to physically drag their father out of the newspaper offices before the cops came, he was two seconds away from murdering the editor right then and there. Later, the newspaper issued an apology article rebuking the previous story as "presumptuous and regrettable" But the damage had already been done to Henry's reputation. Many people whispered of their disgust of him, even though he was once their hero on the track. There was pressure to remove his name from the plaques and signs at the strip but the owners refused to do it, standing firm that he was a local hero and removing his accomplishments would just open up Pandora's Box for anyone else willing to complain about another record holder. Still in all, Hutch couldn't help but see the naysayers side of things. He was her brother and she loved him very much, but even with alcohol not being a factor, he was going fast and reckless on a public road, he knew the consequences that may lay in the darkness ahead.

Hutch slowly took her hand down from the cross and looked into the bleakness of the tunnel beside her with a wavering stare, almost as if she were expecting the mangled ghosts of that night to come walking out from the shadows. Tears began to stream down her face, burning her eyes in the glare of the Maverick's lights. She had lost more than her brother that awful night, and her soul ached in the memories of it all. How could such loss happen in the blink of an eye? Why? Why? Why? It was a question that repeated itself with no answer ever to be found. Sometimes life was nothing more than a bowl of icy heartache. And sometimes you got served much more of it than others. She was tired of eating it.

She spun round, wiping the streaming tears from her face, making a beeline for the car. She shouldn't have come here. This place was loss, wrapped in depression, and tied tight with a crimson bow from hell. By the time she flopped back into the Maverick and slammed the door, she was sobbing uncontrollably. Her shoulders bounced in fits as she rested her arms upon the wheel and hung her head between them. And so she let herself be sad. She let the tears flow till they soaked her lap.

For the next several minutes, she just let everything go, as if she were purging poison from her body. Soon, she raised her head, sniffling. She wiped her face and brought the Maverick back to life with the fast twist of a key. With a quick move, she shifted the car in reverse and began backing up the dark road for what seemed like a solid half mile, placing as much space as she could between herself and that tunnel of death. Then, suddenly, she stopped. She hit the brakes and threw the car into park, letting it angrily idle as she watched the moths dance in the glow of the headlights beyond. Loneliness had never felt so real and jagged more than it did in that brief moment. She threw her seatbelt on and placed the car in reverse, ready to back into an old turnaround spot so she could get herself pointed towards anywhere but there. But she stopped…something was different. Something came to life inside her. She just kept staring out into the road, her memories becoming more like the shades of the blackness that they had came from. She removed her seat belt and let it slide to the side as she pulled back

the shifter into drive…and then it happened. With a fury from the
depths of a place she cared never to tread, her foot buried into the
accelerator. The night shook from the terrifying roar of the engine
and the screaming tires behind it as the Maverick exploded
forwards, barreling back in the direction of the tunnel. Hutch's
eyes narrowed as they cut through the pale yellow of the
headlights, peering and yearning for that exact moment atop white
knuckles and a heart beating out of control. And then she felt it,
with every ounce of her being, she felt the spot with her very soul.
She closed her eyes…She blasted the brakes and spun the wheel
right back into another violent acceleration that sent the car drifting
through the obsidian abounding. In another round much the same
as the first, she went gliding on out the other side of the Dog's Leg,
not even as much as kissing the sides of it. She opened her eyes
and jerked the wheel, slamming the brakes until she skidded to a
stop in the middle of the road. With grave apprehension, she
released her iron grip and her hands trembled as she rested her
wrists upon the wheel. Her entire body began to tremor in the wake
of what she had just done. She felt liberated but imprisoned at the
same time as she suddenly began to burst into tears once more. A
shaking hand soon reached down and caressed the car into park,
followed by the killing of the engine. The sounds of the night once
again whispered to her through the open windows. The serenading
of the crickets and the frogs…a thing she could barely hear over
the ringing inside her own ears. She soon gathered the strength to
look over her shoulder at the tunnel she had just screamed through,
its gaping death-mouth illuminated by the glow of the taillights
behind. A feeling of malaise came over her as she opened the door
and rose up on shaking legs, wiping her tears and walking back to
the Dog's Leg. Squinting, burning eyes peered through the
darkness at the opposite side of the tunnel and the wall that lead
into it. There, perched atop it, was a different cross that read
"Morrison." Hutch stared at it for a solid minute, unable to make
herself go any closer. She then whimpered out the only words she
could, "I'm sorry…"

A nervous finger tapped the side of a hot cup off coffee in the
walls of the Gingerbread House. Ham, stood there, taking shaky
sips of his black brew as he stared in the loneliness of the back

garage with the door hanging wide open. As always, he was the
first to arrive that morning, but his normal routines were cut off by
the sight of no Maverick and no Hutch. All he kept hoping was she
took a quick loop around the area, but the longer he stood there,
the more he knew that wasn't the case. Goddamn was she really
this stupid? Had last night taught her nothing? And then of course
there was the elephant in the room. Had Hank finally pushed her
too far? Had she finally packed her shit, and left for good? Sadly,
Ham couldn't blame her if she had…The last thing he wanted to do
was pity her. After all, she made most of her own bad choices, but
she was still his sister.

"What the fuck is goin' on?" A rough voice echoed into the
garage. Ham felt his blood run cold as he watched Hank enter and
just stop dead at the sight of the empty garage. He was waiting for
him to just come unglued and start throwing things. But instead, he
walked slowly across the stained concrete, stopping several feet
away from Ham.

"Where is she?"

"I don't know…" Ham said quietly. Hank pointed at him.

"Wrong fuckin' answer."

"She'll be back. It's gonna be okay," Ham tried to defuse.

"Ha! In what world do you think this shit is gonna be okay?!
You not remember what she did last night? We have no Maverick,
no Hutch, and a bunch of empty beer bottles she left behind! This
is about as far away from 'okay' as you can get, Ham!" Hank
screamed as he chucked the empty six pack into the trash as hard
as he could. Ham stood quiet, looking at the floor in the hopes
things would die down. They didn't.

"This is your fault, ya know?" Hank said. Ham quickly raised
his head.

"What the fuu…"

"Don't you 'What the fuck?' me, brother. You're always
coddling her! Always stickin' up for her dumb shit. You created a
monster, is what you did!...You're a damn enabler. Where is
she?!"

"What? How the hell would I know?" Ham was becoming
agitated.

"Cuz you're thick as thieves, you two. Have been since she was
old enough ta walk. I don't believe for one fuckin' second you

don't know where she is and she don't know where you are at all times," Hank paused and pointed right in Ham's face, "Now, I'm gonna ask ya one more time…Where is she?" Ham had had enough.

"And what are ya gonna do when ya find er?! Beat her ass again?! You gonna kill her this time, Hank?! Hell, maybe you'd like that!"

"You're treadin' on thin fuckin' ice…" Hank almost whispered as his face became an even deeper shade of red.

"That's okay, I know how ta swim and I'll be damned if I'm gonna stand by and let ya punch a woman in the face again," Ham's voice was shaking. Hank slapped the coffee out of his hand and began walking at him as he spoke in a low growl,

"Well, I see a woman in front of me right now. Let's see how good you make on that promise. You gonna stop me are ya?" Right then Ham swung up and blasted Hank hard in the jaw, sending him stumbling back. The eldest McCray looked a tad surprised by his youngest brother's actions. He stood there and wiped his face, drawing back a hand with fingers covered in blood from his lips being busted open. He drew his attention back to Ham who was standing there with fists held up. Hank smiled.

"Wow…I'm gonna enjoy this," he too put up his dukes, "Sandwich, this is gonna hurt you more than it hurts me." And so the two brothers rushed one another, swinging like mad men, but they didn't even get three seconds in when a voice blasted into the garage.

"Hey! Hey! Hey! What the hell?!" Hayden all but screamed as he ran up to them. Heath was close behind him. Together they grabbed Ham and Hank and pried them off one another as Hayden further scolded. "Hey! What the fuck are you two doin?! C'mon!"

"He started it," Hank pointed at Ham.

"Jesus Christ, what are you, five?" Ham spoke in disgust as he wiped the blood from his own busted lip.

"Holy hell, y'all got me feelin' like dad right now. Seriously what's goin' on?" Hayden spoke as he stood between his siblings with his arms straight out towards them both.

"What's goin on, is this motherfucker over here is abetting a criminal!" Hank pointed over at Ham.

"What? Who? What are ya talkin' bout?" Hayden asked.

"Look around ya, Hayden! Where's the Maverick?! Hutch stole the goddamn thing and she's long gone! And he knows where she went!"

"Stole? Ain't that car in her name?" Hayden looked at Hank oddly.

"Formalities...she owes me money. That car is supposed to pay that debt off. Now where is it?"

"She owes you money?" Heath said in suspicion.

"Well...she owes the shop money. Which means she owes us ALL money. Okay?" He corrected his egotistical slip.

"Where's Hutch?" Hayden asked Ham.

"I DON'T KNOW. And even if I did I sure as hell wouldn't let him know," he pointed at Hank, "You all saw her face yesterday. She didn't beat her own ass."

"She earned that shit and you know it," Hank's voice began to rise again.

"You're a goddamn bully and you always have been," Ham barked at Hank as he began walking towards him again. Hayden grabbed Ham's arm and shoved him back.

"Don't fuckin' touch me, Hayden!"

"Hey! You better start using your nice voice with me, Sandwich, I'm tryin' to be on your side here."

"Oh you're on his side now, are ya?" Hank shoved Hayden.

"Calm your asses down!" Heath yelled at all of them.

"Fuck off, Heath!" They all said back in unison.

"Oh, that is it..." Heath took off his glasses and placed them on the worktop then proceeded to run into the middle of everything, swinging. All four brothers erupted into a free-for-all. The group of siblings turned into a ginger-topped tornado as punches landed, kicks spun, and curses flew. It seemed every shred of pent up animosity that had been bottled ever since Harvey left the shop came flowing out in the worst way possible. Soon enough, the four of them looked like nothing more than a clichéd bar fight in an old western. No one even knew why the other was swinging at this point, but they just kept on trucking, pounding each other into some stupid oblivion, until...The garage came alive with the sound of a roaring engine and piercing car horn blasting over and over. Hutch looked through the windshield at her brothers as they continued to blast one another senseless. She rolled up and slammed on the brakes stopping only feet from where they were and she blasted the horn again. The piercing sound seemed to snap them out of it. Within seconds, they were all just standing there, out of breath, staring at her and the Maverick. Hutch buried the gas pedal a few times, letting the car rev a menacing roar into the garage before she killed the key. Everything was dead silent as all four brothers stood there staring at their sister in the passenger seat. Hutch just shook her head as she stared right back. She stuck her head out the window.

"You buncha dumbasses. Just look at yourselves. All out of breath n' bleedin'…Like a pack of starvin' coyotes fightin' over a dead chicken…Christ," Hutch voiced her disapproval. She then fished out a cigarette and lit the end as she watched her brother's march over like zombies and silently surround the front of the car on all sides. Heath put his glasses back on his face and whistled at the sight of engine that they all now remained transfixed upon. Once again, Hutch leaned out the window and just squinted while her eyes went to the faces of each of her brothers. For a solid minute, they just glared at the motor without speaking a single word.

"For God sake you'd think there was a pair of tits on the front of this car…" Hutch whispered as her cigarette danced in her tooth gap. She looked to Hayden who stood the closest to her and spoke up, "What were y'all fightin' about anyways?"

"Yeah, yeah, Hutch, that's awesome. Why don't ya fire that puppy back up for a second," he spoke, not even looking at her. Hutch rolled her eyes. Christ, was this all it took to diffuse a McCray argument? A pretty engine firing away? It made sense, but this would've been a useful piece of information that saved countless black eyes and broken jaws in the past. Hutch turned the key and the garage was once again flooded with thunder. In some odd, simultaneous action, all four siblings surrounded the car, nodding their heads and half smiling. Even Hank.

"Rev that fucker," Heath yelled over the noise. Hutch pumped the gas hard. The front of the car twisted under the torque and sent a round of explosive bursts screaming through the garage. Hutch let the car idle for a moment, watching the anger on her brother's faces melt with every lurch of the loping camshaft. Hell, if muscle cars weren't the closest thing to magic, she didn't know what was.

She once again killed the key, leaving the silence of ringing eardrums and the smell of exhaust to circulate the air. As the engine died to nothingness, all four brothers suddenly began shaking their heads and blinking as if they had just awoke from some drunk-induced afternoon nap. Hutch arose from the car and slammed the door, watching the phenomenon the entire time as she puffed away on her smoke. She looked directly into Hank's eyes.

"Well?"

"Well, what?" Hank sneered.

"What you think about her? Not bad, huh?" Hutch clarified the obvious, patting the side of the fender. Her brother took a silent moment to look over the Maverick once again.

"Still a diamond shoved inside a turd…but you did alright. Ya did good," Hank said and then walked away, disappearing through the back hall door. Everyone stood in silence for a minute as the sound of the closing door echoed through the garage.

"Jesus…Christ. Was that a compliment? Did Hank just compliment another human being other than himself? Hell hath frozen over," Hayden let out in disbelief. He looked around at the others who were still in obvious shock. Especially Hutch.

"Naw, the day hell freezes over round here is the day Hank apologizes to someone other than a customer," Ham spoke as he spit blood off his swelling lip, "That shit ain't ever happenin'." Hutch winced as a hand patted her shoulder from behind.

"She's a beaut, sis," Heath let out.

"Thanks," Hutch replied. Heath began craning his neck and looking things over some more, "Well…I mean, she does need reupholstered…Needs a paintjob…Could use some carpet…Is that a crack in the rear quarter glass over there? Looks like…"

"Okay!" Hutch silenced him.

"Well…the point is, Cass would be proud. What ya gonna name er'?"

"What?" Hutch looked at him oddly.

"Oh, c'mon, ya put all this damn work into er', she means a lot to ya, right? Ya gotta name 'er," Heath said as he cleaned his glasses with his shirt.

"Okay…I'm gonna name her…Sarah." Everyone was silent for a brief moment. Heath nodded and patted his sister on the back.

"Sarah it is then," he started to walk away but stopped and said, "Hey, Sarah could use a hood too."

"Fuck off, Heath."

"Okay, Okay. I'm just puttin' that out there." Right then, the back hall door came flying open with a roar from behind it.

"Hey! It's Shit O' Clock, assholes! Were runnin' a business here! You can pet the car later," Hank yelled out to them all. He took a swig of coffee and side-eyed them as he turned round and disappeared once again.

"You heard the man! Time to mill cranks and bang skanks! Or in Hutch's case, sweep floors and shovel shit." Hutch gave him the middle finger. "Sorry, Hutch, but until Hank says otherwise you're still the gopher bitch, and will be treated as such. I love ya though," Hayden laughed as he pointed and walked out of sight with Heath in tow. The door slammed, leaving behind no one but Ham who hadn't even made step-one towards the front. He just stood there with his arms crossed, staring at her with a cold glare. She sighed out a puff of smoke and walked towards him,

"Lemme guess, this rumble was because of me?"

"Among other things..." Ham answered short.

"What other things?"

"That was rhetorical, Hutch. There were no other things. It was ALL about you. Hank thought you ran off with that car and wasn't comin' back. Gotta tell ya, there was part of me that thought he was right?"

Hutch flicked ashes onto the floor, "Yeah, well I guess that ain't a stretch for anyone ta think."

"Where were you?"

She thought about throwing out a lie but was just sick of it. She went with the truth this time.

"I was up all night...I went ta the Dog's Leg."

Ham's eyes widened.

"Jesus Christ...What you go there for?"

"What you think?"

"You didn't..."

"I did."

"And?"

"And what? I'm still fuckin' here, ain't I?"

"Holy shit, Hutch is that what actually happened with the shop truck the other night? You tried to tame that tunnel and sideswiped it, didn't you?"

"What?! No."

Ham sighed and placed his hands on his hips.

"You're fuckin' unbelievable, you know that?"

"I told ya I didn't take the truck through there. I'm not lyin'."

"Hutch it ain't that. It's the fact that you went to that place and did the same stupid shit he did. What is it? You wanna go out like him? In forty million pieces spread across a wall like strawberry jam?"

"That's a hell of a thing to say about your dead brother."

"OUR dead brother, Hutch, he was our brother. Jesus Christ…Out of this whole family you lost the most from that night. And I thought you would've learned from his mistake."

"Look, I'm not defendin' what he did."

"Yes you are! By repeatin' his stupidity you're defendin' what he did. Hutch, that road is a public road, always has been. And much like the road that is your life, it has two lanes, a normal lane and dumbass lane. As your brother I'm askin' ya, no I'm beggin' ya ta stop takin the latter of those two. I lost one brother ta that place and I'll be goddamned if I'm gonna lose my only sister to it!" With that, he turned round and began to walk off. But he wasn't done. He spun back round and pointed at her, "If you go back there again and end up takin' someone with you like he did, I swear to God almighty I will spit on your grave."

Hutch's mouth fell agape as he walked away and slammed the door, leaving her aghast at the last thing he had said. She was speechless. He had raised his voice to her many times, but nothing that bad had ever come out. Such poison was usually reserved for the likes of Hank. But even though it cut into her deep, she understood where it came from. Henry had meant a lot to them all, and even bringing up his death was enough to send any one of them on edge. Maybe she had been the fool to go back and try what he had failed, but a piece of her felt that is what she had to do. In her mind, simply looking at the place where the carnage happened wasn't enough. Bowing her head to makeshift grave markers and crying was only half of the healing process. She felt horrible inside for upsetting Ham, but in the end, she regretted none of it. She needed it, and she felt better for having done it. She fought back the tears as she mashed her cigarette onto the floor below her. Her misty stare drew to the pinup calendar above the workbench...Thursday. There remained a little over forty-eight hours between now and the moment of reckoning. The race with Regina was so close she could smell the burning rubber it would undoubtedly leave in its terrible wake. The future had never felt more uncertain.

Much like the days preceding it, that workday went cold, slow, and callous as steel. At least to Hutch it did. All of her brother's, however, seemed to be in better spirits than they had been in months. Maybe even years. They laughed and joked, talked of old racing days, women, and recklessness. Even Hank was in the midst of it all, smiling and chuckling. It was all very strange, but Hutch soon figured it out. It was the fight. There was something about men that when they beat the shit out of each other they suddenly became best friends. And maybe it wasn't just men...She had certainly been guilty of it. She remembered Heath and her beating the hell out of one another on a few occasions and they were thick as thieves for a good while after that. Maybe it was just the release of all that pent up aggression two people had been feeling towards one another. You turned into wolves trying to assert your dominance, but then when the dust of the fight settles down, you remember you're both human, you realize the utter stupidity of it all. You wipe each others tears and move onto treating each other better for the rest of your days...Well, unless your last name was McCray, then you just beat the hell out of one another every six months to reset the feelings. No one was perfect.

Hutch entered the shop area with the most disgusted look of defeat. She tossed a bucket full of cleaning supplies back into the shelves as pissed off as could be. Hayden grinned.

"Still enjoyin' your new position?" He smarted off.

"Am I enjoying it?" She said as she ripped off a pair of rubber cleaning gloves and threw them in the trash, "Let's see, well, I just got done disposin' of a turd the size of a steakhouse potato. I don't know which one of y'all managed to squeeze that thing out, but ya have ta have a good idea of what childbirth feels like."

Hayden was laughing so hard at this point that no sound was coming out.

"Oh yeah that's fuckin' funny! You didn't have to deal with this thing. I tried flushin' six times and it just rolled around in there. It was wider than the goddamn toilet hole! I seriously thought I was gonna have to call animal control on this thing!"

"Hutch, stop! Just, stop!" Hayden wheezed in between his laughter.

"I will NOT stop! I took the butt-end of the plunger and stabbed holes in it and that STILL didn't do the trick! You know what I had to end up doin'?"

"Please don't tell me," Her brother begged, out of breath.

"I had to go get a butter knife and chop that bastard into pieces...Jesus, this might be rock bottom for me."

Hayden was now leaning against a shelf, his face beet red and lungs out of precious air. He tried to pull himself together as Heath walked into the room.

"Hey, what am I missin'?" He goofily looked around.

"Oh, god, don't make her repeat it," Hayden eked out.

"Oh, I was just tellin' the story of how I had to julienne a mud baby to get it to go down the shitter just now!"

Hayden couldn't breathe at this point. Hutch was convinced he was about to die right then and there. Heath looked around the room.

"Okaaaay. What?"

"She...She...She had to cut...Oh, my god, I can't..." Hayden tried explaining in between his hysterics.

"What our four year old brother is tryin' to say is, there was a turd in the shop toilet so massive in size that I was forced to cut it up just to get it to go down the drain," Hutch spat out.

Heath just stood there with an odd look on his face.

"Wow...alright," was all he spoke as he placed a bag on the worktop. Hutch eyeballed him strangely. That wasn't the reaction she'd expected. Especially from him. Suddenly, it hit her.

"Oh...my...god..."

"What?!" Heath said.

"It was you! You gave birth to that fudge ferret!" She pointed right at him.

"How the hell you gonna say that?! Where's your proof?!"

"It's that look!"

"What look?!"

"The baby that shit its diaper look you got goin' on there! Back me up, Hayden!" But Hayden was in no condition. He was literally crying at this point.

There was an awkward pause and then finally…

"Hell, it wasn't that big!" Heath sneered.

"No! No! That thing was…Heath, I thought that thing was a dead rat that drowned when I first opened that stall door."

"Oh, just stop it!" He snapped in irritation.

"Heath! Look at me! It was a behemoth, it was the width of a pop can. Jesus, how did you even pass that thing?! How there wasn't blood in the toilet was beyond me…," Hutch paused. Her eyes got wide, "Wait…wait, wait, wait."

"Oh, now what?" Heath spit out.

"There was no toilet paper in there with it."

"So."

"SO?!"

"Sometimes ya don't have ta wipe," he spoke with confidence.

"What?!"A look of horror brushed her face, "What the fuck you mean sometimes ya don't have ta wipe?! You should ALWAYS wipe! Startin' ta understand why you've been divorced four times."

"Ahhhh…" Heath waved down a dismissive hand.

"Team meetin'!" Hanks voice interrupted with a boom. Everyone stopped what they were doing. Heath cast an odd look towards Hayden.

"What he say?"

Soon everyone was shuffling into the front room, one face more confused than the next. They all lined up as Hank stood there with his clipboard, once again belting out,

"Team meetin, gather round."

"Team meetin'? Did we just wander into a fuckin' K-Mart?" Hutch sneered.

"Funny one, sister of mine…As y'all may or may not've noticed, our work load is pickin' up and borderin' on the edge of 'Oh shit what are we gonna do?' Turns out Twin Eagle Machine is closing down."

"You're shittin' me,?" Hayden spoke in disbelief.

"Nope. Old man Guthrie is seventy-nine and apparently his grandson ain't got no gumption to wanna keep runnin' the place so guess what? Unless people are willing to drive another forty miles just to avoid us for their engine work, we're all this area's got. Now I'm sure someone is gonna end up buying that place out or startin' their own shop when they see the demand in this area, but, until then, were gonna keep seeing that overflow. I guess what I'm sayin here is, we're bringing Saturdays back." Everyone moaned and slipped out curses of disapproval at those words. It was the reception that Hank had already predicted. He immediately barked back at them. "Ahh, shut the hell up with your belly achin'. Christ, you'd think I was askin' ya to shave baboons asses, everyday, for the rest of your lives."

"Well that would be pointless," Heath let out.

"What'd you just say to me?" Hank looked at him with a raised brow.

"The baboons asses? Shavin' ya know? Kinda pointless because their asses are already bald."

Hank just stared at his brother for a moment and shook his head in disgust. "What the fuck is wrong with you?" Heath went quiet and just stared at the floor. Hank went on, "Fact of the matter is, we have to start workin' Saturdays or we're gonna have to start turnin' people away and I sure as shit ain't turnin' people away. Cuz when ya start turnin' people away theeeey what?..." he waited for one of them to finish the sentence.

"They gotta come back later," Heath spoke.

"No, you dumbass! The answer is, They don't come back! They don't come back, and they flip you the mental middle-finger walkin' out the door."

"When we startin' this Saturday thing?" Hayden sighed.

"This THING is starting ASAP. This Saturday onwards…8 a.m. to 2 p.m. ain't gonna kill y'all and if….Hutch you got somethin' you wanna say ta me? Cuz you're eyeballin' more than usual right now."

Hutch was quiet for a second, but then spoke up her obvious grievance.

"I gotta sell that car this Saturday. Remember?"

"So?"

"So…I gotta take it to her."

Hank crossed his arms and sighed.

"And why the hell you gotta take it to her? Why can't she just come here?"

"Yeah, Hutch, why can't she come here?" Ham snarkily backed up his brother's question, knowing full well what she was up to. Hutch cast him a glare as she clenched her teeth in agitation.

"BECAUSE...she's not able to come here. She's indisposed," she drew out her words, never taking her stare off Ham. She then looked at Hank. "She's got a business meetin' with a paper company in Morgan County. Her truckin' company is talkin' with them bout being their full time carrier and she asked me if I would please bring the car there to her at noon."

"Whatever, Hutch. As long as you're bringin' back sixteen grand I don't give a shit. So consider yourself excused for this Saturday."

Hutch nodded while Ham just shook his head. 'God damn she had lying down to an art form,' he thought.

"How the hell we expected to handle all this extra work with two machinists?" Heath let out, pointing at himself and Hayden. Hank said nothing as he walked over and grabbed the broom out of Hutch's hand and placed it into Ham's.

"I'm just gonna put that there..." he then began rifling through the stack of papers on his clipboard while Hutch looked on with bated breath. Soon, he withdrew a spec sheet and handed it over to his sister. "Take it. New project. 302 build. It's yours. Welcome back from the land of shit stains and dirty dustpans, sister of mine...Don't fuck it up." He walked away from her, leaving her with the task of trying to cover up a smile that was about to crack her face in half. She couldn't believe it, Hank was actually letting her build again. She thought for sure she'd be pushing that broom until one of them dropped dead, but here she was, staring at a custom build sheet that was shooting for 400 horsepower. Her heart fluttered and she let that smile loose like the butterfly it was.

That day ushered in the seemingly long forgotten days of old. Granted it had only been a few weeks since she was pulled from her true calling, but to Hutch it seemed like an eon. With bright eyes and a silent song in her heart, she began the task of prepping a brand new block for a life of fiery hell and hazard. Creating another monster that would sling a wayward soul into the vanishing point and beyond. She was right where she was supposed to be, threading bolts, turning wrenches, and fine tuning like the metal maestro she was. Still…something lurked. It was the uncertainty and eventuality of the obvious. And as badly as she tried to let all that darkness be chased away by the constant ring of local country radio and the chatter of her ratchet, it remained there, scratching like a hungry cat at the back of her brain. A constant reminder that no matter how much she pretended, life was not normal again. It would never be. And if she lost this race…it could possibly be over.

The work day ended with no lift in the feelings of doom and dread that loomed over her. After her bothers departed for the evening, she took the time to fix the Maverick's hood. Measuring and cutting a hole for the blower to tower out of. In the end, it wasn't her prettiest work, but the car wasn't being prepped for a show, it was being prepped to win. She lined up the hood and propped it up, bolting the hinges tightly. She slammed it down and sighed in the absolute completion of her work…The car was ready, but was she?

A Race Among the Ruins

The next day came and went faster than she could've ever imagined. Time flew when you were doing something you actually loved. And when she tightened the last few bolts at closing time on that build, she couldn't help but sigh in the knowledge that she may never be touching it again. Heath would have to finish it in the event that she lost this race on the morrow. She simply couldn't return here ever again if she had no car and no money for Hank.

Nightfall came. The eve before the race for the freedom of her aunt had finally arrived. Hutch sat there in bed with a dead-eyed stare, chain smoking what seemed like six packs of cigarettes over the course of a few hours. Her foot shook back and forth amongst her growing anxieties and a symphonic tip-tap of her fingernail on the bottle neck of a beer that had long gone warm resting between her legs. What was she doing? Was she really going to go through with this whole thing? The idea of it all seemed perfect, the waiting part. The parts leading to it. But now, now that she was right on the precipice of the actual event, things seemed bleak and confusing. It all seemed quite unreal. An abstract thought process that she almost felt she'd made up as some coping mechanism to deal with her aunt's disappearance. Was Regina even real? Maybe she was just a mirage. A phantom she had cooked up to deal with the hang ups of her own sexuality and Midge. Jesus, there it was again. That flutter in her stomach. That feeling of euphoria in her chest when she even breathed Regina's name. She was losing it and fast. She was on the verge of trying to decide whether she wanted to race Regina or tell her to forget all this nonsense so they could just run off into the sunset together. Surely, she felt the same about her? After all, the girl had bought her a dress, not to mention shared her bed. As all the thoughts of her helplessly falling for Regina flipped one over the next in the blur of her own sleep deprived brain, Hutch stood straight up. She bent down and dug under her pillow till she felt it. With a moment of reluctance, she slid a familiar manila envelope out into the open air…it contained the race route. In the two weeks since Regina had given it to her, she had never even bothered opening it. She unfolded the creases she had made in it and viewed a message written in bubbly letters "Race route, bitch. Love, Regina xoxoxo." Hutch fought back a tiny smile at the note, but then shook her head and tossed the whole mess back onto her bed. She couldn't do this anymore. She had to get some air.

A wicked roar rolled across the steel garage door on high as the Maverick backed out of the Gingerbread House. Hutch pointed herself south, driving the darkened roads, trying her best to let the nighttime air whisk all of her thoughts away into the culverts and ditches she sped past. But after an hour of aimlessly driving the county, she began to realize the once cathartic act was of little use to her this night. It wasn't just the race and Regina that was consuming her that evening, every bad memory that ever was, seemed to relentlessly cram its way into her beaten brain, vying for a spot at the top of her inner hell. It was pointless, the more she tried to rid herself of all this anxiety, the worse it became. She finally pulled a screeching U-turn and headed back towards home. A quick glance at the gas gauge sent Hutch detouring from her trip back across the lot to the shop. She swung wide and piloted herself to the west side of Piper Jean's, pulling into the lonely pumps at the 3 a.m. hour. She pumped a full tank into the Maverick and then grabbed fuel for herself, in the form of smokes, candy bars, and another six pack. As she opened the passenger side door to the car and placed her bag of sins inside, she felt a chill run up her spine.

She froze for a moment. Something wasn't right...in fact it was so far from right, she was finding it nearly impossible to move from her bent over position just inside the car. Suddenly, the lights above her began to flicker. She shivered and nearly screamed as a voice slithered out from behind.

"Nice ride. You did a doozy of a job."

Hutch tried to conceal a gasp as she spun round to see a tall figure standing there. He was donned in blue jeans and flannel, smiling through a dark beard. Atop his head was a tattered hat that read, Redgrace Logistics. It was him, the red-eyed trucker. He wasn't a hallucination after all...or was he?

Hutch carefully shut the door and just glared at the man as he continued to fake a smile that made her skin crawl.

"I know you," she let out reluctantly.

"Do ya now?" He said. His voice...What was wrong with his voice? It sounded like two people speaking at once and the slither of a snake slipped in between. As she stood there trying not to let the fear on her inside show, she kept staring into his eyes, waiting for a glimmer of red, that same crimson she swore she had seen the day Regina showed up for the first time. But there was nothing there, only darkness.

"What do ya want?" Hutch finally broke the silence that was becoming too much for her to bear.

"Me?" He put his hand to his chest, "I'm just bein' a messenger. She sent me to make sure you're not gettin' cold feet for tomorrow."

"She? Who is she?" Hutch patronized him.

"You know who she is...The one I serve."

"The one you serve?" Hutch raised an eyebrow, "Y'all got some weird-ass employer / employee relationship terms."

The trucker chuckled and pointed a bouncing finger at her, "She told me you were funny. But I already knew that."

"Yeah, I'm a goddamn riot...You can tell her I'm still in for the race."

"Fan-fuckin-tastic," the trucker exhaled. He then turned to walk away but was stopped by Hutch's words.

"You can tell her I'll only accept fresh hundreds when I get done dustin' her ass tomorrow. Oh, and you can also tell her I think she's a bitch for not comin' here and tellin' me this herself. You need ta write all that down or ya think ya can remember it?"

"My, my, such shitty words for someone that saved your life."

"Saved my life? I hardly count paintin' dicks on the side of the truck as a life jacket in the vast ocean that is my existence," Hutch shook her head in disgust. The trucker began to chuckle once more. Hutch became more agitated. "And what's so goddamn funny?"

"You."

"Me?"

"Yeah, Hutch, you. The fact that you think graffiti is what I'm talkin' about when I say she saved you…I don't know whether your heads in the clouds or in the dirt, but it sure ain't on your shoulders."

"Right? Whatever the fuck that's supposed to mean…Look I got less than nine hours ta kill a sixer, sleep, and destroy your boss, er' master, er' whatever the fuck you call her, in a race," Hutch started going off as she rounded the front of the car and fished her keys out, "So if you could just piss off that would…be…" she looked up to see that the trucker was gone, seemingly vanishing into the night air in the span of two seconds. "What the fuu…?" She began darting her head around, looking for any sign of him. There was nothing. The fear she had managed to chase away through anger, had come roaring back, consuming her from feet to throat. She quickly jumped in the Maverick and sped through the parking lot, her eyes scanning the mirrors and windows as she went. Still, she saw nothing, there wasn't even a Redgrace truck in the lot that night.

In the next half hour, she nestled back into her camper. She sat there on the edge of her bed, leg bouncing in unease as she held a beer and stared at the door, fully expecting the trucker to come barging through it at any moment. But after about three beers, her nerves began to settle. She lowered her guard at the door and once again turned her attention to the still sealed envelope that contained the race route. She wasn't sure why she couldn't open it. Maybe opening and reading it would make it all too real. Like there was absolutely no turning back once the reality of the route began to soak into her mind. She gave the envelope a toss to the countertop and laid down in bed, lit a cigarette and began to stare pensively at the far window. And that's where she stayed for the next few hours. She drank and stared and puffed and pondered until the tiny light of the dawn began to flood into the glass. She looked at her ticking clock…Less than six hours remained. She wasn't ready. With a quick jump, she exited the camper and fired up the Maverick, leaving the lot behind in a plume of dust that glistened in the morning sun. Miles sped by, with the chilly smell of the dew slipping into her nose between ash and smoke. She had lost count of the cigarettes she had had in the last day. She was always the nervous chain smoker. She still recalled the days after Cass had went missing, she was literally lighting new ones with the ashen butt of the last….She had to calm down. She had to focus.

One half mile down Marne Lane, she slammed her brakes and pulled over into the weeds right next to a ten foot tall fence that spanned what seemed like a solid mile of roadway. She killed the Maverick and walked up to the steel barrier. There was so much ivy woven through the chain links that you couldn't even make out what was on the other side. Hutch shoved her smoke into her tooth gap and grabbed hold, carefully climbing the fence with a symphony of grunts that soon ended with her feet slamming onto the top of a cargo van on the other side. She stood there for a moment, breathing heavily while her eyes squinted a hawk-like gaze across a sea of battered steel and glistening glass, it was her home away from home as a child…Riverside Junkyard. The very same place where the Maverick had come from. She never had quite understood the name. The nearest river was not beside it, it was a good mile away, but close enough she guessed. She jumped down to the bare dirt below and began making her way to a spot only a few rows in. Her eyes widened a bit as she saw it. A 58" Edsel. She hadn't been back here for over ten years yet it was still there. But then again, who wanted a 58" Edsel. She walked up to the battered car and blasted her fist down onto the trunk lid. And just as it had dozens of times before, it came flying open. Fast hands went to the task of lifting up the carpet and, to her surprise, there it laid. A pump action BB gun.

"The glass killer," she whispered as she picked it up and grinned. She shook it and heard the sweet rattle of BBs still inside. Wasting no time, she climbed atop the Ford and sat cross-legged, pumping the air pressure into the gun as she looked her vantage point over. Wow, how things had changed since Midge and her were last there. There were dozens of cars she hadn't seen before…and they were all fresh prey. She finished pumping the gun and cocked a BB into place as she drew a bead down on the nearest driver's side mirror. The trigger depressed and glass shattered amongst the ruckus of blasting air. She smiled. She could almost hear Midge's excited words ringing in her ear from behind. "Good shot, Red! My turn!" Hutch once again began pumping the gun, letting her eyes drift to a new target. Her mind began to wander back to Midge. The last time she had sat on top of this very car was with her…She hadn't been back till now. And why the hell she was here at that moment, let alone any moment, was beyond her comprehension. Still, the good memories outweighed the bad…or least that's what she told herself as she destroyed another mirror and grinned once more. As she went to pump the gun again, she quickly halted at the sound of something coming. It was an odd shuffling. A tiny barrage of tinkling metal and echoing footfall. Panting soon joined in the fray. Right at that moment Hutch froze as her eyes locked with a rottweiler rounding the row beside her. The dog froze just as she did, but then began walking slowly towards her, baring its teeth all the way. Oddly enough, no growling resounded from the animal, just a constant show of silent aggression. Within seconds, the dog was right under Hutch, still showing its fangs. She began chuckling as the black and tan "beast" rose up and placed its paws upon the passenger side door. Hutch leaned down and began petting the dog's head; her laughter had died back down to a smile.

"Holy hell, Roxy, you're just one mean bitch, ain't ya? You never did quite get that whole growlin' and bitin' thing down, did ya?" The dog kept baring her teeth and wagging her stub tail like mad. The morning air was soon ravaged by the unwelcoming sound of a cocking shotgun.

"You're trespassin'! Put that gun down and back off the dog!"

"Back off the dog? She came to me!" Hutch yelled out to the man pointing the gun at her two rows back. It was old Lloyd Romine, himself. She smiled at the sight of him, standing there, nervously quivering. "I hope you got birdshot in that thing cuz we both know you can't hit red on a barn."

"Who the hell?..." he lowered the gun a bit as the old dog limped back to rejoin his side. He took a few steps forwards, looking over his dusty glasses as the sight of the intruder came into full focus. Surely his old eyes deceived him. "Is that who I think it is?" He stopped a car length away from her and smiled wide, "Hutch McCray...How many years has it been?"

"Round about seven, I think."

"Girl what the hell you doin' in here? Besides begging for a load of birdshot in your ass?"

Hutch stared off for a moment and sighed, "Hell I don't even know. Thinkin' I guess."

Lloyd chuckled. "Thinkin? You sure picked a weird place for it. How the hell you even get in here?"

"Jumped the fence right over there. Stepped right on top of that old van. You really need a higher fence or barbed wire or somethin'. Hell ya may wanna start by not parking tall vehicles next to the fence."

"Ha! Well you act like you done this before."

"I used to. A lot."

"Did ya now?..." he raised a brow as he threw his gun over his shoulder. He took a moment and leered at the BB gun she held in her hand. "What the hell you doin' with that?"

"Relievin' stress," she simply said.

"Holy...shit. Jesus....Christ," he drew out like he had reached some earth-shattering epiphany

"What?"

"You're the glass bandit?'

"The what?"

"The glass bandit. The little shit that used to run round here blowing out mirrors and windshields. Holy hell, girl, you probably owe me four-hundred bucks."

"More like four-ten after this mornin...The glass bandit? You called me the glass bandit?" She looked at him with disbelief.

"Yeah, is there a problem with that?"

"Well yeah, I mean, it's kinda wrong."

"How ya mean?"

"Well callin' me a bandit would mean that I am stealin' somethin'. I was just breakin' stuff. You should called me the glass-killer or the mirror-murderer?"

"You McCrays. Always bein' smartasses…So you want me ta just write you up a bill today or mail it to ya?"

"You can mail it. I'll make good on it."

"I was jokin', Hutch."

"So was I."

Lloyd chuckled and shook his head. "Goddamn you remind me of your aunt…I was sorry to hear about her, by the way."

"Yeah…"

"Ha! Holy hell she knew how to twist my arm, buddy. Every time I'd see that girl comin' I knew I wasn't makin any money. She knew how ta make me laugh though, I guess that's worth somethin," Lloyd reminisced, seemingly to himself, as he stared off for a moment. His eyes drew back up to the roof of the car where Hutch sat in silence. She looked awful. Hair a mess under that tattered hat. A black eye and the look of a person who was fighting life with her hands tied behind her back…and life was bare knuckling it. There was a storm brewing behind those tired, blue eyes and he wasn't about to be the one that denied the peace she needed to rid herself of it.

"So you're just out here thinkin', huh?"

Hutch nodded.

"Well, I don't know what demons you're haulin' round on your back, but if blastin' mirrors is all you need to run em' off, you shoot to your hearts content," he looked down at the tired dog beside him. "C'mon, Roxy. Let's leave her be." As the two old souls began to hobble away a small tear ran down her cheek.

"Lloyd?" she spoke up. The old man spun round. "Thank you," she all but whispered to him. He simply nodded and went back to his departure. That man owed her nothing. In fact, she owed him something. Something in the tune of four-hundred by the sound of it, and he was willing to let that tab not only raise but disappear altogether because he knew when he saw a soul in distress, money began to lose its weight. The gesture reminded her of Ham, the very man that, despite all the things he had done for her, she did nothing but continually disappoint. But then again, she seemed to have that talent for everyone she met. She went to pull the gun up to fire again but couldn't focus as the tears drowned out her vision. The BB gun landed with a thud on the roof of the car as a memory overtook her. Time took her back, but not away. She was right back there on the roof of that very car, not but a few days after she had left Midge dumbfounded by her kiss at the side of the creek. Despite the talk from her aunt, Hutch still stayed in her room for most of the days afterwards, still wearing the dress she had been gifted. She distinctly remembered two days after, Midge coming to her house. It was a four mile bike ride from town, and Hutch told her mom to tell her she was sick. She just didn't know how to face her. She was beyond embarrassed and on top of that, she couldn't bear to hear the words she knew would inevitably fall from Midge's lips - "I don't feel that way about you."

Several BB rounds beneath the setting evening sun, led Hutch into a pensive stare, hypnotized by the twinkling glass and chrome that lay for acres in front of her. She was so deep in thought that she didn't even hear someone coming up behind her till she felt the car rock a bit.

"Thought I'd find ya here sooner or later," Midge's voice squeaked through grunts as she climbed atop the Edsel to join Hutch. Hutch shuddered inside at her presence. She had planned on avoiding her for the rest of her life but only managed four days. She sighed as the tiny brunette plopped down behind her and started fiddling with her own hair, waiting for Hutch to say something, anything. But several moments of awkward silence paved onwards. "So you're not talkin' to me now, Red?" Midge spoke. Hutch said nothing. She didn't even turn her head. The brunette sighed in irritation. "Well, I guess your mom was right. You must be real sick, can't even talk. Must have a toucha the laryngitis, eh? Hell I thought you were just makin' that up to avoid me, but here ya sit, not a word to be found…Hope it ain't contagious."

"What do ya want me ta say?" Hutch spat forth.

"What do I want ya ta say? Well, 'hi' would be a good start. Maybe follow that up with an apology for avoidin' me for most of the week."

"Whatever," Hutch growled as she took a bead and blasted another mirror.

"Yeah, whatever. It's always 'whatever' with you, ain't it Red?" Midge was growing more agitated with every moment. Hutch once again went back to being mute. She sat there pumping the gun up with Midge watching her from behind, nervously brushing the hair from her face as the wind kicked up. "Are we not even gonna talk about what happened?"

"What happened?" Hutch patronized.

"Jesus, Lord…" Midge forced an upset whisper. A tear began to form at the edge of her cheek. "Red…look, I love you," she grabbed Hutch's shoulder. Hutch pulled away and glared back at her. "Yeah. But ya don't love, LOVE me…do ya, Midge?"

"That's not fair. You know that's not fair," Midge wiped at her eyes.

"Yeah, well life ain't fair…Sure as hell ain't bein' fair right now, that's for sure," Hutch turned back round and stared over the yard again.

"What do ya want from me?" Midge whimpered.

"What I want is for you ta tell me the truth. You don't really love me. My kiss disgusted you, and you don't wanna be with me."

"You don't know that…"

"Oh, I know. I can see the fuckin' pity in your eyes when you look at me. So just come out with it."

Midge's lip began to quiver. She shook her head a bit. "Look…we're both gettin' upset. I'm just gonna go. My brother's got a few late games at the park tonight. I'll just…I'll call ya when we get back. We'll talk about this later."

"NO!" Hutch screamed, "I said, say it!! Say you don't love me! I wanna hear it! Say it damn it!" The brunette just sat there in silence, wide eyed and disbelieving. "Wow…you're fuckin pathetic," Hutch spoke.

Midge lost it.

"It's not that easy, Red! You just don't get ta tell people how they feel and don't feel! You think you're the only one hurtin' right now?! You think…you think you're the only one in this friendship who's heartbroken and confused?!"

"Oh, I'm not confused, you led me on."

"I what?!"

"Ya did, ya did. You led me on. You came into my life with that beautiful smile, those, those blue eyes. That hair! My god you bought me a fuckin' dress! A dress! What was I supposed ta think?!"

"I don't know! I guess, you were supposed ta think I was being a good friend and...

"There it is! A friend! I'm just a friend! Nothin' more...You know what, you're a heartless bitch," Hutch cut her off, looking her right in the eye. Midge put her hand on her chest and her mouth fell agape in horror.

"What did you just say ta me?" Midge squeaked out.

"Are ya deaf or just stupid?! I said you're a bitch and I want you outta ma life!"

Midge jumped to her feet and just glared down at Hutch with tears dripping from her chin. She spoke as calmly as she could,

"You know...if there's a part of me that really loves you that way it's gettin' buried deeper the uglier you act towards me. I don't deserve this!" With that, she jumped from the car and started to walk away.

"Hey?! Ya forgot somethin!" Hutch screamed. Midge spun round to see her standing up writhing and ripping her dress over her head. She balled the garment up violently and threw it. The brunette caught it before it hit the ground. "Yeah, maybe ya can give that to the next girl you fuck with. Save ya some money and time!"

"You're unbelievable...This isn't you. I'll talk ta later when ya calm down. See ya later, Hutch," Midge spoke as she walked away.

"No ya won't. Ya won't see me later. Ya won't see me EVER again!" She strung a screech of a yell towards Midge as she retreated to the fence beyond. She dropped to her knees on the top of the car and began to sob so violently she could barely breathe. What had she done? How could she have said those things? Her head spun in the mix of all the despicable poison she had just hurled at a soul that, by all regards, was her one true friend aside from Ham back then. It was true, everything she touched turned to shit. As the memory faded back to reality her tears rained down as hard as they had that horrible evening. The words she screamed kept rolling round in her head *"Ya won't see me EVER again!"* She never knew just how true that statement would become. She never ran after Midge that night and she never saw her again... Not even five hours later, five tons of mangled steel ripped Midge and Henry from her life in the haunting mouth of the Dog's Leg. As Hutch continued to sit there and stare across the tear drenched windows of her own soul, she was hard pressed to imagine a world where life could be anymore coincidental and cruel than that very incident. When she went to Midge's funeral, all she could think of was the horrible words she had spoken to her. They were the last things her best friend would remember of her before everything turned to darkness and infinity. To that very day, Hutch was still unsure exactly what she was trying to prove by being so vile to her. Midge had done nothing wrong, and she knew it...but in the end, it didn't matter. No amount of apologizing to grave markers, crying on headstones, or talking to the sky would ever bring back the crawdad hunting, BB shooting, or bicycle races. It was sickening how final things felt when you looked at a casket.

For the next few moments Hutch just let herself go. She let her mind wander through the horrid memories and the depression that followed them. When she finally began to dry her tears, she knew she couldn't have picked a worse day to do this to herself. She looked at the ever-rising sun to the east...It was time to go. There was a race to be won.

Across an indeterminate breadth of distance, similar feelings of sadness and reflection plagued the mind of another. Regina sat there in her Cougar, hands gripping the wheel tightly as she stared through the window into a circling caldron of blacks and blues. Unlike Hutch, no tears streamed down her face, but she donned the same sorrowful and pensive expression that even the sound of her own rumbling engine could do little to erase. Her memories took her back...

"When are ya gonna tell her?" Regina's voice broke the stuffy and smoke-filled air of a tiny motel room. She lie there in bed, covers wrapped round her with her head resting on Harvey McCray's chest. Harvey puffed away on a smoke, seemingly lost in the glow of the tiny TV that played a rerun of 'I Love Lucy' at a volume so low one could barely make it out.

"Did you hear me?" Regina repeated.

"What?"

"I said, when are ya gonna tell her?"

Harvey leaned over and ashed out his cigarette, "Tell who what?" Regina sighed loudly and jolted her body upwards to a kneel in the bed. She glared at him.

"Jesus, Harvey."

"What am I tellin' Jesus?"

"Stop. Stop trying to be cute. You know who I'm talking about. Lonnie. Youre wife? When are you gonna tell her you're leaving her? When are ya gonna tell her about us?"

"Oh shit, sweetheart, now's not a good time."

"Not a good time? Not a good time?" Regina spoke, trying to hold back her temper, "You're right Harvey, now isn't a 'good a time'. A 'good time' would be me and you riding off into the sunset. Moving to California like we talked about. Doing things in the daylight for fuck sake! A good time is not repeatedly meeting up in a shitty motel room fifty miles away from your house!"

"Just calm down," he tried rubbing her shoulder but she jumped away, leaving the bed entirely.

"Don't tell me to calm down…just tell me you're gonna tell her. That's all I wanna hear right now."

"It's complicated."

"Complicated?"

"How many years have we been seeing each other?'

"I…I don't…"

"Ten…Ten years we've been doing this. Meeting for dinner ten towns away. Me coming to the track to watch you race, but I gotta act like a ghost when I'm there cuz god forbid she finds out. And in the dawn of this affair I had to watch you have another kid with her," she paused for a moment, trying to stave off a tear, "But here I am…Still here. What am I to you?"

"Don't do this," Harvey looked away.

"No, I want to know. Just another track harlot? Is that all I am? Something you put your dick in a couple times a week? How the fuck do I know you ain't got four more of me spread out around here?"

"Stop it!" He looked right at her. His eyes quickly went soft. "I love ya."

"Do you?" Regina spoke as she walked away, disappearing into the bathroom. Harvey was hot on her heels. He walked into the tiny room to see her looking into the mirror, tears streaming down her face.

"Hey, hey, hey. C'mon now," he spoke softly. Rubbing her shoulders. "I love ya. I do truly love ya. How couldn't I? Look at ya. Ten years and you ain't aged a day." He ran his fingers lovingly around her chin and face. Regina stared at her own reflection and wept a little harder. She wasn't the only one living a lie. "Seriously though, ya need ta knock that shit off. Another ten years goes by and people are gonna think you're ma daughter. If they don't already." Regina smiled through her tears as Harvey bent down and kissed the top of her head. She spun round and hugged him tightly, letting the hair on his chest soak up what was left of her sorrow. "Baby, ya make me whole. I ain't lyin' when I tell ya that nothin' in my life has ever made me feel more alive than you do. I still remember the first time I saw you staring through the chain-link fence, all wide-eyed and mesmerized by the roarin' of the engines at the track. I knew I was in love right then and there. And when you looked at me, you knew you were in love too. I could see it." Regina nodded. She pulled back and looked up into his eyes.

"So you're gonna tell her?"

There was a moment of awkward silence as Harvey stood there with his mouth agape.

"I...I, in time, I will. Okay? I just need some more time."

"You're fuckin' unbelievable," she pushed him away and all but ran out of the bathroom. She started gathering her clothes and throwing them on with a scowl on her face.

"Ree? Ree, listen..." he called out her pet name.

"I've been listening Harvey! And all I keep hearing is bullshit. I'm getting the hell out of here. You can call me when ya grow a fucking backbone."

"My daughter is sick!"

Regina stopped her dressing, and just stared at him with a raised brow.

"What?"

"Hutch is sick...Cancer. I don't know how long she's got left."

"Why didn't you tell me?" She asked as she slowly sat on the edge of the bed. Harvey sighed. "I...I don't know. I guess I didn't wanna drag ya down with me. I figured ya didn't wanna hear it."

"Harvey, I love you. You can tell me anything."

"I know...I just, when I'm with ya I just want to forget about real life. Forget about the bullshit for awhile. Oh my god...my baby girls dyin'...She's dyin'," Harvey broke down. He sat into a chair nearby and began sobbing like a baby. Regina felt a pang go through her chest. She had never seen him cry, she didn't even think he could. He was a man's man, but here he was, face in his hands, weeping out everything he had kept hidden from her. She slowly rose to her feet and walked over to him. She ran her fingers through his bed-tasseled hair, trying to console him the best she could.

"How long does she have?" She asked.

"I...well...the doctors said three more months...maybe," Harvey began wiping at his tears. "Oh Jesus Christ. Look at me. This ain't me, I ain't like this."

"Harvey, look at me," Regina put her hand under his chin. He raised his head and stared up at her with puffy eyes. "She's gonna be fine."

"What?"

"I said your daughter is gonna be fine. You believe me don't you?"

Harvey sniffled a tad as he nodded. He grabbed Regina's tiny hand and squeezed it tightly as he spoke, "I love ya so much. When I get through this...I'll tell Lonnie I'm done. I promise."

Those last two words, so tiny yet so larger than life, resounded through her head as Regina came back to reality and the present moment. She swallowed a sickened lump from her throat and sighed as she put the car in gear. The time was nigh.

When Stiggy Met Sarah

Hutch had been flying down the road trying to let the late morning air sweep away the rust of the memories she had dredged. But it wasn't long that she began to realize she had no idea where she was going. She had never even opened the envelope Regina had given her. With a side-eyed glance, she saw it lying there on the passenger side floor, a place it had fallen from the wind rushing in. A quick brake and veer off the road later, she retrieved it and ripped it open with haste, revealing a black and white map with a red line tracing their path. As her ears hummed in the idle of the Maverick, she began to shake her head with absolute disbelief. Surely this had to be a mistake. Not only was this route being run during the day, it was far beyond anything Hutch could've ever conceived. The first quarter shot down a main route and then whipped right onto the interstate, where it ended multiple exits later, with the last exit being the supposed finish line. To top things off, the starting line was right where Hutch knew highway patrolmen frequently sat and shot radar.

"Crazy bitch…" she whispered in disgust, letting the paper fall into her lap. She sat there for what seemed like a stretch into infinity, trying to decide if she should still go through with all of this or drive away somewhere, anywhere but there. But the longer she stared through the window onto that lonely stretch of road, the more it reminded her of life in general. Predictable, mundane, and seemingly unending until you drove over the next hill to see the stop sign, and just like that, your ride was over. With that very thought, she had her answer. She shifted back into drive, and pressed onwards.

Ten minutes had passed since she had arrived at the race's starting point. She had backed up next to a billboard in the gravel turn around where the patrolmen often called home, luckily that morning they apparently had better things to do. It was five minutes till noon and Hutch's anxiety did nothing but creep forward with every tick of the clock. She'd sworn she went through half a pack of cigarettes sitting there waiting on Regina to arrive. She puffed and puffed. Inhaled and exhaled with a speed that rivaled the very car she sat in. The gravel below her was soon littered with the remnants of her stress, and just when she went to light another smoke, she heard it. A low growl from beyond the cornfields that surrounded her. It died down to a purr and revealed itself as a gorgeous 1968 Mercury Cougar. A car that, up until this point, she'd only heard of…She had arrived. The Cougar whipped in front of her and then backed up amongst a whirlwind of dust and rumbling exhaust. As Hutch watched the car reverse until it was even with her, she felt the wicked wing beats of the butterflies in her stomach. And they weren't from the impending race, she knew better. They were from the sight of that golden-eyed beauty smiling at her through the window. Regina killed the engine and arose from the Cougar.

"What a day for a race!" She announced, throwing her hands out to her sides. She walked round to where Hutch stayed put behind the wheel, staring stoically forwards, trying to cover up the fact that she was melting inside from her very presence.

"Red. Red. Red…You actually pulled it off. You finished her, and here she sits, ready to rock n' roll," the brunette looked over the car for a moment, and then drew her attention back to Hutch. "You know, I had a feeling you weren't gonna show up. But look at you, sitting in there all pouty, proving me wrong," Regina leaned in and touched the end of the redhead's nose playfully with her finger. Hutch shook her head and gripped the wheel tighter.

"Let's just get this over with," she growled, not even bothering to look at Regina once.

The brunette laughed.

"I just can't get over how damn cute you are when you're grumpy!"

"Well, I must be downright gorgeous today then, huh?" Hutch smarted off, finally looking right into Regina's eyes. Regina went to fire back but was cut short by the sight of Hutch's face. She grabbed her under the chin and took a second to look at the bruises that lined the redhead's jaw and cheeks, and of course, her black eye.

"Wow, Red, I knew you liked it rough but…"

"But nothin!" She pushed her hand away and pointed at her own face, "This is nothin'. So you can quit pretendin' like you give a shit, okay?"

Regina's beaming smile reduced to a crooked grin. "Okay, Red," She spoke softly. She then went on, "Get out of the car."

"What? No," the redhead looked at her in disgusted confusion.

"I said, get your lanky ass out of that car, now," it was more of a demand than a request as she turned round and started heading back to the Cougar. Hutch sat there for a second, stewing away, but in the end she knew she wouldn't disobey. She flung the door open and arose from the Maverick.

"Okay, I'm out."

"I see that," Regina spoke as she walked to the back of her car. She put her big sunglasses down over her golden eyes and dug out her keys while Hutch crossed her arms in impatience.

"And?" The redhead finally spoke in agitation.

"And *what*, Red? Are you always this damn impatient or is that a redhead thing? I got something to show you. Besides I know you're just dying inside to see this Cougar up close, so get your cute, freckled behind over here," Regina spoke as she unlocked her trunk and flung it open. The brunette was right, she was dying to see it up close. She had always loved that model of Cougar. The lines, the hidden headlights. It was just like the 60's Mustangs but with an added touch of sophistication, and oddly enough, she hadn't seen too many up close in her travels. With hesitation, she walked over, arms still crossed, looking back at Regina with suspicion.

"Hope this '*somethin*' you're gonna show me ain't another damn dress," Hutch growled as she began looking into the interior of the Cougar.

"Oh, we're gonna talk about that again, but no, it's not a dress," Regina's words muffled as she stuck her head into the trunk.

"She gotta name," Hutch asked as she rounded the car and lovingly ran her finger across the line of the fender.

"She does..." Regina rose up and slammed the trunk. She walked back round the opposite side of the Cougar and just stared at Hutch, holding something in her arms.

"Yes? You gonna keep me in suspense? What's this gal's name?" Hutch pointed at the car.

"Her name is Stiggy, Red."

"Stiggy?" Hutch raised a brow, and smirked.

"What's that look?" Regina asked.

"Nothin'. Stiggy is...nice."

"Oh go on, you whore. I know you're dying to say more than that," Regina smiled, "Let's hear it."

"Well...Stiggy? Sounds more like a guy name ta me."

"Right, nothing like Hutch, though?" Regina smirked.

"Yeah, yeah," Hutch rolled her eyes, though the brunette made a point. The redhead went on, "Stiggy? I mean, where'd ya get that? Sounds like somethin' ya would name a teddy bear. Or a dog...It was a dog wasn't it? Ya named it after a dog you had when you were a kid." Hutch seemed oddly sure of herself as she walked on around the car she so blatantly poked the moniker of.

"Actually, Red. Yeah."

Hutch stopped and put her hands on her hips, "Seriously?"

"Yeah, Red. Stiggy was a Border Collie. Loved that dog to death. When I was about twelve she ran out in the road and got flattened."

"Oh shit..."

"Yeah, ya wanna know the real kicker? The car that ran her over..." Regina pointed at the Cougar, "It was this exact car."

"What?"

"Oh yeah. I always remembered that. Then one day I saw it was for sale. Actually bought it with the intentions of setting it on fire, but I ended up sparing it instead. It's what Stiggy would've wanted me to do."

"Wow…that's crazy," Hutch stared onwards with her mouth agape. Regina started laughing.

"What?" The redhead spoke.

"It was a joke, Red. I made that all up. Goddamn you're easy," Regina wiped at her face, trying to calm her chuckling.

"That's not funny," Hutch sneered.

"Oh, but it is. You made it funny, with your doe-eyes and your mouth hanging open. You ate that little yarn right up," Regina smiled on.

The redhead crossed her arms and bit at her lip.

"So…Who is Stiggy named after?"

"Oh Jesus, Red. No one. Stiggy is short for Stigmata. I named the car Stigmata."

"Stigmata?...Is that Mexican?" Hutch raised a brow in confusion.

Regina laughed, "No, hun, it's Greek."

"Greek? What's it mean?"

"Well, through the years it's taken on different meanings, but mainly it's the phenomena describing wounds on the body that are similar to the crucifix of Christ. Unexplainable punctures in the hands, wrists, and feet. Wounds that are thought to be inflicted by a higher force," Regina explained.

"Jesus Christ, I liked the dog story better…" Hutch frowned.

"And what about that thing?" The brunette nodded towards the Maverick, "What'd you name it? You give it a wild and sexy name? The name of a goddess? Something like Regina, maybe?"

"Ha. No…I…I didn't give it a name."

"Right, the girl who so eagerly asked me what I'd named my car didn't name hers. That's believable. Spill it, Red."

"I named her, Sarah, okay," Hutch came out with it.

"Sarah," Regina nodded.

"What?"

"Oh nothin, Sarah is…nice?" She readily mocked Hutch from earlier.

"I see what you're doin' there. That's hilarious."

"I'm just surprised ya didn't name her Midge, that's all."

Hutch went cold for a moment.

"Midge is Sarah. That was her real name?"

"Who was Sarah, Red?"

The redhead was silent as she stared at her car for a moment.

"She was...she was my dog. She was a Border Collie...," Hutch obviously lied.

"Right...of course she was," with that, Regina threw the item she had been holding with a thud onto the hood of the Cougar.

"What's that?" Hutch stared at what almost looked like a book.

"A contract, Red. This needs to be legal...well as legal as an illegal race can be."

The redhead curled her lip and placed her hand on the stack of papers with a palpable apprehension.

"Oh, go on. It won't bite you. At least not as hard as I do."

Hutch began leafing through the paperwork trying to make sense of all the legal jargon.

"Christ, this is gonna take me a day to read," she spit out with irritation.

"Red, honey, I don't have all day. I'm a busy woman. Let me summarize...the main part of that thing is the rules, Cass's rules. Basically everything we talked about the other night. No nitrous. No roll cages. No wingmen. Blah, blah, blah, stretched out into a ridiculously long and nearly unreadable abstract of words that a lawyer with two brains and four eyes would have trouble comprehending. Now, let's fast forward to the juicy bits in the back," Regina spoke as she reached across Hutch and flipped the papers to the very last page. "There," she pointed, "It says, in the event of the first party's loss, that's me, the first party shall award the second party, that's you, in the amount of $300,000.00 and the pardon of said party's paternal aunt, one Cassandra Eleanor McCray. In the event of the second party's loss, the second party shall award the first party the title to the car they raced: 1973 Ford Maverick. You see, Red, it's all simple really, you win, you get the money and your aunt, I win I get your car. All in black and white," Regina spoke as she fished a pen from her pocket and clicked the end of it. She quickly put her signature upon a line next to the words "First Party" and handed the pen to Hutch. "There ya go,

Red. Just put your chicken scratchin' right there beside 'Second Party' and we're ready to rock."

The redhead slowly lowered the papers to the solid base of the hood below. Her eyes feverishly scanned the words in front of her as second thoughts and suspicions abounded. A mild breeze slithered the nearby corn, whipping her hair and the pages below her into a tiny frenzy as Regina stood beside her, her eyes drilling her with impatience through those giant sunglasses she wore. Finally, Hutch signed it with haste and stood up.

"That wasn't so bad now, was it?"

"Wait," Hutch slammed her hand down as Regina went to grab the stack of papers. "What's this at the bottom?" She referred to a tiny paragraph.

"Oh, Red that's the Dress Clause I added in."

"The what?" Hutch looked at her oddly.

"Yeah, it says that if I win you have to wear the dress I bought you," Regina yanked the papers away.

"Bullshit. I'm not doin' that."

"Well ya sort of already agreed to it when you signed your name, soooo tough shit."

Hutch crossed her arms. Her face was turning red.

"Jesus…And how long do I have to wear it?"

"Well, till I tell ya you can take it off, silly. Otherwise you could throw it on and take it right back off, and what would be the fun in that?" Regina smiled as she reached up and pinched the redhead's cheek. Hutch slapped her hand away.

"See, you keep that little attitude up and you'll be wearing that dress till you're in a nursing home."

"Whatever. I ain't gonna be wearin' it at all."

"There's that McCray confidence I know and love," Regina spoke as she walked back and quickly threw the paperwork into her trunk.

"We startin' in the road?" Hutch looked out towards the pavement.

"Nope, gonna start right back in here and fight for pole position, like nature intended, Red."

"Well, who's countin' it down? We flippin' a coin?"

"Goddamn you and Cass and your coin tosses. You can count it down."

"Naw, that's not how we do it."

"Jesus H Christ, Red," Regina mumbled as she dug in her pocket and revealed a coin. "Happy? Heads or tails?"

"Heads."

The brunette flipped the coin, grabbed it, and slapped it on her wrist.

"Tails, slut! You should've took me up on that offer," she then smacked her hands together and looked at Hutch. "Well, you ready to set the road on fire?"

The redhead's adrenaline began to spike, the time was here.

"Ready as ever," she nodded.

"That's what I wanna hear. Can I confess something? I'm a little wet right now. And by a little, I mean I'm soaked. Woo! Sex and racing, am I right Red?"

Hutch simply nodded as she walked back to the Maverick.

"Line em' up!" The brunette yelled. Within the next minute, the gravel outcrop exploded to life with a symphony of sixteen cylinders screaming out a bloodlust for pavement and provocation. The two drivers erased all thought as they backed up and adjusted themselves till the noses of their rides were within a hair's breadth. Hutch looked over and Regina pulled off her glasses, revealing those magical golden eyes once again. They sat there for what seemed like a solid minute, sizing one another up amongst the smell of recalcitrant exhaust that slithered through open windows. Soon, Hutch revved her engine as she watched the brunette slide on a pair of black leather gloves. The Maverick rocked back and forth with the force of the torque, spitting out an explosive cackle that rivaled the crackling of thunder. Regina smirked and revved right back, adding to the roaring show of intimidation, a force so powerful it made the corn on all sides quiver in its terrible wake. The fury of the Cougar took Hutch aback. She still didn't know what Regina had under that hood, but it sounded nothing less than a force to be reckoned with. Soon, the engines died back down to a loping grumble, like two beasts waiting in a growing impatience to feed their darkest desires of fuel and flame. Still, amongst it all, the two women's stares upon each other never broke, never ceased through the mayhem…Regina put her hand up, and Hutch held her breath. It was time. The first finger came up "One." Regina mouthed. Hutch felt her grip tighten on the wheel, her breath ceased in the millisecond between Regina's gestures. But as her hand went to raise on a two count she flipped the redhead the bird and buried the gas with a wicked smile. A swirling storm of gravel and dust blinded Hutch as the Cougar exploded forth, leaving her behind in a state of shock.

"Cheatin' bitch!" Was all she could exhume as she too blasted the gas in absolute rage. The Maverick hit the pavement squealing, drifting sideways as it left behind a white smoke cloud from rubber burning hotter than the ire within Hutch's chest. The redhead spun the wheel and corrected, her eyes squinting through the fading maelstrom of dust Regina had left behind for her. And there she saw it, the ivory, ass-end of the car that was leaving her with a frightening speed into the horizon beyond. Hutch focused, burying the gas into the floorboard beneath. The force sent her back into her seat, spiking her adrenaline and spreading a wicked grin across her face. Within moments, the speck that was the Cougar was a full-blown version of itself as Hutch came within feet of its bumper. Regina was doing exactly what she was supposed to, riding the center of the road with a steady hand, making it impossible to pass her. Hutch waited patiently for her opportunity, which would hopefully come in the form of a car heading in the opposite direction. Regina would have to forfeit her hold on the center or risk wrecking.

Hitting 120 mph-plus, Hutch glimpsed her potential savior on the horizon ahead. At this rate of speed they only had seconds to make decisions that could kill them or someone else.

"C'mon bitch," Hutch mumbled, waiting for Regina to make way for the approaching car...She didn't. The redhead swerved as the approaching station wagon barely missed the Cougar. It blasted onto the berm and lost control. Hutch watched with horror as the car overcorrected and flipped over, rolling off the road entirely.

"What the fuck?!" Was all she could expel as the sickening fates of the poor folks inside that car played on a loop inside her mind. She grit her teeth and laid the hammer down, trying to squeak by Regina, but the brunette was having none of it. She swerved to the left, cutting Hutch out entirely. For the next few moments, Hutch went back and forth, continually forcing Regina to hug the berms, trying to get her to lose control long enough to take the lead...but she was as solid and steady as the road beneath. It wasn't long that

Hutch realized she was definitely dealing with no amateur, and she was ruing the day they first met when she laughed at the brunette's claims of beating Cassandra.

Soon, Regina was forced to move, she had to pass a vehicle and Hutch followed right behind her, literal inches from her bumper. The second the car was passed, the redhead hammered down and nosed Regina, claiming the right lane. She had her in check, but far from checkmate as they roared down the asphalt, nose to nose, fast approaching the next leg of the race...The on ramp to the interstate. Hutch kept it steady, resisting the urge to let her eyes wander over to Regina's, she was waiting, nay, praying for another car to come down the opposite lane to force the brunette back, but it never happened. Together, they blasted their brakes and slid onto the ramp, nearly colliding into one another amongst an orchestra of angry horns from passersbys that they barely missed. The air came alive with the ear-shredding sounds of demonic acceleration and peeling tires as they fought for pole down the ramp...Hutch took her. A beaming smile, less one tooth, spread from ear to ear across the redhead's face when she glanced the rearview to see the shrinking sight of the Cougar's grill. But the time for celebration was far from over. As she drew her attention forwards, she saw a sea of all new peril ahead. It was a slithering serpent of cars, trucks and semis, constantly changing, shifting and passing across one another. This was a whole new world to Hutch, she had never had to deal with such abstract in any other race. Not only did she have to keep Regina at bay, she had to navigate a moving maze of vehicles that were going 65 mph+...Things were going to get interesting, and she had to admit, it was exciting. She felt alive.

Hutch concentrated, screaming head-on into the mayhem, trying her best to erase the fact that the brunette was hot on her heels, and focus on the vehicles surrounding her. With the grace of a dancer, she began twirling round the moving steel herd, slipping in, passing, and gunning it with haste, she was becoming one with Sarah, and Sarah was becoming one with her. It was the bonding she had told Regina of. She felt it slithering through her veins and across her bones. She was going to win. She just knew it.

A sudden jolt sent her forwards. Regina was right behind, giving her a love tap in the rear to remind her that life wasn't so peachy just yet. How in the name of holy hell did she manage to catch her this fast? She was sure she had left her behind. She knew of at least two times where traffic had to have cut her off. Still, she was there, taunting her in the rearview mirror. Hutch quickly decided if she couldn't leave her behind, she was going to have to keep her at bay. With speed, she quickly hugged the nearest semi, trying to wait the brunette out until the final exit ramp to the finish line. Regina was having none of it. They were about to pass an exit and that is when it happened. With a raised brow, Hutch watched as the brunette swerved hard and flew up the exit ramp, leaving her sticking to the semi.

"What the....?" Hutch eked out as she watched Regina blast up the ramp, disappearing from sight as the overpass went by. And in that split second, it hit Hutch. She knew exactly what was going on. She was an idiot. She laid the pedal down as panic set in, leaving her semi safe-zone. And just as Hutch expected, there was Regina on the other side, flying down the entrance ramp taking the lead.

"You slippery, bitch!!" She snarled. She could just picture Regina laughing her ass off as she once again hit the interstate, taking the lead right in front of her. Even Hutch had to admit, it was slick. But the brunette was far from done. Right as soon as she took the lead ahead, she darted in front of another semi and slammed her brakes hard, sending the driver into a panic. He too broke fast, jerking the wheel trying to avoid a collision with the Cougar that now sped away from him. Hutch watched with panic as the rig in front of her began violently swaying back and forth…The driver had lost it. The rig spun sideways, clear across the two lane breadth and went into a horrific barrel roll. Hutch was already so close she could barely slow herself amongst wide, fearing eyes, but then she saw it…An opportunity within the taste of a second. As the semi rolled, it jack-knifed mid air and she blasted the gas, slinking right underneath the arch it created as it tumbled on over. Her heart pounded so hard she could feel it pulse through her fingers on the wheel as she stared with terrified eyes in the rearview at the rig tumbling to a sickening stop amongst flying debris of its own making. She had to keep going.

Hutch's stare shot forwards at the shrinking taillights of the Mercury ahead. She clenched her teeth in anger and laid the hammer down. Most of the vehicles close by had stopped in the wake of the mayhem they had witnessed in their rearview mirrors, so navigating them was a cinch as they pulled off to the sides of the road. They parted ways like the Red Sea as the Maverick exploded down the highway with a wayward roar of fiery redemption. Hutch was beginning to realize that the Cougar didn't hold a candle to her in the dead straight-aways. She caught the car within seconds, and began battling her for the lead. But she wasn't giving it up so easily. The redhead snaked back and forth, trying to get around the Mercury, but Regina always seemed one step ahead, like she could read every tactic coming from Hutch's mind. Soon, the vehicles began to appear once more - The tract of folks who were blissfully unaware of the wreck not even three-quarters of a mile behind. Speeds crawled back down to the eighties and nineties as the two women fought tooth and nail, swerving, skidding, and exploding through the maze of moving steel. They soon hit a wall…a moving one. Ahead, the interstate was blocked out by two semis moving tail to tail in both lanes, and what was written upon the backs of their doors sent a shiver of suspicion up Hutch's spine. "Redgrace Logistics" Something was far from right, she could feel it with every spin of the monster below the hood in front of her.

She backed off the slightest and watched Regina come within feet of her own company rigs. The brunette drifted there, trailing behind them as Hutch kept her distance with a cautious eye, waiting for the worst to happen. And then she heard it. Atop the scream of the engine, there was a wail of a sound piercing across her window. It was a patrolman. Hutch fell deeper into the throes of panic. She thought Regina had said not to worry about the police, yet here they were. She couldn't pull over, not now, not ever, she was too damn close. The finish line was less than a mile away now. With a wide-eye, she watched in her mirror at the officer as he swerved back and forth on her bumper and then suddenly whipped round her. The patrol car was now nose to nose with the Ford. Hutch glanced over, expecting to see a red-faced and angry man shouting "Pull the fuck over now!" but what she saw instead made her shudder inside. It was the red-eyed trucker, or rather patrolman at this point. Or whoever the hell he was; The same man that had so unnervingly confronted her the night before, only now dressed in law enforcement garb. He smiled at her with that devilish grin curling below solid, blood red eyes. Hutch knew she hadn't been seeing things, his eyes were red, red as the blood that now curdled beneath her goose-pimpled flesh. Things were spiraling out of control and making less sense by the second. With a brazen swerve, the red-eyed man blasted right into the side of Hutch. She choked down a scream below clenched teeth as the tires beneath her squealed in a malicious sway of lost control. Still, she held it together, righting the car, trying to keep her focus on both Regina ahead, and the newfound menace beside her. Once again, he blasted into her with twice the force of the last. She held on tight, white-knuckling her wheel, spinning it back and forth till she straightened out.

"C'mon, you fucker," the redhead growled, glaring at her enemy through her passenger side window. Hutch jerked her attention ahead to see the horizon changing. The two Redgrace rigs suddenly parted ways, each one now respectively riding the berm on either side as they made way for a third semi to fill the gap between them from up ahead. A trio of rigs now completely blocked the path ahead with Regina still closely trailing them. There was no way of possibly getting around the rolling wall less taking a haphazard course through the grass surrounding. What was the brunette up to? Once again, Hutch was blasted away from her steady pace by old red-eyes. She had had enough. As soon as she righted herself, she returned the favor, smashing right back into him as hard as she could. He grinned and laughed as he steadied himself amongst smoking tires, then went right back after Hutch...but she knew it was coming. With timed anticipation, she blasted her brakes hard. The red-eyed man went crossing over right in front of her, missing her entirely. She smashed the gas and clipped his back quarter, sending him into a maddening spin that quickly lead into a frenzy of speeding flips and barrel rolls. The redhead sped on by him, watching in her rearview at the frenzied storm of steel and flashing light debris raining down upon the road as the car slid to a stop on its side. There was no time for celebration, she laid the hammer all the way down and didn't let up till she was inches from Regina's backside. And that is where she stayed, carefully watching the Cougar in front of her while her peripheral vision fed to her the landmarks passing by...they were dangerously close to their finishing exit.

"What is this, bitch?…c'mon…c'mon…What are ya up to?"
Hutch kept repeating to herself, still blissfully unaware of what
was about to happen. Regina sat there up ahead, calm as could be,
staring into her mirror at the befuddled face of her redheaded
opponent. It was time. The brunette blasted her horn and quickly,
things began to shift. Up ahead, the center semi pulled forwards
enough for Regina to squeeze in between the rigs off to the sides.
The wrinkles of worry and confusion relaxed for a moment upon
Hutch's face as she realized what was happening. This bitch was
going to follow that rig until they passed the others, and then the
other two semis were going to come back together, blocking Hutch
out entirely. If this wasn't blatant cheating and collusion she didn't
know what the hell was. Still, the redhead sat steady, she wasn't
about to let Regina get away with this. She pulled forwards,
sticking to the Cougar's bumper. If the brunette was going to try
and cheat, Hutch was going to make it difficult for her to follow
through with it. As long as she stayed glued to her, she was going
to follow her right on out of this rolling trap…or at least she
thought. The middle semi lumbered forwards until both Hutch and
Regina were well inside the span of the other two trucks, and this
is where it stopped. The two cars held steady, one glued to the
other, and the other glued to the rig. Regina once again looked to
her rearview and shook her head.

"Well, Red, this is where you kiss everything you knew about
reality goodbye…" with that, she closed her eyes and concentrated.
From behind, Hutch's eyes widened as the Cougar became
engulfed in a dark aura of blacks and blues. It was as if it was
being swallowed by a mist of darkness. Bolts of electricity
surrounded the car and then, suddenly, the vehicle turned into a
swirling mass of darkness and steel that whipped into the air and
slammed into the side of the passing lane rig. Amongst this chaotic
mass of gloom, the Cougar reassembled and was now sticking
vertically onto the side of the semi trailer. All Hutch could do was
sit there with her mouth agape and her mind asunder at what she
had just bore witness to. She watched as the ivory car sped
forwards, sticking to the side of the rig as if it were magnetized
until it reached the cab. It was at this point the darkness overtook
again. The Cougar seemed to invert and turn itself inside out, only
to reassemble once again on the side of the middle rig's trailer.

From there, Regina sped down the length of the steel bed until she came out in front of the side rigs. The car swirled into darkness and reappeared right onto the highway. She sped up the finish exit, leaving the redhead in a state of absolute shock and awe. There was nothing inside Hutch's head. Not one coherent thought could even break into the madness that was the wall of all-out nothing between her ears. She couldn't brake. She couldn't lay down the gas. She just rode there for a brief moment, with reality seeming as quiet as the ringing in her defeated ears. She was absolutely disillusioned with reality. Certainly she was dreaming. She had not yet awoken to the morning to face the actual race head-on…But no, it was real, all of it. And that only solidified the moment she realized the semis beside her were converging. With an impact of absolute violence and atrocity, the two rigs came together, mashing her in between. The middle rig out front slammed its brakes in an act of deliberate destruction. The thundering roar of thousands of pounds of twisted metal caterwauled to the skies as three semis, and one tiny car, became intermeshed in a rolling mass of devastation. Everything in Hutch's world went black.

From on top of the exit ramp, Regina stopped and watched out her window as the wreck raged onwards, sliding and rolling down the interstate until it came to a screeching slide hundreds of feet from where it had began. The brunette didn't smile. Nor laugh, nor cry. She didn't even blink. She just sat there with her face frozen in some unreadable murk of emotionless. The reflection of smoke and flames, slithering from a mountain of shredded steel was all that played across her golden eyes. Eyes that were soon covered by her huge sunglasses as she drove off, leaving the carnage she had created behind her…And somewhere amongst it all, Hutch took a haggard breath and the darkness overtook her.

Miles and miles to the north, Harvey McCray sat on the same worn down cushion of his smoke-tarnished couch, cigarette in one hand and a remote in the other. Bent over and glassy-eyed with the spine of his sickly frame poking through his shirt, he expelled a raspy sigh while surfing the channels of the same old bullshit just like he did every day as of late. It had been days since he'd expelled a word to another real, live human being other than Carla, the Hospice nurse whose job was to basically check and see if he were dead yet. Though weeks had trudged past, the thoughts of him and his daughter's last encounter still weighed heavy on his mind, evoking emotions that made it seem as if it were just yesterday. The anger. The sadness. The hell within. He knew deep down simply keeping her away from him would do little to curtail what lie ahead.

He almost felt as if he was going into a trance the more he plucked away at the buttons beneath his ever gaping mouth. Soon, it rested upon a channel, but it was not one he had decided upon. He closed his mouth and grimaced with an angry leer as he pushed the channel button over and over to no avail.

"Goddamn batteries…" he whispered, shoving his cigarette butt into his mouth. The smoke danced on his writhing and pursed lips while he pried the back off the remote and began digging through the rubble beside him. But no sooner had his hand found the pack of double A's did something odd happen. The TV channel changed. His eyes shot to the flickering as channel after channel breezed by with no ebb in the inanity. Surely he was seeing things. With a raised brow, he looked to the battery-barren remote in his hand and right back to the rapidly changing stations ahead. Then, without warning, it stopped on a channel. The volume lurched up and echoed inside the dankness of the gloomy trailer, making Harvey cringe under the sound it emitted. On the screen, the local news broke through the program, bringing forth a brief breaking story…

"*Chopper 6 is bringing us live shots of a massive three rig pile up that has brought traffic on 70 westbound to an absolute standstill. The accident occurred not long after noon, but what is making this tragedy more compelling than most is the fact that it stemmed from what is allegedly being reported as a high speed chase between two vehicles. Several eyewitnesses have reported the cars involved as an early model, white Mercury Cougar and a blue Ford Maverick….*" Harvey's heart began to drop. He sat farther up on the edge of the couch as the reporter went on. "*It is still not known why exactly the chase was happening, whether or not it was a race, road rage, or a domestic disturbance. Authorities have confirmed that the Ford Maverick in question was involved in the accident and is among the wreckage while the Mercury Cougar still remains at large. At this point, it is strongly believed that no one involved in the wreck has survived. Emergency medical and Highway Patrol are still working to clear the area so we will have more details tonight at 6."*

There seemed to be a ringing inside Harvey's ears as he felt his head go dizzy and numb, trying to fight the urge to fall forwards onto the floor. He could hear the whisper of the newscaster's last words mumble "*Just tragic…Awful..*" right before the program resumed. The remote slipped from his hand and was soon joined by his still lit cigarette that fell from his mouth onto the dingy carpet below. She was dead. Gone forever, his only daughter. Just as he went to put his hand on the sides of his head, his eyes widened at the sight of a high heel shoes stamping out the cigarette in front of him.

"Harvey, baby, you need to be more careful. You're gonna burn the house down, silly." Harvey began to shiver as he rose back up, his watery eyes now staring into the golden gaze of Regina. She smiled. "Why, sweetie, what's wrong? You look like someone just died." He wanted to scream. He wanted to throttle her into the floor along with that cigarette. He wanted and wanted, but he simply couldn't. In the end, he just sat there, staring up at her without a word on his lips. "Nothing? You have nothing to say after that?" Regina released. She shook her head and sighed. "You used to be so much more full of life. Angry and vengeful when I took something from you. Now look at you. Sitting there shivering. Tears welling." She squatted down and sat in his lap, wrapping her arms around his fragile body. She pressed her cheek to his as they both stared at the TV, she lovingly ran her fingers through his thinning hair. I Love Lucy was playing. "Awww look babe, It's Lucy. Remember when we'd sit and watch this for hours? We would hold each other, just like this, and everything in the world was right. We could've been like them you know? Like Lucy and Desi. Before you went and ruined it…Before you went and ruined everything. You know after you did what you did, I began to question who the demon actually was…you or me." Harvey closed his eyes; a tiny tear rolled on the top of his cheek. He began to tremble even more, fighting the urge to cry. That's what she wanted…whether it be tears or words flung in ire, she wanted his emotions to break…He was doing his damndest to stop giving them to her. After a brief moment of silence between them, he squeaked out a query,

"How much is enough?...How much more are ya gonna to take from me?" Regina sighed and squeezed him tighter to her as she watched the canned laughter explode behind Lucy's smiling face. "Oh, Harvey...everything. I'm going to take everything."

Welcome to Furnace Number 12

A darkness swirled. A shade blacker than black. Not the hue of the mire behind the lids of closed eyes, but much deeper and far more terrifying. And amongst it all, there was no sound. No anything. Not the murmur of a pulse or even the soft binge and purge of breath round the beating heart...No emotions stirred, yet, consciousness still seemed to exist in this nothingness...And then it happened. The rush. The feeling of wind across the flesh and through the hair. The return of life...Or was it death? The in between? Perhaps it was all three as the mind's eye reveled in the dark beauty of a spiraling cascade of colors. Shades of gray, indigo, and crimson, crossed forth through a fiery ring as the equilibrium returned and the feeling of descent began. And so she fell...She fell for what seemed like the whole of her life replayed over again till she hit the bottom, breaking every splinter of bone inside her...And just like that, the same blackness that had prefaced it all, began anew. Her eyelids peeled back in the pain of a stinging acidity. A twinge that was undoubtedly a product of the aroma her nose was now delivering to her. That smell...sulfurous and bleak, yet so familiar to her heart. Was it the smell of fire from the wreckage? Was she still in the Maverick about to be burned alive from the flames of ignited diesel fuel? She went to scream but couldn't make a sound except a pathetic gasp she swore she only heard in her own mind. And then she heard it... a voice...

"I think she's comin' round..." It was unfamiliar and oddly distorted. The voice of an EMT? A doctor perhaps? Of course it was. It had to be. My god, she was alive. The crash hadn't claimed her after all. As the blur of her stare began to lift away, she saw the outlines of three figures standing over her. The incarnate colors of darkness now gave way to vibrant greens, yellows, and blues. The same voice returned...

"Hun?...Hun, can you hear me?...I think she's dead."

Another voice responded.

"What's that some kinda joke? Of course she's dead, dummy." Hutch's brow wrinkled at the last words that rolled into her ears.

"What the hell?" She squeaked out as she began to blink, letting her eyes fully come into focus. A violent fear jolted as her eyes popped wide and stayed fixed onto the sight she beheld. Above her stood three...things, for lack of a better word. Creatures. Human-like, yet far from it. The one that hovered closest had green flesh, a bird like beak for a mouth and downward curling horns hugging the sides of its head. It stared down at her with an equally worried gaze. It spoke.

"Now try to keep calm, hun. I know we're a lot to take in, but just take a breath and relax." What the hell was this? Surely she was having a nightmare of sorts. Her eyes shot from the green creature to the other two as she fought the urge to scream. The second one was yellow. It glared at her atop an under-bite. It shook its head in agreement with the one who had just spoke. Her eyes then shot to the third creature. It was cloaked in blue flesh. This one was perhaps the oddest of all. It had a trunk and stalky body that made it appear like a tiny elephant that learned to walk upright. It even had large flappy ears gracing the sides of its head. No stare came back from this one. Where eyes should have been were no more than two X's that appeared to be burnt right into the flesh of its face. Hutch's stare slowly returned to the green creature. She was obviously losing it. All she could imagine was herself lying somewhere getting pumped full of Grade-A drugs to kill the pain of the wreckage she had just been pulled from, these three things were apparently side effects of said drugs. A crazy smile stretched across her face. She might as well roll with it.

"That's it. I told you you were okay," The green creature spoke to her, "Now, what's your name?"

"There is no Hutch, only Zuul," Hutch smiled and drew out, quoting one of her favorite movies. The creature raised a brow and looked back at the others.

"Well, what the hell does that mean?"

Before the others could even think to answer, Hutch grabbed a rock and blasted it across the creature's face, knocking it back several feet away from her. The redhead jumped up onto shaking legs with another rock in hand and a menacing stare to match it.

"Get the fuck back! All of you! Wake up. Wake up. Wake up. WAKE UP, HUTCH. You goofy bitch," she ranted out while tapping the sides of her head.

"Hun, there's no wakin' up," the green monster spoke and took a step towards her.

"I said, get back!" Hutch once again went on the defensive. The green creature threw its arms up in surrender.

"Okay. Okay," it spoke, still slowly approaching her.

"Jesus, Izz! Would ya just leave her alone? Every time a new one drops down here ya gotta play the smothering welcome party. Give her a minute!" The yellow monster bellowed out to the green one.

"Holy shit, now that yellow thing is talkin'," Hutch spoke of the creature. It eyeballed her with an angry leer.

"Hey girly, I'm not a *thing*."

"And it's got feelings too…wow, Hutch, what do they have you on?"

"Hun, who the hell are you talkin' to?" The green creature asked.

"Myself, goddamn it! They must have me on some damn good drugs. I just need to ride this out."

"Who's they?"

"You know? They, the doctors, or whatever…I got in a car accident and…wait, why the hell am I explainin' this all to you, you're not even real. What the hell are you anyway?"

"Were demons, hun," the green one said. Hutch wasn't amused.

"Oh…OH okay, yeah you're demons, makes perfect sense, with your pointy horns and beaks and whatever the hell that is," she pointed to the blue creature. It looked around and then pointed a stumpy hand at its own chest in question. "Yeah I'm talkin ta you," Hutch affirmed, "You're demons, annnd I'm obviously in hell," she sarcastically exclaimed as she fell down onto her rear, still quite confident that she was dreaming. The demons looked around at one another.

"Well, yeah you ARE in hell. We all are," the yellow one spoke.

"Fuck this, I'm leavin'," Hutch dropped her rock and returned to her feet.

"Hun, that's not a good idea…" the green one was fast on her heels.

"Stop callin' me hun," the redhead spoke with annoyance as she headed for the dark horizon.

"Seriously, stop," the demon pulled at her shirt.

"Get off me!" Hutch's walk transformed into an all-out run. She ran and ran, never once looking back for what seemed like a mile. Finally, she slowed to a walk, but instantly jumped in fright at the sound of a familiar voice behind her.

"Are you done?" Hutch spun round to see the same trio of demons standing right behind her.

"What the hell?! Stop following me!" Hutch yelled.

"We didn't follow you anywhere. You didn't GO anywhere. You're stuck here. Get it?!" The yellow creature growled back. Hutch began to stumble around a bit, gathering in her surroundings. The creature was right, she had ran off but didn't, it was as if she were just running in place.

"I'm stuck here…I'm stuck here.." she began chanting as she pulled at her hair with a stare of hopelessness. She then blurted out, "Where is HERE?"

"HELL!!" The demons yelled in a synchronized annoyance.

"Well, more specifically the mine of furnace number 12 in Hell," the green one explained.

"Hell?...I'm in…Hell?" Hutch nearly whispered as she turned back around and looked across the charcoal landscape. And what she saw there made a memory come rushing back. Black above black…the inverted sunset. The stench of hopelessness and malaise hung heavy in the eye of the gloom. Purples and blues danced upon the horizon as a stinging sulfur once again wafted into her senses…and she remembered that night. The night she smoked with Regina. The vision that came. Her head jerked to the demons behind,

"Where's Regina?"

The demons began looking at one another with concern. The green one started to speak.

"I…ummmm…"

"Where is she?! Answer me, now!!" she bent down, leering angrily, inches from the green demon's face.

"Well, she's not here. Not in the pit anyway."

"Then where? How do I get out of here?"

"Hun, you don't get out of here."

"Bullshit! I got in here, then there has to be a way out."

"Don't tell her Izz," The yellow demon voiced.

"Ah ha! So there is a way out! Where is it?"

"The gate, but…"

Hutch grabbed the green demon by the throat, "Where is it?! I will pop your green head right off your shoulders, you little shit!"

"That way! That way! Okay?!" The demon choked out, pointing like mad off to the left. Hutch released her grip and went running as fast as she could.

"Wait! Waaaaait!!" She could hear the fading pleas of the demons she left behind. The sound of their voices were soon consumed by something else entirely, pinging and hammering. Steel upon rock. As she ran, Hutch began to take in the odd sights around her. She suddenly realized there were more demons, lots of them, everywhere. They ignored her, working tirelessly, swinging hammers and picks, blasting away at the ground below. The redhead came to a halt as her wandering stare brought full-circle a jaw dropping sight. She walked to a ledge and looked over. Below her was a vast hole in the earth that seemed to stretch for miles, and in it were even more demons. Thousands of them. Some green, some yellow. Some of them were tiny, others large, and still others looked almost human-like, gray skinned and sickly.

"What the hell?" She whispered to herself as she watched them all dig into the red and black rocks below. It was a seemingly never-ending mine, and what exactly they were digging for was beyond Hutch's comprehension. All she could think about was how it reminded her of the strip-mines she had visited as a kid.

"Heyyy?! Stopppp!!" A voice began fading in through the steel symphony below. Hutch jerked her head to see the group of demons she had left behind, catching up with her. She once again bolted off in the direction in which she had been pointed. Several moments flew by as she jogged along the rim of the chasm until finally, she saw it - A gate, a couple hundred feet away from the side of the mine pit. It was nearly thirty feet tall and twice as wide.

Made of round steel machine work that darkly reflected the red glow of the pit behind. Hutch hastened her steps and ran right up to it, blasting the steel with her fists, screaming out.

"Open the gate! Open it, damn it! Regina! Regina!" She wrapped her hands round the steel and began shaking with all her might, trying to get the attention of who or what was responsible for keeping it locked. "C'mon!!...Regina! I need to talk to Regina, now!!" Her voice boomed over the miners' symphony below. She tugged and pounded. Pleaded and screamed, but no one came. She finally slinked down onto her bottom, back against the cold metal that kept her imprisoned in whatever the hell this was. As she began to fight off her tears she heard it. A crunching from behind. Footsteps. She gasped and jumped to her feet, facing the gate once more as a figure came from the gray and black beyond.

"Hello? Hello? I need to see Regina," Hutch spoke to the human shaped entity. Finally, it came into clear sight, stopping inches away from the steel barrier. A wicked lump filled her throat as she realized she recognized the figure...but it wasn't Regina. Long antennae twitched upon a cricket head, all sitting neatly atop a human body.

"Absalom..." Hutch whispered in a weak despair. A terrible symphony of disengaging lock-work screeched into her ears as the gate opened, leaving nothing between her and the imposing monster...or man. Or whatever the hell he was. They stared at one another for what seemed like an eternity. The redhead almost expected him to speak but to her dismay, nothing came from his mouth but a hushed shuffling of twitching mandibles. Hutch took a deep breath, trying to find her courage. She was a McCray, damn it.

"I wanna see Regina. Take me to her."

But the monster said nothing. He just continued to loom there, staring with those black within black globes for eyes. "I said, I wanna see Regina...Now."

Silence.

Hutch's patience was wearing thin as she spoke again,

"Regina...Regina...Regiiiiinaaaaaaa. Regina Redgrace. Pretty damn sure ya two know each other. Dark hair, gold eyes? She's about yay tall? Could use the bitch as a lawn ornament?"

Still Silence.

"Welll?....Nothin'? Fuck this. I'll find her maself," Hutch spoke in frustration as she rounded the man-thing in front of her. She didn't get far...A crushing monster of a hand grabbed her throat, lifting her high into the air. The redhead punched and kicked, dangling there in his grasp like she were nothing more than a toy.

"You...son of...a," was all she could choke out, never ceasing her barrage of fists and feet. Just when everything started to go black, he released her with a thud to the rocky ground beneath. She rubbed her throat, gasping and coughing between an indiscernible orchestra of obscenities aimed at the beast that continued to leer down upon her. She looked up in time to see him bend down and grab her by the boot. With no effort, he began dragging her away from the gate, out into the darkness from where he'd come. Hutch clenched her teeth, angrily writhing, trying to free his iron grip upon her foot. It was no use. Soon, she gave up and relaxed as the wicked rocks beneath chewed away at her back. She watched the upside-down sight of the gate slowly closing, shutting out the concerned faces of three demons behind. Hutch went to call out to them but closed her lips. What were they going to do for her at this point? Hell, she didn't even know their names. The trio of creatures stepped up to the gate and wrapped their fingers round the bars, peering through them till the redhead was nothing more than the gray gloom that engulfed the outside of the mine. The yellow demon looked over at the green one.

"Well, ya think she'll be back?"

"I think we all know the answer to that..." the green one said, then cocked its head, noticing an item laying there in the rocks by the steel. The demon picked it up off the ground. It was a hat. Hutch's hat. It had fallen off her head amongst the panic.

"What's it say Izz?" The yellow demon asked.

"I think it says...Mc...McCray...something."

"What's it mean? That her name maybe?"

"Not sure...but it sounds familiar."

From the small of her back, to the tips of her fingers, Hutch felt the nasty bite of the ground beneath chew away at her as she was dragged and dragged. Dragged and Dragged for what seemed like miles. For a reason she couldn't place, there was just no fight left in her. She stared brokenly into the sky...Was there a sky in Hell? Was she even in Hell? She hadn't the slightest clue any longer. All she knew was that if it were a sky above, it was starless, blacker than black. Darker than the nothingness behind one's lifeless eyelids. Every now and again she would look to the sides…it wasn't much different, just a brackish gray fog that blanketed everything to the cobalt earth below. Her gaze soon led her to the monster that dragged her along. A thousand questions abounded. Who was he? What was he? Who was he to Regina? Hutch went to open her mouth in what she knew to be a futile inquiry, but it just stayed silent and agape as the fog lifted, revealing another familiarity. She craned her neck and beheld the sight of a beaten Plymouth Superbird. Absalom's chariot. She was quickly righted and rolled into the open door of the front seat. Her bleeding back seared in agony as the cold vinyl kissed her ravaged flesh through the torn holes in her shirt. The redhead leered with suspicion through her dangling hair and the filthy windshield ahead, waiting for Absalom as he made his way over to the driver's side. She flinched as the hinges screeched and the whole car rocked to one side beneath his massive weight.

"Where are ya takin' me?" Hutch's emotionless voice cut through the stale air of the interior. But as expected, the cricket-man had less than nothing to say to her. As if she didn't even exist, he turned the keys to the car and it came alive with a roar that rolled to a rumbling idle. Hutch tilted her head as she listened to the valves click and pistons pump…this engine sounded strange. There was an overbearing hum mixed with a moaning screech amongst it all. Like a forgotten soul trapped inside the machine…It was haunting. Suddenly, her head whipped back as he blasted the gas, sending a rooster-tail of rocks behind them. Hutch watched in the rearview as the fog they had come from disappeared into the horizon, giving way to the obsidian and purple flames flitting in the skyline. As she looked all around her, she realized it encompassed them, just like it did on her drug-induced trip that night with Regina. It was to that end that she began to wonder if the remnants of the drug still lingered inside her somewhere, perhaps in her spine, only remerging in the violence of the accident. It certainly would explain all of this crazy shit.

A lifetime seemed to pass as Absalom drove further into the darkness. And no matter how much ground they covered, the flaming horizon never seemed to draw any nearer than when they first departed. Hutch would occasionally look over at him, watching his grotesque mandibles twitch, wondering what was going on inside of that head of his, if anything. But even if she'd wanted to, she hadn't the time to ask. She felt him lay off the gas and make a turn to the left and there it was. Something loomed ahead, steadily blocking out the glow of the inferno behind. Through the lowly glow, Hutch began catching glimpses of wrecked cars on both sides of them. Some were so mangled they were unrecognizable. Still, others only had minor marks and dents. As she watched the vehicles grow in number in the reddish-purple glow of the landscape, she began to feel like she was being led straight into a junkyard of sorts. Whatever it was, Hutch had a bad feeling about it all.

An unnerving surge of goosebumps spread cross her flesh as Absalom slowed the car to a crawl with his headlights illuminating a large gate not unlike the one at the entrance to the mine. Giant steel hinges moaned and reverberated across the windshield of the Plymouth as the threshold opened wide for them to enter, seemingly by its own will. Hutch glanced at the cricket-man, looking for some sign from him as they pulled into a courtyard of sorts with walls built high from the scraps of cars. The engine was killed as were the headlights, leaving only the low light of the flames beyond to see by. She watched with apprehension as the towering cricket-man exited and circled the car, throwing open her door. He grabbed her by the arm and yanked her outside, making her march ahead of him while he tightly grabbed a handful of her hair.

"Ow! Yeah…okay. I'm walkin'….shit!" Hutch blurted out as Absalom trudged forwards, pulling her hair back so tight it stretch her scalp. Through watering eyes, Hutch looked above in awe at the sight of a huge archway they were walking beneath. Just as the walls surrounding, it too was forged from the bodies of fallen vehicles, linked, welded and patched together, making an abstract of ungainly architecture. The redhead jerked her head at a sound. Amongst the slithering silence, a chattering emerged. It was here, then there, bouncing off the ruins of the cars. Laughter. Hissing. She gasped a few times as she caught fleeting glimpses of glowing eyes and red flesh, darting in and out of the darkness as Absalom led her onwards.

"There's my gingerbread girl!" A bubbly voice shot into Hutch's ear, sending her weak in the knees. The cricket-man halted her. She peered with squinted eyes through the gloom across what appeared to be another courtyard, and there, at the far edge, she spied a tiny woman. It was none other than Regina Redgrace. She sat there on a throne made of scrap metal with a backrest of cars piled upon cars, spiraling in a towering twisted mass that defied all aspects of gravity and sanity. Her golden eyes danced above a joyous round of laughter as she sat there, crossed-legged with her cheek resting on her hand. A tiny demon-like creature was massaging her bare feet while another fanned her gently with a car fender.

"Oh, Red, I didn't think your face could get anymore precious than when I pulled you over with that cop car but, girl, you have reached the next level," she smiled. The redhead just stood there, mouth agape as she watched several red-fleshed demons come from the scrap heaps beyond and circle subserviently round the base of Regina's throne. One of them handed her a plate of what Hutch assumed to be grapes but they looked more like tiny glowing rocks. The brunette began snacking on them as she scowled and yelled at Absalom,

"Let go of her. NOW."

Hutch felt the release and relief as the giant unhanded her, but she barely noticed amongst her own confusion. She just stared at Regina, partly terrified, partly pissed, but mostly heartsick.

"Well, Red. What do ya want?"

Hutch looked at her with disgust. Finally, her words came to her.

"What?...What do I want? You brought me here."

"Right, because you called out for me. Now, why are you here?"

"Why? What the fuck?! What happened?! Where am I?!"

"Oh sweetie...you know what happened. You lost the race. Now you're in Hell," she explained with a playfully pitying look on her face.

"If I lost, I owe you a car, not...not my goddamn soul, or...Wait?...Who are you? WHAT are you?"

"Oh, baby, I think ya know the answer to that. I mean, do the math. We're in Hell. We're surrounded by demons and all number of ill shit. I'm probably not the CEO of a trucking company. Well...I mean I am, but you know what I mean."

Hutch just stared at her blankly for a moment.

"So…you're the devil?"

Regina almost choked on what she was eating. She laughed so hard it echoed across the twisted walls and arches of her palace of scrap metal.

"Ohhhh, no, no, no, babe. You're thinking a little too big. But I'm flattered. Really, I am."

"But…but?" Hutch felt herself getting lightheaded. She looked around. "What the hell is this place?"

"It's Hell, sweetie."

"No, this place we're in. All the cars? What…"

"Trophies, Red."

"Trophies?"

"Yep. Each and every car you see is a race I won."

The redhead once again began looking around at the vast number of cars. There had to be over a thousand. "So as you can see, Red, I've won a LOT. Actually, I've never lost. And now, I have your car." Hutch looked at her. "Yeah, its right up there, behind you."

The redhead spun in a panic and looked high to the peak of the archway they had entered through. Sure enough, there was the mangled body of a pale blue Maverick stitched into the chaos. She spun back around to face Regina.

"Yeah, I put it right up there so I can look at it all the time. Kinda like a deer head over the fireplace."

"So ya beat me, good for you. Ya got my car. That's all I was supposed ta give ya, now take me home."

"Oh, Red, sweetheart, I don't think you looked over that contract very well."

"Contract?"

"Yeah, the one that you signed giving me rights to your car, your soul, etcetera, if you lost, which you clearly did. Not for lack of trying though…that part where you tried boxing me out was a nice touch." Hutch was becoming more aggravated by the second.

"I signed a contract for you to take my fuckin' car, nothin' else!" She pointed at the brunette.

"You sure about that? Let's go over that again," Regina said. She then called out an unfamiliar name over her shoulder, "Bishop!" A lanky, red demon came bounding out of the shadows.

"Yes, mum?" He spoke with a broken, British accent.

"Would you be a dear and fetch me the McCray contract."

"Of course, mum." As the creature began to slink away Regina stuck up a finger.

" I'm sorry, no, the *Hutch* McCray contract…don't want you to grab the wrong one."

Hutch raised a brow at the statement as the demon began digging away at a huge pile of disheveled papers off to the side of Regina's throne. Within seconds, the red-fleshed fiend pulled forth a beaten book.

"Ere' it is, mum. Hutch McCray."

"Thank you, Bishop. Now would you kindly read Ms. McCray the part that she apparently read right over?" The demon bounded over to within a few paces of Hutch. The redhead's stare went back and forth with suspicion between the creature and the brunette that smirked behind him. The demon cleared his throat.

"Oi, yeah, ere' it is…in addition to relinquishin' the title to their 1973 Ford Maverick, party two also forfeits their soul n' servitude ta party one ta work in the mines of furnace twelve for n' undetermined length of time or until party one pardons them of said services."

"Well there ya have it, Red. You sort of belong to me till I say you can leave," Regina smiled.

"What?! Give me that!" Hutch yelled and snatched the book away from the demon. Her eyes scanned the open pages, praying the little, red bastard was making it all up.

"Go ahead and read, sweetie. It's all there in black and white, tucked between the lyrics to the Star Spangled Banner and a recipe for raspberry cheesecake. Yummy." Hutch's eyes darted around the page. The brunette was correct. It started right after the words "*the land of the free and the home of the brave.*"

"You know your lips move when you read to yourself, Red?" Regina pointed out.

"Shut up," she snapped as she read the rest. "This is bullshit!" Hutch violently slammed the book together and kicked it into the air. She pointed right at Regina. "You tricked me, bitch!"

"Oh, there's that temper you McCrays are famous for," Regina scolded, "I didn't trick you at all, Red. You just signed it without even reading it. You should reeeeally be more careful, silly."

Hutch felt her blood boiling hotter than the flames rising in the eternal distance beyond. But something cooled them a tad…she was hurt more than anything.

"I trusted you…" the redhead spoke.

"Ewww, yeah you probably shouldn't have done that. I am a dark soul after all."

"Well I didn't know that…" Hutch spoke.

"Let's be honest, Red, if I had told you I was a demon before all this, would you have believed me? No. No ya wouldn'tve. Ya would've said 'oh Regina, ya goofy bitch' and shrugged it off like it never happened. Though, I gotta be honest, a few times I actually pointed out that clause you just read to people and you know what they did? They laughed and they STILL signed it! Ha! Boy, you should've seen their faces when they got down here. They were pissed. More at themselves than anything, I think." Regina finished the plate in front of her and wiped her hands. A tiny demon retrieved it from her lap and ran into the shadows.

Hutch just stood there shaking her head and trying to resist the urge to run over and pop the brunette's head right off her shoulders. She couldn't believe this was happening. Was this even happening?

"Oh, Red, don't look so glum. It's not like you're the first person who hasn't read that contract before signing it."

"My aunt…" Hutch muttered.

"What, babe?"

"My aunt? Where the fuck is she?"

"Oh Red, you lost, remember? You don't get Cass back. That wasn't part of the deal."

"You said she was working for you ta pay off a debt. So she probably got herself in the same bullshit I'm in right now. My aunt is down here somewhere," Hutch adamantly spoke.

The brunette shrugged her shoulders. "Maaaaybe. Maaaaybe not."

"Yeah, just sit over there and play your cutesy bullshit mind games with me, but I'm tellin' ya right now, I know she's down here. And I'm gonna find her and when I do, me and her are gettin' outta here together."

"Well, there ya go, babe, you got it all figured out. A girl with a plan. But in the meantime, you got work ta do. A LOT of work," she spoke then looked past Hutch. "Take her back to the mine."

From behind, Absalom lumbered out from the shadows, grasping the redhead.

"Wait! No! We're not done here!" Hutch yelled as she struggled to free herself from the iron grip of the cricket-man.

"You know what? We actually aren't done here. Let her go!" Regina spoke.

Hutch looked surprised as the giant released her and she turned back to look at the brunette with bated breath.

"The dress clause, Red."

"The...what?"

"Yeah, I almost forgot the other part of our deal. If I won, you had to wear that dress you refuse to take from me."

"You've got ta be fuckin' kiddin' me?"

"Oh, I'm not kidding. Bishop! Fetch the dress!"

"Right away, mum!" The demon did as he was told, rummaging through the scrap behind. He soon ran up to Hutch, totting a cotton sundress.

"Ere' ya go, love," Bishop spoke to her. Hutch just stared at the article of clothing lying there in the demon's boney grasp. She looked up at Regina.

"Well?" The brunette said. Hutch sighed and ripped it from Bishop's hands.

"Thank you for your gift!" Hutch smarted off to her as she just stood there holding the dress at her side.

"Red, it's not a handbag...Put it on."

"Fuck you."

"Put it on or I'll make these crims put it on you," she pointed to the red demons surrounding her, "You don't want that."

"Oi, I think I might fancy that, actually," Bishop spoke.

"Shut up, Bishop," Regina rolled her eyes.

"Yes, mum."

"C'mon, Red. Your shirts torn up anyway."

Hutch glared at her for what seemed like a solid minute.

"Fine..." the redhead spoke, hastily stripping down to her underwear. She quickly threw the dress over her head and let it unfurl down past her knees. She stood there, scowling, face peppered with black soot, hair disheveled, and black boots beneath it all.

She was definitely a sight.

"Would ya just looked at that? Sexy!" Regina smiled, following it up with a wolf whistle. "Now spin."

"What?" Hutch snarled.

"Give us a twirl, Red. Show off what god gave ya!"

"Jesus Christ…" she mumbled as she turned in a full circle, arms crossed.

"There ya go! Work it! Work it!" The brunette laughed, "Oh, Red. You know how to make me laugh."

"Now what?" Hutch growled.

"Now? You go to work."

"What the fuck?! No! Hell no!" Hutch began fighting as Absalom grabbed her once again. He tossed her over his shoulder and began walking off with her.

"Bye, Red. Happy digging, babe! Try not to rip that dress!" She waved playfully as the redhead disappeared out of sight, kicking and screaming the whole way. Bishop slinked up to the side of the throne, looking at Regina with concern.

"Oi, I think that one's gonna be a problem, mum."

"Oh, Bishop, baby, you have no idea how much trouble that one is."

High above and an uncountable amount of dimensions away, a telephone began to ring inside a nicotine stained trailer. Harvey McCray had since turned the TV off, staring like a ghost into the yellowing walls across from where he sat. He was unmoving, like a wax sculpture forever posed in the throes of some unimaginable grief. The phone just kept ringing and ringing, singing a song of inevitability into his humming ears as a life-age of memories and countless regrets played across his numbing mind. She was gone. Hutch was gone. His only daughter. That's why he couldn't budge to answer that phone. He knew on the other end it would be an officer, or Hayden, or Hank, telling him the news…He just wasn't ready to hear it from another human being. Regina had won…Yet again, she had won. And he knew she was never going to stop. With a steady rise, he peeled himself off the couch and unhooked his oxygen line from around his neck. He let it drop to the floor beside the tank, and just like that, he grabbed nothing but his cigarettes, his keys, and a bottle of Jim Beam he kept wedged in the cushions…and he walked away. For the first time in months, he stepped out into the blinding light of the day in nothing but his robe and tattered slippers, walking unsteadily down his steps and right into the driver's side of his pick up truck. He lit a cigarette and fired the engine up, And just like that, he backed up and left, leaving the dark confines of his trailer far behind as he drove out into god only knew where.

Miles and miles passed with the open breeze of the summer air caressing his dehydrated flesh, his mind began taking him back to his heydays, open roads, and car races, drag strips. Fast women and fast cars. Hell. Heaven. Everything that made him smile before the cancer began to ravage his body. Ten minutes later, he was pulling onto Banner's Ridge Road. He stopped the truck a few hundred yards in and just glared down the lonely stretch of road, his cigarette nearly burnt down to the butt. And then, without a word, he tossed the smoke out the window, and plowed the gas as hard as he could. The truck exploded forth, throwing him back in his seat as he went from zero to ninety miles an hour, taking the old girl to her limits. Soon, nothing was inside his head. All the memories that had passed by not that long ago were erased into a black haze inside his mind as his eyes watched the wall of the Dog's Leg come into view. With a smirk on his face, he unhooked his safety belt and impacted the wall with a violence that shook the entire county. He left this world just as his son did thirteen years ago - In a flash of burning and twisted metal.

The ride back to the mine was as foreboding as the drive away from it. Perhaps even more so. Hutch just stared out into the abstract of fog and towering flames beyond, wondering just what in the hell she was going to do at this point, if anything. Of course, there was that small part of her that was still expecting to wake up. To find her eyes popping open to the sight of her camper ceiling, dizzy-headed and waking up from some drunken stupor or bad trip. To realize Hell wasn't a real place at all and that maybe even Regina herself had never existed. But with every passing moment, those thoughts faded further and further into the gloom she so hopelessly stared off into.

With a swift and violent act, she found herself being ripped from where she sat by the monster of a man-thing that was Absalom. He led her through the gate to the mine and gave her a shove that sent her rolling head over heels. She came to a stop, cheek slamming hard against the cold rocks beneath. A sudden rage boiled inside of her that quickly outshined the searing pain she now felt. She pictured herself jumping up and running back at the cricket-man to give him a taste of McCray justice. But she couldn't bring herself to do it. The not-so-distant memories reminded her of how such an act ended with her being dragged like a wet rag. Her anger detoured down into a bleak feeling of malaise that lay on her stomach. She just continued to lay there with her face in the dirt and ears engulfed with the terrible sound of the closing gate. A loud clunk signified the latching of the threshold and Hutch's heart sank all the more. Clanking steel, breaking rocks, screeching and squalling, and all manner of demonic tunes, now wafted up to her from the mine below.

"Somethin' told me you'd be back," a voice startled Hutch. She jerked her head up to see the same green demon from before standing there with the other two close by. It spoke again, "Well, how was your meetin' with Regina, hun? Don't look like it went too well." Hutch sighed in disgust. She clenched her teeth and pushed herself up to a stand, dusting off the ash and blood that clung to her knees through her dress.

"Ooooo, fancy new duds, hun. She give you that?" Hutch groaned and rubbed at her bruising cheek and temple as the green creature kept on, "Hell of a consolation prize, that dress. Well, at least ya got somethin'…"

"Holy shit, would ya just shut the fuck up?" Hutch finally spat at the demon. It closed its mouth, looking a tad bit hurt. "And give me ma hat back." The redhead spoke as she violently ripped her cap off the demon's head, putting it back on her own. With that, she walked away, leaving the demons behind.

"Wait! Where are ya goin'?!" The green one said.

"Home!" Hutch never looked back.

"You ain't a fast learner, are you? Haven't we been through this?"

"I don't know, have we?" Hutch smarted off as she stopped in front of the gate. She placed her hands and feet firmly in the steel crossbars and began climbing.

"That's a bad idea," the green demon shook its head as it watched her ascend, "You seriously think none of us have tried that already?"

"Ahh, let er' go, Izz. She'll find out," the yellow demon growled.

"Yeah, listen ta your buddy there," Hutch yelled down as she reached the peak of the fence. She straddled the steel and waved down at them, "Well, I'd say it's been fun, but it ain't...at all," with that, she threw her other leg over and began crawling down the other side with the tiniest bit of hope on her breath. Her feet hit the rocks below and she looked back through the bars to see the demons she had left behind. But they weren't there...Nothing but a familiar sight stared back at her.

"You havin' fun yet?" A voice came from behind. Hutch jerked and spun round to see the trio of monsters now standing behind her.

"What the..." her head spun back and forth in confusion. It was as if she'd went nowhere at all. "But I just..." she spoke, pointing at the gate.

"Ya just what? Ya climbed the gate and ended up right back in the mine? Oh, you're kidding?" The yellow demon smarted off. It then walked up to her and threw a pickaxe that landed down at her feet. The creature pointed at the tool, "Ya wanna save your own dumb ass? Start diggin'. Or ya can just keep climbin' that gate over and over or runnin' out in the middle of nowhere for all I care. You'll be a crim in no time," the demon then walked off, shaking its head as it descended and disappeared over the edge of the mine. The green demon slowly walked up to Hutch. It picked up the pickaxe and handed it to her.

"Diesel's right, hun. Best start diggin'."

The redhead just stared off with glassy eyes while she half-heartedly gripped the wooden handle of the tool. Both remaining demons watched her in silence for a moment. They had both seen that look before. The point where you realize you're stuck, trapped until possibly the end of all time in a pit of sulfurous ash and rock. The point where you realize you'll never feel the sun warming your bare flesh or smell the blossoms of spring or the fresh-cut grass of summer. It was all gone. Never to return. And a part of you dies. The first part of many.

The green demon gently grabbed Hutch by the hand, "C'mon, hun. It's okay. I know how ya feel, I've been there, but this mine ain't gonna dig itself." And so the redhead let the demon lead her off with nothing but lost hope, and a tick of curiosity, propelling her steps.

With awe, Hutch once again beheld the vastness of the mine. She had only briefly looked it over before, but now the full breadth of its dominion took her aback. She could barely see the other side as it was swallowed up by a haze of gray and red mist that hung in the air like the soiled breath of a forest fire. The whole thing seemed to have no bottom. It funneled down to what perceivably was the basement, but she could barely make out a thing down there. It was a wash of blacks and grays like the surrounding area outside the borders of the mine. Hundreds of rail systems attached themselves to the crooked canyon-like walls, guiding mine cars along their track. They fed downwards into the heart of the pit, leading to a destination unknown by the likes of Hutch. The redhead's stare soon led her back to her own path. She watched her step as the small, green creature led her down through a labyrinth of craggy outcrops, switchbacks, and piles. They passed many groups of other demons toiling away. Some digging at the rocks, some filling the mine cars, and still others working the mine cars, themselves. It was all controlled chaos, like some matte finish painting from the dark mind of an artist long dead, it was bathed in hues of red rage and blue-gray dejection. It was the farthest thing from anything she could've ever imagined herself witnessing firsthand in her life or afterlife. And it was now apparently her cell for God only knew how long.

Hutch and the other demons soon found themselves on a flatter area. The green demon released her hand.

"Well, let's see what we can dig up here, hun. Been kind of a dry spell for us lately. Maybe we can turn it around. Maybe you'll be good luck," the green demon started to swing a pick into the ground below. It split apart, revealing a fresh, shiny golden hue that could be seen all over the mine like a system of veins. This rock seemed to be giving the entire mine that reddish orange glow that kept it from being pitch black. Hutch watched the demons work for a moment.

"I never told ya my real name…" the words just sort of fell out of her.

"Oh, ya mean, Zuul isn't your real name?" The yellow demon grumbled in sarcasm, slamming away at the rock.

"Naw…it's Hutch."

"Ha! Shit, I don't know which one I believe less, Zuul or Hutch," the yellow one once again opened its mouth.

"Hey, asshole, I ain't lyin' to ya. It's the name ma dad gave me," suddenly something hit Hutch hard, "My dad….Ham…Hank…"

"What's she goin' on about?" The yellow demon asked.

"I don't know," the green demon responded.

"My dad. My brothers…They gotta know by now…I died. Oh shit…I'm dead. I'm fuckin' dead." She dropped her pickaxe.

"Wow, that just now hit ya?" The yellow demon scoffed.

"Calm down, hun," the green demon said, trying to sooth her.

"Calm down? Calm down?! How the fuck do I do that?"

"Start digging. Keeps your mind off of things," the green demon kept picking away at the rock.

"Dig? That's your answer, just dig?"

"Hey, nothin' else ta do."

"Great…what the hell are we diggin' for anyway?" The redhead questioned.

"You ain't diggin' for nothin'. You're just talkin'," the yellow demon interjected.

"Oh, don't listen ta him…were diggin' for all number of different stuff. But mainly firerite. That's all that glowin' orangish stuff everywhere. See?" The green demon pulled a lump of the mineral out of the rock and held it up to Hutch. The redhead stared at it with a bit of awe on her breath. The glowing insides of the rock seemed to churn over and over in a dance of amber hues, like autumn leaves tumbling one over the next. She reached out and touched it, it felt slightly warm. "Pretty ain't it?" The demon smiled.

"What's it for?"

"Fuel."

"Fuel? For what?" Hutch's interest was beyond piqued.

"The furnaces for the hellfire."

"The hellfire?"

"Yeah, hun. I know you've seen it. That towering wall of flame that's everywhere on the horizon down here? That's the hellfire." The green demon explained. Hutch just stared blankly. The creature spoke again, "Okay, picture your household stove. We're sort of in the middle of one of the burners, but you and me, we're like the size of…bacteria. We dig the fireite and put into the carts. The carts are pushed to the bottom of the pit and led through the lower shafts into the furnaces that fuel the hellfire. Simple."

There was a bit of silence as Hutch let the explanation sit in.

"So…were basically minin' coal to fuel the fires of hell?" The redhead spoke, hoping she was wrong on some level.

"Bingo! Give this broad a balloon!" The yellow demon smarted off.

"Jesus…we're in the furnace of Hell …"

"Well…one of many."

"Huh?"

"We're in just one of thousands of furnaces, hun. Hell's pretty big."

Hutch just stood there, once again taking the sight of the mine all in. She shook her head at a thought, "So we're in the basement of Hell? The crotch, no the asshole, of Hell? And our job is to mine shitty rocks? So we're shit-stained workers not even good enough to be in the REAL Hell. Wow, yeah that makes me feel great."

"Hey now, it's a pretty important job, keeping the fire's of Hell goin'," the green demon tried to make light of the situation.

"Yeah, and what happens if the fires go out?" Hutch asked.

"Ha! Actually, I don't know. But it can't be good. The whole expression 'when hell freezes over' and all that. Definitely not good. I'm Izzy, by the way," the demon ended on a salutation that was long overdue. The creature extended its claw-covered hand out to Hutch for a handshake. The redhead apprehensively obliged.

"Izzy…okay," Hutch simply nodded. The green demon then turned and pointed, "And that grumpy asshole back there is Diesel." The yellow demon just grunted. "And this blue guy here, that's Hieronymus."

Hutch stared at the tiny, elephant-like creature. A slight smile turned up on either side of his trunk. An odd crunching noise fell forth as two spindly arms came out from the demon's back. They bent up and round to his head, each holding an eyeball in hand that hovered right in front of his eyeless face. The eyes looked around and focused on the nervous redhead.

"Holy shit…" she swallowed a lump from her throat.

"Yeah, he's kinda different. And quiet, if you haven't noticed," Izzy smiled.

"What's his name again?"

"Hieronymus. But I just call him Hiney."

The blue demon scowled a bit at the nickname.

"Yeah, I don't think he likes that," Hutch said. She then forced a smile and threw a little wave at the blue demon. Another round of crunching came forth as a third arm wrapped round him and coyly waved back at her.

"Jesus…how many of those does he have?" She muttered.

"Four, that I know of," Izzy said. Hieronymus then withdrew his eyes, picked up four pickaxes in each of his extra appendages and started to dig.

"Hell, that just seems downright unfair," Hutch spoke as she kept watching the bizarre creature mine away as she too began to swing her axe with a sigh on her breath. The rock was surprisingly soft. It broke away almost like top soil beneath her swings, revealing an abundance of amber rock that illuminated the area all the more. She gathered up an armful of the mineral and tossed it into the nearby cart.

"There ya go, hun. You're getting' it," Izzy smiled.

"Goddamn I'm missin' jail right about now…" the redhead muttered as she once again began swinging into the rocks.

The Princess

Away from the unending orchestra of clanking steel and thundering toil, a tiny coo of pain wrapped in pleasure, exuded from Regina's lips. She sat there, topless, facing backwards upon her throne as Bishop pressed a glowing, white-hot key into the flesh of her back. Her lips writhed beneath an orgasmic moan as the red demon recoiled the metal, leaving the impression of the Maverick's key forever burned into her skin. Bishop blew at the blackened victory brand, chasing away the smoke that still rolled from it.

"All done, mum," he spoke to her. He backed away submissively as she turned around in the steel chair, facing him with an emotionless gaze. A group of tiny demons scampered to her side, holding her shirt and bra. She grabbed them up but didn't immediately throw them on as she stared off through the archways of mangled cars to the fiery horizon beyond.

"The flames….they're dying," she spoke a redundancy that made Bishop's blood boil. It was always this way. Every damn earthly July she would rob the brimstone from the firerite mixes and use them for her own selfish conquests. The flames of Furnace 12 would inevitably began to die and they would have to pull double time lest someone from higher up came knocking on the door to see what the problem was. And neither one of them wanted that. They were in this together. Or at least that's what Bishop kept telling himself. In the end, the red demon just kept his mouth shut and watched Regina with a growing concern as her attention drew from the fires, to her own bare stomach. She began to lovingly rub her hands across her flesh, remembering at time when things weren't just about her. A memory overtook her…

Regina sat there, the chill of stainless steel biting at her bottom through her underwear. And even crueler yet, was the chill tickling her spine through the open back of a medical gown she desperately wanted off. For the first time in her existence she felt vulnerable, and she didn't like it. Her feet dangled and twitched off the edge of the table, rubbing across one another in the anxious thoughts of what was to come. How did she end up here? She never once pictured herself in a doctor's examination room, staring at the mundane white, block walls peppered with biology cross-sections and dioramas of human body parts - These paper and plastic reminders of one's own mortality and feebleness. Were these macabre things supposed to make you feel better about your visit? Surely not. But still, she eyed them with a curiosity she never imagined herself to have until that moment in time. Because, for once, they actually applied to her.
Suddenly, the room came to life with a rush of air. Regina winced inside at the doctor's return. It felt as if he'd been gone for weeks, hell maybe he had. Dr. Higgins…That was his name, right? Jesus, it sounded like the name of a puppet cat on public access TV. His practice was tucked between a hardware store and a bridle shop. It was about as small-town as you could get. She was quite sure he was probably moonlighting as a veterinarian on the weekends, helping the neighbors' horse give birth all while talking about his hunting dogs and CB radio hobby. She wasn't referred to him. She didn't find him in the phone book. She just happened upon his office while driving around in lieu of the events that worried her enough to give the place a second look. With a smile as genuine as the age that was beginning to gray his beard, he spoke,
"Well, Mrs…Redgrace. We found out the problem."
"Oh, God. Is it cancer? It's cancer isn't it?" She interjected with fear. The doc had to keep himself from chuckling,

"What?! No. No. No. You leaped to the worst thing pretty quick there. No, you have vomitin', mainly in the mornings, uh, frequent urination, um, lightheadedness, what else was on here…?" he started thumbing a page on a clipboard he held.

"Stomach cramping."

"Right. Stomach crampin' too. So you wanna take a guess at what's wrong with you?"

"Cancer?"

"No! Ha! No. Where do ya come up with this stuff? No…You, little lady, are pregnant."

A hush fell on the room as Regina's eyebrow rose so hard you could almost hear it over the Beach Boy music humming through the door glass.

"I'm…I…what?"

"Pregnant. You're with child. Congratulations." The doctor waited for a happy response, but nothing came. Not even a smile.

"Well…How did this happen?" She asked.

The doc couldn't contain his chuckle this time.

"Well…Um, I think ya know how it happened?….Don't ya?" Regina was quiet for a moment. The doc's confusion sat in further. "Well…you were with a man, right? There's a Mr. Redgrace, right? You and him, you two…had relations? Yes?"

"No…I…I KNOW how it happened…I just…Oh my god…this can't be happening. Not to me. Not now," her voice began to crackle into a sobbing of tears.

"Oh no now, don't cry," the doc grabbed a handful of tissues and handed them to her. "It's fine. You're gonna be fine. I know being pregnant can be overwhelming and…"

"Do you?! Do you know?! And how many babies have shot out of you?!" The doc, leaned back, eyes widened. He had no rebuttal. "I'm sorry…I'm so sorry," she almost whispered as she dabbed at her eyes. "Why does this keep happening to me?"

"Ummm, why does *what* keep happenin', Mrs. Redgrace? Pregnancy?"

"No! Not that…This!" She pointed at the tears running down her cheeks. The doc was even more confused. "It was that feather…it did this…Forget it. Thanks Doctor," she spoke bluntly and began to retreat out the door.

"Mrs. Redgrace!?"

"What?!"

"Your clothes," he pointed to the pile of garments on the far chair, "You don't want the town gettin' a free show do ya?" She felt stupid. God, she was losing it. She walked back in and grabbed them.

"Well...I'll leave ya to it then," the doc nodded as he left her alone in the cold sting of that awful white room. She dropped her gown to the floor and just stood there, half naked, staring off with tears still pooling. Her head cocked as she caught eye of a chart hanging on the far wall. She slowly walked up to it, gazing upon the artist renditions of different stages of pregnancy - A visual aid showing how babies changed over nine months. With an unsteady hand, she traced a finger down the timeline, ending with the final weeks and the tiny human that was ready to come into the world. Her face softened as she expelled a sigh and ran a hand across her stomach, cupping it gently. She held it there for what seemed like the whole of eternity, wondering what exactly was going on inside of there. And then something happened that she never expected. She smiled. It was tiny but it was there. Almost involuntarily it crept onto her face and reheated the cold tears that still lingered.

Minutes later, she was fully dressed and walking through the lobby, but she stopped at the sight of an information pamphlet amongst a slew of other pamphlets. She plucked it up and stared at it. It was titled in bold, *"So, you're pregnant?"* Yes, she was...and she had no idea how she was going to break the news to him.

"Why the hell is it so damn cold down here? I thought Hell was supposed ta be hot?" Hutch blurted out as she swung away at the rocks. *"Hot as hell."* She remembered the expression. It carried no weight in this place. It wasn't hot. It actually wasn't cold either, it was...well, it was nothing. The only thing that even felt like anything was this strange crawl beneath her flesh. A sensation that ran a chill up her spine every time she watched the cobalt flames rage with an eerie silence in the distance.

"So what's your story?" Hutch suddenly spoke towards the green demon after a moment of silence.

"My story?" Izzy asked.

"Well all of y'alls, I guess. How the hell you end up down here?"

"Probably the same way you ended up down here. You lose a bet?"

"Yeah. How'd you know?"

"It's always a bet when it comes to demons."

"I lost a race."

"Right. Well, that's how a lot of us got here, hun. We raced Regina, and we lost. You always lose. No one beats Regina."

"Bullshit. No ones unbeatable."

"Diesel? Has anyone ever beat Regina?" Izzy yelled over her shoulder.

"Hell no," he answered back without hesitation.

"Yeah, well that's cuz she's a cheatin' bitch. Rigged our agreement. Rigged the race. Hell she's probably been riggin' everythin' from the first day I saw her."

"Ahhh, don't let it bug ya too much. She may act happy-go-lucky and full of life but she's far from it. She's being punished too. Just like us."

"How ya mean?" Hutch raised a brow.

"Well, she's what they call the Furnace Master here, the one who makes sure we're doin' our jobs. But she ain't here on her own freewill. She was sentenced to this. Ya see, we're in a prison within a prison. The King put her down here."

"King?"

"King Redbane, her father. Regina is a Hell Princess."

"Get the fuck out…" Hutch's jaw dropped, "She's the princess of Hell?"

"No, hun. Not THE princess of hell, just A princess. She's one of many, but most of the others aren't in the type of trouble she's in."

"Trouble? For the love of shit, this is Hell. What did she do that was so wrong?"

"Way I heard it, going topside. Flirtin' with humans. Trying to be one."

"She's Hell royalty but she wants to be a human?" Hutch shook her head.

"Well, it's that old 'grass is always greener' thing. Fish wants to be a bird. The sea wants to be a mountain."

"So a demon goin' topside and minglin' with people is a no-no?"

"Yep…To be honest most of this is rumors. Main thing is she's down here serving out her time. Hell, she ain't even supposed ta be going topside anymore but you see she ain't obeyin' that. If the King knew, he'd probably be throwin' her down in the deepest depths he could find, but she runs a tight ship. Keeps lips sealed and everyone looks the other way."

"Damn…" the redhead mumbled as she gathered up another armload of rocks. All of a sudden, a loud noise almost brought her to her knees. It thundered into the mine, refracting off the walls like the blast of a giant horn sending out a call of warning. She spun round to see a dark cloud flooding over the edge of the mine down the way. A maelstrom of lightning began whipping through the mess and the redhead's eyes adjusted to the sight of a rectangular object emerging from it all.

"You see that?" Izzy pointed.

"What the hell is it?" Hutch squinted.

"That's the bread and butter of Redgrace Logistics."

As Hutch looked onwards, she could see it was the back of a semi truck, creeping to the side of the mine. She heard the blast of the air brakes as it came to a stop with its tires only inches from careening over the edge. The doors swung open with a violent screech. Hutch's eyes widened in horror as she watched dozens of human-like figures plummeting out of the truck, into the mine. They rained down, bouncing off rocks and rolling into balls on their descent into the terrible pit.

"What the fuu….?" She couldn't even finish as she watched them begin to rise up from where they had fallen.

"They call them grays," Izzy stepped to the edge of the mining spot, watching alongside Hutch. The figures looked like humans covered in ash. They started fanning out, slowly marching along, much like the zombies in movies Hutch had watched late at night with Ham. This wasn't the first batch. She remembered she had seen others when she first looked into the mine.

"What are they?"

"Lost souls…Well, sort of. That's what Regina's been up to with her trucking company. She found a way into Purgatory and she's been gathering souls from there, shipping them in her trucks back to this gateway, and dumping them."

"Why?"

"More souls to mine and help with the effort."

"Goddamn, how many souls does it take to mine the coal for these furnaces?"

"Oh, hun. Were mining for more than firerite," Izzy cryptically spoke as she walked away and began swinging into the rock once again. For the next few moments, Hutch stopped her toil and just watched with awe at the demons that had befriended her. If this was truly hell, they were nothing like she'd imagined dark souls to be. They were full of vivid colors and lines that made them look like living cartoons. To that end, they put her mind of Rat Fink style characters like the ones she'd seen on fenders and flags alike at the strip. It was all so surreal. She spoke up again,

"You said you raced Regina? Which means y'all were topside before? You were people?"

"Hard ta believe ain't it?" Izzy said.

"Jesus…so every demon in this mine used ta be a person?"

"Well…most I think."

"Shit. That means ma aunts probably in here somewhere," Hutch stopped her digging. A bit of hope was on her tongue, "Do you know a Cassandra. Most called her Cass."

"Hmmm, well the name doesn't sound too familiar but…"

"You think anyone else would? She's gotta be down here. Regina told me she was working for her."

"Hun, it's possible, but you gotta understand somethin…"

Right at that moment a loud clank sang out from Hutch's dropping pickaxe. Both Izzy and the redhead's eyes met in curiosity over the sound.

"What the hell is this?" Hutch dug under the normal firerite and pulled out a deep red crystal. She held it up for the demons to see.

"Are ya shittin' me?! She's swingin' for a few hours and already finds one!" Diesel voiced an obvious distain.

"Oh, hun, you found one. Good for you!" Izzy smiled.

Hutch turned the beautiful rock over and over in suspicion.

"What the hell is it?"

"Remember when I told ya we were mining for more than firerite? That there is brimstone."

"And?"

"And?! It's like finding a diamond!"

"Well, I don't think I got much use for jewelry down here, so unless this thing can whip me up a cigarette and a beer I'm just chuckin' it over here," Hutch spoke as she went to hurl it into the nearby cart.

"Stop!" Izzy grabbed her arm. The redhead glared at her with question. "That thing is important. You don't just throw brimstone into a cart."

"Okay. What makes it so special?"

"Brimstone has all kinds of uses. Powerful uses. Upper level demons consume it to become stronger and faster. Regina uses it to open her gateways to the earth."

As Hutch listened, her nose began to work overtime at the smell of something familiar. She pulled the rock to her face and gave it a huge whiff.

"Holy shit...I think I smoked this once," Hutch looked unnerved.

"Ya, what now?"

"Topside, before all this mess. Regina let me smoke somethin'. Smelled just like this. I saw crazy shit. I saw this place...The hellfire in the distance."

Things were silent for a moment as Hutch silently reminisced on that night in her camper. Suddenly, she donned a look of irritation, "Fuck this stuff." She went to toss it into the cart, but once again Izzy stopped her throw.

"What the hell is wrong with you?! I told ya not to do that!"

"Hey! Ya done told me this shit is only good for demons like Regina, so why the hell would I keep it?! I don't want her ta have it!"

"It's got other powers, okay?"

"That so? Start talkin'," Hutch pointed down at her.

Izzy sighed. "Maybe I oughta go ahead and tell you about the change...Look around the mine. What do you see?"

Hutch dropped her pickaxe to her side and leered around. "Demons minin'?"

"What about the demons though? Notice anything about them?"

"They're all little assholes like you?"

"No, the colors."

Hutch once again began scanning the mine with curiosity. She did notice.

"They're all green and yella."

"There you go."

"So what?"

"That's the process down here. See, when you first get here you start off as a human, like you. But overtime you….you change."

"Into a demon?"

"Yeah."

"Jesus Christ…" Hutch became agitated.

"You first change into a green demon, like me. A greenie. Then you slowly shift into a yellow, or blondie, like Diesel over there. And then…." Izzy trailed off.

"And then I turn inta one of them red things, right?" Hutch said.

"Yeah. You turn into a crim."

"A crim?"

"Crims. Reds. Crimsons…they're the worst of the worst. Whatever bit of humanity was left in them is all gone."

"We're talkin bout those same things Regina surrounds herself with?"

"Yes."

"And y'all are tryin' ta avoid bein that? They were all fawnin' over her, fanning and rubbin' her feet. I'd rather be doin' that than slavin' away in this shithole."

"You don't wanna be a crim," Izzy shook her head.

"And why not?"

"You become a true demon then. There's no comin' back from it. And I think the worst part is ya remember everything. Everything about your life. Who you were. And it does nothin' but torture you to the point of madness."

"So? I remember all that shit right now."

"Not for long…" Diesel mumbled in the background.

"What the hell does that mean?" Hutch glared with suspicion. Izzy sighed.

"I was tryin to tell you earlier, when you asked me about your aunt, when you start to turn, you forget some things. And then after awhile, you forget a lot of things. Pretty soon you don't remember much at all. The life you had is some distant thing. And all you get every once in awhile are strange flashes of memories that may or may not even have happened to you…Even our names…and the names we have now? Not sure where they came from. Probably just made them up at some point. So you see, you're aunt may be down here, but I doubt anyone but Regina would know who it is. It could be any of these demons."

Hutch looked hopelessly across the breadth of the mine at the thousands of imps toiling away.

"Hun?...Are you okay?" Izzy asked.

"Oh yeah, I'm fine. I'm in Hell. I'm gonna turn inta a demon and lose my memory. And I'm never gonna see my aunt again, the only woman who ever really gave a shit about me in my pathetic life...Things are fuckin' fantastic," her voice cracked a little at the end and her eyes glassed over with tears she quickly covered up.

"Well ya know, you don't have to become a crim if you keep finding those," Izzy pointed at the brimstone rock the redhead still held tight.

"Boy, ya find a silver lining on every shit-stained cloud don't ya?"

"Well, I figure this place is bad enough without me addin' to it. Might as well smile. You should try it sometime"

"Yeah...don't hold your breath on that."

"Hey? Are ya gonna use that goddamn rock or not?! Every second you two stand here and cackle like hens is one step closer to ya turnin' green," Diesel growled.

Hutch looked down at the glowing stone in her hand.

"How do I...? Do I smoke it?"

"No ya don't smoke it, ya fuckin' hippie!" Diesel sighed and threw his pickaxe to the ground. He lumbered over to the redhead. "Here..." he grabbed her hand and thrust upward till she was pressing the stone to the center of her chest. "Now, hold it right there. It'll start pourin' into ya." The yellow demon stepped back from her and watched as she sheepishly stared down at the rock, waiting for something to happen. But nothing did.

"Am I doin it right? Should I close my eyes er' somethin?"

"Shut up. You'll feel it," Diesel silenced her, "And when you do feel it, only take a nip. You don't wanna drain that thing dry. You'll be in deep shit when ya go ta turn it in later." Hutch had no idea what he meant by that. Several more unnerving seconds paved the way as she stood there, waiting with grave apprehension. Would it hurt? Would it bring her to her knees? She soon began to read the looks of confusion being exchanged between the demons that stood in front of her. Something was definitely amiss.

"What the hell?" Diesel bellowed, "Give me that thing! What ya do girly, dig yourself up a dud?" He ripped the stone from Hutch's hand and looked at it with disgust. He began listening to it and shaking it violently.

"Oh hell, there's no such thing as a dud brimstone, Diesel," Izzy crossed her arms.

"Well there is now!"

"Hey, maybe it won't work on her for awhile. She did say she smoked it with Regina while she was still topside. Maybe it's built up in her system or somethin," Izzy suggested.

Diesel made a face.

"Naw! She done dug up a paperweight."

"Well try ta use it on yourself then!" Hutch growled.

"Oh, wow I never thought of that!" Diesel sarcastically spat. "I can't use it! It's bonded ta you!"

"To me?

"Yeah! These things bond to whoever touches them first. Then ya gotta turn them into the crims. Crims are the only ones that can break that bond. So here!" The yellow demon chucked the rock. It rolled and stopped at Hutch's feet. "Enjoy your pet rock! And don't lose the damn thing. When the crims come ta collect, they're gonna know you had one. They can see it in your eyes."

The redhead stood there in confusion, watching the grumbling demon as he returned to his work post, mumbling things like "What a waste." and "Should've been me." Hutch's stare returned back to the face of Izzy, who was smiling, as always.

"Am I a freak?" Was all Hutch could expel.

"What?" Izzy raised a brow.

"The stone. It didn't work on me. Does that mean I'm some kind of freak or what?"

"Oh hun, no, no, no. Don't you worry your head about it," Izzy said as she bent down and picked up the glowing stone. She handed it back to its finder, gently patting the redhead's hand as she wrapped her fingers around its glimmer. "There. Now hold onto that until shift change. It may not have helped you, but Regina will be thrilled with it. That's a big one."

"Well, I'm sure glad I'm here ta make her happy," Hutch said as she rolled the rock around in her hand and felt the anger began to rise. "You know what? Fuck Regina." With that, she reared back and hurled the rock as hard as she could towards the center of the pit.

"What the hell, girly?!" Diesel yelled as he watched the stone disappear into the depths below.

"Hun, what did you do?!" Izzy panicked. Hieronymus grit his teeth and whimpered behind her.

"What did I do? Are ya blind? I threw that rock down in the hole. And if I find anymore, they're gonna be followin' it. Fuck her and her brimstones," she spat out as she returned to digging into the rocks with a newfound violence. Izzy slowly turned to look back at Diesel with worry on her face. Diesel pointed at her.

"I told ya she was gonna be trouble, didn't I? Redheads are always trouble."

Far outside the iron gates of the pit, Regina still hadn't moved from her victory throne of scrap metal. Bishop stood there beside her, watching from the side of his eye with an odd apprehension gnawing away at him for his boss's silence. The hush itself was nothing new. He had seen her stare into nothingness for earthly months on end but this was something different. Something was astir inside of her, and he didn't like it one damn bit. He broke the silence.

"What's our next move against the McCray's, mum?"

Regina said nothing. She just kept staring off at the beaten car she had taken from Hutch.

"Mum?" the crim spoke with reluctance.

"I heard you, Bishop…"

"An'?"

"And what?!" She turned and snapped, her golden eyes drilling into him. The demon recoiled a bit like a dog being put in its place.

"I just wanna know whu' the plan is, is all, mum."

"The plan is, we keep digging until we find it," she looked towards the car again.

"Right…but…it's just…"

"Yes?" Regina stared at him again.

"We been diggin' for a long time is all, mum. Whu' if there ain't anymore down ere'?"

"They're out there, Bishop. We just need to keep digging. We need more bodies. Just keep doing what you're doing and trucking them in."

"Mum, we got ten thousand in the pit n' hundreds more comin, but…'

"But?"

"Well…we're runnin' outta brimstone, mum. Ya know that. Ain't gonna be enough of the stuff to keep that gate open very much longa. N' July is almost up, and well, I know how you feel about July."

"Do you? Tell me."

"Well…." the crim twiddled his finger tips across one another. He knew he was treading on dangerous ground, "It's just that…You been playin' this game a long time with him. You took so much from him. And now you took his daughter. Why ya think ya ave' ta become a bright-eye again ta end him?"

"Bishop, Bishop, poor, simple, Bishop," Regina sighed as she leaned back in her chair, shooing away crims that had been fanning her, "You don't understand vengeance at all, do you?"

"Well, oi think oi know my share of ow' it works but…"

"No you don't. Not on my level you don't. What you understand is revenge. It's not about running blindly in and ripping someone apart, limb from limb, and it's over just like that," she snapped her fingers, "No…vengeance…it's…it's a dance. A long, slow dance. Hips swaying, limbs entangled. It's a fine wine you savor. An orchestration. A melody that builds upon itself with every single note written in shades of blue-sky beauty and then retraced in malevolent, cast-iron. And then, you fawn over that opus, you hold it close to your breast until every single pitch is a part of you. Then, and only then, are you ready to ruin someone. And when it's all over, when the finale finally arrives, you see it in their eyes. Fear, despair…and the most satisfying thing of all? Regret. Them knowing that all of this hell could've been avoided had they chose not to be such a despicable creature," she finished with what seemed like her own regret weighing her tongue down amongst the poetic explanation. Bishop was deathly silent beside her. Soon, she turned back and looked at him again. "Now…do you understand what vengeance is?"

"Yes, mum."

"I wish I could believe that…The McCray's are off limits. I'm done with them for now."

"Old red-eyes ain't gonna like that, mum, havin' ta wait another year. I understand this is some orchestra to ya, but 'ow long ya gonna keep him from gettin' his payback?"

"If he has a problem, he can come to me with it. Does he have a problem with me?" Regina looked deep into the eyes of the demon beside her.

"No, mum."

"Do YOU, have a problem with me, Bishop?"

"No, mum."

"Good. Now round up the others and go to the pit to help him with the next collection. And you tell him Hank McCray is not to be touched. Understand?"

"Yes, mum."

Shift Change

The constant swinging "clank" of Hutch's pickaxe was becoming as monotonous as the silence between the group. Even Izzy had shut her mouth long ago, leaving the redhead to wonder if anything was worth being said at all at this point. She had no idea how much time had passed since she first climbed down the side of that pit. It seemed like a full work day had come and gone but without a clock in sight she had absolutely no idea. Of course the very thought of a clock was laughable. Did demons keep time in this shit-hole? She highly doubted it. She felt it more likely that time, itself, meant absolutely nothing to any of the beings around her and, perhaps, that's what scared her more than anything…Knowing that she would eventually become one of them, never caring about time either. Knowing a moment would arrive when time was not even a memory, and all that remained was the swing of the axe and the smell of the sulfurous rock beneath.

With every passing moment, she could feel her fatigue begin to build…and, with that, she began to question things all over again. Could she even sleep? Was sleep as distant a thing as time? She also felt hungry and her craving for cigarettes would not wane. Surely these things were of no use to a dead person? Still, they remained as persistent as her unquenchable thirst to break down the gate and ring Regina's tiny little head off her tiny little body.

Just when she dared go to speak out an inquiry of her weariness, her ears were introduced to an all-consuming sound. Not quite unlike the siren from the unloading trucks, a loud bellow of a horn blew down into the pit and every soul looked up. Hutch eyed Izzy with reluctance as the noise faded off like the storm warning sirens she dreaded as a kid.

"What the hell was that? More trucks comin' in?" The redhead questioned.

"Shift change!" Diesel yelled as he threw his pickax to the ground and began climbing up the side of the mine. Hutch watched as the sides of the mine came alive with thousands of bodies crawling upwards in a slithering unison.

"C'mon, hun. Up we go," Izzy followed behind Diesel. Hutch looked to the strange blue demon, Hieronymus.

"What's happenin?"

The creature just smiled at her and walked on past, ascending with the others. "Wow, that was helpful. Thanks," Hutch spat out in disgust as she followed his lead. She swore the climb out was worse than the hours of labor she had just put in, her attire wasn't helping either. Her dress kept getting caught under her boots and stuck to her knees, but soon enough it was over and she was standing on the main grounds of the mine, right at its edge. She noticed all the toiling souls were forming a ring around the pit as far as she could see, posting up in single-filed lines. She forced her way towards the front through grumbling demons she'd never met, and wedged herself in between Izzy and Diesel.

"Someone wanna tell me what the hells goin' on?"

"Shhhh!" Several demons shushed her.

"Shift change. Collection time," Izzy simply whispered, never taking her eyes from the direction of the gate. Soon a symphony of opening hinges sent a cringe through Hutch as she watch a deluge of red bodies begin to flood into the mine.

"Crims…" she whispered to herself, "What do they want?"

"Somethin' you ain't got," Diesel whispered, "It was nice knowin' ya, girly."

"Don't say that!" Izzy admonished him as silently as she could.

"Hey, she's the one that chucked the brimstone, not me."

"Shut up. Shut up. Here they come," Izzy reached back and slapped him on the arm.

Hutch watched as the group of crims fanned out, all holding open bags as they walked to each line. One of the bigger red demons came up to their group. He lumbered over on all fours like an ape and then stood tall, glaring down at Izzy with a smile. He was an odd looking sort, body like a primate but a head that looked like someone had stretched translucent red flesh over the skull of a wolf. His pointy ears laid back and twitched as he spoke,

"Well, Izz. I know you got somethin' for me. You always do."

Izzy held out her arm and opened her hand to reveal two small brimstones she had found.

The big crim's smile crumpled.

"That's it?"

"Yeah."

With a grunt he grabbed them from her hand and stared into her eyes.

"Are you sure that's all ya found?"

Izzy looked right back into his crimson eyes, never batting a lash.

"Yes. That's all I found."

The crim growled in further disappointment.

"So my best stone finder gives me two pebbles that could barely start a car, let alone keep a gate runnin'?"

"I'll do better next time."

"Not only are these things tiny, but I swear you drained them too much. You takin' more than you should?"

"No. Never."

"Ya sure bout that? I doubt a damn hoot-owl could make these things out on a moonless night. Look at how dim they are."

"I took my fair share, I said."

The crim grumbled and tossed them into the bag. He pointed right at Izzy's face.

"I'm gonna have eyes on ya, greenie. You been that color too long ta not be takin' too much. I catch you drainin' more than you should, your ass is punchin' a one way ticket straight to the furnace pit, ya hear?"

Izzy just nodded. Her growing nervousness became palpable to Hutch. She didn't know what the furnace pit was but it instantly sent a chill through her. The crim fiddled with the collection bag for a moment and stepped onwards. He locked eyes with Hutch and something odd happened. He smiled again.

"McCray! Last time I saw you, you were tastin' the business end of a semi. Actually three, semis."

Confusion instantly settled into the redhead. She looked at him with a suspicious glare.

"You not remember me?" The crim tilted his head.

"Should I? All you red things look the same ta me."

"Ha! Well now that just hurts my feelings a lil' bit."

Hutch kept staring into his ruby eyes. A flashback overtook her.

"You're the trucker...the red-eyed trucker."

"Sure am! Buuuut that ain't the first time we've met. Naw, me n' you, we go back a few years. Still don't remember me?"

"No." Was she supposed to? She hadn't recalled meeting a seven foot tall red-demon in her past travels.

"Shame...but damn, you still look good. Pity you chose to beat beavers 'stead of polishing poles."

Hutch felt her anger rise. She tried to keep it down.

"Are we done here?"

"Naw, I'm afraid we ain't," he said as he unfurled the bag open once again, "What you got for me?"

Hutch stared at the bag then looked over at Diesel.

"I'm talkin' ta you McCray, not him!" The crim bellowed. "Let's see those stones."

"I don't have any."

The crim sighed and dropped the bag to his side.

"Bullshit. You didn't find one of those little red boogers on your first shift?"

"No."

"Ya know, I don't think I believe that. In fact, I think you're holdin' out. AND I also got the sneakin' suspicion that one of these new friends of yours gave ya the stupid-ass idea of hoardin' the stones for your own benefit."

Izzy started shaking her head with a 'no'.

"Really, Izz? Cuz maybe that's why you ain't got no more stones than that pathetic lot you just handed over. Maybe you were lettin' McCray here keep most of the ones you found? Maybe ya got some soft spot for your new bright-eye pet."

"No," the green demon squeaked out.

"I hope not. Cuz I'm about to find out. And if I'm right, you're ALL goin' to the furnace pit together. You can hold hands and sing kumba-fuckin-ya while the flesh burns off your bodies." Right then, the crim looked deep into Hutch's eyes. "So McCray, ya say ya didn't find any stones, eh?"

The redhead sneered and cast him an unblinking glare. Diesel, Izzy, and Hieronymus all shook as the crim searched deep through her stare, looking for the truth. Suddenly, the crim's, face went back to normal. He sighed.

"I guess you weren't, lyin McCray. Ain't that a bitch. You'll be lookin like this one in no time with that kinda luck," he pointed down to Izzy whose face was more than flabbergasted. The crim stepped up to Diesel.

"I ain't got nothin'," he confessed.

"Ha! Well there's a fuckin' shocker! Just look at you, blondie. You're startin' ta get a little orange shade comin' in and we both know that ain't a goddamn sunburn. You know, when you first came down here I thought ta maself, there's a dude with the balls ta last. Attitude six lanes wider than the road he died on. I figured you'd be green for eternity. But no, here ya stand, bout to jump headfirst into an empty swimming pool," the crim shook his head. Diesel just scowled up at him with nothing to say. The crim wasn't finished. "Now this one over here…" the crim pointed to Izzy, "That's the one I figured would be wearin' red by now. Nope, she's still greener than an elm tree in June. And she's been here longer than you. Pathetic." The crim leaned in till he was inches from Diesel's face. "Ya wanna know what I think, blondie? I think you wanna be a crim.

Diesel shook his head 'no'.

"No?! Really? Cuz ya ain't doin' much ta convince me otherwise." The crim rose back up with a smile. He patted the yellow demon on the shoulder. "Don't worry, blondie. I'll make sure I put a good word in ta the boss about ya. Maybe you can be her new car detailer. After all, you're gonna need somethin' ta keep ya occupied when all those bright-eye memories come rushin' back inta that pea-brain of yours. Now get outta ma sight," The crim shoved Diesel aside and walked up to Hieronymus. Hutch watched as the tall demon gave the tiny blue one an odd nod and just walked right on by him as if he were exempt from the collection process. The redhead went to open her mouth about it, but instead, another inquiry came falling out that bothered her even more.

"Who is he?" She spoke as she kept her eye on the boss crim.

"Not sure, hun. Most just call him red-eyes," Izzy looked up and answered.

The redhead's mind began working overtime

"No one knows his human name?" She spoke.

"Nope. That's just what he's called around here. You mean you don't know him? He seems to know you."

"Yeah, no shit...How long's he been down here?"

"Since before me," Izzy said.

"Well I gathered that much, but how long've you been down here?"

"Uhhh...I don't know."

"Christ...You demons and your damn old-timer's disease. Bout as worthless as a double headed nail."

"Excuse me, but don't ya think we should be focusin' on somethin' else right now, girly?"

"Like what?"

"Like how in the hell he couldn't tell that you had brimstone."

"I didn't have brimstone."

Diesel bit his upper lip, trying to hold back a yell, "Yes, you did. You had it in your hand and then chucked it. I told ya they can tell when you've touched it," he hissed out a whisper.

"Well...maybe I just gotta good pokerface."

The yellow demon pointed at her, "BullSHIT. There ain't nothin' special about you. You know how many times I seen others try to bluff the crims, Too many to count. And they ALL get caught. Now, what are you?"

"What?" Hutch raised an eyebrow.

"Ah, leave her alone, Diesel," Izzy spoke.

"Izzy, stay outta this!" The yellow demon pointed.

"Oi, there a problem over ere', mates?" A familiar crim shuffled up to the three.

"No Bishop..." Diesel put his head down and looked away. The others followed suit, hoping the crim would leave without making a scene. Hutch was the only one to keep her eyes glued to him. She leered down as he chuckled a bit.

"Blimey, ya made a right cock-up of that dress already, love. Maybe you oughta just slip it off. Probably draggin' ya down anyways." he creepily expelled with a hungry look in his eye. Hutch wanted to punt him like she did the book he read from earlier, but she just stayed calm.

"Why don't you leave us alone and go back ta bein' Regina's bitch?" The demon's eyes went dark, almost as if the redhead had struck a deep nerve in him. It was so bad she was half-expecting him to lunge, but he tried concealing his rage with a toothy grin.

"Listen ere' you lanky cunt, you're lucky you're ew' you are, otherwise you'd be 'avin a bad time roight about now."

"A bad time? Shit I already thought I was havin' that. I'm stuck in the port-o-pot of hell right beside you. Does it get any worse?"

"Oh, it can get way worse, love…"

"What the fuck is goin' on back here?! I already checked these shit-eaters for rocks. Let's get a move on. I gotta get back topside. Times a tickin'," the red-eyed crim came back through, interrupting Bishop's stare-down with Hutch. The crim backed away with an evil glare and followed the other red demons towards the next group. Things were unnervingly quite amongst the fold for the next few moments. Izzy finally spoke.

"That was Bishop."

"Yeah. We've met," Hutch affirmed, still eyeing the crim down where he stood at his next post down the way.

"He used to be the furnace master here…till Regina."

"What?" Hutch's stare went down to Izzy.

"Yeah. That's the story anyway. Regina was tossed in here and supposed to be doin' work with us commoners, but she took over. Ha! Can you picture that? Hell Princess of Level 12 shoveling rocks into dirty mine carts…I don't know what she's promising him or these other crims for going along with all this, but it must be worth their while." Izzy's words echoed inside Hutch's head for a moment. No wonder he'd gotten riled at her insult. He was boss here once. Now he was playing second fiddle to Regina and no doubt looking the fool most times in front of the masses.

The redhead's eyes soon locked into another crim that stood out among the rest. He donned a cowboy hat.

"Who's that?" Hutch pointed.

"That's Yellow Duck. He's one of red-eye's second hands, " Izzy spoke, "Wanna guess how he got his name?" The question seemed rhetorical as Hutch viewed the broad-shouldered crim in the collection lines a few rows over. One side of his face bore the remnants of when he used to be a blondie. It was a large, yellow mark shaped like a duck, of all things. Izzy started in again,

"Some say he didn't quite change all the way. A piece of goodness is still in him."

"Bullshit. A crim's a crim," Diesel grumbled under his breath. As the redhead's stare kept drifting between the odd crim and the eerie horizon ahead, her eyes squinted at the sight of something in the beyond. It was strange looking. A towering and spiraling presence that now had her full attention.

"What the hell is that?"

"The hellfire, hun. Didn't we talk about this?"

"Not the flames. THAT," Hutch pointed to the outline of the huge mass in the fog below the fires.

"Oh…the Helix. It's part of the Leviathan."

"Ahhhh, the Helix and the Leviathan. Yeah those things. Stupid me, I knew that," Hutch looked down at the green demon with disgust. Izzy smiled.

"She's being a smartass, Izz," Diesel had to state the obvious.

"Oh? OH! Well, ya didn't have ta be mean about it. The Leviathan is Regina's race track, hun."

"Are you shittin' me? Jesus she has her own personal racetrack?" Hutch seemed to only utter to herself as she continued to study the odd structure, trying to make sense of it. She lifted a finger, "So…what is that thing then? A tunnel or somethin'?"

"It's a spiral, hun. A corkscrew."

"What the hell you mean? Like it goes upside down?" Hutch couldn't believe what she was hearing.

"What part of helix, spiral, and corkscrew are ya not gettin', girly. YES, it goes upside-down." Diesel hissed before Izzy could respond.

"Holy…shit," the redhead went quiet, picturing the outline of the race-leg in her mind, likening it to the roller-coasters she once rode as a teenager at Cedar Point. She wanted badly to scream out her disbelief of the idea that a car would run through that thing and go upside down over and over, but then she recalled what she saw right before her crash and the argument went placid, slipping back into the darkness beneath the towering Helix.

"So…how long is it?"

"The Helix?"

"No, the whole shebang? How long is this track of hers?"

"Oh, I don't know, hun…each leg is about nine to ten miles so…maybe fifty miles?"

"Christ…whata monster…" Hutch could feel her curiosity blooming with each passing moment. She wanted to see more. She HAD to know more. She went back through the dialogue just expelled and did the math. "So this thing has five legs then?"

"Right. At the end of each leg is a finishing point. The whole thing is actually in the shape of a giant star and this mine is smack dab in the middle of it all."

"So you've seen this thing?"

"Seen it? I helped build it."

Hutch went to open her mouth but she was cut off by the trumpeting call of the same horn that had ushered in the crims' collection.

"Shift change, maggots! Get back to it!" Old red-eyes roared to the groups that stood around the immediate area.

"C'mon, hun. Back we go," Izzy tugged on Hutch's dress, turning round to head down the side of the mine.

"Wait? What? I thought this was shift change. We're just headin' right back into the pit?"

Diesel scoffed, "Girly, you're not catchin' onto this whole hell thing very quick. Shift change is a cute phrase for 'stop working for ten minutes, then move to another spot'."

Hutch sighed, "Well shit."

And so the change commenced. They descended right back down into the mine only to end up not fifty yards from where they'd been before. It all seemed absolutely redundant.

Hutch finally spoke up after working ten minutes in their new mining spot,

"Ya said you helped build that road?" The question had been eating at her like a rat on rot. Izzy chucked a small batch of firerite into the nearby cart and sighed,

"Yeah. I helped build Leviathan. So did Diesel."

"Why you always gotta bring me into these goddamn conversations?" Diesel moaned.

"I wasn't bringing you into nothin', I was statin' a fact," Izzy shook her head and returned to digging.

"So…it's basically just a big playground for her then?" Hutch asked.

"Among other things, I guess."

"How ya mean?"

"Well…it's more than a playground. Part of it's the main leg to the gateway topside. Remember the truck that came in here earlier ta dump bodies?"

"Yeah."

"That's where it came from, hun. They drive from the gate, which is the top point of the star, down to the lower right leg and then up into the bottom cross of the two legs. That there is called the crotch, there's a straight road that leads from there to the backside of the mine, right there," Izzy pointed to where the truck appeared earlier. Hutch stopped digging and began visualizing the whole process. And to that end, an idea began to spark.

"So…after they dump the cargo, they head right back out and go topside?"

"Most times. Yeah."

Diesel slammed his pickaxe into the rocks and stood there staring at Hutch. She kept glaring at the south side of the mine, poking at her bottom lip in some trance of thought. She finally looked over and noticed the yellow demon's eyes drilling into her.

"What you lookin' at?"

"Someone who's got some stupid-ass idea brewin'."

"What? Maybe I got somethin' goin', but it ain't dumb."

"Yeah? Well let's hear it."

"Well…the way I figure it, why can't someone find a digging spot near the drop-off over yonder, and then when that truck comes through, hitch a ride on it and get yourself back topside."

"And there's that stupid-ass idea," Diesel growled and began digging once more.

"What?! Is it so bad? What's ta keep me from doin' it?"

"What's ta keep you from doin' it? Let's start with common sense, girly! Ya don't think someone ain't already tried that? Guess what happened to them? At the bottom of the furnace.

Startin' to think that red hair of yours burned out all your brain cells.

"Oh, is it really so goddamn stupid? What's worse, sittin' here diggin' rocks for all of eternity, or tryin' ta get the hell out of here?"

"Diggin' rocks," Diesel answered fast.

"Oh, bullshit…"

Diesel stopped his digging and pointed.

"Look, all you greenies are the same…"

"I ain't green yet!" Hutch interrupted.

"No, but you're gonna be if you keep this shit up. You're all the same with your delusions of grand escape. Hell, I know all about it. I was like you once. We ALL have gone through the motions. Denial. Grief. Back to denial. Then escape plannin' and other stupid shit. Best ta get over all that before you get yourself into a situation way worse than diggin' rocks and listenin' to this one cluck like a rabid hen all day," Diesel pointed at Izzy.

"Hey!"

"Sorry, Izz. Ya talk too damn much."

"So what then? I'm supposed ta forget about everythin'. About my family? About my life?"

"You don't have a life, girly! Ya crashed and your light went out, remember? Trust me, the longer you're down here all that stuff will slowly fade and you won't remember much of it. It's better that way."

Hutch went silent for a moment. Her life hadn't always been the best, but the thought of losing all her memories was nauseating. If she didn't at least have those, then what the hell did she have? A pickaxe and pile of rocks. This was all a nightmare come true.

"There's got to be somethin'…." she half whispered.

"What?" Diesel said.

"I said, there's got to be somethin! Some way out of all this shit!"

"There is, hun," Izzy said.

"What is it?"

"Ya just keep diggin'," Izzy smiled.

"Jesus Christ, are ya serious? Ya keep tellin' me that shit, but how the hell is it supposed ta do anythin'?"

"You work for the rapture."

"Holy shit, Izz, don't try and sell her that bill of goods."

"For real, don't come at me with that shit. I heard enough of that when I used ta go ta church…So you're tellin' me that you think J Christ himself is gonna swoop down in here and pluck you up if ya just keep diggin' like a good little demon?"

"Not, Jesus, not God. Hell I don't know what it is, to be honest. But it's somethin'," Izzy said. Diesel scoffed from the back. "Don't give me that!" Izzy pointed at him, "You've seen it too."

"Seen what? What is it?" Hutch asked.

"It's nothin'. It's bullshit," Diesel dismissed.

"Nothin, ma foot. It's like…it's like this lightning bolt hits ya, and then poof, you're gone. Transported somewhere far from this pit. Never ta come back. I think it's just the universe grabbin' you up out of here, knowin' your debts are paid off. Ya know?" Hutch wanted to laugh as much as she wanted to bat the demon upside her head. Her attention drew to Diesel.

"Ya seen this happen?"

Diesel stopped digging and hesitated.

"Ya, have. Haven't ya?" Hutch still couldn't believe it.

"Look, I don't know what it is, okay? She's right. This bolt of light hits a demon and then they're gone. We never see them again. I don't know what it is. No one down here does. And if the crims know, they certainly ain't sayin'. Hell it could be takin' ya somewhere worse. Or just erasing you from any and all existence."

"Look, hun, you can listen ta whoever ya want and believe whatever ya want, but I know it takes ya somewhere better."

"How do ya know?"

"I…I have faith," Izzy confessed.

"Yeah, well I'm fresh outta that. There's gotta be another way."

"Ya could always race Regina."

"Shut up, Diesel," Izzy hissed.

"Hell that's what got me into this mess in the first damn place…Wait? What? What da ya mean, race her? Like again?"

"Well yeah, just ask Izz about all that," Diesel smiled. Izzy was visibly angered. She sneered and waited for Hutch's inevitable query.

"What's that all about?" The redhead stared down at the green demon.

"It's nothin, don't listen ta him."

"Don't sound like nothin' ta me. You tellin' me you can race her anytime? For what? How?"

"Not anytime…" she began to hiss, but straightened up, "Look…Regina plucks folks out of this pit to race her now and again. Sometimes at random, and then sometimes a brave soul will just up and volunteer,"

"A stupid soul…" Diesel corrected her. Izzy scowled and looked back to Hutch.

"And?" The redhead urged the story forwards.

"AND…if you beat her, she'll let you go. Free and clear. She promises you a fresh, human skin to inhabit and a new life topside."

"And if you lose?"

Izzy stopped digging for a moment. Lines wrinkled her brow as she thought about how to answer.

"Ya get thrown in the furnace pit. No one ever sees ya again. Ya fade and become part of the ash…and that only happens if you actually make it far enough to be declared the loser."

Hutch's brow raised.

"How ya mean?"

"That road out there…it's dangerous, hun. It's a monster in itself. Most demons meet their fate out there and they never return."

Hutch leered at the greenie for a second. And the suspicious question just dropped out of her, "Demons can die?"

"Yes."

It hardly seemed believable. Hell, not even plausible. How could something that was dead, by all rights, die again? But before she could dwell on it for too much longer...

"So you know anyone that raced her?" Hutch asked.

Izzy nodded her head in self-disgust.

"Who?"

"Me…I almost had her, hun. I was this close," she pinched two fingers together.

"You didn't have shit. You're lucky you're still standin' here," Diesel grumbled.

Hutch's confusion set in. "But…you're still here. I thought ya said you become furnace ash."

The redhead waited for the greenie to explain.

"Yep, I'm still here…She musta had a soft spot for me or somethin'…She just let me come back here."

"Has anyone ever beat her?" Hutch asked.

"Have some of these rocks been gettin' in your ears, girly? Didn't we already discuss the part where no one beats Regina. And no one ever will."

"Well she thought she could," Hutch pointed at Izzy.

"So? She's a dumb-dumb. Hell, most of us are here because we thought we could beat her, but it takes a real dipshit ta try it all over again. Like I said, she's lucky she's standin' here. And if you got any sense, you won't go chasin' the same magic dragon she did."

"Well, I learned my lesson. Never again. I'm just waitin' on my rapture ta get me out of here."

"Ya know, Izz, I don't know what's crazier, racin' Regina or thinkin' some magic lightning bolts gonna get ya out of here."

"Where do demons go when they die?" Hutch suddenly let out.

Both Izzy and Diesel stopped working, "What?" They expelled at the same time.

"You said demons can die. They die out there on her raceway. Where do they go?"

"No one knows, hun," Izzy let out soberly.

"They have to go somewhere…right?"

"Do they? Maybe it's just nothingness. You're just gone," Izzy said.

Hutch couldn't wrap her head around the idea.

"How's that even possible?"

"Don't know, hun. But it's best not to dwell on it much. Keep diggin', and wait for that rapture."

Hutch put a finger to her lips as she thought inward and onwards,

"Demons can die…" she mumbled then spoke up, "But…but I'm not a demon."

Diesel let out a short laugh.

"What? I'm not!"

"You're a demon."

"I'm not a goddamn demon. Look at me."

"You're a demon," he egged on something he knew to be a fact. Hutch's face was turning redder than the firerite she mined.

"I am NOT a fuckin' demon! I don't look like you, or you!"
She pointed at Izzy and Diesel, "And I definitely don't look like
him," she pointed back at Hieronymus. "I'm a human, okay!"

"Oh, well that settles it then. Ya look like a person ya must be
one. I certainly can't think of anyone else down here that looks like
a person that ain't human. Oh, wait, yes I can, the hell princess that
got you down here!!"

Hutch went dead quiet. Jesus, he was right. She didn't even want
to let out a peep that would affirm his smartass words, but her
silence was more than enough.

Hank's Rough Night

"Well, at least you ain't hidin' it no more," a voice cut through the open office door of the Gingerbread House.

"Who said I was?" Hank retorted back to his brother from where he sat on his throne, downing a bottle of whiskey. Ham crossed his arms and just stared, emotionless.

"How long?"

"How long what?"

"How long ya been back at that?"

"Does it fuckin' matter? Hell, does anythin' matter? I think we got bigger things to be worried about right now, Sandwich."

"You're right. We do. And where are you? Sittin' here alone drownin' yourself. We got decisions ta make as a family. We got a long road ahead."

"Yep and it's paved with shit."

The room was silent for a moment. Suddenly a tiny chuckle emerged. "McCray McCurse month," Hank whispered as he swigged down another gulp of amber.

"What?" Ham asked.

"I said, fuckin' McCray McCurse month, Ham. You know? The jolliest time of the goddamn year. The month where God himself floats down from heaven, pulls up his robe, and takes a hearty angelic shit all over anyone that shares our namesake."

Ham rolled his eyes.

"You ain't gonna stand there and roll your fuckin' eyes at me, when you know goddamn well I'm speakin' truths."

Ham stayed silent. Hank waved a dismissive hand at him, "Ahhh what the fuck do you know. Hutch would agree with me."

"Yeah, well, she ain't here right now, is she?"

"No…No she ain't. But if she was. She'd be on my side, I can tell ya that." Hank took another swig then pointed at the chair across from him. "Sit." Ham reluctantly headed towards the chair, looking at it as if it were the last place he was going to sit, ever. He plopped down and watched as his brother retrieved a shot glass from the drawer and began to pour the whiskey into it.

"Oh, no. I'm good."

Hank's fiery eyes shot up. "This ain't for you, stupid. Whiskeys a man's drink. If I was gonna offer ya somethin I'd hand ya a Zima, faggot." Ham just shook his head and crossed his arms, leaning back in the chair as his foot began to tap in nervousness. Hank took a shot from the glass then spoke as he slammed it back down.

"Did you know?"

Ham's brow raised. "Did I know what?"

"Did you know what she was up to? Did you know she wasn't headed out this mornin' to take that car to be sold? Did you know she was goin' out to race that sawed-off cunt?" Hank's voice paced faster with each question as he poured Ham a shot and slid it across the table. Ham just sat there, staring into the tiny vessel, watching the amber swish round as it chased away the force that had sent it there. He was treading on dangerous ground. There was no way he could be silent for too long lest he give away the obvious answer, and he had no idea how Hank would react. He knew damn well what she had set out to do that morning, but in the end, Ham opted for the watered down answer. He took the shot and cringed as he spoke.

"I knew she was up ta somethin'."

A deathly silence slithered into the room as Hank just kept drilling an emotionless stare into the eyes of his brother. Ham couldn't even dare to swallow the remnants of the shot that still burned his throat as he waited for his sibling to say something, anything. But he did nothing. He didn't smile or frown, or even breathe for what seemed like an entire minute. But then it happened. He began to chuckle a bit.

"You knew she was up to somethin'?"

Ham wasn't quick to answer. It seemed ominously rhetorical. Hank just chuckled on some more as he swigged down another drink. He repeated, "You knew she was up to somethin'...I bet ya did. I bet ya did. So, in a way, what you're tellin' me is, this is your fault."

Ham's eyes went dark.

"Fuck you." He slid the shot glass back across the desk.

"No, fuck you!" Hank yelled as he grabbed it up and hurled it back. It missed his brother's head by inches and shattered against the block wall. Ham did his best not to wince as it whizzed by, but inside he was trembling to beat an earthquake. Hank pointed,

"You knew she was up to somethin', but you said nothin'?"

"And what the fuck was I supposed ta say?"

"Anything, Hamlet! Anything was better than nothin'! You're gonna sit there and say you ain't ta blame, but if you'd said somethin, we wouldn't be in this situation right now."

"How's that? Hutch would've done it anyway. You know that."

"I would've set that goddamn car on fire if I even had the slightest inkling she was gonna go do that stupid shit!"

"Oh bullshit, that car was worth money, you wouldn'ta set it on fire. Fact, I think that's what this is all about, that sixteen-grand goin' up in smoke on the interstate, not our sister."

"You watch your fuckin' mouth, before you end up where she is. Sit the fuck down!" Hank bellowed as Ham got up, about to leave the room. Ham paused and sneered. He slunk back down and just glared at his brother with disgust.

"This, right here, this is why I drink."

"What? Fighting? We all fight."

"Not the goddamn fightin', Ham...it's beyond that. It's the assumptions...the insinuations...the fact that you'd sit there and assume I'd choose money over my own blood...Look, I've done a lot of things I regret. God knows I'm a shit, and there's a neat little hammock hanging in hell for me. I've let my temper do the talkin' and the doin' and the fightin' and I'm just...just tired of being called the bad guy even when the shoe fits most times. That's why I drink..." Hank finished, and took another swig.

"No."

"No?"

"That's not the reason you drink. You're just a nasshole…"

"Oh, I'm an asshole, huh?"

"No. Not an asshole, a NASSOLE. With a N. A Nice-Asshole. You're an unredeemable shit that peppers his actions with half-ass apologies and fairy dust. You'll be horribly nasty to someone, then come back and sugar coat with one small good deed to try and make up for it. And all it does is send mixed signals to the people who care about ya. I don't know who the fuck you are. Never have. And the worst part is, I don't think you know either. And that, brother of mine, is why you drink. "With that, Ham arose and went to leave the office, hoping the conversation was over. It wasn't. As soon as his foot set down on the dark hallway floor, his breath left him. From behind, Hank came charging, tackling him and slamming him into the far wall.

"You sonuvabitch!" Ham barely got out as he tried defending himself from his brother's terrible onslaught. They hit the ground rolling, kicking, swinging and cussing a hurricane of obscenities, looking like two raccoons fighting over a trashcan. Soon, Ham freed himself and jumped up, putting up his dukes in ill attempts to fight off his monster of a sibling. Hank didn't even swing, he lunged and shoved as hard as he could, sending Ham flying backwards. He blasted into the front counter and flipped right over it onto the other side, his breath once again went screaming out of his lungs. Before he could even get to his knees, he felt the force of Hank's grip upon his shirt collar and he ripped him to a stand. The elder McCray couldn't even get a swing in as Ham came back to life and laid a nasty right hook so hard it loosened his brother's grip and sent him stumbling back across the lobby. Now whether it was the anger or sadness that caused him to almost black out with rage, he'll never know, but Ham ran forwards and kicked his brother as hard as he could right in the chest. Hank went flying backwards, slamming into the back counter. He frantically grabbed onto anything he could, but just ended up with a handful of coffee pots and foam cups on his descent onto the cold floor below.

"Stay the fuck down!!" Ham pointed and yelled at Hank. They were both already out of breath. The entire lobby was a flit with their labored gasps and Ham's stumbling steps.

"Get fucked," Hank mumbled as he began to right himself, back onto his knees. Ham ran up and shoved him over, slamming him back against the side of the cabinets again.

"I said, stay down! I mean it, damn it! Stop this bullshit! You're gonna get yourself hurt!" Ham began unleashing a series of screaming pleas. He didn't want this to go any further. For several awkward moments, the two siblings held their ground. One standing with his fists up and the other in a crumpled pile below him. Not soon after, Hank put a hand out.

"Help me up…" he grumbled out in a defeated tone. With grave apprehension, Ham leaned forwards, reaching out for his hand. Their grips entwined, but when Ham went to pull, something came out from the side. With a force that rocked his teeth, Hank blasted an empty coffee pot across his face. Shards of glass went flying everywhere, raining down as Hank jumped back to his feet, swinging and bellowing a song that even a demon couldn't decipher. Ham's world was nothing but a spinning slideshow of fists and fury, but somehow he maintained his stand. He put one hand across his swelling face and the other up to guard the brutal blows being dealt by his brother. Hank was weakening. That kick must've taken out his battery because the swings Ham now received were not signature Hank the Tank, but they hurt no less. The younger McCray soon found himself being pinned against the back counter. He got a few swings in, but nothing that sent his brother in a tailspin like before. Things were getting uglier by the minute. Blood was flowing, and as they traded punches, they traded each others crimson back and forth, from knuckle to cheek.

"This is your fault, I said! You're always babyin' that girl and this time it bit us all in the ass!" Hank bellowed as he drew back another trembling fist. He went to lay it down, but the room came to life with the sound of a ringing telephone. The brother's stares drifted sideways with looks of curiosity as Hank kept his fist hovering amongst the orchestra of the chattering business line. No one called this late. And with the recent events barely in the rearview mirror, whatever lay on the other end of that line couldn't be good. Hank released his grip on Ham and let him slam back against the cabinets. The towering McCray limped to the front counter and ripped up the receiver.

"McCray Machine…" he let out with hardened steel. Ham just stayed put, slumped over the back cabinets as his attention drew fully down upon the conversation he could only hear the half of.

"Yeah…Okay….When?...I see…Yep…," Hank let out intermittent acknowledgments amongst the chattering from the other line. He then began writing down something on a notepad. "I'll call later….Yep…I'll see you then…" and then "click" he hung up the phone. A cold, dead silence crept in. Not even the brothers' labored breaths could do anything to chase it away.

"Well?...What was that?" Ham tried not to show panic in his voice.

"Nothin' good," Hank spoke bluntly, walking on by, back into the office. He soon remerged with what was left of his whiskey bottle.

"What the hell was it, Hank?"

Hank pointed at the phone as he rounded the counter, "McCray, Fuckin, McCurse Month." With that, he swigged from the bottle and walked out the front door, leaving Ham standing there, his face painted with a darker shade of worry than before. Ham soon trotted over to the blank notepad his brother had scrawled on. He grabbed up a pencil and rubbed the lead sideways across the pad till he revealed the impression of what was written previously. It was an unfamiliar address and number. He quickly grabbed the phone and dialed the digits from the pad. A few rings soon lead into, " Dillon County Coroners office…"

Ham just went catatonic. "Hello?" The voice said over and over amidst the silence. He slowly lowered the receiver with a chilling click.

Out and away, Hank was already miles to the north of The Gingerbread House, leaving it behind as he sped through the hot summer night, his mind racing at twice the RPMs of the truck with the deadest look upon his face. Despite his callous stare, things boiled behind those emotionless eyes. Echoes of the past. Regrets. And cold inevitabilities that were now coming home to roost at the fault of one simple phone call. Everything seemed less than real. A dream inside a dream. Hutch…Now this? How was this happening? He wanted to laugh at the whole thing. Laugh so hard he'd have to pull over just to catch his breath amidst the stupidly of it all. But he did nothing. He just stared out into the belly of the headlights, becoming entranced by the grainy roll of the pavement as it swept in the uncertainties of what was to come. He drank down some more whiskey with a confidence that almost made him forget that the very act was illegal. It didn't matter. None of it did. For the moment, that whiskey was the only thing keeping him from coming unglued and running head-first into the next pair of headlights he saw. So he just kept at it, foot to the floor and lips to the glass until he could catch some piece of something, just anything that would keep him sanely grounded to this world and the travesties it kept dumping into his lap. Soon, he chucked the empty bottle out the passenger side window. It spiraled through the night air and became briefly illuminated by the refraction of blue and red lights speeding down the road.

"Shit..." was all Hank could grumble out as the patrol car came within feet of his bumper. For a split second he thought about punching the gas, leading this poor bastard on a chase through the back roads till one of them ate a tree at one-hundred plus. But no, things were already shit covered enough as it was. For once, Hank thought about someone other than himself. He pulled off the road into the weedy ditch, his fingers tapping out an impatient beat upon the wheel as he waited for the officer to come front and center. And so he did.

"Well, how's it goin' tonight?" The patrolman looked at Hank with an unnerving smile.

"Been better," Hank mumbled, keeping his stare ahead.

"I bet it has...I bet it has," the officer spoke a line of dialogue that felt eerily true to form. Hank finally looked over with the odd reply. He was now staring at a lanky man, full dark sunglasses pulled over his eyes above a mustache-crowned smile. It was after 10 p.m. Why the hell was he wearing sunglasses?

"Boy, the sun is pretty damn blinding tonight, eh?" Hank smarted off.

"No McCray, your sunny disposition is what's blindin' me.

"You know me?"

"A little bit...but your reputation precedes ya, that's for sure."

"Look, I don't want no trouble. Had my fair share of that today"

"I see that. Looks of your face, ya had a little disagreement with someone...Top that off with two of your kin in horrible accidents in one day? Ew-eee, that's gotta chaff your ass."

"Yeah..."

The officer looked up and down the road during an unsettling pause. He spoke again,

"What'd you chuck out the window back there?"

Hank knew that was coming. What a dumb-ass move on his part. He'd been better off to have just shoved that bottle under the seat and taken his chances, though he knew the entire cab had to have smelled like a tavern sink drain on a Saturday night.

"Oh that? That was your mom's diaphragm. Yeah, she won't be needin' it anymore. Say hello to your new step-dad. We should go fishin' sometime."

The officer smiled wide.

"You always talk to law enforcement like that?"

"Only the assholes."

"Let me see that registration and license."

"Thought you already knew who I was? Why you need all that?"

The officer sighed.

"Step out of the vehicle, McCray."

"Aw, come the fuck on. I got too much bullshit going on right now to be dealin' with this. You know I wasn't speedin'. So what's this all about?"

"Get out of the truck I said."

"No...my happy-ass is stayin' planted right here. And if you think you're gonna man-handle me outta here, you best radio your buddies, cuz you're gonna need em." The entire truck lurched sideways as the officer violently grabbed the door and ripped it right off the hinges. With a grunt, he heaved it into the roadway where it skipped and sparked, disappearing into the cornfield beyond. Hank couldn't even react, he just sat there mouth agape, staring through the frame of his cab where a door used to be.

"I said, get the fuck out of there," the officer's voice suddenly transformed into a slithering echo of demonic resonance. He stood there, shoulders raised and chest puffed out in a display of all out rage while he removed his sunglasses, throwing them to the ground to reveal the glowing red eyes behind.

"What the fuck...?" Was all Hank could mouth. He quickly darted inwards, grabbing a 44.mag he kept hidden beneath his seat. The gun took fast aim but was backhanded from his grasp. Hank was ripped from the cab and tossed across the road like the door that had preceded him, all before the firearm could even hit the ground. The searing pain of blasted joints and ripped flesh was soon washed away with adrenaline as the eldest McCray jumped to his feet just inside the cornfield. He ran back out through the broken stalks into the road with a vengeance leading the way. The officer laid into him faster than he could've ever anticipated. Two quick jabs to the gut sent him keeling over. The demon then gave him a hard kick to the back, sending him onwards, flipping in a pile till he crashed right back into the truck he was just excised from. Hank tried to get right back up, but was grabbed from behind. The demon pinned his arms behind his back and pressed him against the truck bed.

"Jesus Christ, McCray. You're gettin' sloppy in your age! I gotta say, I thought you were gonna put up a bigger fight than this. I guess a decade gone can slow a man down."

Hank swung his head back with all his might, blasting the demon in the face so hard that he let go for a split second. It was all he needed...With a quickness, he spun round and laid a right and left hook across the reeling face of the red-eyed officer. He then turned round and retrieved a piece of metal pipe from his truck bed that he proceeded to lay into the demon with a rage he hadn't felt in years. Swing after swing, sent a bone crunching symphony into the nighttime air but it was short-lived. The red-eyed brute grabbed the pipe in mid swing, his human hand nearly folding under the blow. Their eyes met.

"My turn." He ripped the pipe from Hank's hand and began returning the favor, in kind. Hank felt his breath leave him as the pipe blasted him over and over. He did his best to keep his arms down, allowing his shoulders to take the brunt of the blows being dealt. Within seconds, he was knocked to the ground in front of the truck. The demon swung the pipe high into the air and let it drop, but Hank was quicker. He rolled out of the way and jumped to his feet, sweep-kicking the demon's legs out from under him. Hank laid his boot right against red-eye's head, driving his face into the headlight with a sickening smash. It did little to stop his onslaught.

The demon dropped the pipe and roared in rage as he jumped back to his feet, meeting the human head on with a spear of a tackle.

Several minutes of all out violence paved forth as the two took turns beating the living hell out of the next. And things went visceral fast, as punches turned to clawing, clawing turned to biting, and biting led to blood flow. Both of their hands and faces were now redder than the eyes of the beast that was determined to end this McCray if it was the last thing he ever did. Soon enough, he once again had the upper hand, pinning Hank's arms and slamming his face into the hood of the cruiser.

"What the fuck are you?!" Hank bellowed out.

"Who the fuck am I, is more like it. Don't you remember?"

"I have no fuckin' clue who you are, you piece of shit!"

"Well, let me refresh your memory, McCray," the demon hissed as he ripped a butterfly knife from Hank's back pocket. He flipped it open and held it inches from Hank's face.

"Go ahead. Do it! Do it, you lil' bitch," Hank yelled into an evil chuckle. The demon yanked him up and spun him round, plunging the knife deep into his bad hip. The cornfields slithered under the sound of Hank's ear shattering yell. He fell into a pile on the side of the road, quivering with the knife still embedded to the handle. The demon slowly walked over and stood above him, leering down with that same crooked smile he had shown up with.

"Memory any clearer, McCray? Is it coming back ta ya?!"

"Just end this…You son…of a…bitch. I'm tired…of your bullshit games," Hank stuttered out in agony, clutching his hip tight.

"Ahhh, c'mon. After that you STILL don't remember? That's the second time my knifes been in that hip! September 86'? Grayson Road?"

Hank's eyes went soft a bit.

"Yeah, now it's coming back ain't it? Your sister made you stop, and ya did…for an hour anyway. But ya came back didn't ya? Yeah, all that pent up rage just didn't sit well on your gut did it? You came back and you laid into me again, but this time when the dust cleared…I didn't get back up did I? You're a killer McCray…I know the things you've done.

"No…"

"No? So that wasn't you dumpin' me in one of those lonely Starne's strip pits, car and all at 3 a.m.?...I heard you hit a little snag though. You were headed home and a cop hit his lights. Now, you had a knife wound and all my blood still smeared on your clothes, so what did ya do? You hit the gas hard and purposely ran yourself into the first tree ya saw ta cover that mess all up...Worked like a charm too...No one really noticed I was gone. Not even a missing poster...Fuck, I shouldn't be surprised. I was a shit in life. Still am. Hell, so are you. Guess we got that in common, huh, McCray?"

"I don't have anythin' in common with you, ya fuckin' asshole," Hank groaned as he drew up the .44 mag from the weeds of the ditch where it had been thrown earlier. Red-eyes smiled even wider. The night came to life with the thunderous sounds of gunfire as Hank pulled the trigger, over and over, till the gun was empty. Six holes opened up across the officer's chest, as he stumbled back across the roadway...but he never fell to the ground. The sound of chuckling could be heard as Hank dropped the gun to the rocky berm and watched with disbelief as the man, or whatever the hell he was, stood straight up and spoke,

"Nice try, McCray. But ya just don't get it. You don't win this round. Tonight you finally met your match. Bet ya never thought that would happen, did ya?" The demon walked over and retrieved the pipe from earlier and started batting it lightly against his palm. "Yep, I'm gonna enjoy this. Probably too much. I'd promise ya I'll make it quick, but we both know that's a lie."

"You come back from the dead so you could kill me with that pipe or talk me to death? Take your pick cuz I ain't gettin' any younger and I'm sure you gotta long list of dudes you gotta get back to butt-fuckin'."

"Well you're just a shit-heel right ta then end ain't ya?"

"You expect anythin' less? You certainly don't want me ta beg do ya?"

"Well now that would be nice, but I guess ya can't have everything. I would like ta know one thing before I make your face look like leftover ground beef, why'd ya do it?"

"Why I do what? Come back and beat ya ta death that night? I was doin' what mother nature wouldn't, eradicating a bottom feeder. People like you don't deserve ta live. Ya never change."

The demon smiled off an angry scowl and raised the pipe high above his head.

"Like I said, we got a lot in common, McCray. See ya in Hell."

Right then, the pipe he held was ripped out from his hands. Hank watched as it swung around, blasting the demon right in his side, sending him flying like a broken doll through the air, right through the front windshield of the cruiser. The impact was deafening and tires screeched as the vehicle lurched backwards several feet under the force of it all. The demon disappeared into the car amongst a torrential downpour of glass that rained down in an eerily beautiful blast radius, sparkling in the blue/red glow of the lights abounding. Through the madness, Hank's eyes adjusted to the demon's attacker. A tiny, golden-eyed women stood there holding a pipe that was nearly as long as she was tall. He watched in disbelief as she walked over to the cruiser, reached in through the broken window hole, and yanked red-eyes out with one hand, holding him up like he was a nothing. Her short stature kept her from lifting him off the ground completely, so he just dangled there, his feet dragging the ground below a face that was still dizzied in the events of what had just happened.

"Get in the car," she spoke cold and callous. She then threw him down onto the pavement. He slid for several feet and then jumped in terror, quickly getting into the passenger side door of an ivory-white Mercury Cougar. Right then and there, her eyes met Hank's. They stared at each other for what seemed like an eternity wrapped neatly into a second.

"You," was all Hank could let out.

"Me," Regina simply said. She then dropped the pipe with a clang at Hank's feet and walked back to her car. The silence of the country road was once again ravaged, this time by the wicked sounds of a demonic engine and the screeching tires beneath it. Within a moment, she and red-eyes were gone, leaving Hank just lying there, reveling in his own confusion and elevating terror…No one was going to believe him.

Escape

"Hayden?" The name slipped from Hutch's mouth as she stood there holding her pickaxe to the ground. The demons looked around at one another in confusion at the sight of the redhead staring off into space, her head cocked like a curious dog. "Hayden, I can barely hear ya," her voice opened up again. Diesel raised an eyebrow and looked once again at Izzy,

"You gonna ask, or am I?" Diesel grumbled.

"Hun?" Izzy spoke softly. Hutch kept her odd stare into nowhere, a small smile gracing her lips. "Hun?...Hutch?....Darlin', what are you doin? Who you talkin' to?" Izzy pressed softly on.

"Girly!!!" Diesel finally shouted in annoyance. Hutch jumped and started blinking like mad. Her stare drew down to the demons.

"What?...What?!"

"I should ask you that. Who's Hayden?" Izzy questioned.

"Hay...Hayden?" She stuttered, obviously still half out of it.

"Yeah, hun. Hayden."

"Hayden...He...he was here."

"No...No one was here."

"But I heard him. He was talkin' ta me...he...he said..."

"What he say?"

"I...I don't know."

"Jesus H Christ, think of the firerite she could've mined during this worthless conversation," Diesel grumbled.

"Hush up," Izzy scowled. She looked back up at Hutch. "Who's Hayden, hun?"

"Hayden, he's ma brother."

"Oh, you had brothers topside?"

"Yeah, Hayden, Heath, Hank, Ham,…"

"Holy shit, girly, was your mom a Saint Bernard or were you just part of the Irish Seven Dwarves?!"

"I'm Scottish! And…I had a big family, okay?" Hutch sneered.

"Obviously…"

"Well, that's good you remember them…it's good you're remembering," Izzy nodded.

"Of course she remembers. I don't see a lick of green on her, unless she's hidin' it up that dress."

"And?" Izzy spoke.

"AND?! Izz, are ya serious? Most people that drop down here are greenies by the second shift change and here she is, several shift changes later and she's still whiter than paper in a blizzard. Somethin' ain't right."

Izzy put a hand under her beak and stared at Hutch in suspicious wonder.

"What? Don't look at me like that," Hutch became irritated as she once again began swinging her pickaxe to the brackish earth below. "You act like I have some kinda control over all this. I gotta tell ya, I ain't in no rush to become a green, bird-thing like you, but it ain't like I have a say in the matter either." Hutch gathered an armload of firerite and rounded the nearest mine cart. She began dumping it in as she went on in agitation at the still silent Izzy. "If you got somethin' ta say, say it."

"I just…I don't have anythin' to say, really. Diesel's right about the greenie thing, but…who knows. Maybe you just won't ever turn. Gotta be a first time for everythin', even down here." Izzy put out her two cents and began digging into the side of the mine once again. Hutch just stood there, throwing in a few more pieces of firerite she accidentally dropped on the trip over. As she released the glowing ore, she leered across the way to spy Diesel unearthing a sizeable chunk of brimstone. She stood there, waiting for him to say something. To shout, "Hell yes!" do a victory dance and then absorb part of its energy. But none of that happened. What did happen, however, made Hutch's brow raise so hard it hurt her face. He turned his head slightly to see if anyone was watching, leading Hutch to duck down behind the cart till she could barely see over it. He hit the stone with his pickaxe, driving it right over to where Izzy toiled away in ignorance. And then it happened…

"Damn, Izz! Ya found another one!" Diesel spouted off.

The green demon turned round to see the glowing brimstone at her feet. She smiled.

"Well, would ya look at that! I did!" She quickly grabbed up the rock and held it to her chest, sucking in some of the incense from its core. Her skin tone transformed back to a truer, more vibrant green as she rolled the rock back to the floor, saving it for next shift change. Hutch's eyes narrowed as she rose up and trod back over to her lonely pickaxe. She plucked it from the ragged ground and walked over till she was beside Diesel. He cast an odd stare. She had never worked this close to him, she was obviously up to something.

"Can I help you with somethin', girly?"

"Well, maybe." Hutch began striking the earth as close as she could to where he toiled. "I gotta weird feelin eatin' at me that over here is where I could find me some good brimstone."

Diesel stopped digging and glared up at her.

"Uh-huh. And why would ya think that?"

"Well, it's just that…" right then, the redhead's words were cut off as the whole mine came to life with the echoing call of the shift change horn. The three demons quickly dropped their tools and headed off, leaving Hutch leering at the back of Diesel's head as he hastily retreated up the craggy summit. Her look of agitation only grew as she too tossed her tool down and all but ran after the yellow imp, catching up with him as soon as he crested the top of the hill. She grabbed him by the arm and held him back as Izzy and Hieronymus walked on to join the ranks of the collection lines.

"What the hell you doin'?! Let go of me!" Diesel jerked away from Hutch. He brushed himself off and kept walking but the redhead was right beside him.

"What the hell was that?"

"*That* was me tellin' you off for not knowin' the boundaries of personal space, girly," the yellow demon hissed.

"Not that. Back there, before the siren. You diggin' up brimstone and throwin' it to her." Diesel slowed his steps. "Yeah…you've been had. I knew there was somethin' weird about her findin' all that shit."

"Don't tell her. Ya can't," Diesel's eyes went soft, if only for a moment.
It was the first time ever that Hutch saw even the slightest bit of raw emotion coming from the otherwise curmudgeony demon. Hutch dropped her attitude a bit.

"Why are ya doin' it?"

Diesel sighed.

"Look around ya, girly. We're surrounded by a prison of black and gray. That girl up there is the only thing in this pit that has any light left. She's the blue sky that casts out the dark, and I'm gonna keep her shinin' as long I can. I know she's annoyin' sometimes…hell, a lot. But she's the only thing that's kept me sane this far. It's too late for me, but it sure ain't for her. Might as well put that stone to good use," Diesel explained his actions as he stopped in line in front of Hutch. The redhead had to admit she was touched, though she refused to show it. But more so, she was surprised that such a negative soul could show such selflessness. Still, she found a gaping flaw in the beauty of it.

"That's sweet n' all, but did ya ever think of what happens when ya finally go and turn inta one of those red things? Who's gonna throw her brimstone all day to keep her green?"

"You are."

Hutch's brow raised. She pointed at herself. "Me?!"

"That's right. You obviously don't need those stones, you still ain't got a lick of green on ya. Might as well make yourself useful."

"Well, my plan is ta get out of this shithole. So you can count me out."

"Jesus, girly. You're not goin' anywhere. We all think were gettin' out of here. It's a pipedream."

"And this rapture thing she keeps goin' on about? What about that? That a pipe dream?"

"I don't know…"

The screams and commands of the crims were falling down as they came quickly through the lines, collecting what they could with a haste Hutch hadn't seen before. Within seconds, the red-eyed crim came rushing up to Diesel and her.

"I'm not even gonna waste ma precious time with you shitworms. I ain't ever seen anyone as useless at findin' brimstone as you two." Hutch barely took in what the crim said as she was too preoccupied with his physical condition. Someone had worked him over. He was bruised and beaten and even walked with a limp to compliment it all.

"Rough night?" She mouthed off.

"Sure was, firebush," he spoke as he walked on by. A chill from the past rushed up her spine at the nickname he spat out. It played verbatim and true to tone from a night she remembered oh-so-well. Both panic and anger sat in as she spun round.

"Sid?! Sid Caldwell?!" Hutch had finally put a name to him. His human name. The demon stopped dead in his tracks, as did all the crims around. Looks of worry brushed their faces as their appointed superior looked over his shoulder back at the redhead. A toothy smile wiped clean the malevolence and melancholy that had soiled his face.

"Thata girl…that McCray memory ain't as alcohol-stained as I thought," he spoke as he walked back to where she stood. "You missed me didn't ya? It's okay, you can say it. I missed you too," he placed a claw under her chin only to have it smacked away. "Haha! I gotta say though, you were way better lookin at sixteen. I'd rather had a slice of that teenage, peach pie. I'd have fucked you straight, firebush."

"Where's ma aunt?" Hutch growled.

"Well that went off subject real fast. No *"Fuck you Sid. You're a nasty, dickless, toothless, prick I wouldn't touch with a cane pole?'* You just went right ta brass tacks. Where's Cass McCray? That is the sixty-four thousand dollar question, ain't it?" He chuckled.

"Well? I'm waitin'. You nasty, dickless, toothless prick."

"HA! Jesus Christ, McCray! You really don't know what's goin' on here at all, do ya? She ain't told you yet, has she?"

Hutch's eye went soft a bit.

"No…why don't *you* tell me."

"Aww, naw. It's a little too fun watchin' those lines of wonder wrinkle on your forehead while ya slither round in that dress just screamin' the words inside, *"Where, oh where is my Aunt?! Why won't anybody tell me?!*" Besides…I can't tell ya. I'm already in hot water with the boss."

"That why you look like shit? She work ya over? How's it feel havin' a woman beat your ass?"

"Actually, firebush, all this is from your brothers."

"What?" She tried desperately to conceal a look of worry as the demon opened his mouth inches from her face.

"Yeah, see, I took a little trip topside recently and did what Regina shoulda done a long time ago. I took out Hank first. I gotta admit, he put up a fight. That's where all these gunshots came from. Then I worked my way down the peckin' order right down to your favorite brother, Hamshit, or whatever he's called. He squealed like a fuckin' pig when I disemboweled him with my bare hands. Pathetic." With that, he shook his head and turned round to leave. Hutch jumped down, grabbed the closest rock and chucked it full force, blasting him right in the back of the head. She could barely hear Diesel saying "What the hell, girly?!" over the ringing of the rage inside her head. All the other crims squalled out as the rock split in half and sent the boss crim bending forward under the impact.

"You done fucked up, McCray," Sid hissed out as he went into a full charge back at her. All the demons surrounding spread out, trying to get away from the violence that was about to ensue. The giant crim tackled the redhead so hard her hat flew off her head. They slid along the craggy ground for several feet under the impact with Hutch gritting her teeth as the earth tore at her dress and the flesh beneath. Before Sid could even swing, she plunged her finger deep into one of his gunshot wounds and hooked it in tight. He howled out in pain and leapt up from the ground with Hutch still hanging on with teeth clenched and fire in her eyes.

"Fuckin', bitch!!" He yelled and backhanded her off himself. She hit the dirt once more, flat on her back, and Sid was once again on top of her. As she threw her hands up, trying to defend herself, he bit her pinky finger right off and swallowed it. The entire mine erupted with her screams of agony. She grabbed another rock, blasted him across the face and kicked him off. Within seconds, she pounced on top of him, clawing and screaming like a rabid animal as blood rained down from her severed finger, turning the crim's face into a truer shade of red.

"Fuck you, you fucker!" Her voice cracked under the strain of her blinding rage. Sid punched her in the gut and pushed her off. He violently grabbed her hand and laughed as he spoke,

"This time I'm bitin' off the whole hand, firebush!" Right as his teeth went to mash down, the entire mine turned to a bright shade of blue. The crim's grip was ripped from Hutch as he went flying some fifty feet across the way, skidding and sliding across the rocks from the force of a blue beam that blasted him along like he was less than an insect. He came to a rest in a pitiful pile as Hutch rose up and looked to the source of the beam that had saved her hand. And there he stood. Hieronymus, the tiny, blue demon that hadn't spoken a word since her arrival. A glowing indigo star hovered in front of him, the source of the blast that had sent Sid reeling. It hummed under a powerful energy and then seemed to absorb right back into the flesh of the demon's chest. All the souls present, even the crims, stood in awe as the blue demon recomposed himself. He walked over and one of his skinny arms appeared from his back. It reached down, plucked up Hutch's beaten hat from the dirt below, and carefully placed back atop her head. The sounds of crackling sinew resounded as the arm retracted back into his body while the redhead just stared at him, speechless and exhausted. Suddenly, Sid's voice made her wince.

"You only get one of those, ya blue-balled fuck. I don't care who ya used to be, it doesn't mean you're untouchable." The crim pointed, limping back towards Hutch. The blue demon said nothing. His eyeless face made him hard to read on an emotional level. He simply turned round and walked back down the edge of the mine.

"Yeah that's right, you better walk away," Sid proclaimed, still in an obvious state of apprehension, "Well don't just stand there! Get back in line! Collection ain't over till I say it's over!" Sid roared out. Everyone soon fell back into their places, except the redhead. Hutch paid him no mind. She just kept her stare and mouth slightly agape in the direction the blue imp had gone. Suddenly a devilish whisper rushed into her ear,

"And as for you, cunt. He ain't gonna be able ta protect ya forever. And he sure as shit can't protect what ya got left topside. Tonight, I'm goin' back up there and finishin' the job. I'm gonna kill your cousins. I'm gonna kill your nieces and nephews. Hell

I'm gonna kill their fuckin' pets. And I ain't gonna stop till everything with the McCray name attached to it is a mass of blood and bone quiverin' in the palm of my hand…And as for your precious aunt? Good luck ever seein' her again." With that cold promise still ringing dead as winter in her ears, the crim lumbered away. Bishop had been right. Things could get worse in this place. She had to get out of there…

Minutes seemed as hours, if time even existed, as the collection finally ended and everyone was made to return to the hell of digging. Hutch was deathly silent despite the attempts of Izzy trying to get her to talk on the descent back into the mine. She was numb. Beyond numb. The thoughts of her dead brothers circled in her mind and only intensified at the idea of Sid going back to slaughter children simply to spite her. As a young girl Hutch always wondered, as kids often did, if monsters existed. Now she knew. And he wore a suit of blood-red rage. Even the throbbing pain of her missing finger was barely noticed by her as she began scanning the mine with her mind working on shoveling the proverbial shit away long enough to formulate some kind of normality; enough to get her headed in the direction of freedom. But where was it? She was trapped. And her head began to spin in rage and despair alike at the thought of herself being caged like a rat, alone but not, in the thoughts of the hell that was yet to come.

"Don't worry, hun. It'll grow back," the redhead finally heard a voice that wasn't a muffled version of itself. Hutch shook her head.

"Huh?" She wetted her lips in question as her eyes fell focused on the green demon gingerly wrapping her hand tight, covering the stump that was her pinky finger.

"The finger, hun. It'll grow back, I said. In time."

"What? How?"

"You're a demon, hun. Demons heal. Some faster than others. It'll be back."

"Goddamn I said I'm not a…" she didn't even want to say the word. She wasn't. Was she? Was she like Diesel? Like Sid? A soul destined to kill without mercy and do the biddings of unholy kings and queens? No. No it couldn't be true. She had to keep it together. She was a human…Wasn't she?

"Look…I know that has to smart, but ya best get back ta diggin', girly. You've got into enough shit already. Hell you're lucky I'm still hangin' around ya. What were ya thinkin'? Pickin a fight with a crim. A boss crim no less?! You better hope he doesn't report that shit to Regina or we might all be done for," Diesel admonished her as he went back to swinging into the rock and ruin. Normally, Hutch would've been all over him, telling him off even though he was right. But she couldn't even hope to formulate words at that moment. All she could do was stare out through the mine, trying to keep her mind off the pain that was slowly taking over…But beyond that, something else lingered. An itch. A ridiculously awful itch creeping round her inner thigh. She began to dig at it with her good hand, gritting her teeth at the annoyance of how all-consuming it was.

"Jesus, ya got fleas now, girly?" Diesel noticed her actions as he dug. Soon, she ripped up her dress to look at the source of the problem, and things went from gray to obsidian. There was a patch of flesh on her inner thigh that was a true shade of green. Her skin was changing. She was changing.

"No. No. No. No. No…" she began to babble as she let her dress fall back down. She could feel her whole body start to spin in the fear of what was happening. This couldn't be real. And just like that, her eyes rolled into the back of her head, and she passed out under the stress of it all. A dream of a memory flooded her mind…

1990…

"Of all the damn dives, this is the last one I expected ya to be in," Hutch said as she bellied up to a bar beside a slouched over Cassandra McCray. It *was* a dive. The dive of all dives in Dillon County. The Red Rabbit. The Red Shed seemed a more appropriate name. Hutch used to think it was an old abandoned shack some farmer built too close to the main road years ago when her wondering, young eyes would peer out the car window. She'd only recalled being in the place one other time and she was too drunk to remember that it apparently was built to house about fourteen people tops.

Cass sat there for a moment without a word on her breath as she puffed on a cigarette. Her niece watched with concern as the smoke slithered away, revealing a face that her aunt hardly ever displayed in public. Sadness. Her puffy eyes were wreathed in red from tears fallen and wiped away for hours on end. She looked broken...destroyed...as if someone had sucked her very soul out through her chest and replaced it with river mud and lead. Was she even in there?

"Ya wanna talk about it?" Hutch finally broke through the uncomfortable silence between them. It was all she could come up with. Asking her if something was wrong was quite redundant at this point. Cass took another puff on her smoke and straightened up a bit, chasing away her disheveled scarlet locks with an unsteady hand. She didn't even look over at Hutch, she motioned for the bartender to fill her shot glass with another round of the Jameson she'd apparently been pounding for the better part of that night. Hutch watched as the barkeep filled the glass.

"This is the last one I'm pourin' you, alright? Now that your sister's here, she can get ya the hell outta my hair," the short troll of a women belted in the gruffest voice.

Hutch wrinkled her nose. Her sister? Jesus, either she was looking old or Cass was looking young, she couldn't decide which; she was too busy eyeing the peppered chin stubble on the woman in front of her. The barkeep slammed down the bottle, jarring Hutch's ogling. She pointed at the redhead with a hand that was missing two fingers and her voice cackled again, "Well?"

"Well what?" Hutch smarted off.

"Ya want somethin'?"

"What?"

"For fuck sake...a drink, darlin'. Ya want a drink?"

"Oh...yeah...a beer."

"A beer...could ya be more specific?"

"Surprise me, okay?" Hutch barked. The woman leered at her and shook her head while she prepped a glass. Hutch's attention went right back to her aunt whose head was now buried into the wood of the bar top.

"Hey?" She began shaking Cass. "Hey?!" Her aunt's head popped back up. She again was quiet as she reached for the whiskey and downed it. The sound of breaking glass erupted as she tossed the shot glass over the bar to the floor beneath. It shattered at the bartender's feet just as she was returning with Hutch's beer.

"Well, red, that's comin out of your bar tab," she hissed as she slammed down the beer and went to cleaning up the mess. Hutch's stare went back and forth between the barkeep and her aunt's now emotionless face.

"Sloppy cunt," the woman mumbled as she turned to throw the glass shards in the bin.

"Hey!?" Hutch barked, "Show a little respect. You know who this is?" She pointed at her aunt. The barkeep shrugged her shoulders in disgust.

"Should I?"

"This is Cass McCray."

The woman shook her head.

"The Scarlet Harlot? The Queen of Highland?"

"Oh, she's one of those track tramps?"

"No. She's got records on the those boards. She's a driver."

"Was a driver," a voice mumbled from a tattered booth. Hutch turned round to see a small group of inebriated men yucking it up.

"What was that?" Hutch's eyes were afire.

"I said she *was* a driver…How long's it been? Five years? She's washed up. Look at her."

Hutch pointed and started to go off, but she felt a hand shoot out and grab her wrist.

"Stop. Stop. Stop," Cass quietly spoke. She guided her niece back round on her stool, but not before Hutch let out, "Motherfucker, you better be gone by the time my ass leaves this stool." The men erupted into further laughter. "Fuck that guy," Hutch spoke to her aunt as she drank the first gulp of her beer.

"Well…he ain't wrong," Cass spoke again as she lit a fresh smoke. Hutch slammed her beer down.

"What is this, a pity party for Cass? You need to sober up, and quick."

"You sound mad."

"I sound mad? Are ya shittin' me right now? You not remember what the hell last night was?"

Cass's eyes drifted to the ceiling in thought.

"Your race against Menendez?"

"Menendez?"

"Chicken Menendez, or whatever that goofy shit calls himself."

"Oh…him…that."

"Oh, that," she angrily mocked, "Yeah, well you didn't show, so you forfeit, so who the hell do you think Chicken comes looking for to collect his money tonight cuz he couldn't track ya down? Next of kin. Me….You're lucky I had a stash to pay him," She took another drink, "Or should I say I'm lucky I had a stash to pay him."

"He wouldn't have done shit to you?" Cass mumbled.

"Yeah well after 86' I don't fuck around like that anymore." Cass started chuckling, much to Hutch's surprise. "What the hell's so funny?"

"86'…I miss that kinda stuff."

"Oh ya miss gettin' the shit beat out of you? Almost gettin' killed?" Hutch snapped at her.

"Maybe…" she said as she took a deep inhale of her cigarette.

"Jesus…what the fuck is wrong with you tonight?"

Cass said nothing as she blew a huge plume of smoke above their heads. She watched it dissipate in an almost child-like awe as her niece sat there fuming beside her. Cass spoke,

"Ever notice how folks are always yearnin' for the past or the future. Everybody's always like *Remember when*" or "*I cant wait till*". Nobody's ever livin' in the here and now….Not you…Not even me. But I sure as hell used to."

"So let me get this straight, you gettin' punched in the face over and over, is you livin' in the here and now?"

Cass had nothing to say. Hutch felt as if she were just talking to herself. Was Cass just a ghost sitting beside her? Or was she the ghost. After a moment, she watched as a tear rolled down her aunt's cheek. She turned to her niece again.

"Kid…promise me somethin'?"

"Sure," Hutch reluctantly spoke.

"I gotta do somethin'…and it's the hardest thing I've ever had to do, and I want ya to promise me, no matter what, you won't hate me when it's over."

Hutch's forehead wrinkled. What the hell was she going on about?

"What…?"

"Just promise me, you'll understand. Promise me…promise me that we'll always be family."

Hutch just sat there with her brow raised. She shook her head and took another swig of her beer. "Hutch, please," Cass's tone went stone cold.

"Okay. Okay, alright, I promise."

"Okay then," Cass nodded. She handed her smoke to her niece. The sound of a slow Charlie Daniel's song began echoing through the shitty speakers of the corner jukebox as Hutch took a puff.

"Hey! Turn that up!" Cass yelled out. The barkeep shook her head and surprisingly obliged the command, though Hutch figured it was more of an attempt to drown Cass out than to make her happy. Instantly, the bar began to reverberate loudly with the sounds of a soulful country beat. Hutch just watched Cass as she swayed back and forth in her seat and drunkenly sung along with old Charlie, like every word was eating her heart alive that night. Something was wrong. So wrong that a horrifying anxiety began to gnaw away at Hutch's insides. She'd never seen her aunt like this. When the song finally wound down, Cass dug into her pockets and slammed down a wad of cash onto the bar top. She then hopped off her stool and hauntingly spoke,

"Life is just a long, dusty book full of hellos and goodbyes." With that, she quickly walked away from her niece and out the rickety door. It was the last time Hutch ever saw her.

Hutch's eyes popped open wide and took in the sideways sight of the three other demons glaring down at her with looks of concern. Before they could say a word, she popped up to a squat and began rubbing her eyes, trying to free herself from the mist of ether she had just aroused from. She had no idea how long she'd been out, but her ears became consumed by the shattering sound that had awakened her. It was the horn that sounded off at the far end of the mine, the same one that ushered in the deliveries of the grays. She watched as the first truck backed up quickly to the edge of the mine, and her head went aflutter with the idea she had proposed aloud from some shift changes prior.

"Hun, you need to get back to diggin'," Izzy's sweet voice came through the tail-end of the siren surrounding. As the dizzying noise died back into the tone of swinging picks and grunting souls, Hutch jumped to her feet like she'd been kicked. And before the demons could say another word, she shot off in an all-out run, leaving them scratching their heads in panic.

"Where's she goin'?!" Izzy's worried voice let loose. Diesel didn't answer at first, he was too busy watching the redhead zigzag through the hoards of digging demons, headed straight in the direction of the semis on high. It hit him like a mallet.

"Shit, girly…what the hell are you thinkin'?" He almost whispered to himself.

"Diesel?" Izzy opened up, "What's she doin'?"

"Nothin' good. C'mon!" He dropped his pickaxe, motioning for the other two to follow as he broke into a run in the direction Hutch was headed. What seemed like several minutes were more akin to one as the trio sliced through the craggy maze of the mine face, jumping and evading around slews of fellow miners, trying their damndest to bridge the gap between themselves and the ginger that was bound to get them all thrown in the furnace ash.

"What's she doin?! Where's she headed?!" Izzy's panicked voice kept echoing behind Diesel.

"Just keep runnin', damn it!" Was all he could muster. On ahead of the demons, Hutch was reaching the far side of the mine. She began climbing the face like a rabid animal with her eyes transfixed on the back doors of the semi trailer above. She could almost smell the diesel fumes as she pressed onwards, up the nearly sheer face, grasping rocks and ruin in her aid to get her to those beautiful steel doors aloft. With only paces to go, she sprung up, her good hand grabbing a fistful of the truck trailer's bumper bar. She smiled wide as she hung there, ready to pull herself skyward to victory, but something was wrong, she felt as if she weighed three times as heavy. With a quick crane of her neck she looked down to see Diesel hanging there, his hand wrapped tightly round her ankle, below him Izzy did the same, and Hieronymus on her. All three demons linked themselves together, hanging there, all their weight pulling down on Hutch's leg.

"Don't do it, girly! Just let go!" Diesel yelled up.

"You let go! I'm gettin' the hell out of here! You ain't stoppin' me, damn it!" For several moments, the redhead grunted and rocked, trying to get her other hand up high enough to grip the bumper. She let out a little scream as her bad hand finally caught a hold and she went to pull herself up with all three demons still tethered to her. Whether it was her rage or some newly found demonic strength, she would never know, but she managed to pull herself and the trio up onto the ground below the trailer. Diesel let go and he and the others crawled on up, huddling and hiding behind the rear axle of the trailer next to Hutch.

"Well, now what, girly? What the hell is your brilliant plan?" The yellow demon hissed out a whisper below the rumbling idle of the semi.

"Shut the hell up, I'm thinkin'."

"Well ya better think faster, this truck is about to unload and drive off, and were gonna be sittin' here with our pants down."

Right then, they all sealed their lips as they watched a set of red legs walking down the trailer beside them. It was the crim coming round to open the doors. Hutch watched as its feet jumped up and perched on the bumper bar, it was time.

"Go. Go. Go," she quickly and quietly hissed as she rolled out from under the truck, running towards the cab ahead. The other demons scrambled out, clumsy as could be, following her as fast as their little legs could take them. The redhead jumped up and held the door open as she ushered the trio inside ahead of her. Within moments, she too had climbed into the truck, slowly shutting the door behind her. She plopped down into the seat and the fear overtook her. She had driven countless cars and trucks. Made them do things that most humans couldn't, but a semi was another matter all together. The redhead had basically grown up walking amongst them in the lot of Piper Jean's, but had never once sat-ass in one. She was quickly wishing she had.

"What the hell, is this a damn airplane?" She muttered out in panic as she viewed the countless abstract of dials, buttons, and gauges before her.

"Girly, you tellin' me you got this far and don't even know how ta drive this thing?!" Diesel belted out.

"No! Naw, I got this! Okay?!" The redhead became agitated. She ran her fingers in a worry she could barely conceal round the steering wheel and onto the gear shift with Diesel glaring down over her actions.

"Don't hit the brake!" He yelled into her ear as her foot began to lower.

"What?!"

"The second you touch that pedal those rear lights are gonna pop on like a Christmas tree and that crim is gonna know we're in here.

So you better be ready to tear ass out of here as soon as you hit that thing."

"I got it! Shit...." Hutch threw a dismissive hand in the demon's face. She then began to mumble to herself "You got this...I got this. Okay. Here we go. It's just like a car..." She quickly blasted the brake and clutch, throwing the beast into gear. With a massive blast of the gas she screamed out a victorious war-hoop "Woooooo! Here we go, bitches!" And the semi went...but in the wrong direction. Every soul in the cab panicked as the entire rig flew backwards towards the mouth of the mine.

"Shit, girly! What the hell?!" Diesel roared out as Hutch slammed the brake as hard as she could. She could feel the rear trailer axles dive down over the edge of the mine, lifting the back end of the truck off the ground. They now dangled there on a pivot, the massive pressure of the trailer slowly pulling them backwards as the weight shifted towards the mouth of the mine below.

"Do something!" Diesel yelled.

"Like what?!" Hutch screamed back, throwing the semi into drive and slamming the gas. The rear tires barely touched the ground and did nothing but spin like mad in the fruitless hopes of gnawing into anything solid. Right then, Hutch caught wind of movement in the rearview.

"Shit," was all she could muster as she threw the door open in time to see the driver crim. She spun and kicked him as hard as she could, right in the face, sending him reeling back and tumbling head over heels.

"Ya got bigger problems than that!" Diesel yelled as he pointed a yellow finger out the door. A thunderous sound emerged as Hutch watched the horror of a huge crack shooting out from the edge of the mine towards the front of the truck.

"Over here too!" Izzy yelled at the sight of a similar crack rushing round the passenger side. Hutch started rocking in her seat, plowing the gas and spinning the wheel back and forth.

"Where the hell is he goin'?!" She spat out as she watched Hieronymus crawling out the open passenger side window.

"He's probably bailing! Just like we should be! It's over, girly! Just let it go before we all go over the side of this shithole." But Hutch refused, she kept at it, like she was possessed, spinning the wheel and shifting gears in some insane attempt at a miracle...and one was on the way. Outside the cab, Hieronymus was far from retreating. The little blue demon crawled round and plopped right down behind the truck cab. All four of his otherworldly arms unfurled from his back and shot forth like vines, intermeshing through the madness. They ripped off wires and hoses alike and then went to the main task at hand. Within moments, the tiny creature had somehow unlocked the kingpin to the trailer releasing its hold upon the truck ahead. The terrible sound of moaning steel and screaming rock erupted as the trailer slid down the weakening ledge, falling to the bowels of the mine below. The rig ahead righted itself, blasting down flat upon all ten tires with Hutch's eyes popping wide in the absolute surprise of it all.

"Go! Go! Go!" Diesel commanded to the redhead. She fumbled, grinded the gears, and mashed pedals, but the rig was going nowhere in her mad rush of confusion. "Get out of there!" The yellow demon pushed Hutch out of the captain's seat. He plopped down fast, righting everything she had wronged within a split second as if he had done it a thousand times before. He thrashed the gas and the rig took flight, plowing ahead of the ever widening crack forming a halfmoon along the edge of the pit. Hutch sat there beside Izzy, staring at Diesel in confused amazement as he led them straight and true towards the presumed back gate of the mine. His short stature wasn't helping however. He could barely see over the steering wheel.

"Uh, little help here!" He yelled out for someone to let him know if he was headed in the right direction.

"Girly, you're gonna have ta take over!"

"Yeah and that worked out real well before!" She protested.

"Just take the damn wheel and I'll do the rest!" He demanded. She leaned over and grabbed hold as he punched the gas and continued to shift up the gear range as quickly as he could.

"What's goin' on up there?!" He looked up to the redhead.

"You're fine! Just keep mashin' that gas!" She reassured.

"Christ! This is the stupidest thing anyone has ever talked me into!" Diesel growled.

Hutch looked down at him.

"I didn't talk you inta shit! You came along all by yourself! And almost fucked things up in the process, might I add!"

"Oh, I fucked things up?! You're the one that almost sent us backwards over the edge of the pit!"

"Guys…" Izzy spoke in between.

"I had it under control!"

"Oh yeah, you really did. All that steering wheel spinnin' and pedal mashin' saved our lives!"

"We're here ain't we?!"

"Guys…?" Izzy once again opened up.

"We ain't gonna be here for long! Might as well enjoy what's left of this ride cuz after that stunt you pulled back there, every damn crim down here is gonna be after this truck!"

"You two, shut the hell up and watch the road!!!" Izzy finally lost it.

"BRAKE!!" Hutch screamed as she finally looked up. Diesel blasted the brake but it wasn't enough. The truck slid across the rocky lot and blasted into the rear of another backing semi. The entire truck ahead jackknifed under the impact, sending Hutch into a tizzy.

"Shit! Shit! Shit!" Was all she could bellow as the demon below her grit his teeth amongst the madness.

"What the hell's goin' on up there?!"

"You ran us into another rig!"

"What's this 'I' shit?! You're the one steering this thing!" Diesel yelled from under the dash.

"Oh my god. Oh lord," was all Izzy could mumble as she rocked back and forth, staring out the window.

"Reverse! Reverse!" Hutch screamed as she saw two crims jumping out from the truck ahead. Diesel did as he was told, mashing the pedals and shifting while Hutch spun the wheel, trying to get the semi righted.

"They're comin!" Izzy pointed out the obvious.

"I see that! Just shut up!" Hutch kept steering, watching the advancing red imps in the headlights as the demon below her reversed, in kind. "Brake and forwards!" She commanded. The truck's gears grinded and it lurched back and forth, sending off in a slow crawl back towards the back exit of the mine. They hadn't got more than twenty feet when the crims ahead had reached them. The unsettling sounds of metal tapped away as the imps jumped onto the hood and crawled like spiders to each side of the truck.

"Please go away. Thank you," Izzy tried to stay calm as she rolled up the window in the crim's face. Shattering glass and the roar of a pissed-off demon commenced shortly afterwards. Red hands came clawing inwards, trying to grab the greenie.

"Get off her, you bastard!" Diesel shot out from under the dash and punched the crim as hard he could in the face. The red demon reeled, but held onto the mirror as he came back for more.

"You're a dead dog, blondie!" It screamed a promise at Diesel. The two went to trading punches, pushes, and curses all while Hutch tried to keep the semi moving in Diesel's absence. She soon learned she had bigger problems as the other crim was now at her window. She let go of the steering wheel and held the demon at bay with one hand as it tried biting at her face over and over. The redhead's other hand went to slinking around the cab, looking for anything she could to fend the imp off of her. And quickly enough, she found it. A violent blast of chemicals shot into the open mouth of the crim as Hutch unloaded a fire extinguisher with the malice of the devil himself. She then turned and blasted the now white-faced menace with the butt-end of the tank and watched him fall into a writhing ball on the ragged ground below. Things were still far from placid in the cab as the redhead turned to see Diesel and the other crim still going at it.

"Here!" She tossed the extinguisher to Izzy. The greenie grit her teeth and aimed true into the face of the red imp, dousing him till his face looked like the cap of Everest. One final kick from Diesel, sent the fiend rolling back out the window, but once again, it still held onto the mirror for dear life.

"Oh, no ya don't!" Diesel grabbed the extinguisher from Izzy and blasted the tank as hard as he could on the weakening fingers of the crim. It quickly let go, bounced off the fender, and rolled under the gas tank to the ground where it was immediately crushed by the advancing tires of the rig. Izzy winced and closed her eyes as bones crushed beneath heavy rubber. Diesel wasn't as sympathetic. He leaned out the window, shaking a fist in the air as he yelled,

"Who's the dead dog now, ya red-titted bitch!"

"Diesel!" Izzy admonished him.

"What?! He bit the shit outta me!" He showed her his bleeding hands. "Not to mention, he tried rippin' you apart." Suddenly, he realized he wasn't helping move the truck. "Shit, girly!" He jumped in between the seats and was going to go back to his duties when Hutch stopped him with an open hand.

"It's fine. I got this."

"You sure about that?"

"I have to be. We can't keep driving like that," she went to shift and a horrible grinding emerged.

"Up, not down!" Diesel yelled as the redhead flinched and corrected.

They all became deathly quiet, watching together in a somber state as they passed the abandoned, jack knifed rig at the back of the mine. Diesel spoke.

"This is bad girly, real bad. Keep that gas punched and you best be pullin' a plan outta that freckled ass of yours."

"The plan is ta get to that gateway and get outta here."

"Uh-huh. That sounds a little too easy."

"I didn't say it was gonna be easy. I didn't even ask y'all to come for God sake."

"Yeah, but I bet you're glad we did...Jesus Christ. When we get busted for this…"

"IF!" Hutch tried correcting him.

"No! WHEN we get busted!...No one's ever done this. I can't imagine what the punishment is. Hell she's gonna have to invent a punishment for this one!"

"Just calm down."

"Oh Christ, I gotta redhead tellin' me to calm down now."

Right then, they all flinched at a flutter of movement by the passenger side window. A blue ball filled the gap and in dropped Hieronymus. He plopped into the seat beside Izzy and stared out the window as if nothing had happened.

"Hiney!" Izzy squealed and hugged him tight.

"And where the hell were you while we did all the heavy lifting?!" Diesel griped.

The blue demon just sighed and kept his head forwards, taking in the sights of a giant gate not unlike the one on the opposing end of the pit. Hutch kept it steady as she leaned forwards, watching the archway of the imposing threshold go over top of them. They were now out of the mine and a chill passed through them all. Hutch leered through the mist that now began to slither in from the bowels of the black beyond. She could make out a roadway, though it wasn't much of one. Ruts and tread-marks left a tell tale path of a hundred semi's past and ten times as many souls hauled in like cattle. The doubt and the dread began to set in as heavy as the otherworldly fog abounding, but she did her best not to let it creep onto her face. She had no idea what she was doing, and she was taking three souls into that beyond with her.

"Well?' Diesel growled.

"Well what?"

"You know where you're headed?"

"I'm trying, okay? This is isn't exactly a Sunday drive ta Shoney's."

"Oh well, it's nice ta know we're in good hands…Hopefully Regina peels the skin off me first cuz I just wanna get it over with."

"Would you stop?!"

"No! Not till ya admit ta me that ya have no idea where the hell you're goin?!"

"You helped build this damn thing! Shouldn't YOU know where were headed?!"

"I didn't help build much, girly. And what I did build, I don't wanna see again."

"Whatever…I know where I am goin'…I have a navigator, remember?" Hutch pointed a finger over at Izzy.

"Me?" She pointed at herself with dread.

"I don't know anyone else in this truck who's ran around this entire road. This stretch we're on now, it had a name, like the split or cock, or somethin'."

"The crotch. The crims call it the crotch," Izzy corrected.

"Yeah they would…So this things a star shape?"

"Yeah. Keep drivin' and you'll come to an intersection."

"Which way do I go when I get there?"

"Left, hun. You need to go left. The other leg goes above the road like an overpass. Then you hit the lower right point and head north, clear to the very top of the star. The gateway is there. I've seen it."

Hutch smiled a little. She slapped Diesel on the shoulder.

"Ya see? We got this. Ain't nothin' to it."

The yellow demon sighed and scowled.

What seemed like a mile passed by with the pace of an eon's breath. Hutch began to slow the rig as a massive structure loomed on high in the distance. It was Regina's playground, the Leviathan. Highway Hell. It did exist. It wasn't just folk tales from the mouths of the imps. The ground became smooth as she traversed the rig from the haul line to the surface of the main road. The faint glow of the flames in the beyond cast an eerie dance of shadows across the high-rising overpass above. It had all the makings of a forgotten highway that perished and went to eternal rest in the ether, a beautiful display of death and life forged in a hundred different shades of tempered ash. Hutch couldn't help but awe in its terrible presence.

The redhead slowed the rig down and then, finally, came to a complete brake. Diesel's eyes popped with surprise, but quickly turned to a leer of irritation as he watched Hutch look back and forth across the unholy road ahead.

"What are you doin'? It's left, girly. An armless ape could do this. Let's go."

But Hutch said nothing. She jammed the semi into park and then flung open the door, quickly leaving the demons by themselves to revel in their own confusion.

"What the hell is she doin'?" Diesel mumbled as he watched her walk out across the glow of the headlights. She stared on high into the twisted metal of the overpass and then drew her attention to the road she now trod. With reluctance, she bent down and pressed her hand flat to the surface of the highway. It was as cold as forged steel against winter's breast, but seemed to emanate an odd tingle into the flesh of her now trusting hand. She couldn't help but revel in the feeling of it. All of the time she'd spent toiling away in that pit she had missed this almost as much as her family. The road. Just a road. The lonely yet familiar feeling it gave. A path that could take you anywhere your heart desired and escape the problems that plagued you.

"It's pyre-slag" Izzy's voice startled Hutch as she called down from the window of the rig. The redhead looked up, hand still on the road.

"What?"

"Pyre-slag. What we paved it with. It's what's leftover from the firerite burn. The stuff is tough as nails." Hutch rapped on the road a few times gently with her knuckles. It was definitely harder than your standard asphalt.

"Wow, that's so amazing. Now can we get goin' before the crims show up?" Diesel tried keeping his calm. Hutch sighed and made her way back to the still-open door of the rig. A slam of a door and several gear jams later, they were headed left, and south, to the lower right point of Leviathan.

The road was quiet. Quieter than death. As were the occupants of the truck that traversed it. No one spoke a word as they watched the path ahead snake back and forth in the oddest directions. This beast of a track was definitely not a straight course. She didoed and froed with a dance of freedom Hutch only remembered from scenic highways and ill-planned country roads.

"This is part of the Serpent. Well the mild parts," Izzy finally broke the chill of the silence.

"The Serpent?"

"Each leg has a name. There's The Mirror, The Labyrinth, The Straights, The Swan Song, and this is the Serpent. Can ya guess why this one is named the Serpent?" The green demon's inquiry was quite rhetorical. Hutch just half smiled, but it melted away as the road straightened and made way for a sight ahead. It was a giant, perfect circle, not unlike the looks of a roundabout. Hutch looked to Izzy for direction.

"That's the lower point. Almost all the points look like this. You can either stop in the center or go round the circle and keep going." The redhead spoke not a word and did the latter. Taking the outer-belt of the circle till she was now pointed what she presumed to be northerly.

"There ya go, hun," Izzy nodded. "Now you're on the straights. Home stretch to the top point and the gateway."

Hutch breathed a slight sigh of relief, though it was murdered right then and there by Diesel.

"Home stretch, my ass. Makes it sound like we made it. Girly, what you're headed down is the most traveled leg on all of Leviathan. Might as well call it crim road."

"They might be in between shifts," Izzy tried diffusing.

"Shifts?! Ha, crims don't have shifts. Even if they are in some lull right now, other eyes are prying. And that damn cricket is always somewhere."

"Absalom…" Hutch mouthed to herself. She then spoke aloud, "Who is he? The cricket-man?"

"Don't know, hun. One of Regina's henchman. If not her right hand man," was all Izzy knew.

"Pet, more like," Diesel grumbled.

"So ya have no clue who he was?"

"Girly, I can't even remember who I was. Ya think I have the slightest damn clue who that two-legged bug was before all this?"

"It was just a question," Hutch gripped the wheel tighter and stared ahead.

"Hell, if anyone would know that answer it should be you."

"What's that supposed to mean?"

"C'mon, you knew who red-eyes was before he became the biggest asshole crim to walk this pit."

"That was just a coincidence."

"No. I don't think it was. I still think there's somethin' off about you. You're not like the rest of us down here. You're more than just a key branded on Regina's skin or a debt that's owed."

Hutch felt her anger rising.

"What are ya gettin' at? You sayin' I'm one of her pets now?"

"I don't know what ya are, to be honest. You been lookin' like a bright-eye way too long, I know that. I'm startin' ta think she's keepin' you that way."

"And why would she be doin' that?"

"I don't know, girly. You tell me."

The accusations the yellow demon threw her way just kept adding to the throb of rage growing in her head. But was he right? She couldn't help but wonder amidst it all, but did her damndest not to show it. The yellow demon went on,

"And what was with you back at the pit? The way ya just up and freaked, then fell over like a sack of potatoes?"

"It was nothin'…"

"Yeah, didn't look like nothin ta me."

Hutch finally boiled over.

"Jesus! You wanna see what I freaked out about?! I'll show ya!" She yanked back her dress to show Diesel the green on her inner thigh, "There! Ya see!...Wait? What?" Her angry glare went to confusion right along with the other demons in the cab. The spot on her thigh was no longer there. The alabaster skin she had always known was all that remained.

"Is this a free show, girly, or am I suppose ta be seein' somethin' else right now?" Diesel eyed her inner thigh, then looked up at her. Hutch slowly pulled her dress back down and shook her head.

"I...I...there was...never mind..."

"You goin' daffy on me? That would explain a lot, I guess."

"I ain't goin' nuts, okay? I don't think...Look, if you wanna turn back now, there's the door, but you better know how ta land on your feet cuz I ain't slowin' down," she pointed towards the passenger side of the rig.

"Ah hell, girly, I ain't goin' anywhere...to be honest, this is a nice change of scenery. Better enjoy it though, cuz it ain't gonna last long."

"We're gettin' out, alright?"

"Keep tellin' yourself that..."

Hutch sighed and began fiddling and digging through the dash clutter till she unearthed a cassette.

"What are ya doin'?" Diesel griped.

"Drownin' you out," the redhead said as she shoved the tape into the dash and turned up the volume. Alabama began blaring away so loudly it made everyone jerk in the cab. It wasn't Strait, but it would do, Hutch thought to herself. Hell, who was she kidding? It could've been polka music and she would've been fine with it. It seemed like her ears hadn't felt the kiss of music for a decade, and she couldn't help but smile as the sweet sounds filled her senses, bleeding out the very real danger they were in. If only for a moment. A short one at that. Before she even knew it, the tunes cut short, distorting into a tattered symphony of mush that spiraled into her watching the tape deck spew out a dark bird's nest of ratted ribbon.

"Goddamn it!" She yelled as she pushed away at the eject button and fruitlessly tried shoving the tape innards back into the jaws from which they so ruthlessly spewed. Soon, the riddled cassette became the least of her worries as she suddenly spotted a set of headlights, then another, and yet another. From seemingly nowhere, lights came passing by, beaming from cars and trucks and all manner of vehicles you'd see passing on the interstate.

Hutch started to panic, but before she could voice her grievances, Izzy spoke up.

"Don't worry, hun. They're nothin'. No crims behind those wheels." The redhead didn't respond immediately. She just stared at them as they passed. A few even came round the semi, headed in the same direction.

"What are they?"

"Ghosts. Or something like it. Reflections of car and driver that may or may not have met their end upon the highways and byways above."

"Translation, dingy here has no fuckin' clue what they are. None of us do," Diesel threw in his two cents.

"So...they can't touch us?"

"Oh no, hun. Make no mistake, there as solid as they look. And believe me, they're a pain in the ass when you race on this beast. They're all over the place down here. And you never know quite when they might pop up to ruin' your day," Izzy explained. Hutch said nothing, she let herself be sucked in by the dance of the cars as they switched lanes and went about their business as if they were ten thousand miles away from Hell. It seemed yet another grim refraction of what she missed about being topside. The simplicity of how the vehicles moved to and fro without care, reminded her of home. Strip away the darkness and flame in the foreground, and she could've sworn she was back on route 70, just making her way home with the other schlubs. And it wasn't awful. Not one bit. For several minutes, she reveled in some awkward silence as the demons stared over at her, wondering if she were still there...but something broke the daydream. Ahead, a set of lights seemed unlike the rest. They were much brighter, barreling down amongst a phalanx of neat rows of amber runners. It was another rig. Hutch felt her skin crawl.

"Now we got trouble, girly," Diesel said as somber as could be.

"Don't worry your head, hun. Just act natural. They won't notice"

"Oh yeah, act natural. We got a blue demon, a blondie, a greenie riding shotgun, and a bright-eye drivin' us all. Yeah, ain't nothin' weird about that. We'll be fine."

"Will you shut up, so I can think?!" Hutch growled, never releasing her stare from the blinding lights ahead. Diesel's eyes began darting around the cab, looking for something to use, and, quickly, he found it. He ripped down a red jacket that hung round the back side of the seat.

"What are you doin?" Hutch looked down at him as he threw the garment on and cinched the hood tight till only his eyes showed.

"You two, kiss the floor, till this truck gets by!" Diesel yelled at Izzy and Hieronymus. He then looked up at Hutch, stretching his arms out to the sides. "Does this thing make me look like a crim?" The jacket was three times too big. He was swimming in it.

"You look like a pile of old laundry," Hutch replied.

"Ahhh, move it!" He yelled as he jumped into her lap and took control of the wheel. She ducked down as the other rig came roaring past. The two crims piloting the semi looked briefly into the passing cab to see a wrinkly mass of red steering the truck. They slowly looked over at one another, exchanging an odd leer. From back in the truck, Diesel jumped down and ripped the hoodie off himself.

"You think they bought it?"

Hutch grabbed the wheel and kept staring into the rearview, watching the other semi disappear into the beyond. She kept waiting with bated breath to see its brake lights illuminate, but nothing happened.

"Well?" Izzy threw in. The redhead finally breathed a sigh of relief. But, before she could even speak, a loud squelch belted out from the dash. The sounds of a rough voice echoed through the cab from the speaker of the CB radio.

"Gatebound Freightshaker, you got your ears on?"

"Shit. Shit. Shit. Is he talkin' ta us?" Hutch looked to Diesel as she eyeballed the rearview once again.

"Well he ain't talkin' to himself!"

"Great save back there! I told ya ya looked like a pile of laundry!"

"I'm sorry, I didn't see you makin' a move to do shit!"

The radio interrupted their argument.

"Freightshaker, do you copy?" The crim seemed to be growing agitated with the silence.

"Answer him!" Izzy yelled in a panic. Diesel grabbed the CB and tried handing it to Hutch.

"Oh, hell no! They're gonna see right through me. You do it."

"Goddamn it…" he pressed the button, "Copy that." He responded.

"Freightshaker…everythin' okay back there?" The crim asked.

"Roger, crotchbound," Diesel winced at his own word choice.

"Crotchbound?" Hutch silently mouthed with a look of terror. There was a moment of silence on the airways. So long in fact that the four began looking around at one another, thinking it was all over.

"Copy that, Freightshaker," the crim finally came back. Everyone breathed a sigh of relief as Diesel went to place the CB back. But the speaker belched once again.

"Freightshaker? ….Why you runnin' bobtail?"

Diesel grit his teeth in defeat.

"What? What the hells that mean?" Hutch questioned.

"It means, where the fuck is our trailer? You know, the one you lost over the side of the mine?" Diesel pointed to the back. A chill ran up her spine. She had forgotten all about it, obviously so had Diesel. Hell maybe they all had. Diesel cooked up some bullshit, and fast.

"When we dropped the grays we got two flats and a blown pigtail."

There was another sickening moment of silence and finally,

"Roger that, Freightshaker." Once again everyone breathed a sigh of relief. But miles to the south of them, the crim changed his CB channel, speaking to someone else entirely.

"Redrum, this is Yella Duck…we gotta problem."

A raspy and familiar voice came back, "Copy that."

Breaker Breaker 1-9

"Holy shit! Can you believe that?! I think we might make it, girly. Thanks ta my quick thinkin'. Stupid-ass crims, fell for the old blondie in the hoodie trick."

Hutch listened to Diesel's self-appreciative ranting as her paranoid eye flipped back and forth between the rearview and the ghostly stretch of road ahead.

"You're awful quiet...thought you'd be tickled to death. This crazy-ass scheme of yours might pay off," the yellow imp spoke to the redhead.

"We ain't outta here yet! So save your dumbass hootin' and hollerin' for later! You're makin' my brain itch," she snapped.

"What's this? Role reversal?! Five minutes ago your glass was half-full now you handed it off ta me. Sometimes I think you just like ta argue. Like if I said those flames on the horizon were blue you'd say they weren't."

"Of course I would, they're purple, a colorblind nightcrawler could see that!" She took one hand off the wheel.

"And there ya go again," Diesel crossed his arms.

"Worms don't have eyes, hun," Izzy spoke.

"Boy, nothin' gets by you, does it?" The redhead muttered in disgust.

"Breaker, breaker, one-niiiiine…" a voice suddenly slithered through the CB radio. It sent a pang of fear through the cab. "This is Redrum. Firebush, do you copy?"

A chill of nausea ran through the redhead as she stared at the blood soaked rag that used to be her finger. The demons all looked around at one another amidst a growing anxiety.

"How'd he know?" Diesel whispered. Hutch grabbed the CB and held it up to her mouth, ready to drop one-hundred atomic F-bombs, but she paused. She shook her head and slammed the receiver back to the dash.

"Fuck him…" was all she muttered as she mashed the gas even harder.

"Firebuuuuush. Look darlin', I know how wet that pussy gets when ya hear ma voice but my god, baby, you need ta get that hand outta your panties and on that radio so we can talk."

Hutch's lips began writhing with a wave of silent obscenities as she tried desperately to avoid the temptation to call back. A few moments of silence paved the way and then…

"Look, I'll play along and keep talkin' so you can finish, but just promise you'll flick that snowpea with the bloody finger stump I gave ya."

She was livid. She wanted to jump through the airways and come out the other side, boot-first, right into his shit-eating mouth. Still she kept her hands firm on the wheel.

"That was a real subtle escape ya made back there, firebush. Droppin a trailer over the side of the mine and jackknifing another rig drew no attention whatsoever. You oughta write a playbook on how NOT to escape a furnace mine."

No one said anything in the cab. Sid started in again. "Man, you are awful quiet…didn't think that was possible. I know you're there though. That's okay, I'll talk and you can listen. I'm headed southbound with an entire convoy at my ass at about five klicks and closing. If you don't stop that rig by the time you see our headlights we will be forced to engage you…And by engage, I mean mash you head-on, side swipe you, flip you, do whatever it is we have to do to make sure you ain't nothin' but a million little pink pieces all over this shithole she calls a road. Now, do you copy that?"

Hutch just looked at the others briefly. She couldn't help but feel shitty at that moment. She hadn't made them come along, but she was still the reason they were there just the same.

"Well if you won't copy, I'm sure that yellow pile of dogshit you got ridin' shotgun will." Diesel's eyes popped wide. "Yeah that's right blondie. You don't think we didn't notice some yellow, green, and blue missin' from our lovely pit? You know blondie, I'm gonna make you a promise, you get that bright-eyed bitch ta pull over and we can work somethin out. Now, I'm not unreasonable, I just want Red ta pay the piper. We're gonna chuck her ta the bottom of the furnace and stomp out that green girlfriend of yours, but I'll let you go back unscathed to the pit. Back to slingin' axes, maybe with a brand new coat of green on ya, what da ya say? A fresh start."

Diesel looked into the faces of the Hutch and Izz, their eyes searched his in some frightened moment of unease. The yellow demon grit his teeth and grabbed up the CB in his trembling hand. He pushed the button.

"Get fucked, ya nasty, toothless, dickless prick."

Amidst the rumble of his cab, Sid chuckled to himself. He responded,

"Shame…" he then switched channels to the crims following his lead. "Hit her with everything. Run her off this road, even if it means rollin' your rig."

"Copy that, Redrum…but what about the cargo?" One of the crims questioned.

"Fuck the cargo. If she wants more grays she can go get em' herself."

"Roger that, Redrum. Over and out."

Sid's last words still echoed in Hutch's ears as her brain scrambled and pulled at a million different ideas, trying to pluck one down that wasn't rotten and rife with uncertainties. But no such fruits existed. She had no idea what to expect from the convoy that was barreling down on her with every spin of the winding obsidian beneath her tires. Izzy looked around in an anxious silence, her wide, doughy eyes looking for reassurance from the other three, but there was none to be had. Hutch wanted to tell her it was going to be okay, but she wasn't going to lie to her. She couldn't even lie to herself at this point... She just kept a dead stare peeled towards the horizon ahead...and, within seconds, she saw it, a line of headlights strung across the entire breadth of the highway ahead. Sid's posse of semis had arranged themselves into a rolling wall of steel, with nary a mirrors reach between each, ready to mow down anything in their path.

"Girly?" Diesel mumbled out as he watched on at the ominous sight ahead. "What's your plan? Tell me ya got one?" Hutch heard his shaky words, but her mind was somewhere else. Off in some dark place...A void where all her feelings seemed to go numb. But inside that place there was something else there with her...all the hate, the fear, the sadness she had carried around with her since she had come down to this god forsaken pit, just seemed to hit her all at once. And in that instant, she went crazy. She let go and her foot buried to the floor. She didn't know which rig ahead was Sid's, but she picked the middle one, and stayed a steady course right for the center of its headlights.

"Girly?...Girly?" Diesel's voice became shakier by the second. "Hutch?!" He yelled. But she didn't even flinch. And it was at that moment Diesel knew she had made up her mind. Izzy crawled ahead against the pull of the forwarding rig and dug her claws into the dashboard. She peered over it amidst a growing dread, squinting in the blinding glow of the rigs that were menacingly close.

"Diesel? Diesel, make her stop!!" She cried out. Hutch heard nothing at this point. She only felt the absence of sound; a vibration that coursed through her foot, rattling the bones clear up into the center of her numbing mind. Diesel knew he couldn't stop her. He just looked over at Izzy and spoke as calm as could be.

"She's gone, Izz. Duck down and hold tight." With that, the trio of demons hit the floorboards as Hutch's emotionless face cracked into a crooked grin of insanity.

"That's it, bitch. Come to daddy. Come right into my arms," Sid whispered as he mirrored Hutch's wicked smile behind the wheel of his own rig.

"Redrum?" A shaky voice of a crim came through Sid's radio. He grabbed it up in anger.

"What?!"

"She ain't slowin'. What's our move?"

"Don't let er' through!"

"Boss?" Another crim voiced out its concern.

"Everyone listenin', I said hold this goddamn line! She's bluffin!" With that, Sid smashed the CB down. "You wanna play chicken, cunt! I gotta cock for ya! Come get it!" He yelled as Hutch's headlights became all he could see. And then it happened….a bellowing nightmare of a scream erupted as one of the crims lost its nerve. The demon blasted the emergency brake, locking up all eighteen wheels, sending its rig into a chaotic overcorrection. The semi blasted the truck to right of it, and then to the left, creating a domino shockwave of mayhem through the other rigs.

"You stupid fuck!!" Was all Sid could get out before the gap between the convoy and Hutch was breached. Amongst the split second of the chaos, the redhead saw it…an opening between the colliding rigs…and she took it. She plowed onwards, with a shaking RPM needle, right between the front semis. A screaming symphony of steel shredded the ear as she buried deep. Mirrors ripped off, sparks flew, and tires exploded. The three demons all rolled under the dash amidst the terrifying impact as Hutch mashed the accelerator, forcing her way between the snaking semi trailers ahead. Before she could even reach the end, she felt the pressure release as one of the rigs jackknifed, starting a cataclysmic chain of events. Nearly the entire convoy became a spinning and rolling mass of twisted steel, intermeshing into a spider web of all-out destruction. The side windows of the redhead's rig shattered as it was whipped around one full turn, nearly flipping it over under the force of the impacts abounding. The sound was deafening. Like bombs setting of more bombs inside the belly of a steel beast. And it all happened within the spread of seconds.

Hutch kept an iron grip around the wheel as she mashed the gears in a rage, trying desperately to find the first gear. Soon, she clutched hard and knocked it into place, blasting the gas as she once again took off in the direction she'd been headed. But something was off. The rig was struggling. Like the whole damn thing was sinking in sand. She instantly feared the tires were all blown as she screamed out, "Goddamn it! Go, you bastard! Move!" Diesel rolled out from under the dash, feeling himself as if he couldn't believe he was still in one piece. He soon noticed Hutch's struggle with getting the rig back up to speed and looked out the window to the rear.

"Holy shit!" He yelled out at the incredible sight. One of the convoy rigs had rolled onto its side and became tangled up on the back of their rig. The trailer teetered across their fifth wheel, still dragging along the truck that towed it. The back of the trailer had blown open, spilling out the contents of the grays within. They all began shuffling around like the zombies they were, only adding to the chaotic scene unfolding before the yellow demon's eyes.

"What's happenin' back there?!" Hutch yelled out.

"Nothin good! You got a passenger!" Diesel answered.

"Hutch leaned up and craned her neck out the window to see the problem.

"Holy shit!"

"That's what I said!" Diesel darted back into the cab. He jumped onto Hutch's lap and looked out the driver's side along with her.

"Jesus H Christ, girly, this ain't good!"

"Well, no shit!"

"Mash it!" He commanded as he jumped down off her lap.

"What the hell do you think I'm doin'?!" Hutch yelled over the redlining engine. The rig managed to creep up to about 20 MPH but it just wouldn't go past that.

Half a mile away, things were stirring behind them. Not all the rigs had met a mangled fate. In fact, one was making a violent u-turn, headed back for the pileup. Another rig had since come back and rolled on by.

"Redrum, this is Yella Duck, do you copy?"

"Right behind ya! Anyone else still standin?!"

"I think that's a positive on the negative, Redrum."

"Shit…let's dump these trailers. They're weighin' us down!"

"Copy that."

"Shit! Shit! Shit! This thing is gonna overheat! We gotta do somethin'!" Hutch screamed.

"Jesus…oh, hell," Diesel mumbled to himself as he looked around nervously. "I got this! C'mon! Follow me!" He slapped Hieronymus on the shoulder as he climbed out the passenger side window. The blue demon reluctantly followed the yellow one outside. The two crawled carefully back onto the fifth wheel where the wrecked rig was still holding on tightly. Together, Hieronymus and Diesel began pushing the side of the mangled trailer. Putting their feet down and thrusting, doing everything they could to free it up, but nothing was giving.

"Damn it, H! What the hell are we gonna do?!" Diesel belted out. He quickly scaled up the trailer, plopped down on the top, and began looking around for something. What the hell that was exactly he hadn't a clue.

"Maybe we can free up the truck at least? That would get rid of most of the weight," Diesel spoke to Hieronymus and pointed off to the side towards the mangled truck that the trailer dragged along. With haste, the two ran down the trailer till they were looking over the side at the fifth wheel mechanism. Diesel reluctantly leaned over the side and began jamming and pulling at the release lever. "Shit, H! Damn it, it ain't budgin!" He grunted and griped, tugging with all his might. Soon, he felt a persistent tapping upon his shoulder from the blue demon. "What?! What?!" His voice soon died to a coo as he glared over his shoulder in the direction Hieronymus was pointing. Back from where they'd come, he saw it, two sets of headlights bearing down through the shadowy mass of the convoy pile up. "That ain't good. That ain't good at all…C'mon! Pull this while I pry!" Diesel yelled as he jumped right down into the fifth wheel. He wedged himself tight and began pushing and tugging while Hieronymus pulled above. Amidst it all, the truck blasted a bump on the side of the highway, jarring it loose from the grasp of the claw. The rig and trailer separated violently and a long blue arm stretched out, yanking Diesel to safety. Together, the two demons watched as the truck rolled over in a maelstrom of sparks, coming to rest as a battered ghost upon the obsidian abounding. The weight release caused a massive shift in power. The rig ahead lurched forward and the two demons nearly fell off the trailer from the force of it all. They quickly steadied their feet and ran back down the battered trailer, jumping back to the rig ahead.

"Well, ya must've done something right!" Hutch praised as she felt the truck gathering steam.

"Never mind all that, we got company! Floor it!"

Hutch couldn't even pull a worrisome inquiry from her mouth before the impact come. They all clenched their teeth as the rig was rammed hard from behind. The truck began fishtailing under the impact and the redhead once again began white knuckling the wheel, trying to keep them from careening off the road. Over and over the hits came, some worse than others. Hutch let out a war hoop as she kept her foot to the floor, her anger growing with every cheap shot from behind. Soon, her ears were overcome with the sound of another rig rounding the beaten trailer she still helplessly drug along. She looked over, and there he was, smiling that tooth-filled grin he lacked in life.

"Fiiiiirebush," his voice came over the CB. "C'mon baby, pull over. I just wanna talk. That's all."

Hutch grit her teeth and yanked the wheel, driving her rig over into his. Sparks flew and rubbing tires screeched out a bitter symphony of burnt rubber. Sid backed off to the side and hovered there, his howling laughter squelched through the CB waves. "Girl, I knew you liked it rough, but goddamn!" Right then, Hutch's passenger side window came alive with the terrifying sounds of another rig creeping up. "How bout we get really freaky? Get a little threesome action goin'. Whata ya think Yella Duck?"

"Copy that, Redrum. Let's make us a sandwich," the voice of the other crim came blasting through her radio. Before Hutch could even think, the two trucks came swerving into her, mashing her tight between them. The redhead kept a tight hold on the wheel as she did her best to chase away the fear that desperately tried to rip her apart, not unlike the trucks surrounding. As the sparks danced and metal groaned, the speedometer waned with every pulse of pressure the two rigs relentlessly dished out to her. With all her might, she spun the wheel hard to the right, but it did nothing. She stayed perfectly wedge between the trucks, their speed slowly withering down to 40 MPH. Diesel had had enough, he reached up, ripped the CB right off the dash, and threw it with all he had out the window. It connected true, right into the face of Yellow Duck. The crim nearly fell from his seat, jerking the wheel as he did so. The rig screeched out and away from Hutch, allowing her to blast the gas and fend off Sid from the other side. From there, she kept swerving to the left and right, blasting into each rig, keeping them at bay as she gained traction once again. Another half mile seemed

to go by like ten until she finally began to tire. Diesel could see it
in her face, like she was about to just hit the brakes and give it all
up even though she'd came so far. But then something else was
there…A glisten in her eye. The yellow demon looked over the
dash to see the headlights of an oncoming vehicle. It was one of
the countless phantom cars on the Leviathan. He looked at the
redhead for a split second, just long enough to see her grin as she
whipped the truck to the right, driving Yellow Duck over into the
oncoming car. The sound was deafening. Pieces of shrapnel flew
into the cab as Hutch closed her eyes, leaving herself nothing but
the sounds of the carnage she'd created to fill her senses with
victory. And victory it was indeed. The car and the rig flew
backwards, into the broken trailer she still drug. It dislodged and
whipped round her driver's side with a violence even she didn't
expect. She opened her eyes in time to meet Sid's as the spinning
trailer smashed into his rig, causing him to lose control. Hutch just
stared ahead, a tiny smile creeping up the side of her face as she
listened to the terrible sounds of the trucks crashing behind her.
And then it all went calm. The hum of the highway below was the
only noise that filled the cab as all the demons looked round at one
another in disbelief. And then…

    "Yee-haw!! Fuck yeah, girly!" Diesel erupted in a triumphant
cheer. Izzy jumped up and hugged her tightly.

    "Ya did it, hun!"

    "Okay. Okay, that's enough of that. Don't be gettin' all mushy
on me," she pushed the green demon away as she caught the sight
of something looming in the distance. "What the…hell?"

    Izzy rose up and gazed upon what Hutch was entranced by. It
was a glowing aura of light. A halo filled with a dazzling array of
indigo and red that fluttered over one another like the waves of an
ocean upon a backdrop of obsidian.

    "Is that…?" Hutch couldn't even finish her sentence.

    "It is," the green demon smiled.

    "It's…it's beautiful," the redhead wouldn't even blink for fear
she'd miss one millisecond of its ever-growing luster. She went to
mash the gas harder but something caught her ear. Something
hauntingly familiar. A chill ran up her spine as the full onslaught
of the noise came into fruition in the form a roaring engine that
seemed to run on the vile screams of the damned. Hutch's head

snapped to the side to behold the horrible sight of a battered Plymouth Superbird. The coal-black and bottomless eyes of Absalom met Hutch's as he leaned over the seat and stared up into the cab. Even though she had defeated an entire convoy of crims, she now felt vulnerable…Helpless and terrified. It was as if the cricket-masked monster was sizing her up, looking for her Achilles heel. Everyone in the cab was as deathly silent as Hutch. No one knew what to expect from the man-thing, but one fact hovered with an even greater gravity…Wherever Absalom was, Regina was always close behind. Hutch tightened her grip on the wheel as the cricket slowly leaned back in his seat. She was sure he was about to make his move, and he did. He blasted the gas and took off like a shot. Hutch watched him disappear beneath the grace of the glowing gateway ahead. Suddenly the bottom of the halo flashed with a bright light surrounded by bolts of electricity. He had passed through the threshold, into the topside beyond.

"What the hells he up to?" Diesel finally broke the uncomfortable silence.

"I…I don't know…" Hutch kept her eyes fixated on the spot where he'd gone through.

"Hun…Stop," Izzy spoke up.

"What?"

"I just…I got a bad feelin'. Just stop this rig."

"You are fuckin' kiddin'? We've got this far and you want me to pull over and what? Give up?"

"No! I just…I gotta bad feelin'."

"Well the feelin' is mutual, but I ain't stoppin'. We're too damn close," Hutch spoke as she mashed the gas, piloting a steady course for the gate ahead. The doorway was much larger than she'd first thought. The closer she came, the more she could grasp its grandeur. It had to have spanned some one-hundred yards in breadth and at least that in height. She once again became enthralled with its majesty.

"Hun, please stop. Please," Izzy's voice cut in once again. Hutch shook her head and stayed the course, Never once looking in the direction of the sniveling green demon. But she wished she had. Five-hundred feet and counting from the mouth of freedom, a blinding light once again exploded through the hell-born kaleidoscope…It was the Superbird reentering the Leviathan at

200 mph-plus, with it's beak pointed dead center of the rig. If Absalom couldn't run the truck off the road, he was going to split it in half. It all happened so fast, yet so slowly. No one even had the time to react, though they could hear the future of their own screaming inside their heads. The car blasted into the front of the rig, crumpling into a ball as it pushed the nose of the semi inwards with an explosion so loud it could be heard back on Earth. The truck went up onto its front tires, speeding along for some fifty feet before the force sent it on over into a terrifying death roll. Car and semi, intertwined into a mass of sparking and crumpling steel that whirled and reeled for the eternity inside a nightmare. Nothing seemed real. Hutch seemed to go numb in the ten seconds it took from impact to finish. Darkness overtook them all as the pile of twisted metal slid to a pitiful stop about one hundred feet from the mouth of the gate. All was silent. Even the hum of the massive portal did not exist. It all seemed like a replay of the events that had led her there. A visceral playback of her wreck topside replayed with a terrifying slow motion inside her brain, mixed with all the colors amidst the darkness that had funneled her into the pit. The helplessness. The loneliness. The dread. All of it came to a climax that popped her eyes open wide. She was now staring up through the cab into the black roof of Furnace 12. With no thoughts to embrace and a tingling of numbness throughout her entire being, she climbed up through the truck and flung herself out onto the door. She cast a melancholy stare across the scape of the highway, to the gate, and then back to the macerated heap of metal that was once the rig. Her eyes soon transfixed onto the hunk of steel that still clung to the front of the truck. Somehow, the giant wing of the Superbird still stuck out of the entire mess, overshadowing a chilling sight beneath. There, amidst the wreckage, was the top half of Absalom. She couldn't quite tell if he was cut in half or just stuck down in the car, but, like her, he was still much among the living…Or the damned, or whatever the hell their existence was. She watched the mandibles of his face writhe back and forth as he tried with a weak grip to force himself out of the carnage to no avail. With a quiet slither, she lowered herself down off the rig and limped over to him, standing above him with a wayward stare. In that instant, she still felt nothing. No pain in her body. No emotion in her soul. But that all soon

changed. With a clenched fist she flew into a rage, blasting him in the face with the hardest punch she could muster. This led into another punch, and another. Soon, a maelstrom of blows rained down like thunder. She screamed out a horrifying bellow of pain that only accentuated the hate she felt toward him. There was no way to stop. She couldn't. She didn't know how. She just kept screaming and pummeling him till her knuckles dripped with blood and her yells turned to crackling gasps of angst. But then something happened, a piece of his face flew off and the next punch she went to drop hovered there along with her gaping mouth. Something lay beneath the skeleton face of the bug. Something…human. Through the small hole in Absalom's face, she saw it. A set of lips. She lowered her fist and began to tremble at the sight of it. With grave apprehension, she leaned down and grabbed hold of his other mandible, ripping it off with a grunt to reveal the entire mouth and chin beneath. The smooth, alabaster flesh glowed in the light of the humming gateway beyond as she played with her own lips and toiled in the thoughts of what lay beneath the rest of the insect-man's mask. With all the courage she could muster, she grabbed hold of what was left of the bug's face and ripped it clean off, unveiling the face below. All the life that may have been still left within her shell, retreated at that very moment. She felt sick and dizzy. Surely this was all a dream? Memories flooded back to her in a chaotic tumble of pain and sorrows once buried. The face…that face. She knew it. She knew it like the cold kiss of January and the hot embrace of July. It was her brother, It was Henry.

"It wasn't supposed to happen this way. You weren't supposed to know," a small voice startled Hutch from behind. She looked over her shoulder to see Regina standing there. Her face painted in the shades of some calloused regret. Hutch could do nothing but just stare at her for what seemed like an eternity. And then,

"What the fuck did you do to him?" Before Regina could answer, Hutch spun round and began shaking the man in the wreckage. "Henry? Henry, it's me?! It's your sister! It's Hutch! Say something!" She quickly became hysterical as her tears rained down on the emotionless face of the man she knew to be her dead brother.

"He won't answer you. He can't," Regina took a few steps forwards.

"You shut the fuck up! What did you do to him, goddamn it?!"

"He…" Regina started to speak but her words were cut short by a violent slap across the face. Hutch recoiled her hand.

"You did this to him…you turned him into this. I know you did. That's what you do, you ruin everything. You break everything you touch," the redhead spoke coldly, pointing a shaking finger right into the brunette's face. For a moment, Regina was at a true loss for words. The two just stood there in the light of the gateway, one eyeing the other with fire in her eyes and the other's eyes becoming softer by the second. The brunette went to speak once more, but was shut down by another slap from the hysterical redhead.

"Whatever is about to come out of your mouth, save it. Save it for someone who gives a shit…And from what I'm seein', that's nobody," with her cold words finished, she quickly spun round and ran back to where Henry lay entangled in the metal abstract of the wreck he'd created. She began trying to fight her tears off as she pulled and pried at the wreckage that entombed her sibling, to no avail.

"I'll get you out of there…You'll be okay…FUCK!" She lamented as rage and melancholy fought for the throne of her heart. Henry spoke not a word. He didn't even blink as his cloudy eyes stared straight through her like she wasn't even there. It only made her sob even more as she let go of the metal that tore at her flesh. She buried her hands in the blood of her palms and began wailing as the memories of her brother and that fateful night came screaming back. Amongst the sound of her own sorrow, she heard a set of tiny footsteps shuffle up behind her.

"He ended up this way trying to right and wrong that wasn't his to bear," Regina started in, fully expecting Hutch to jump up and lay into her once again. She didn't. She did nothing but cry and cry. But Regina knew she was listening, so she kept on. "He knew the things that happened…instead of trying to make them right he tried to make them go away." Hutch slowly turned and looked over her shoulder.

"What the fuck are you talkin' about?" Regina slowly shook her head. She looked as if tears of her own were about to fall but nothing came.

"You wouldn't understand…he made his bed of guilt and now he's lying in it…That night. It wasn't supposed to happen the way it did. I didn't know that car was coming on the other side of the tunnel…neither did he. He took me right before the straight-away and laid into the gas. I don't know what he was thinking. There was no way he was going to make that cut through there at that speed. I don't know…sometimes I think he knew that…Maybe he just wanted it to all be over. He just couldn't live with the secrets anymore."

Hutch sniffled and wiped at her face in horror.

"You were there that night?"

Regina nodded.

"And you did nothin'? You just watched the carnage and left?"

Regina was deathly quiet for a moment. Taking the time to remember the horror she beheld. "There was nothing to save. You know that. You know what that wreck looked like…I stopped and killed the engine and just looked at that mass of metal he'd created. I remember how quiet it was. Or a least at first…When reality began to sink in, all I could hear were the deafening sounds of the crickets. They sang and sang and sang, like nothing had happened, completely oblivious that five people were gone…just like that. And for a moment, I envied those insects. Apparently, so did he…From the quiet of the ruins, Henry McCray arose wearing a mask of the bugs that had serenaded him into darkness, and behind him followed the car he so despised in life. I left him there on that lonely stretch of road…but he followed me. He followed me everywhere I went until I let him become the slave he thought himself to be…" Regina ended her chilling version of events that had transpired that horrible night. Hutch knew she was telling the truth, but she still didn't know what the brunette meant when she talked of Henry righting a wrong that wasn't his. Still, she asked no questions. She slowly leaned in and kissed Henry on his cheek. Then, without even looking at Regina, she rose to her feet, and began walking away into the darkness of the highway, away from the gate. Her heartbreak was palpable. Even Regina could feel it in the air as she watched the redhead walk away into the distance like she was never coming back. Soon, the awful sounds of a limping diesel truck could be heard in the distance. It was Sid. He slowly passed the redhead, glaring down at her with an angry leer till he saw Regina up ahead. He stopped the rig and jumped out, ready to fetch the woman that had made a fool of him.

"Stop!" Regina commanded.

"What?!"

"I said leave her alone…give her a minute."

"Give her a fuckin minute?! She just helped scrap an entire fleet of your rigs! We might have two good trucks left topside and you're tellin' me ta give her a minute?!" Sid protested with an anger he could no longer keep at bay. Regina just glared away at him for a moment as he kept moving his stare between her and the fading redhead in the distance.

"Go ahead. Go after her. See what happens," she spoke with malice. The crim stepped it down a notch, lowering his shoulders until he was in a more submissive state. The beating he'd received was still fresh in his mind. "That's what I thought," Regina spoke again. She then slowly walked over to the wreckage, keeping her golden stare drilled into the man in the metal. She stopped just a pace away.

"We need to get him back together. I'll get the others. We'll dig him outta there," Sid spoke, but his journey back was cut short by Regina's words.

"No."

"No?" The crim raised a brow.

Regina shook her head a bit. She wetted her lips. "I'm letting him go."

"You ain't serious?…He's one of the best servants you got and you're gonna release em? Just like that?" Regina looked back at him. She spoke not a word. Sid went on. "Wasn't he part of your grand design? Your plan? Your revenge?"

"Things change…" Regina all but whispered. She then leaned down and placed her open hand across Henry's face. A violent storm of lightning whipped around his body and surged in and out of Regina amongst a glowing aura of indigo light. She clenched her teeth as if the very act of what she was doing was ripping her own spirit into shreds. Within moments, a beam of light blasted out of his chest, sending a radiant ray of blue into the darkness above.

And just like that, his otherworldly shell of a body went limp and the light disappeared. Regina recoiled her hand slowly and looked down upon the empty shell with a glare Sid had never seen from her. Remorse. Several uncomfortable and silent moments paved onwards as the crim stood behind her, waiting for her to say something.

"Throw his shell into the furnace and salvage what you can out of the rigs.

"Yeah, but…"

"I said clean up your fucking mess!" Regina screamed out. Her words made Sid cringe inside. Suddenly, his eyes caught a glimpse of color among the twisted steel. Three familiar demons peered around the cab of the wrecked rig with a growing terror.

"What are we gonna do with them?" Sid pointed.

Regina's stare drifted over to the trio. They all darted back behind the truck.

"Gather them up and take them to her."

Sid's eyes grew in shock. He couldn't believe what he was hearing. He opened his mouth to protest but thought it best not to push her buttons any longer.

"And then what?"

"Take all four of them back to the mine and get them started on cleaning up that mess Red made…We're still moving forward. We need to find it."

The sounds of clacking metal once again filled Hutch's senses. They were all back in the nightmare of the mine, but her head was still somewhere else. It was still back at that wreck…back with Henry. Oh, how she missed him. She had always wanted to see him one last time…but not like that. The headstone they had laid across his grave had more life in it than that shell she had seen only hours before. It was hard remembering a man so full of life and hope be reduced to the thing that served Regina. But even with all that in mind, Hutch couldn't help but wonder what was happening to him. If Regina was in the process of putting him back together or burying him in the deepest pit of Hell. Deep down, she hoped for the latter. She couldn't bear to look at him like that any longer for there was always that little feeling gnawing at her in the background…Hoping beyond hope that he could be saved and once again returned to the person he was on Earth. But she knew it was all wishful thinking.

"Girly, that axe ain't gonna swing itself," Diesel's gruff voice shot into her ear. She did little but sigh as she stared off across the mine. Izzy looked over at Diesel.

"What happened to her back there? She ain't said a word since the accident."

"Maybe it jarred somethin' loose...hell I don't know. She should be smilin' and whistlin' showtunes. We're all lucky we're not at the bottom of the furnace right now after that stunt she pulled."

They both kept staring at her for another moment.

"Oh my god, girly, I found a pack of cigarettes over here!" Diesel suddenly yelled out, trying to get a rise out of her. Hutch didn't even bat an eye. "Hmmm, nothin. That ain't good."

"Somethin' definitely happened to her back there," Izzy said.

"Of course somethin' happened to her back there, she was a dog dick's length away from going home. We all were. But you don't see me moping around like a zombie. Might as well paint her gray, she'd fit right in with all these other purgatory puppets shufflin' round here," Diesel went back to swinging away at the rocks.

"You saw what happened back there didn't you? The rapture?" Izzy whispered.

Suddenly Hutch's brow raised. She snapped out of her trance.

"What did ya say? What did she say?" Hutch looked at Diesel.

"Uh, nothin', girly, it was nothin'. Get ta diggin' before Regina changes her mind about turnin' us into firerite."

"She said she saw a rapture. I heard her. You saw it?"

"We all saw it, didn't we Hiney?" Izzy smiled. The blue demon nodded.

"Yeah whatever, it was whatever," Diesel gruffly spoke.

"It wasn't whatever, it was a rapture. I told ya they were real," Izzy said.

"Who was it? Who got it?"

"That cricket-man. Absalom. Regina just put her hand down and poof! He went somewhere else," the green demon explained with an almost child-like enthusiasm.

"Oh my god...Regina? She...she made that happen?"

"Well...um, I guess I never thought about it. Maybe?"

"What the hell?" She looked to Diesel for confirmation, but before he could speak a terrible sound exploded. A chunk of metal blasted into the side of the beaten semi trailer beside them in the mine. A huge hook attached to a cable landed right at Hutch's feet. Her gaze narrowed and slowly traced back up the steel line to the top of the mine where a group of crims glared down at her.

"Stop your fuckin' gabbin' and hook that up, firebush!" Sid called down to her.

"Fuck off," Hutch yelled back up.

"Hey, the boss said ya need to clean up your mess. So get to cleanin'."

She chucked her pickaxe to the rocks and grabbed up the giant hook. She started mumbling a gamut of obscenities to herself as she began twisting the cable and hook round the axles of the trailer till she was sure she had it secured. With that, she locked down the hook over the cable and tugged on it.

"There! Happy?!" She yelled up and walked away.

"Ecstatic…Pull er' up, boys!" Sid commanded to a truck the cable was tethered to. The rig lurched forwards, belching a cloud of black fumes into the air. From below, Hutch watched as the trailer flipped over and began being drug up the side of the mine, expelling a terrible screech as it scraped across the rocks. She quickly turned her attention back to the demons beside her.

"So Regina can rapture folks?" She went right back to it.

"I don't know what Regina can do, okay? She was just leanin' over him I think. I don't know if she did it, or he did it, or whoever did it. It just happened," Diesel started getting agitated.

"So he was for sure raptured?"

"Am I stuttering? YES! A blue light blasted from him and he was gone! Why is this so important to you?"

"He was my brother!"

The demons all became quiet. Their demeanors downshifting into an apparent confusion.

"He was…what?" Diesel spoke.

"My brother. Absalom is my brother. Or…was my brother. Jesus, I don't know…"

"But how? Why?" Izzy asked.

Hutch just shook her head.

"I don't know…I don't know about anythin' anymore. I just wanna go home. This is all bullshit!" With that, she grabbed her pickaxe back up and chucked it as hard as she could at the side of the mine. It buried deep into a boulder and a series of cracks spread out from it.…but they didn't stop. Hutch tilted her head as she watched the cracks from her rampage spread like spider webs across the sheered face of the mine. And then it happened. A thunder from above. She couldn't even move as she watched the horror of the entire south side of the mine break off and avalanche downwards upon them all, bringing with it the trailer the crims were towing out. The sound was deafening and all-consuming as she beheld the wall of rock plummeting down. She tried to turn to run, but was swept up and engulfed…everything went black. She awoke to the sound of her own coughing and panicked breath and was introduced to a darkness she'd only seen but a few times in her life. That is, if her eyes were even open. Had she gone blind? She wasn't even sure at that point.

"Hello?!" She spat out and winced as the sound of her own voice reverberated painfully back into her ear. "Shit…" she began fumbling around, feeling her body to make sure she was in one piece. Miraculously, she seemed to be fine. Her confusion sat in further as her hands were introduced to a cold and smooth surface beneath where she sat. She fully expected to feel the jagged rocks around her but it wasn't so. She went to get up but quickly realized she couldn't. Her leg was stuck under the rock, she could feel it as she pulled and grimaced in the blackness abounding. The panic further set in.

"Izzy?...Diesel?...Hello?" She spoke at normal tone as to not evoke the painful echo once more. She thought for a second then spoke again, "Hieronymus?" Nothing but absolute silence greeted her back. "Goddamn it…" she started pulling on her leg once again, clawing at the rocks, but she couldn't even hope to budge them. Then, she gasped as she heard a shuffling across the way. She had no idea where she was, but somebody or some-thing was in there with her.

"Hello?"

The shuffling came once again and she winced inside. Her eyes squinted as a blue light illuminated the area. She could finally see where she was. She was currently entombed in the trailer that had fallen back down the mine. The ceilings and walls were buckled inwards but luckily not enough to crush her. She was towards the back of the rolling container. It must have swallowed her up and been covered by the cave-in. The rocks spilled in through the broken doors, pinning her leg down where she sat. As she took it all in, she began wishing it was dark again, it made things less real. But through her panic she didn't even realize how the hell a light was shining until she looked across the way. There, at the other side of the trailer, sat Hieronymus. Hutch glared at him with confusion as his whole body glowed with a soothing indigo aura.

"Oh great…it's you. Nothin' like gettin' stuck for the rest of eternity with someone who can't talk." As expected, the demon remained silent at the far end of the trailer. Hutch once again began pulling at the rocks as if her tenacity was somehow going to free them. She soon heard footsteps clanking across the steel and, within moments, Hieronymus was there, standing beside her.

"Yeah?...Ya want somethin'?" The redhead spoke to him in irritation. He just continued to stand there, staring at her with that eyeless face of his. "Jesus Christ…" she mumbled. Right then, a crackling sound emerged as the blue demon's four spindly arms sprouted from his back. They shot forwards, working their way through the rocks until they were interwoven amongst them. Within seconds, he dislodged the pressure, allowing Hutch to pull her leg free. She shuffled backwards and sat against the side of the trailer wall, grabbing her ankle and massaging it amidst the fading pain. Hieronymus retracted his extra arms back into his body, then mirrored Hutch's actions, plopping down on his bottom directly across from her. The two stared at each other for a long awkward pause.

"Thanks…" Hutch finally whispered.

"You're welcome," a voice emerged from the demon. The redhead winced at the surprise. She didn't say anything at first, she just sat there, staring at him thinking, for perhaps a second, she'd imagined the whole thing.

"Did you just…talk?"

"Did I?" The blue demon responded. His voice was surprisingly calm and almost robotically soothing. Not at all what Hutch had expected. "I'm always talking, it's just that most don't know how to listen. But you can hear me now, can't you?"

The redhead was still at a loss for words for the moment. Her confusion was only exacerbated by the fact that the mouth of the creature in front of her wasn't moving as he talked. In fact, the only thing on him that did anything was a mysterious star that appeared on his forehead. It glowed with every syllable he expelled.

"Why ain't your mouth movin'?" She voiced.

"It doesn't need to. Cover your ears," he said. Hutch plugged her ears with her fingers, not fully knowing what to expect. "Can you hear me?" his voice echoed inside her head. She gasped and unplugged her ears as she realized his voice was most definitely not coming from his mouth. It was as if he was projecting his very words right into her head. And in a way, that's exactly what he was doing. She could hear him giggle at her reaction.

"How are ya doin' that?"

"Ahhh, so you are ready to listen?"

"Well, I kinda ain't gotta choice," Hutch scoffed. She then got an odd look on her face, "Can you hear what I'm thinkin'?"

"I can only hear what you allow me to hear. Go ahead, talk to me."

"But...I am. Ain't I?"

"Not with your mouth. With your mind."

"But...how?"

"Surely you've thought about something before you say it?"

"Ya don't know me very well, do ya?"

Hieronymus giggled once more.

"You've talked to yourself inside your head, have you not?

"Well...yeah."

"It's a lot like that...try it. Talk to me."

Hutch raised a brow. She was beginning to think this whole thing was ridiculous. But still, she tried it anyway.

"Can ya hear me?" She thought.

"Excellent! You're a natural!" Hieronymus praised. Hutch blushed a bit. It was crazy, no, downright insane, like nothing she'd ever experienced before.

"I did it!" She thought.

"You certainly did...Now...I fear we're going to be down here for awhile. What do you want to talk about?"

"Ummm....I don't know."

"Oh, come now. Let's talk. It's been a long time since I talked with anyone. Ask me something….anything."

Hutch thought long and hard about that question. And it just came out, "Where's my aunt? Do ya know her? Cassandra McCray?"

"I'm sorry. I don't know where she is. I've never met her. Only she knows the answer to that."

The redhead sighed. This demon seemed special. She hoped he would have better insight as to where Cass might be.

"By she, ya mean Regina?"

"That's correct."

"Yeah well, she don't seem to want to tell me," Hutch thought. She looked off into the dancing shadows of the demon's blue aura, getting lost within them for a moment. Another question abounded.

"What's your story, anyway? Who are ya? What are ya?"

"Me? I am a Pentalpha"

"A what now?"

"Pentalpha, a sage demon. We're given as gifts to the offspring of the Kings and Queens. We become the young, royal demon's advisors and confidants. Lieges, if you will. My master was a princess named Remylionsynthe."

"Remylionsynthe?" The name rolled through Hutch's brain. Foreign yet beautiful.

"Yes. She was the most alluring creature I'd ever seen. And I was proud to serve and guide her. She was named after the crimson and black flowers that grow in the darkest depths of Hell. They blossom every six-hundred human years. She was conceived upon their blooming."

"So you were her nanny?"

"One might say that, but it would be trivializing the gravity of what we truly do. We are responsible, in great part, for what type of demon the royal youth grow up to become. And the most difficult chapter of that process is the Beguilement."

"What's that?"

"A final tribulation. A test that will determine whether the young royal is worthy to one day rule over his or her own level of Hell. The Beguilement by design is simple, the outcome is far from such. The princess or prince must first choose a human form and go topside. From here, they must integrate into society, blending in, using the teachings they were bestowed before their departure."

"Teachings from you?"

"Correct. Those teachings are ones of the utmost importance."

"And how does a demon like you know enough about people to teach how ta be one?"

"Simple. We too were humans, once. Just like the greens, the yellows, and the reds. But we have a far different transformative process. We change from green, to yellow, to blue. We are very rare, Hutch. We were humans who had third-eyes or extra sensory perceptions in life. And we lost our way…but we are reborn in the blue flesh you see before you."

"So…your princess…all she had to do was go topside, get a job, and live a human life?"

"No…her main task is to seduce a human. All young royals have to do this. They must make a human fall in love with them, but they are not allowed to fall in love with the human. For ten earthly years they must hold this bond and then break it. Severing all ties to return to Hell, thus proving to the Kings and Queens that they have no human emotions whatsoever."

"She just has ta dump the guy? That's it?"

"Love is not so simple…For all of the terrible weapons human possess, love is the most difficult to conquer."

There was a moment of silence between them. Hutch's mind fluttered through the thoughts of falling in love, then having to break it to pieces. Most humans would have grave difficulty…but a demon, surely it was a cakewalk.

"And?…Did she pass the test?"

"She…she was doomed from the beginning."

"How so?"

A sigh echoed inside Hutch's head from the demon in front of her. He stood up and walked over to her.

"Maybe it's best I show you. You need to know. You need to know at least this one truth."

Hutch was confused. Her forehead wrinkled with apprehension as the little demon raised his stumpy arm, extending it towards her.

"What's happenin?"

"Touch my hand…I'll show you."

As the redhead began to reach forward, she winced at the sound of the blue imp's voice. "But I must warn you. There are things here you can not unsee…are you prepared to deal with that?"

She reluctantly nodded.

"Show me." She grabbed his hand and an abstract of blinding light engulfed them, swallowing them up and spitting them out into another place entirely. Hutch gasped and released her hand away from his. Her senses adjusted to the maddening sounds of car tires screeching in rage and the smell of burning rubber that rained down softly. She could feel the sting of exhaust caress her throat as she looked around in confusion. The bitter dark of the trailer had disappeared and was replaced by a starry, summer sky above. Her heart melted at the sight of green leaves and the kiss of warmth enveloping her flesh like the embrace of a long lost lover. Where were they? *When* were they?

"Are we?…is this? Englewilde? Jesus, they shut this place down years ago," her shaky voice inquired.

"Yes. The place where it all began," Hieronymus spoke as he watched Hutch gaze around in cautious awe. Her eyes took in rows of makeshift bleachers haloed in clouds of cigarette smoke drifting through the blinding lights on high. Beyond this was a dusty, dirt lot packed to the gills with rows of cars and people commingling, passing joints and beers to one another. It was an abstract of stoned smiles and carefree camaraderie cut down the center with a short fence caressing the edge of an ebony mile. It was a far cry from the dragstrips she knew today. No one was peddling T-shirts and hotdogs or handing out flyers for magazine subscriptions. Here she could no longer see the plastic of the commercial creeping in. It was just good times and good vibes. It was just cheering crowds, the summer night, and two slabs of American steel duking it out one green light at a time. As she became lost in the sights and sounds of a time she never got to be a part of, her confusion once again returned.

"Why'd ya bring me here?" She looked down to the blue imp beside her.

"This is where my princess found her human. This is where she started her Beguilement."

"Wait?...What? Here in my town?"

"There she is now…" Hieronymus pointed to a women standing by herself at the chain-link fence. Her dark locks twisted in the breeze atop an orange mini shift dress, spewing out two beautiful bare legs and bare feet that twitched with anticipation in the grass below. Though her back was to them, Hutch could tell she was transfixed by the bellowing cars peeling out from the pit. Her hands clenched tight into the fence was a dead giveaway, for she too had stood along the strip many a time as a kid with that same awed stance, wondering what it was like to be behind the wheel of the monster. To feel the power engulf you. The redhead's eyes squinted down in suspicion as she made her way across the lot, closer to the unmoving girl, but right then the brunette turned around. Hutch froze in her tracks as two golden eyes drilled right through her soul.

"Shit…" the words barely wheezed from Hutch's lungs.

"Don't worry. She can't see you. This is just a memory," Hieronymus assured her.

"Regina…" Hutch spoke, "Regina is…Remylionsynthe? Regina is *your* princess?"

"WAS my princess," he corrected her.

"But…but…" words just seemed to leak from Hutch's mouth as Regina turned back round to watch the next two cars blast off the line. The crowd roared, but then it all went silent inside the redhead's mind as she caught the glimpse of someone else familiar to her weary gaze. A tall man walked with a confident saunter through the grass and stopped just three paces away from where Regina remained entranced. He rested his race helmet under his arm for a moment as he too watched the next cars rumble up to the line. Hutch watched as the man threw side-eyed glances towards Regina, smiling a flirtatious grin till she finally looked his way.

"Come…let's get a closer look," Hieronymus began waddling forwards, leaving Hutch behind for a moment. Soon enough, she trotted on till she was once again beside the demon. They were so close to Regina she could reach out and touch her, but it wasn't the tiny brunette that Hutch had her eye on at this point.

"Dad? Daddy?..." she cooed out like a child to the man making eyes at Regina. And it was. A thirty year old Harvey McCray with a full head of hair and a beaming smile as wide as the track he just came from. The redhead was at a loss, she'd only seen pictures of her father so young, and her childhood memories of how he looked only stagnated as the years swallowed the past. She tried to reach out and touch him, but stifled her own shaking hand, trying to hold back a tear as she did so.

"He can't hear you, Hutch. Remember, this is only a memory." The redhead heard the words just as much as she ignored them. A million questions seemed to buzz away in her troubled mind, but she was shaken away from them as she heard her father finally speak.

"You a Chevy girl or a Ford girl?" Harvey broke the ice.

Regina looked over at him, seemingly shocked that anyone wanted to talk to her.

"I...I..." she stuttered.

"She has no idea what he means?" Hieronymus spoke to Hutch.

"What?" Regina asked for Harvey to repeat himself.

"I said, are ya a Chevy or Ford girl?"

"I...I like both," she finally answered.

Harvey's head rose up, belting out a hearty laugh.

"Hey, I like that answer."

"You do?"

"Suuuuure. I'm the same way. I get so damn sick an' tired of hearin' people gettin' in fights about what's better. It's all American Muscle. Now see, if you're like me, and a few choice others, ya can see the beauty in any of these beasts, regardless of what they say on the grill."

Hutch couldn't help but smile at that. It was her dad's mantra, passed right down the line to her. She always did, and still appreciated damn near every muscle car she'd met.

Regina and Harvey watched together as another set of cars tore off the line. Her heart raced as Harvey cheered like a madman.

She then watched as another car rolled into position. She read the emblem.

"What about Dodge?"

"What?" Harvey smiled.

"What if I'd said I was a Dodge girl?"

"Oh well, I'd have to offer ya I ride home then cuz I know ya probably walked here."

Regina looked at him oddly.

Harvey couldn't keep a straight face. He howled with laughter,

"Little track humor there."

Regina obviously still didn't get it.

"Ya walked…ya know because you're a Dodge girl and your Dodge is one hundred percent likely to be broke down? I know, I know, it wasn't funny…Well, maybe a little funny."

Regina smiled. She looked to the cars again.

"Who do you thinks gonna win this one?" She asked.

"The Dodge," Harvey said without a pause.

"The Dodge?" Regina looked surprised.

"Sure."

"Why?"

"Well ya gotta look beyond the cars. The driver is the soul of the beast. See how the Chevy driver is ticking over there? Revvin' and inchin' up. He thinks he's bein' intimidating…but he ain't. He's nervous. A confident driver doesn't have to intimidate anyone, he already knows he's gonna win. Now look at the Dodge…Driver is just sittin' there. He's patient. He's in the zone. Nothin' in this world exist right now cept' the gas pedal and the light in front of him. Yep, that Chevy ain't winnin'. Fact I think he'll false start." No sooner had Harvey finished, the Chevy roared to life before the Dodge. A round of boos erupted from the crowd along with the words "Foul Start" from the announcers booth. Regina looked over at Harvey and grinned.

"I know, I know. I'm amazing. It's like I can see into the future. It's a blessin' and a curse, really," Harvey playfully gloated.

"A real fortune teller, huh?" Regina batted her eyelashes.

"Maybe."

"Well, if you're so good, tell me my future."

"What, ya mean like where you're gonna end up in life?" He smiled.

"Naw, that's too far. Let's just start with tonight."

"Okay," Harvey grinned and raised a brow. He took off his gloves and threw them to the grass along with his helmet. He extended his arm towards the brunette. "Give me your hand."

Regina gave him a look.

"C'mon now, I won't bite," Harvey assured her.

She soon presented her hand. He grabbed it, gently rolling it over. With a soft touch he traced his finger along the lines of her palm and spoke,

"Hmmm, interesting."

"Is it?"

Harvey closed his eyes in fake concentration.

"Sure is…mmm, hmmm, yep. Later you're gonna end up at The Velvet Lounge down on route 64…round about ten-ish. There, you're gonna meet a handsome race car driver, bout my height, with fiery red hair and you two, well you're just gonna hit it off and have yourselves a great night."

Regina smiled as Harvey wrapped both his hands around hers. "I'm Harvey. What's your name, darlin?"

"My names, Re…" she caught herself as the hell-given moniker almost slipped through her teeth, "Umm…Re…Regina….My name is Regina."

"Well, Regina, this might be forward but, you're just about the most gorgeous thing I've ever laid my eyes on."

"Stop!" A loud voice cracked like thunder inside Hutch's head. It was Hieronymus. As soon as his words erupted everything halted. The entire scene that surrounded them paused like a movie and Hutch began looking around in confusion.

"What? What's happenin'?" She questioned.

"Look," the demon pointed, "There it is, the moment when she failed. Look into her eyes, Hutch." The redhead reluctantly inched forwards, looking into Regina's eyes. "Closer," the demon almost commanded. She moved in till the flesh of her nose almost caressed Regina's. What was she looking for? "Do you see it? The sky within the amber," Hieronymus spoke. Hutch blinked a few times in obvious confusion, but then she did see it. An almost unnoticeable sparkle of blue, deep within the gold of Regina's beautiful eyes. "What is it?"

"Humanity…emotion. A sparkle of a relic that's hidden deep within the souls of every demon. You see, demons were angels once and they still carry a tiny shard of angelic grace. Even the ones that are forged in Hell are passed that heavenly splinter. And when you can see it, it means something is alive there."

"Love." Hutch spoke as she looked to her father.

"Love," the demon concurred. With that, the memory faded away to bitter shades of black. Hutch could feel a chill race around her body as the warmth of the summer air was stripped from her. She wanted to weep for so many reasons, but held her tears as her stare stayed fixed to the darkness that used to be the face of her father.

"He was right," she spoke cryptically.

"Who?"

"Hank...my brother. He said he saw Regina and my father together years ago. I laughed at him." Hutch turned around to face Hieronymus. "What happened to them?"

"Her love for him only grew with every passing day. She became child-like under his charm...One could say almost like a slave to it. Her love of cars, of racing, the Leviathan, it's all because of your father. She wanted to love everything he did. He taught her how to drive, to become one with the road. She became the very opposite of what she was meant to be in the Beguilement, and she knew it, but love blinded her to that fact. She knew her days were numbered, but she ignored them with the beautiful ignorance of a child. She knew there would be no level of Hell to reign over upon her return and she would never feel the embrace of her father ever again. So she did the only thing she thought she could...She became a human."

Hutch's brow raised, "A human?...How?"

"The question you should be asking is why? Why become a human and live one life just to be sent back to Hell to be punished forever for that short stay? It was true love. A love incomprehensible to most, let alone your father. He never loved her half as much as she loved him. I believe that he had every intention of doing what he did that first night they met. Maybe he should've...he would have spared her all of this."

"What? What do ya mean? What does that mean?"

The demon shook his head.

"That story isn't mine to tell...When she returned to Hell, she was banished to this place and I along with her. For a time I was her mechanic. I helped her make the cars down here what they are."

"Then what happened. How'd ya end up in the mining pit?"

"I tried getting in the way of her plans. She didn't like that. So she cast me out."

Hutch nearly fell to her knees at the deafening sound of pounding. It throbbed all around, echoing over and over. It stopped.

"What is that?!"

"There isn't much time, Hutch." One of the demon's spindly, hidden arms came out from his back. The hand on the end of it held a sight that cast a strange calm over her. It was a feather that glowed with a gorgeous indigo aura. "Take this." The redhead reached out, stopping just short of the object. She could feel tiny bursts of electricity shooting out from it into her fingertips.

"What is it?"

"The thing that Remylionsynthe desires most. I found it long ago. She has a plan for it. But that plan will change. She will love again."

"I don't understand…"

"You will, Hutch. Take it. It's yours now," he beckoned it closer. The loud sound once again emerged, deafening Hutch twice as much as before. "Hurry! Time is running out!" The redhead grabbed the feather from him. She gasped as she felt it course through her hand right into every nerve-ending of her body. A power pulsed through her now, something she couldn't quite explain as she stared in wonder at the feather that was responsible for it. The sound came down thrice. "Quickly, Hutch! Hide it!" She began fumbling around, trying to place it under her dress, but it just glowed right through the fabric. "Hold it to your chest!" The demon commanded. She did as she was told, pressing it so hard it hurt, not knowing what was going to happen. With a warm burst, it disappeared into her flesh. She released her shaky hand and looked to Hieronymus with wide, fearing eyes. "It's yours now. Use it wisely." And just like that, the sound fell down again. A metallic blast came forth, along with the turgid and salty smell of the mine. Hutch fell back onto her behind and her eyes adjusted to the sight of six exhausted crims walking into the back of the semi trailer. They had freed her from the cave-in. Right then, her anger elevated as she watched Sid push his way between the rescue party and walk up to her. The red demon leaned forwards with a smirk.

"The boss wants to see ya."

Deal with the Demon

"What are you trying to do to me?" A simple question refracted off the beaten and broken cars of past victories. Hutch heard the words from the mouth of the woman she loved as much as she hated, but she had no answer. Instead her eyes drifted around, looking into the sneering faces of what had to be every crim in that godforsaken place, all scattered about Regina's courtyard. The redhead could feel the shaking of the demons she now called friends as they pressed up against the back of her legs in fear. She had no idea as to why they'd be dragged into whatever this was.

The silence paved on for what seemed like a solid minute as Regina sat there, picking away at her fingernails in irritation. She had a completely different look about her. Her face was no longer bright and confident, it seemed matte finished and pale, like part of her life-force had been borrowed and never brought back. Her eyes were a darker shade of gold, almost bronze, or at least it looked that way from where Hutch stood across the way. The brunette poked her tongue around the inside of her cheek and then bit at her lip, staring towards the false sky above.

"What am I going to do with you, Red?" Regina finally spoke again. You started a fight at collection time. You managed to destroy nearly my entire fleet of semis with your escape attempt. You caused a cave-in in my mine TWICE. And Sid, tells me you've yet to bring me ONE fucking brimstone, which leads me to believe you really suck at your job, or you're throwing them into the pit to spite me," she became more agitated with every accusation she threw forward. She took a breath and tried calming herself. "So I guess the real question is, why the hell am I keeping you around?"

"Good question," Hutch suddenly spoke up, "Why ARE you keepin' me around. Why don't ya just send me back topside so I'm out of your hair?"

Regina scoffed and laughed. "Oh wow, that's cute, Red. Is that your little plan now? Drive me so insane that you think I'll kick you out? Oh, baby, look at all these bumbling, red assholes I have to deal with. It's like having a hundred of you around all the time. Trust me, you're not going to get out that way."

"Then how do I get out?"

"Well, you could always hijack another one of my trucks and ride out into the sunset," Regina quipped with a smile. Hutch was not amused, but the brunette spoke before she could throw her two cents in. "You know, something has been eating at me, Red...What if you had made it out?"

"What?" Hutch asked.

"Made it out threw the gateway. What if you *did* go back? What happens then? Do I have to remind you, you died? You think you're just going to walk back into everyone's life and it's all going to be normal? Open the door to that Gingerbread House "*Hi, everyone! I'm back!*" Yeah, see how that goes over...And what did you seriously plan on doing with the three stooges behind you there? They're not exactly going to get a job at Waffle House hocking hash browns looking like that. They need meat suits, Red. You really didn't think any of this out, did you?...No of course you didn't."

The redhead just glared at her.

Regina smiled once again, "You know, I'm surprised you want to leave at all. Considering the feelings you have for me."

Hutch's face went soft.

"Wha...What?"

"You do love me, don't you, Red?"

"What?! No! I…I..No. No," the redhead shook her head in defense.

"Awww…you do. You really do. And you think I love you back, don't you? Honey, all that stuff up topside was…a game. It was just us having fun."

"I'm not in love with you," she held back a tear.

"Oh Red, sweetie you can say bullshit all you want but you can't deny it. I see it in your eyes. The way they light up every time you see me. Your heart elevates and those butterfly wings beat so loud inside you I think you're gonna lift right off the ground and fly away. It's…it's kinda sad." The crims surrounding began to chuckle at Regina's cold words. Hutch grit her teeth, fruitlessly trying to hold back her tears. She could feel her anger welling up until she was about to explode. And so she did,

"Fuck this!" She grabbed her chest and a magnificent blue illuminated the area, silencing the crims into a death-hush. Every soul present stood as still as statues as the redhead held high the feather Hieronymus had given her. Regina's eyes burned with a desire Hutch had never seen before. Like a mad woman who'd been starved and beaten for weeks, being shown a horn of plenty.

"Where'd you get that?" The brunette's voice barely eked out. Hutch had no idea what the feather even was. All she remembered was Hieronymus's words echoing in her mind. "*It's the thing that Remylionsynthe desires most.*" And she was going to use it to her advantage.

"Don't worry about where I got it," Hutch spoke.

"Give it here, Red. Please. Just…Just hand it over."

"Okay…you let me go home, and I'll give it to ya."

"Oi! This is bullshit, mum! We spent ages lookin' for that! Just take it from er!" Bishop's voice erupted above it all. He ran in and lunged at Hutch.

"Bishop, NO!!" Regina screamed out. It was far too late. The crim grabbed hold of the feather and it shot a blast of blinding electricity into his body. The demon flew backwards, rolling onto his back, engulfed in white flames. His screams of pain deafened them all as the flames ate away his flesh until he was nothing but a shuddering pile of bones and sinew lying on the ground. Even though she'd hated him, the scene almost sickened Hutch. She put a hand to her mouth in horror.

"No one move!" Regina's voice boomed. She then jumped from her steel throne and walked to the middle of the courtyard. She stopped three paces away from Hutch and looked around to the crims in anger. "You fucking idiots, that thing is a bearer instrument. You can only take it if she chooses to give it to you." The brunette took a breath and let it out, trying to conceal her nervous twitching with that signature smile. She adjusted her collar and brushed off the wrinkles in her suit like she was buying some time, trying to think of what to say next.

"Okay…" she spoke calmly, "What do you want?"

"I already told ya. I wanna go home."

"But what is home, really? Isn't home where you make it? It could be topside, it could be down here, it…"

"Enough bullshit. Ya know what I mean. I want to go back to my family. Back to my shitty job and my shitty camper, drinking my shitty beer, and smoking my shitty cigarettes."

"Wow…that's a lot of shit," Regina smarted off. Hutch was not amused. Her icy stare just drilled onwards as she held the feather firmly. The brunette backed away, almost submissively; her lips curling a bit as she did so. It was so odd watching her fumble around like this. She almost behaved like a bumbling teenager, trying to come to the realization she had to leave childhood behind.

"Can you do it, or not?" The redhead asked.

"Yes."

"Good…"

"Okay then…so just hand it over and we can get you back home."

Hutch recoiled the feather as Regina walked towards her.

"No."

"No?" Regina stopped in her tracks.

"You've played enough games with me. You're takin" me topside, *then* I'll give ya this thing."

Regina nodded with shame staining her face.

"Okay, Red…"

There was an uncomfortable pause between them as Hutch's brow began to wrinkle with thought. She looked down and around to the demons cowering behind her. The same ones that had befriended her when they could've just left her on her own so many times.

"I want them freed too."

"What?" Regina became terse.

"And my aunt too. Wherever she is, I want her back home." Hutch's hard stare returned to Regina's. "Deal?"

The brunette's docile gaze hardened back to wrought-iron. Her eyes went dark.

"No," she simply said. Confusion flooded Hutch's chest. She swallowed a lump from her throat.

"What?"

"I said, no. You're raising the bar higher than I wanna jump, Red. You can trade for your freedom, or the freedom of the others, but you're not getting both." With that, Regina walked away, back across the courtyard, and plopped down on her throne.

"Well? What's it gonna be?"

All of the confidence that feather had spurned was now quickly washing down the proverbial drain that was Hutch's heart. She looked back to the demons once again and began thinking about her aunt. Had she seriously come this far just to be transported back to her shitty existence empty handed? But then a thought emerged. A plan. A scheme. A negotiation of sorts. She could only hope it would work.

"I said, I want my freedom, my aunt's and theirs."

"I'm sorry, did I stutter at any point when I said you're not getting both? Did I stutter, Sid?"

"Naw, boss. Ya didn't," the tall crim concurred.

"I want another shot at beating you," Hutch held out the feather again.

Regina raised a brow.

"Come again?"

"I want a rematch. You and me, on this raceway of yours. You win, you get the feather and we all have to stay. You lose, you still get the feather, but we all get to go home."

"No, girly, Jesus," Diesel whispered behind her.

"You're telling me you're willing to risk losing the only bargaining chip you have at freedom on the slim chance that you can beat me in a race just because you won't leave them behind?"

"That's right."

"And who told you about the race course? About Leviathan?"

"A little bird."

"Of course she did," Regina's eyes drilled into Izzy. The green demon, quickly hid all the way behind Hutch. "And did this little bird also mention if you fail, you could end up dead, permanently?"

"She may have mentioned that."

"Mm'hmm, and did she mention that NO ONE has ever won?"

"Maybe…but there's a first time for everything, right?"

"Maybe…" Regina said. She paused for a moment. "I'm going to bet she didn't bother telling you that that road out there is more than just a road. It's a monster in itself. An ever changing creature that even, I, it's creator has little control over. It's forged from more than pyre-slag. It's saturated with the pain, misery, and loss of every soul that's ever traversed it. Mine most of all. You see, Red, it's not me you'll have to worry about out there as much as the road itself. It gets inside you. Changes you. Turns you into something you're not. Some have gone mad mid-race, veered their cars into the first thing that could extinguish them. Others have become so saddened that their tears blind them from seeing the way. A piece of me dies every time I go out there…And there's not much left of me…"

Hutch took in every disturbing word that fell from the brunette's lips. She knew she wasn't lying. There was a terrifying sincerity in her voice that chilled the redhead to her core. Still, she stood her ground and said the only McCray thing she could.

"Sounds like a good time."

The courtyard was deathly silent for a moment as Regina stared off, seemingly at nothing at all. Hutch had no idea where her mind was drifting at that moment in time.

"Okay…"

"Okay?" Hutch's brows rose in surprise.

"If this is what you want…I'll race you, this one, last time."

The uncomfortable silence crept in once again. Hutch lowered the feather and looked around.

"What happens now?"

"You pick out a car, Red," Regina said. She looked to the crims. "Take her to the yard." Just like that, the crims surrounded Hutch and her demons with Sid breaking through the group.

"Put that away 'fore someone else gets hurt, huh?" He pointed towards the feather. She glared at him while she let it absorb back into her chest. The light faded away and she breathed deep. "Of all the turds in this toilet that could've found that thing, it had to be you," the boss crim shook his head with a laugh. "Fate sure is funny, ain't it McCray?"

"Sure is," she gruffly agreed. Sid nodded.

"Well...follow me," the crim turned and began walking across the courtyard. Hutch paused a moment, looking round to the three demons behind her. They cast her nervous stares, well, except for Diesel, he was clearly pissed. She felt she should say something but the words just weren't there, so she just followed Sid like she was told. As Hutch walked across Regina's unholy circle, all the crims followed along, surrounding her like they were protecting her...or planning on murdering her. And that was the problem, the redhead truly didn't know which it was. As she looked around to the sneering faces of the red demons, she couldn't help but wonder if she was being led out somewhere in the darkness of the beyond to be slaughtered and buried amongst the ash of the firerite.

"Choose wisely, Red. I'll see you later," were the only departing words Regina had to offer as her golden eyes locked with the blue skies of Hutch's. Their gaze remained unbroken until it was swallowed up by the pillars of broken cars Regina called trophies. Hutch's gaze returned forward, to the back of the beast she so despised. Sid's demeanor seemed different, and she didn't like it one damn bit. Ever since that feather had come to light he seemed softer, almost normal. Well, normal for Sid.

"Where ya takin' us?" Hutch growled.

"Relax. Didn't ya hear the boss? I'm takin' ya to the yard."

"What's that?"

"You'll see, firebush. You'll see."

They walked and walked for what seemed like a solid mile into the brackish foreground beyond Regina's lair. Hutch could barely make out Sid at this point even though he was only paces away from her. The thick fog of the beyond had rolled in, turning all the crims into ghostly shapes that seemed to float more than walk into the unknown ahead. The only thing that remained true were the flames in the distance, burning away like they always had. There was no smog or shadow that could ever hope to conceal them. Hutch became lost in their flickering as they trudged onwards, staring into the writhing blue and white, flipping like the tongues of serpents, ascending into the false horizon. However, something began to break their dance apart. Shadowy and twisted rows sprung up across the fiery landscape, imprisoning the inferno behind a patchwork of black bars. It was a fence. A towering one, that spread as far as Hutch could see through the smog in either direction. It looked much like the fence at the pit, and to that end, made Hutch's fear elevate in the thought that they were all getting chucked right back into the hell of their perpetual mining shift.

Sid stopped an arms length away from a huge gate that towered some twenty feet into the air. The redhead watched as he reached out, sticking his finger knuckle deep into a lock mechanism upon the threshold. With a grunt, he turned his digit as if it were a key, and a series of clicking introduced an ear piercing symphony of scraping metal as the giant door opened and swung inwards. The boss crim stepped back and leaned against the gate, extending his arm out with a beckoning hand.

"Welcome ta the yard, firebush," Sid spoke, waiting for her to walk through the open gate. The apprehension to even speak was grave, let alone move at that moment. She stood there, eyeing the darkness behind the gate and the creature that was trying to get her to walk blindly right into it.

"What's in there?"

"Look, I ain't got time for this shit. I got messes to clean up that you made. Now get your happy, freckled ass through this gate fore' things get ugly, huh?"

Hutch just glared at him for a moment. She then looked to Izzy. The green demon nodded as if she knew it was all okay. And so, together, they all walked through. Bitter shades of rust and darkness, painted the air in a matte finish Hutch could barely see through. As she traversed deeper, she flinched at a sound on high. She looked up to see broken glass globes on the ends of lamp posts. They popped and hummed as an amber light came to life inside them. With each pace she took, another row of them would spring to life and hum away. More and more lit, until dozens of them spread across the expanse, chasing away the malaise in the air, clearing it until the redhead could behold the sights around her. And what a sight it was...

Cars. Dozens of them. No hundreds. Spread out as far the melancholy of the lights could reach. They were all placed into neat rows, two deep, bumper to bumper, with headlights pointed towards the emptiness of the corridors in between. Hutch stopped, blinking in awe of what she was now taking in. It took her back to Riverside. She could almost feel the sluggish summer breeze and the blinding refractions of sun rays across broken mirrors and chrome. And just like the junkyard, many of the cars donned the same expressions. Some were slightly broken and battered some looked quite drivable, but all shared a common thread, they were all covered in a film of dusty ash, a product of the furnace burn. The redhead ran her finger across the hood of the nearest vehicle, smearing the tip gray with an ashen smudge. She rolled the dust between her fingers and looked to Sid who still stood at the gate with the other crims.

"Well, I'll leave ya to it, McCray," he spoke as he grabbed the gate and quickly slammed it shut. Hutch gasped and ran full bore, slamming into the gate with her hands wrapped tight round the bars.

"What the fuck?! What are ya doin'?!"

"Relax, firebush. Ya tried escaping twice. Ya seriously think I'm gonna leave you all the way out here without lockin' ya up? No fuckin' way. Hey, ya know who I didn't have to lock the gate on?"

Hutch looked at him oddly. Sid pointed to Izzy.

"I didn't have to lock it for that one right there. Why? Cuz she's got manners. She never tried ta escape…Actually I just knew she was too yella ta try anything. But ya get the idea," Sid spoke. He quickly turned and grabbed an odd looking bundle from another crim that stood beside him. It looked like a battery of some sort with a leather bag attached to it. "Oh yeah, you're gonna need this," he said as he tossed it through the gap in the gate bars. As it came to a rest at the feet of Izzy, Sid raised a brow and grabbed Hutch's hand. "Holy shit, would ya look at that? Your finger grew back."

The redhead yanked her hand away and looked. He was right. It was back. She held her hand out and moved her pinky in terrified awe.

"Yeah, I feel real bad about that. I was thinkin' next time we get in a fight, we'll make it even. I could lose a finger inside of you. Hell, maybe three. Ya think ya could take that many?" The boss crim burst into laughter. Hutch lunged forwards in rage, reaching through the gate, clawing like a mad woman towards his face. Sid, just kept chuckling as he turned round and walked away with the other crims following him. Hutch's anger was soon overthrown with panic.

"Wait. Wait! How the hell am I gonna get out of here?"

"Pick a ride and yell out the gate for help. Happy huntin'," the crim's voice faded out along with the sight of him. All that was left was the thick wall of smog they'd all come from.

"Fuck you!" She screamed out through the nothingness.

"I love you, too." Sid's smart-ass remark whispered back. Silence set in as Hutch pulled her arm back through the bars of the gate. She turned to face the three demons behind her.

"Jesus, what did I get myself into?" She whispered in defeat. She slowly walked by, leaving the trio as she meandered up the first row of cars. Diesel was quick to answer.

"That's a damn good question, girly. Ya know I don't think this is about you caring about us at all? I think this is about your pride. You don't like being beat. She made you look stupid in front of everyone. Or maybe ya just care about your aunt and we got thrown in the mix so you could sleep better at night."

"Seriously? Are we gonna do this right now? You talk about me being hard ta get along with…"

"Well if it ain't your pride, you're just a dumbass then."

"Oh really?! How ya figure?" Hutch stopped and glared down at him.

"Seriously? Ya had freedom right there in the palm of your hand. All ya had ta do was give her that damn thing, but you chose ta push her buttons."

"I think what she's doin' is sweet. She's bein' selfless, Diesel. She could've just left us," Izzy spoke as she gathered up the bundle Sid had tossed them.

"She should've. You call it whatever ya want, I call it being a royal dipshit."

"Whatever…I ain't got time for your shit," Hutch said as she began walking the row once more.

"Well?...Is it true?" Diesel picked away.

"Is what true?! No, It's not my pride! Okay?!"

"Not that! I'm talkin' about what she said back there. Do you love her?"

"What?! No!"

"Then why would she say that?"

"She says a lot of things, if ya hadn't noticed. A lot of bullshit things," Hutch stopped and began looking around.

"Right, girly, right....Where'd ya get that feather anyway?"

The redhead looked towards Hieronymus for a brief moment.

"I...I found it in the trailer back there. The cave-in musta knocked it loose."

"Good god. Must be the luck of that Irish in ya."

"How many times do I have ta tell ya I'm Scottish?"

"Potato, Patahto...which happens to be a favorite of your people if I'm not mistaken."

Hutch's eyes suddenly went soft and she started bawling into her open hands. The demons looked around awkwardly at one another as she wept uncontrollably.

"Look, girly...I...It was a joke."

"It's not that," she sniffled and wiped at her nose.

"Then...then, what is it?"

"Never mind. Fuck it. It's nothing," there was no way she was about to lament that she was coming undone from her feelings for Regina. That she was hopelessly obsessed with her since the day she'd first laid eyes on her. And she was still that way. Despite all the things Regina had done, she still was senselessly and tragically in love with her and she had no idea what to do about it.

"You see what it did ta Bishop?" Izzy tried changing the subject, "The feather, I mean."

"Oh no, Izz, I didn't see it turn him into leftover spaghetti. He deserved worse. He got off easy if ya ask me. All the shit he's done."

"Where do ya think he went?" Hutch thought for a moment. The question had been brushed before, but she truly did wonder, especially with her brother leaving this pit.

"Jesus H Christ, girly what's with you? Why are ya all emotional all the sudden? Who gives a shit? Hopefully he got reincarnated as a fly on a dog turd. I don't know."

Hutch sat down on the hood of the nearest car. She buried her head in her hands and began bawling once more.

"Jesus, do somethin'," Diesel looked to Izzy, hoping she could handle this better than he could. The green demon grabbed Hutch's dress and gently tugged.

"Hun? Hun, you've got to pull it together. You need ta pick a car."

The redhead sniffed back her tears and wiped at her face. She leaned back, placing her hands on her knees, looking back and forth across the endless rows of ghostly cars that surrounded them.

"What is this place anyway? Where'd she get all these?"

"To be honest...I don't know, hun."

Suddenly, a voice came to life inside Hutch's head,

"They're all emotional imprints of her soul. Phantom version of the cars she loved or hated through her time on earth. Memories in the form of steel," Hieronymus telepathically spoke to Hutch. The redhead looked down at him, almost in shame.

"Did I do the right thing?" She asked inside her head.

"You did exactly what you thought you had to."

Hutch reluctantly nodded and turned her attention away from the blue demon, back to the task at hand. She rose up and began walking, not saying a word as the demons slowly followed behind her. There were so many cars there. Mostly of American make, and mostly muscle. She had never seen so many amazing cars congregated in one spot, not even at the track events back home. If these truly were imprints of all the cars that impacted Regina since her time on earth, Hutch couldn't help but wonder what her own mind's yard would look like. She loved cars, but she gravely doubted such an assemblage of vehicles would reach this number from her own memories. As she traversed, bumper after bumper, hood after hood, she was reminded of that day in Riverside when Cass and her were looking for a project car and found a sad, little Maverick. She slowed her steps as she came to a four way crossing between the rows. And then she saw it.

"Oh my god..." she hastened her steps and ran to a familiar looking car. A 1970 Torino stained in the same somber shades of ash as the rest of the lot. Hutch stopped right in front of the bumper, her chest pounding with fear and reminiscent joy alike. It couldn't be? Was it? She leaned down and ran her finger through the grime, uncovering a true blue paint shade beneath. An uncontrollable shaking took over her body as she rounded the fender and squatted down, tracing her hands over the snake emblem that proved to her it was indeed a Cobra edition Torino. Cold clicks resounded, followed by the opening of the door to the silent beast. A familiar scent seemed to escape between a mixture of forgotten dust and time, right into Hutch's nose. She plopped herself down into the driver's seat and half-heartedly batted the purple fuzzy dice that hung from the rearview mirror. It was his. It was Henry's car, his REAL car. Not the one he'd been sentenced to drive upon his death. Tears lightly graced her cheeks.

"You alright, hun?" Izzy stood on tiptoes, looking through the window.

"I'm…I'm fine. It's just…this was my brother's car. But…but I don't understand. He died in this car. This car was mangled. It was in a thousand pieces."

"It's a memory, Hutch. A physical manifestation of something it was before it was destroyed," Hieronymus's voice slithered inside her head. She understood, and to that end, perked up.

"Wait…if every car in here is from her memories, that means Sarah is down here somewhere," she spouted as she jumped from the Torino and took off down the row.

"Hutch, wait! Hutch!" She could hear Hieronymus's voice fade off and away as she ran with rabidity down the rows, looking intently for hoods with blowers towering from them. She saw a few, but each time they weren't attached to the Maverick. She ran and ran down row after row, her head darting in an excitement that soon trickled into a creeping dread as what seemed like two-hundred cars were passed without a sign of the beast she'd created with Cass. Regina's yard soon spiraled into a prison cell of a labyrinth she became hopelessly lost within. Hutch began to feel her head spin, everything looked the same now. The cars were nothing but a spinning mass of steel with tires spread beneath. She finally let out a scream of defeat and plopped down on her bottom, leaning against the bumper of the closest car. She pulled her knees into her chest and fought of the urge to cry once again as she cast a defeated stare into the foggy headlights across from her. She flinched for a moment as the silence was broke by tiny footsteps around the row. It was Hieronymus. Her eyes stared with sadness into the X's of the demons face.

"I can't find her…" she spoke inside her mind.

"Some things just aren't meant to be."

"Is that supposed ta make me feel better?"

"This place is much like the dreamworld, Hutch. And like a dream, you will be shown things you may not want to see. Things you desire most will be out of your reach. Even though these are Regina's memories, every chooser sees the yard differently. If you can't find that car, it is fate telling you you shouldn't."

"Which one am I supposed ta choose?"

"The first step in hoping to best Remylionsynthe, is by choosing a car that is a bad memory for her."

"Then…then Henry's car. She felt guilty for his death. I could see it in her face."

"No. Think, what is her greatest weakness? Her only weakness?"

Hutch thought for a moment. Her mind took her back to the memory Hieronymus had guided her through.

"Love," she answered.

"Yes. She loved your father," he responded. Hutch sat there for a moment, her forehead wrinkling in thought, dredging through the memories of the cars she had seen in her own life. She rose to her feet and began searching again.

"There you are, girly. You find one yet?" Diesel's voice came around the corner as Hutch trudged on.

"No…but I'm close," she mumbled as she paced onwards. The demons once again followed behind her in absolute silence as her head panned the dust and rust of the hellish corridors that were Regina's memories. And then she saw it, a beak pointing out from the gloom ahead. She stopped in front of the car and let out a breath of dejection as she wiped away the grime, revealing the blood-red paint beneath. The last time she'd seen her, the tow company was hauling her off to the impound lot and, as far as she knew, that car was still there topside. She couldn't believe she was down here. Regina's memory was apparently strong.

"Ruby…." Hutch let out the car's name. She looked to Hieronymus and spoke to him the only way she knew how. "She was my father's car for years. She was his pride and joy when he met Regina."

"That's the one, Hutch. You've chosen wisely."

The redhead turned back round and stared at the sight of the car she'd bested countless racers with on the winding backroads of summer. It was covered in a film of ash and dust that was far thicker than any of the cars surrounding. Like it had been left alone and forgotten in someone's barn far longer than the earthly years past the day of its own manufacturing. It was covered in so much filth that it looked as if someone had tried to literally bury it. Hutch began brushing the dust off the hood and windshield. It fell in sheets to the ground below, so heavy it made an audible racket as it cascaded and crashed off the laces of her boots.

"Jesus Christ…" she mumbled as she kept at the task. Izzy joined in, brushing off the passenger side the best she could all while an archaic creak resounded as Hutch opened the door and looked into the cockpit of the beast she knew all too well. She had dropped at least two engines in this thing and just as many transmissions ever since she'd taken ownership of it. She was hard on cars to say the least. But treating her gingerly wasn't going to win her races. She sighed as the memories flooded back like the ghosts they were. All the faces of defeat. The cold hard cash that slapped the palm of her hand. The smell of the alcohol she used to loosen herself up. It was all there, unseen by the eyes of any but her. It all felt surreal.

"So this is it, huh?" Diesel grumbled, "Jesus, girly you know how ta pick em'. Well I guess I might as well get used to being down here, cuz this thing looks like dogshit on wheels."

"You watch your mouth!" She pointed at the yellow imp. "This dogshit on wheels is your key ta gettin' outta here. Show a little respect," Hutch ended her scolding and flopped down in the driver's seat. She gently ran her hands across the dash and then onto the wheel where she gripped tightly. Diesel stuck his head over the door at the hinges, eyeing the redhead oddly.

"Beggin' your pardon there, girly, but it seems like ya have an unhealthy attachment ta this thing and you've only been around it for two minutes."

"I've been round this car longer than two minutes…this car was my dad's. He bought it brand new off the lot in 67'. It was his baby…Well, it used to be. Got it from him in 87'. I've driven it ever since. I know every inch of this car. Every bolt."

"Right…and what the hells it doin' down here?"

"It's another one of Regina's memories."

"So this is the car you raced her topside in?"

"No."

"No?...So she raced your dad too then?"

Hutch thought about that question for a second.

"You could say that."

All of a sudden, a banging startled the redhead. It was Izzy pounding on the hood.

"Hey, pop this thing," she said. Hutch reached down and pulled the lever, obliging the demon outside. The creak and clang of hinge springs erupted as she watched the hood rise up, blocking the dingy view ahead. The redhead slowly pulled herself out of the car with a grave apprehension wrapped tightly round her chest. She was almost afraid to look under the hood for fear there'd be nothing there at all. Just an empty hole full of wires and hoses and the hellish ground staring up at her from beneath. She cautiously rounded the door and peered into the unknown. But to her surprise it was not empty, it was indeed filled with an engine, though it was not the engine she'd expected. With confusion, she leaned in and ran her fingers across the air cleaner assembly, looking deep into the abstracts of what lie beneath. It was a 350 HO. The very same engine the car had come stock with when her dad had bought it. Her confusion was soon overthrown by despair in the thought of the power this car would deliver. The car would scoot, no doubt, but it was a far cry from the horsepower of the 454 she had in it when she last saw it topside. Hutch nervously poked at her lips and remained in deep thought, never taking her eyes from their intent scanning of the engine compartment for what seemed like several minutes.

"Are ya just gonna keep staring at the thing or are ya gonna get it movin?" Diesel finally grumbled at her.

Hutch stood up quick, blasting her head on the underside of the hood.

"Shit…" she let out, rubbing her head through her hat. "Okay. Yeah…yeah, let's turn her over." Hutch tried believing in her own words as she rounded the door and jumped back into the seat. Much to her surprise the keys were in the ignition.

"Uh, hun?" Izzy spoke.

"I got this. It's cool, the keys are in it," Hutch dismissed her.

"No, hun, listen…"

"I got it okay?" She pumped the gas a few times and turned the keys with bated breath…Nothing happened. Not even a hopeless symphony from the solenoid. Hutch sighed. She leaned forwards and began bumping her head off the steering wheel.

"Jesus, this isn't happenin'," she whispered to herself. "Well what the hell now? I'm sure the auto parts store is open right down the street. Hell, maybe we can ask someone for a jump." She rose from the car in irritation, blurting out as much sarcasm as she could.

"Hun?" Izzy tried interrupting her.

"Wait…seriously maybe we can rob a battery from another one of these cars…"

"HUTCH?!" Izzy screamed.

"What?!"

"Would ya shut up a second and listen? You need this," Izzy raised up the strange module Sid had given her back at the gate. Hutch pointed.

"Is that a battery?"

Izzy sighed.

"No, hun. Look," she jumped up inside the engine compartment and scurried over to Hutch. She presented the module to her. "See down inside here?" The green imp pointed into one of eight cylinders bound together that made up the unit. There was a small glass cap bolted down inside. Beneath shined a luminescent amber and red. Hutch leered at it suspiciously. "You see that?" Izzy started again, "That look familiar?" The redhead grabbed the module away from the demon and looked it over.

"Looks kinda like brimstone in there," she said.

"Bingo. It is," Izzy said as she grabbed the unit back from Hutch. "Not just brimstone though, it's highly concentrated brimstone. Ya see, that's what I was tryin' ta tell ya. This car ain't gonna start. None of them are. Not without one of these, puppies."

"You're tryin' ta tell me that that little thing there is gonna make this car scream ta life. What about gas?"

"This IS the gas, hun. The electric, the fuel, everything…it's like…like a soul, sort of. It brings the car ta life with none of the things it needed topside. It turns the car into something else entirely."

Hutch scratched her head in confusion. Izzy spoke again, "Regina's car? You had to have noticed it isn't normal. The way it sounds."

"The way it sounds?! Hell, how bout the way it moves? I saw that thing disappear and reappear. Go sideways. Just all kinds of crazy shit," Hutch barked.

"Exactly. This is what her car runs on. It's the same thing my car ran on when I raced her."

"Okay…but…but how does even work? Do we have to hook it up or?"

"Yep. We just hook it up," Izzy replied. She sat the module down by the carburetor and began fiddling with the spark plug wires.

"Do ya even know what you're doin' there?" Hutch raised a brow.

"Yeah, yeah! It's fine," she began finagling once more, rubbing at her head and mumbling to herself. After a solid minute, it was quite obvious she had no idea what she was doing.

"Just admit you don't know what you're doin?" Hutch crossed her arms.

"Okay, alright?! It's foggy in my mind. Regina had a crim hook it up for me. I thought I remembered how he did it."

"Greeaaaat…" Hutch sighed.

Right then, Hieronymus lumbered up and gently pushed Izzy out of the way.

"Hiney?! I got this, just give me a second!" She protested, but Hieronymus was hot at work. All four of his spindly arms came from his back, dispersing hands that went to the task at hand. All the others watched with raised brows as the blue demon clipped wires, unscrewed bolts, all while one of his arms held a watchful eyeball on the work.

Hutch looked at Izzy.

"I think he's done this before."

"Huh," the green demon huffed, "Yeah, well, I would've figured it out."

Diesel and Hutch rolled their eyes.

For the next several minutes, Hutch nervously paced around the vehicle while Hieronymus did his thing. She brushed off the remaining ash and grime from the car as best she could and began checking the tires and so forth. To her surprise, the tires seemed immaculate. Full tread and not a sign of dry rot on them. In fact, despite the dirt that covered her, Ruby seemed as beautiful as the day her father had brought her home. She remembered well the stories of how pissed off her mother had been the day he'd brought home that car. But her dad just didn't care. When he saw something he wanted, he got it. Although, the choice of that car had shocked the family. Regardless of her father's incessant preaching of "brands don't matter" the McCrays had been primarily a Ford family, and he was no exception. Hell, all of their drag cars had been Fords. So to see him drive a GM home was a tad odd, though no one mentioned it. She was quite sure the aesthetics of that car were what drew her father to it. And she really couldn't blame him. She had fallen in love with that car the first day she sat alone in it at six years old and pretended to be driving it. She dreamed of open roads, trees screaming by, and legs long enough to actually reach the pedals. It was a thing she'd done many times after that without her father's knowledge. One minute she'd be playing in the dirt with Tonka trucks, then the second no one was looking, she'd jump back in Ruby and take her for another "drive".

"Pooj, I found sand all over the seat in my car today. Ya wouldn't know anythin' about that would ya?"

"No, daddy."

"Alright then."

It was a conversation that took place a dozen times over between her and her father at the dinner table. Looking back, he had to have known, but maybe the thoughts of his only daughter taking that much of an interest in fast cars made him keep his cool and overlook it. In addition to those memories, Hutch recalled the day he 'retired her' so to speak. It was 1980. He drove her into the backyard garage and began ripping her innards out. He was at it for that entire day. Taking out the seats, headliner, carpet, parts of the dash. Hutch remembered her mother asking her to go out to the garage and fetch him for dinner. She peered through the crack in the door to see her dad violently ripping out the guts of the car. Even then, she never did quite understand what prompted him to do that. The interior was a little worn, but it seemed a bit redundant. He claimed he was simply 'remaking her' by getting an

414

all-new interior and then building that 400 motor for her. In the end, he never did put that engine in the car. Hutch ended up doing it. She also had to track down every piece of interior her father had disposed of. Which was pretty much all of it, with the exception of the steering wheel and main dash. Harvey didn't want her to have that car. She had the money but he refused to sell it to her. Cass was actually the one who ended up buying it. She lied to Harvey and told him she was going to make it her new ride over the fastback, but then turned right around and sold it to Hutch. That was a sore spot for years between them all. But he finally seemed to get over it.

Hutch rounded the back of the Pontiac and brushed off the license plate to reveal an alphanumerical pattern that outdated her ownership of the car. She sat there studying it for a moment, only to come to the absolute conclusion that this car was no doubt a memory of Regina's about her father. Hell it was likely this was the very car he taught her how to drive in. She soon rose up, her head wrinkly in the memories she'd never seen of her father and Regina laughing and smiling within the confines of the red beast before her.

"All done," a voice echoed in her head. She flinched to see Hieronymus standing there, retracting his arms into his back. She nodded to him. Moments later, she found herself in the driver's seat, once again turning the key, only this time with twice the apprehension of before. She could barely wrap her mind around the fact that a bundle of brimstone attached to the engine was going to do anything less than blow it to smithereens. Still, she hoped for the best as the ignition was turned. An explosion commenced as the monster roared to life faster than Hutch had ever witnessed her to do in the past. It startled her as her heart skipped a beat with an involuntary pump of the accelerator. Was this really happening? As she looked through the dingy windshield to the grin on Izzy's face and a thumbs up, she knew it was absolute. That same grin proved to be contagious as Hutch throttled the gas pedal over and over, sending out a wicked thundercall to the dead air of the yard surrounding. Ruby rocked under a torque the redhead had never felt before. There was power there, a power far beyond the earthly 350 that lay inside her. Hutch had seldom felt a wrench of torque such as that even from the likes of pro stock cars. With wide eyes, she rose from the car with the strange, stinging odor of sulfur bellowing from the galloping exhaust. It caressed her nose, reminding her of the smell from the furnaces of the mine. She bent down and looked with awe into the module that Hieronymus had secured to the motor. It was a rampant lightshow of detonating fire through the tiny glass windows of each cell that made up the unit. She just stood there, letting it entrance her as she listened to the idle purr of an engine that was no longer the mortal mass of steel remembered from the past, but one quite literally possessed by hellfire and brimstone. Though it purred out a tune of unbridled power, something lie beneath. A song of melancholy and ash. A dirge of a somber heartbeat amidst whispers and screams. The redhead couldn't help but let her grin grow larger as she became lost in the thoughts of what this monster could do. That car was no longer the Ruby she once knew, she was something else entirely.

An infernal flurry of honking echoed across the smog of the plain between the yard and Regina's lair. It bounced into the ears of Sid and he let out a sigh of discontent at the thought of having to let her out. He trudged to the gate with an entourage of scuffling red behind him to see the blinding lights of a car only feet from the steel bars. Through the dim windows he could see her there, confident as could be, waiting for her release with Izzy beside her in the front and Diesel and Hieronymus in the back.

"Took ya long enough," Sid grumbled as he looked through the bars.

Hutch leaned out the window and glared at him.

"Cut the small talk, asshole. I gotta race ta win."

The drive back across the smog-drowned expanse was not nearly as somber as when she had walked it earlier, though there was still that tiny tinge of doubt lingering as the headlights finally refracted off the ruins of Regina's lair. Hutch came to a stop just outside the main courtyard as she saw Regina walking out to meet her. The brunette didn't look pleased. She scowled as she violently motioned for Hutch to cut the engine. The redhead did as she was told. For the next few, uncomfortable moments, the tiny brunette began circling the car with a slow and wayward gait, her golden eyes maniacally drilling into the vehicle that Hutch had chosen to bring to the start line.

"Damn, girly. She don't look happy. What did you do?" Diesel whispered from the back seat.

Izzy shushed him as her eyes too began following the furnace master around. She had to admit, she had never seen her this distraught. It was subtle, but she was upset. Soon, Regina walked in closer on the driver's side.

"Well? What da ya think?" Hutch let out. The brunette said not a word. Her attention seemed to be fully focused into the interior, her eyes piercing a stare right through the redhead as if she weren't there. She leaned down a bit, resting her arms cross the open window sill. With the same unbreaking leer, she leaned in further till she was inches away from Hutch's face. The redhead was having trouble reading her. She couldn't tell if she were about to cry or about to scream out in rage. For the next minute, Regina just continued to pan the interior, soaking it all in like it were a poison she had to suck out from her own bones once before. She leered into the backseat at Hieronymus for a second, but then her eyes soon locked right into Hutch's.

"Well? Do ya approve or not?" Hutch sneered. The words were met by a slap across the face from the brunette. The sound seemed to echo through the car, causing the demons to wince almost as badly as the redhead. Hutch grabbed the side of her face in shock as she glared at Regina. She slinked away from the car and backed up slowly, once again looking at Ruby in her entirety. She shook her head and walked away.

"Follow me," was all that came out of her mouth. Hutch turned round to look at the others while she rubbed the side of her stinging face.

"Jesus, girly what did you get us into? Did your dad run over her dog in this thing or somethin'?" Diesel threw out an absurdity. Hutch had no answers. She looked into the rearview mirror, right into the backseat where Hieronymus sat as quietly as could be. She wanted to talk to him, ask him one last time if this was the right car for the job. But what was the point? The choice had been made. The redhead shuddered as she heard the fiery roar of the Cougar come to life and refract off the windows of her own patiently waiting beast. A scream of burning rubber erupted as Regina peeled out clear across her own courtyard, nearly losing control as she did so. If the slap hadn't been enough, Hutch now knew she was good and pissed. But what she didn't know was if that was a good thing or bad thing. Would her emotions cause her to make mistakes out on the track or would they sharpen them into spikes that would close the coffin tighter on Hutch's hopes of victory. Time could only tell.

The redhead watched the ivory Mercury turn from headlights to taillights within an eye's blink and then she became deafened by a loud horn blowing behind her. It was Sid. He pulled up right behind the Pontiac in one of Redgrace's rigs, ready to push it forward if Hutch didn't get her shit together. The redhead fumbled for the keys and brought the beast back to life. She soon found herself rolling across the gloom of the nothingness ahead, slowly chasing the red glow of Regina's backside while the bright lights of the semi escort blinded her from behind.

Emotions drifted from uncertainty, to fear, to anger, and then right back to uncertainty once more as the slow journey commenced across the foreboding expanse ahead. What was once a rocky plain devoid of landmarks, slowly turned into a road beneath them. It was slightly narrow, not quite unlike the crotch road at the bottom of the mine. Hutch honestly had no clue where they were headed. She had lost all sense of direction long ago. She wanted badly to ask Izzy what was happening, where they were headed, but words just seemed as unwelcome as the ashen black that surrounded them.

Several more unnerving minutes paved the way and then the smoky fog began to lift, revealing a sight that jarred Hutch to absolute attention. It was the gateway. They were once again at the northern tip of Leviathan. The redhead eyed the gateway as it writhed and retreated back and fro across itself. It was so painfully beautiful, though something was different about it. It didn't appear as bright and as lustrous as before. It seemed as though it were dying off, fading away, back into the ether from which it undoubtedly came. Though her eyes became entranced, they were pulled away by the thought of her brother. She looked off to the east, but the rig and his mangled car were long gone. Not a shred of metal or a bolt reflected in the radiance of the light ahead. It was if the whole thing had never happened, but Hutch knew better.

The glow of brake lights ahead grabbed the redhead's attention back to the road as Regina threaded the roundabout beneath the glory of the gate ahead. As Hutch piloted Ruby onto the surface of the road, she could feel the vibration of the otherworldly threshold pulsing up through her tires and into her flesh. It was power incarnate, so pure even the hum of the hell-fired engine couldn't mask its droning harmony. The red Pontiac rolled onwards, coming to a stop right beside the Mercury that waited patiently behind a dull orange line traced across the intersect of the roundabout. The starting line. Hutch slid the beast into park, sighing nervously as she looked overtop Izzy, through the window of the Cougar beyond. Regina sat there, staring forwards into the bleak vanishing point of the highway ahead. God only knew what was running through her mind at that moment, but Hutch was quite sure she wanted no part of it. Suddenly, the air sucked from the vehicle as both doors were violently thrown open.

"What the hell?!" Hutch yelled as she was ripped from the driver's seat by Sid.

"Sorry, firebush! Gotta rid your car of rodents. Get the hell out!" The crim shoved the seat forwards, beckoning for all the demons to evacuate the car. Hutch stood back and watched as the trio piled out of the car with worried looks on their faces. A small band of crims began escorting them to the rig nearby.

"There ya go! Pest-free interior! I'll send ya a bill in the mail," Sid smiled and patted the top of the Pontiac.

"What are ya doin' with them?" Hutch sneered.

"Relax, firebush, we'll take good care of your little pets there. You'll get em' back when you all go back ta the pit together."

"Ya mean when we all get ta go home together."

"Jesus Christ, firebush, you are one clueless bitch. You might as well just hand her that feather and go back to the mine. Save us all some time. Hell, you ain't even seen the race course. You don't even know what the hell your gettin' yourself into. But, good luck. You're gonna need it," Sid waved a hand at her as he walked away. Hutch just stood there in thought for a moment. He was right, she was flying blind. Or was she?

"Wait," her mouth came open as she made a beeline for Regina's car. She made a fist and began beating on the window. It came down fast.

"This better be good," the brunette growled, never once looking at Hutch.

"I wanna guide."

"A what?"

"Izzy. She's raced this thing against you before. I want her to come with me." The brunette finally took her stare away from the road and drilled it right into Hutch's. She said nothing. "Seriously? Every odd is stacked against me. What's it gonna hurt ta give me this one goddamn thing?" The brunette took her eyes away. She remained silent again. "Please." It was a word that didn't leak from the lips of the McCray's often, at least with any sincerity. Regina looked back up to her again, she threw her hand out the window and motioned. The crim Yellow Duck came running up to the car.

"Boss?' He asked.

"Get the greenie. Put her in Miss McCray's car. Gently, please."

"Right away," he took back off towards the rumbling rig beyond. Hutch was dumbfounded.

"Thank you," was all she could muster.

"Don't thank me, Red. Thank those blue eyes and those long legs of yours," Regina grunted. Hutch had no idea what to say to that. She was almost confused. But it took a backseat as she watched Yellow Duck usher Izzy back into the Pontiac and shut the door. The redhead looked to Regina.

"What are the rules?"

"Very few. You're in my house now, Red. But they're pretty simple...You see the light there?" Hutch looked to a post beside the start line. Dozens of crims climbed up it like monkeys, snarling and laughing. A glowing red light pulsated on a box among them. "When it turns green, you go. Whoever gets to the next star point first, wins the leg. Leviathan has five legs. Simple. Best out of five."

"That's it?"

"That's it...You got one minute. Make the best of it." With that, Regina rolled up her window, leaving Hutch alone to ponder the next sixty seconds. She looked to the light post and then to the straights ahead of her. The panic began to set in as she ran back to the car and jumped in, quickly strapping herself in.

"What's happenin, hun?" A voice made Hutch gasp. She'd already forgotten about Izzy.

"What's happenin' is me and you are gonna win ourselves a race."

"Me? What am I gonna do?"

"You're gonna be my eyes. I never seen this thing before, so you're help guide me through it. Okay?"

Izzy nervously nodded.

"Okay?!" Hutch asked again.

"Yeah! Okay! Okay! I'll do ma best."

Hutch pointed at her.

"No. I need more than your best. Now, grab onto something, kid…" she stopped for a second then smiled. "Shits about ta get rad."

"Oh, you have no idea, hun," Izzy shook her head.

Leviathan

The Straights

And so the metal beasts took their leave
Spinning tires amidst mayhem's breath
Shooting through the darkness of The Straights
Into certain gloom, yet uncertain death

Though the demon was first to take the lead
The Gingerbread Girl was fast to steal
She left her rival far behind
In the glow of the gateway's zeal

In and out of phantom cars she weaved
Through a path she once trod before
Though she laid down the lead, felt the pulse through the tread
The wolf was once again at her door.

They fought for the lead for mile upon mile
Between clenched teeth and a monstrous smile
Redlining the needle upon the face of the dial
Though the demon won out when she used her beguile

As The straights came to a deafening close
The redhead could see the line that marked the repose
But the princess screamed by her to claim the win
And she was waiting at the finish with that signature grin

"Oh, Red, honey, you had me and you blew it," Regina chided as she hung out the window, slowly circling the roundabout with Hutch behind her.

Hutch could do nothing more than give her a dirty stare as they came slowly rolling round to the start line of the second leg.

"This ain't good..." the tiny voice of Izzy almost whispered. Hutch looked over in the passenger seat.

"What? Chill out. It's ONE loss. We got this."

"Hun, The Straights is the mildest leg down here. It's kind of a gimme."

"Oh, is that so? And did you win that leg?"

"Well...no...I..."

"Well there ya go! Jesus, sittin' over there judgin' me and you didn't even do it. What the hell? Ya know I didn't bring ya along so you could throw pig shit on my parade. Maybe you should ride with Regina..."

"Oh stop! Just stop!" The green demon barked, "Look, I'm sorry but you're gonna need me."

"Oh, am I?" Hutch had her doubts.

"Every leg from here on out is nuts, like batshit-crazy nuts. That back there," she pointed to the darkness of The Straights, "That was nothin. That was like a normal drive down a highway. The other legs...they're...."

"They're what?"

"Well, let's just put it like this, I wish I'd had a guide when I did them, okay?"

Hutch just shook her head and tightened her grip on the wheel, "Whatever..."

"No, not whatever. The Serpent is next."

"Yeah, it was just a windy road from what I saw."

"It's more than a windy, backroad, hun. The Helix."

"The what?"

"You remember, outside the mine, ya saw that thing and ask me what it was? You ready to go upside-down?"

Hutch raised a brow. "I...I...how the hell?"

"Exactly. Ya have to trust this car."

"Oh, that sounds easy, I just trust the car and defy gravity. No problem," Hutch smarted off.

"The pulse? You feel it right? That lifeforce rushing in from the car. Into your hands and feet. Into your heart?"

Hutch did feel it. It was an electric dance of joy and dread.

"What about it?"

"You have to channel that to your mind, hun. You tell the car what to do, not the other way round...You wouldn't believe the things ya can make a car do on this road."

"Are you two done chattering yet?' Regina hollered out through the open window as they both sat there idling at the next start line. Hutch said nothing, she just eyed the red light on the post and then looked towards Izzy. The greenie spoke,

"Just trust me..."

Hutch nodded and revved the engine.

"Lets do this shit..."

The Serpent

And so red gave way to green and fire
The machines took flight on burning tire
Into the winding belly of the beast
To the star point's finish that lay to the east

Apprehension and dread began to swirl
In the heart and the mind of the Gingerbread Girl
But she stayed the course and took the lead
Dancing through corners with tempestuous speed

Further they went, into the bowels of the snake
Tunnels and spirals came fast in its wake
And soon the redhead saw it ahead on high
The towering Helix that blotted the sky

She looked to the greenie and she gave a nod
So she blasted the gas, sent a prayer to God
The car went sideways and soon upside down
But she stuck to the road as she went round and round

424

Six giant loops were traversed with a scream
Like the rollercoasters she'd rode as a kid in a dream
But lo when she found the flat ground once more
The demon passed by and doubled her score

"Two and zero, baby!" Regina laughed as she hung out the
window and pounded the side of her door. Hutch barely heard the
victory whoop, she was still coming off the high of riding the
Helix. She still had no idea how she'd made it through there
without dying. As she sped the roundabout she looked to Izzy. The
greenie had a half a crooked frown on her face. She could tell the
demon wanted so badly to speak, but dared not.

"Don't even open your mouth," Hutch assured her suspicions.
The two rumbling cars once again stood side by side, facing into
the unknown stretch that Izzy called The Mirror. Hutch had no
damn idea what that meant, but she was sure it was nowhere near
as complacent as it sounded.

"Well, Red…is this where you get off? Personally, I already got
off, but what I mean is, is this where I end you?"

Hutch just shook her head, not even bothering to look over at
Regina. "Ahh, babe, are you pouting. That's so adorable. I would
get out a pinch your wittle cheek if I didn't think I'd get my hand
bit off," she laughed on.

"Cut the shit," Hutch finally spoke, "I got this. Your ass is
mine."

"Oh, you tease. Don't go making promises you can't keep."

Hutch looked over to Izzy as she waited for the light.

"On a scale of one to ten, how fucked are we?"

The demon spoke, "Twelve."

The Mirror

The third leg was a go and the monsters roared out
The redhead held tight and pushed through her doubt
Her garnet steed cut deep through the sting of the mire
Into the rotting intestine of reflection and fire

The road that lay ahead disappeared in darkened breath
Revealing paths once traveled before she was taken by death
She was consumed by memories painted in shades of fall
Till she realized this road she traveled was no road at all

The Gingerbread Girl's car became worthless in this place
Her mind was the only engine that could help her win this race
Surrounded by every awful memory she'd ever had to weather
She felt the pain of it all once more as her flesh turned into leather

She felt herself age to the grave, then back into the womb
Her heart rotting amidst the memories bound to seal her doom
Sarah's death. Her mother's wane. The pain of her father's wrath.
Cass's leave. Henry's crash. The tears she cried on the path

The heartbreak came all at once, but she fought with all her might
And pushed out the sadness, turning darkness back to light
The road reappeared to her eyes and the finish line was there
She crossed over it before the demon, without a moment to spare

Ruby's hell-fired engine waned and her transmission wound
down to a steady spin. Hutch looked in the rearview in disbelief at
the Cougar behind. She'd beat her. She actually beat her. She
wanted to jump up and down. Get out of the car and raise her fists
into the air, becoming the giddy girl she tried desperately to cover
up at that moment. But instead…

"What the hell was that?! Some warnin' would've been nice!"
Hutch suddenly began drilling Izzy about the race leg. The demon
winced, throwing her little hands up as if she were trying to
physically bat the admonishment away.

"There wasn't anything to say, hun. Nothin' can prepare you for
that…nothin'. Sometimes it ain't about the car down here…" Izzy
spoke, never looking at Hutch.

"Well, no shit…" Hutch grumbled. She pressed the brake and
crept to the next start line.

"Besides…ya did it," Izzy added.

"Did you?'

"Did I what?"

"Did you win that leg when you raced?"

The greenie was quiet for a moment as she listened to the roar of Regina's car come full circle.

"No...I didn't," she answered hauntingly.

"Guess who's back in the game, bitch," Hutch had to poke at Regina. The brunette came to a stop, then slowly looked over. She was shaken. Her face was as ivory as ghost-flesh amidst a gaze of utter emotionlessness. Hutch's smile waned into nothing at the sight of her adversary. Seeing anyone, much less a demon princess, with such a look didn't exactly inspire happiness. As Hutch glared on, she couldn't help but wonder what the hell Regina had seen in her memories. They were obviously much harder for her to stomach.

"Congratulations, Red," was all that leaked out of Regina's mouth. Hutch couldn't even tell if it was sincere because of how dead it was. The redhead looked to Izzy who, in turn, just shook her head and shrugged her shoulders. Jesus, what had that girl seen? But there was no time for conversation, the light ahead illuminated, and the fire ignited once again.

The Labyrinth

Engines fired the machines out into brackish haze
Deep in the belly of the track intertwined just like a maze
The redhead found panic in the sight of tunnels ahead
In the face of a towering wall painted in the shades of the dead

Fast, she chose the middle road before she could even think
And just like that, she was all alone before she could even blink
The path ahead threw hairpin turns she could barely hope to tame
And it was not long she realized how the Labyrinth got its name

U-Turns and corners and shifting walls came fast
Every way the redhead went, looked just like the last
She looked to the greenie for guidance on which paths to chase
But everything was different from the time she had ran the race

From behind a terrible noise erupted to tear the mind asunder
The sound of a giant machine that rivaled the tongue of thunder
A monstrous truck with monstrous tires came rolling in her wake
Determined to crush her flat as soon as she made a mistake

The redhead took a breath and found inner peace inside
She outsmarted the beast and quickly turned the tide
A brake averted a crush and the truck broke through a wall
Leaving a path to freedom where the finish line stood tall

Hutch could barely chase off the trembling that had consumed her from head to toe as she sped across the finish line and entered the fourth star point. It was lonely there. Far too lonely for a victory cry or even a sigh of relief. She slowed Ruby to a crawl and crept through the roundabout, looking for signs of Regina, but she was nowhere to be seen. A moment later, the Pontiac crept to the start line of the fifth leg of Leviathan. Hutch looked over at Izzy. The greenie cast her the same questioning gaze as they waited in an uncomfortable death of dialogue amongst the rumbling idle of the red beast. Just as Hutch finally went to speak, an echo of hellfire crackled in the distance and the ivory monster made her way back into the race. Regina crossed the finish line and whipped through the roundabout on screeching tires that were as angry as the woman who gave them life. Within a second, the demon princess was nose to nose with Hutch, ready for the final bout. The redhead looked over to Regina, but she didn't look back. A baleful scowl painted the side of her face as she stared coldly into the blackness ahead. It was obvious she was sickened by her own failure, so Hutch just kept her mouth shut as she turned back to face the mouth of The Swan Song and the spiraling obsidian within it. A sudden touch made the redhead flinch as she looked down to see the tiny hand of Izzy gently patting her leg.

"You got this, hun. We're almost home."

"What's in this last stretch?"

The greenie drew her hand back to herself before she finally spoke one word,

"Lies."

The Swan Song

Explosions of fire and tire murdered the hush
Sped the racers fast back into the rush
Hearts went aflutter to awaken the soul
Through curtains of sable, ash, and coal

But amid the dark a light came through
With the smell of rain, leaf, and dew
Then sun shined bright and hell faded away
To usher forth the beauty of a new day

The Gingerbread Girl was back on earth
Driving the roads she'd known since birth
Her heart warmed fast as the wind whipped by
It was just a girl, her car, and the wandering sky

She drove through summer and back through spring
With a smile bright enough to make angels sing
Every memory that ever made her heart swell
Kept playing on repeat in this trickery of hell

She then remembered what the demon had said
This place was built of lies and dread
The redhead screamed and light turned to ash
The mirage fell away and then came the crash…

Hutch's mind remained afog as the beauty of the beast collapsed around her, revealing once again, the cold, pyre-slag surface of Leviathan. Regina was right beside her, neck and neck as they traveled at speeds that the needle couldn't even ascend into. There seemed to be nothing ahead and nothing behind, like they were moving on some arcane conveyer belt through the very absence of time itself. And then it happened, a feeling of dread. Hutch felt the hair stand up on her arm as she looked over at Regina. Their eyes met for a fleeting moment and time stood still amidst the chaos on Highway Hell. The demon's wrought-iron stare softened as she kept her gaze locked with the redhead's for the next few seconds.

It was so subtle, yet so powerful. It was as if her humanity had sprouted from the rusty earth just long enough to show Hutch that something was alive in there. It was a look of sorrow, regret, and ultimately, submissiveness as Regina let her foot off the gas to allow the redhead to take the lead. Hutch didn't even have the time to process what the brunette was doing when she heard Izzy scream beside her. She spun her head to catch the horrifying flash of another car, speeding head on, right into Regina. An explosion rocked Ruby to one side as the two cars intermeshed and roll off the road in a pile of twisted steel. Hutch went numb…everything had happened so quickly. She couldn't even catch a grasp of one single, coherent thought as she watched the cars behind her roll apart and come to a sickening stop in her rearview. She gasped as she looked ahead to see the top star point illuminated by the gateway. It was the finish line. The real one. She had won....hadn't she? Right at that moment, she buried the brake and slid sideways till she came to a complete stop in the middle of the very road she had almost conquered. With panicked breath, she kept looking back between the finish line and the twisted wreck behind her, trying to make the right decision, if such a thing existed. Finish the race or run to Regina's aid.

"What are ya doin, hun?! Finish it! The ends right there!" Izzy yelled at her. Hutch all out ignored the greenie. She threw open the door and ran back to the wreck, but began slowing her steps as she beheld the grimness of the scene up close. It seemed all surreal in the frame of her review mirror, but now it was quite bitter in taste. In a panic, she ran over to the Cougar. It was now ragged and beaten, a former shell of what it was only moments before. All the windows were denoted and blown to fragments from the uncountable rolls it had taken off the roadway. It lie there, upon its top with one of the front wheels still rotating under the force of the impact. Hutch dropped to her knees and began searching for Regina, almost certain she was probably thrown from the vehicle amidst the mayhem. To her surprise, that wasn't the case. There she laid in a pitiful crumpled pile, the exiled Princess of Level 12. She was reduced to a bloodied and unmoving body that laid in absolute silence upon the headliner of the Mercury.

"Oh shit…God, no…." Hutch began whispering in terror as she crawled into the mass of steel. She wrapped her hands tightly around Regina and pulled her out from the wreckage through the blown-out rear window. The tiny sounds of tinking glass played a melancholy tune as she rolled the tiny brunette over onto her back and looked down upon her broken body with horror. There were giant gashes in her abdomen. Her clothes were torn asunder there, and parts of her innards were beginning to fall out. Her eyes were closed amongst a thick coating of her own blood that stained nearly every inch of her sober face. She looked peaceful. Like every awful thing that had ever turned her into the monster she'd become had lifted away from her, leaving behind a bliss only found in the mouth of eternal sleep.

"Regina?...Regina?...Regina, wake up…Regina?!" Hutch pulled her up and cradled her in her arms for a moment, trying to get her to awaken, if she was even still in there. But there was nothing. Not a breath, not a twitch of a brow, nor a pulse of life of any kind emanated from her tattered little body. Hutch's eyes began to well with the sting of sorrow as she rocked back and forth where she sat, clutching tightly to Regina. She looked through the blur to the smoke rolling out of the other car….The other car…The redhead felt a chill as she beheld the make and model. It was a 67' Firebird, just like Ruby, only it was painted in the shades of ash and ruin. Like it had been set afire long before it had been in this wreck. It lay on its side about a hundred feet away in its own state of disrepair. She wanted to run over and murder whoever or whatever was inside of it. This was the absolute last thing she'd expected to happen…to be sitting here, holding onto a dying demon instead of racing across the finish line to victory.

A few more minutes passed by with Izzy, Diesel, Hieronymus, and all the crims waiting in silence at the star point, well, almost all the crims. Sid and Yellow Duck were nowhere to be seen among them. Hutch finally wiped at her tears and slid her hands carefully under Regina, hoisting her up. The brunette dangled in her arms like she hadn't a bone left in her body, while she slowly walked back towards the finish line.

"Pooj?" A sickly voiced called out through the gloom behind her. She almost dropped Regina. That voice. That name. It couldn't be. Slowly, she turned around and was overcome with a new level of horror as she watched her father crawling from the wreckage.

He had been the death driver. The soul who had caused the hell she now held in her arms.

"Dad?...Daddy?!" She let out in confused terror.

"Pooj...put er' down. She ain't nothin' but trouble. Win your race...Just leave er',"

Harvey McCray muttered as he coughed and stuttered around, trying to get up on his feet. Hutch looked down onto Regina's broken and pitiful body. She looked back to her father.

"Daddy, I can't...I...love her. I can't just leave her like this!"

Her father began shaking his head, still trying to stand up. He fell back on his hip.

"No...No, Pooj. That's what she does, she gets in your head. You know what she is. Ya have ta trust me."

Suddenly a small coo of pain and disorientation erupted from the brunette. Her golden eyes barely opened.

"Re...Red?" She spoke.

"Yeah?"

"Red...don't listen to him. He's not what you think he is," she barely eked out.

Hutch became all the more terrified.

"Wha...What do ya mean? He ain't my dad? That's not my dad?"

"No, he's your father, but...but you can't trust him. You can't." Hutch's head went into a spin. This was all happening too fast. She had no idea what to do. She squatted down and gently leaned Regina against a nearby rock along the highway. The brunette coughed as Hutch went to stand up to face her father once again. Regina's hand shot out and grabbed her wrist tightly.

"Red...get me some brimstone. It'll help me heal. Please."

"Don't do it, Pooj!" Her father crawled closer and pointed, "You give her that, she's gonna heal and end us both...She's a killer, Hutch. A cold-blooded killer."

Hutch pulled her hand away from Regina. The brunette began shaking her head as she covered the gaping wounds on her stomach.

"No. It's him. Your father's evil, Red."

"He's evil? You're a demon, for god sake. I...I...is this some game?!"

"Pooj, honey, listen. Just get away from her."

"Red, don't let him come any closer…"

"Shut up! Shut the hell up! Both of you!" Hutch screamed as she wrapped her hands tightly round her head. She began sobbing in the wake of the emotional tug-of-war. She had become the tattered and muddy rope in the middle. The man who raised her on one end and the woman she loved on the other. "Just…shut up," she once again spouted through a curling lip.

"I don't know what game you two are playing but I won this race. You wrecked and you forfeit! So unless you think ya can crawl fast enough to beat me over that finish line, I want to go home and my aunt is comin' with me. Where is she?"

Regina's face went soft with the same look she had given when she told the story of Henry's death. "Red…I…"

"Where is she?!"

Regina's lips tightened for a moment.

"She isn't here. I'm so sorry…I lied to you, Red. I…"

"No. No. No. No. What are you tellin' me right now. What the FUCK are you sayin' to me?! WHERE IS SHE?!"

"You need ta ask your father where she is…" Regina spoke soft and defeated. They both looked to Harvey.

"Dad?"

He put his hands up in defense.

"Hey…your aunt left. You know that. She left us. Abandoned us all just like your mom."

"Tell her, Harvey, or I will. Tell her now!" Regina screamed.

"I told ya, she ran off!"

Regina looked up to Hutch,

"She's in the old Starne's mines at the bottom of the deepest pit! Over a hundred feet down in a watery grave!"

Hutch's brow wrinkled. Her confusion barely fought back a wall of hysterics. She looked at her father.

"Wha…What? What is she sayin'?"

"And she isn't the only one down there is she, Harvey?" Regina added.

"Pooj…Pooj, she's crazy. I told ya she gets in your head. Don't listen ta her. She's trying ta drive a wedge between us. We need each other ta get out of here!"

"Confess, Harvey! Tell her what you did! Tell her what you are?"

Harvey's eyes went slightly mad looking. An insanity glowed within them as he glared at Regina. "Tell her, or I'll show her…you know I can."

Harvey tried softening his face, recomposing himself. He stuck his hand out towards Hutch.

"Pooj?...please…"

Suddenly, Hutch felt the iron grip of Regina's hand grasping onto hers. A flash of light blinded the redhead, and she was transported to another time. A memory. She could hear it long before she could see it. A fog surrounded her, gray and stitched with prisms of green that gave way to trees and weeds. A gentle wind flicked her hair and tickled her neck as everything came into focus. It was just like when Hieronymus had taken her back, only there was no track or screaming crowd. A somber tone floated on the breeze as she looked around her into shades of green and earth. She was surrounded by forest and the undeniable smell of July. There was an old rutted and grass-devoured dirt road down the middle of everything, one that hadn't been traveled by the likes of many for years. Along it, a lake or pond of sorts. Narrow, it ran the length of the road for some eighth of a mile. Hutch recognized it. She'd been there once before. It was part of the old mines off route 82. A place her father took her fishing once despite the adamant "No Trespassing" and "Danger" signs peppering the entire area. But it was different for her father. The signs didn't apply to him. He had become friends with the owner through the shop who now resided in Pennsylvania. Harvey had personally rebuilt several engines for Gerald Starnes's hotrod obsession. He was the heir to the Starnes Mining Company, and he let Harvey use the land for fishing and hunting with the promise he wouldn't bring friends or tell anyone about it. The enormous tract of land had been abandoned since the early fifties when the coal began running thin and the company decided to focus on other areas towards the southern half of the state. It quickly was reclaimed by the forest that it had chewed up and spit out so many years ago. By all rights, it was now wild and truly abandoned on some level and Harvey held one of only a few keys accessing the gates on the land.

Hutch scanned the area from where she now stood beside the edge of the forest. Her ears were overcome by the humming of cicada and a group of crows across the way. But her attention was now swallowed by the sight of what lay beside the edge of the tattered road. It was Ruby. The Firebird sat there in an eerie silence. Her father mirrored the car's state of being, sitting idle in the driver's seat, staring off as if he were somewhere else entirely. He was waiting on something. She could see it behind the ghostly haze of his primeval stare. Slowly, she walked from the forest, looking towards the direction the nose of the Pontiac pointed. There was a sound; an engine. The steady hum and gallop of valves and pistons brought forth the sight of another car coming down the haul road. A white car. A 1968 Mercury Cougar. Hutch shuddered as she watched Regina pull up beside Harvey. Her window rolled down, exposing a look on her face that was almost impossible to fully read by the likes of any mortal. She threw the beast into park and killed the engine. Hutch swore every bird and insect in the area stopped right along with that engine as she crept ever forwards till she was right between both of their cars. Her forehead wrinkled and she raised a brow as she looked into the eyes of the brunette. They were not golden. They were blue. Blue as the pure summer sky that shared the white clouds aloft. Regina spoke.

"Hi."

"Hey," was all he could muster. They looked deeply into one another's eyes for a few moments.

"Where have ya been?" Harvey asked.

"Around."

"Around? I haven't seen you in months and that's all ya gotta say?"

"Things…things got complicated. Okay?"

"Complicated? What things? Ya know ya can talk to me."

Regina looked away and nodded. He went on. "Look…I know you don't deserve this. I'm sorry I've treated ya the way I have. I've kept ya hangin' on for so long and I'm so, so sorry….is there someone else? Ya find someone else? Is that why ya been avoidin' me?"

"No…No it's not like that."

"I'm leavin' her…"

Regina looked into his eyes with question.

"What?"

"Lonnie...I'm leavin' Lonnie, Ree. I...I mean it this time. I can't stand the thought of losin' ya....Okay?"

"Okay," Regina lit up. She smiled so wide a tear ran down her cheek.

"Well don't just sit there, come over here and pop a squat beside me," Harvey smiled, patting the passenger seat of Ruby. Regina grinned and nodded, but the smile quickly faded as her hand went to grab her door handle.

"Hey...I've got something to tell you. It's...it's part of the reason I've been away."

Harvey put his hand up and smiled.

"I know what you're gonna tell me."

"You do?"

"Yep. I can see it. Ya went and got more beautiful since you've been gone. I can see it from here and I'm okay with it," he joked. Regina wanted to laugh but all she could muster was a smile with obvious distress behind it.

"No...I...seriously, Harvey. Promise me you'll love me no matter what? That you won't leave me."

"Ree, what's got ya ruffled? Yur shakin' a little. C'mon, get over here. We'll talk about it," he motioned.

"Promise me," she insisted.

"Oh, okay, I promise ya."

"Close your eyes."

"Oh, Ree, c'mon now, what's goin on? Now yur gettin' me all ruffled."

"I said close them."

Harvey sighed and shrugged his shoulders. He closed his eyes with a shake of his head.

"Alright then," he spoke in defeat. As he listened to her slowly getting out of her car, he spoke again,

"Is this some kinda surprise?"

"I guess you could say that."

The door to the Cougar slammed and Hutch was taken aback by what she saw. Regina stood there in a gorgeous sundress. She looked as marvelous as she ever had. But this time there was a glow about her, and a protruding belly that was some eight months pregnant. With brows raised in awe, she eyed the brunette as she carefully walked behind Ruby and rounded the passenger side door. She opened it and flopped down beside Harvey who still waited with closed eyes and bated breath.

"Well? Can I open em'?" He asked.

Regina licked her lips and fidgeted in apprehension. She nodded to herself.

"Yeah. Go ahead."

Harvey smiled and looked over, popping his eyes open wide. They immediately drew to her huge baby bump. His smile waned a tad.

"Ree...Uh...umm. Ya, um? What happened? What's going on?" He fumbled for words. It was impossible to tell what he was thinking. Regina was immediately fighting back tears. It wasn't the response she'd hoped for.

"I'm pregnant, Harvey."

"Well...yeah I can see that, Ree. But...but. Who's is it?"

The brunette's mouthed fell agape in shock. A tear escaped.

"Wha?...Harvey it's yours. She's ours."

From right outside the window Hutch watched with nearly the same shock as Regina. It was beyond uncomfortable. Silence paved the way for what seemed like an eon.

Harvey finally spoke,

"She?"

"Yeah. She. We're having a girl...I wanna name her, Marnie...Isn't that cute?"

"Ree, I thought ya said ya couldn't have kids. Ya told me when we first got tagether that ya couldn't have kids. That...that you were barren. Ya told me that," Harvey's words grew all the more agitated.

"I know! I did tell ya that. I'm sorry. I didn't plan this! Okay?!"

"Ya sure about that?"

"What?"

"Ya sure ya didn't plan this? Tryin' ta trap me. Ta get me ta leave Lonnie once and for all? That's what ya always wanted."

Regina bit her bottom lip, trying to maintain her composure.

"Harvey...not to be crude, but I've been letting you drop loads in me for eleven years. If that was my master plan, it would've happened long before this."

"Jesus...Ree...I got six kids. I can't be havin' another one. Why would ya do this?"

"Why would *I* do this?! ME?! I'm not the fucking virgin Mary, Harvey! This ain't divine conception!...Oh my god...this isn't how I thought this was gonna go," Regina tried calming down. Her tears began welling all the more.

"Well, how did ya think it was gonna go?! That I was gonna wrap my arms round ya and say 'Oh honey, it's fine! I really wanted a seventh anchor weighin' me down! Jesus Christ!" Harvey spat out coldly as he threw open his door and jumped from the car.

"Where are you going?!" Regina shrieked, wiping at her cheeks.

"I'm goin' for a damn walk, okay?" He said as he fished a cigarette out and lit it with an angry, shaking hand. He slammed the door, "Just...just sit there. I need a minute. I'm sorry...I just need a minute." And with that, he walked off down the haul road. Hutch watched him for a moment, but her attention quickly drew back to the inside of the car where Regina burst into a sobbing fit. She threw her head into her hands and wailed like nothing the redhead had ever heard in her life. It was pure heartbreak. Hutch could almost feel it radiating into her own chest as she watched the brunette's shoulders bounce along with the weeping she expelled in violent waves. Hutch wanted so badly to get into the car with her, wrap her arms around her, and tell her everything was going to be okay. But she couldn't. And even if she could, she knew she'd be lying.

For several minutes the redhead watched Regina bawl and bawl, till she finally wound down to a whimper. She sniffled and wiped at her face, then began digging around, looking for a hanky or a napkin. Her hands soon went to the glove box in front of her, but it was locked. With a shaky hand she grabbed the keys from the ignition and quickly found the breadwinner. With a turn, she opened the dash and immediately grabbed a handkerchief that sat right up front. She pressed her swelling cheeks into the fabric and dabbed at her eyes with the hanky...but she soon realized, it wasn't a hanky at all. Her brow wrinkled and lip twisted as she pulled the pink linen away from her face, watching it unfurl into a pair of wrinkled women's panties. She let them fall to the floorboard in disgust. Her sorrow was soon turning to distrust and anger as she looked into the glove box only to spy yet another pair that she knew wasn't hers. With an angry lunge, she grabbed hold of the other pair and yanked, but it was caught on something. Regina's face once again retreated back to disgusted curiosity as she saw the panties were pinched tightly at the edge of the glove box. Suspicion ran high as she leaned forwards, looking at the seam the garment was wedged into. The entire length of the glove box seemed to be lined with another piece of metal that shouldn't have been there. A false wall, in a sense. She picked at the edges of it, trying to pry it open but finally she just gave the panties a horrendous jerk. A piece of metal popped and the entire fake door went flying open, dropping its entire contents into her lap. Like slow motion, a deluge of panties, Polaroid pictures, and over a dozen fake Carnation flowers, rained down, filling her lap to the brim. Her breath left her as she stared down into the mess of hell she had just unleashed upon herself. Shaking hands soon drifted down, sifting through the debris. She retrieved the first Polaroid her fingers ran across and she held it up to her terrified gaze. It was the dead and naked body of a young woman, sprawled out upon the grass with strangulation bruises round her neck. Her eyes were open, permanently frozen in the horrible sight of her own fate. Between her legs, a single green carnation was perfectly positioned. It was Loretta Park. She was the third woman that had been found dead within a two year period in the tri-county area, slain with a carnation on her body. She was the case that finally made authorities label the murders as the work of a serial killer. Five more would follow her.

Regina could feel her heart elevating with every anxious move as she picked through the rest of the pictures, catching glimpses of other murdered women in varying sexual positions, all sharing the same ligature marks and carnation flower positioned on their naked flesh. Hutch leaned into the driver's side window, watching in terror at the sight of Regina shuffling through the murder memorabilia that filled her lap and cascaded down to the floor below. The brunette could barely breath as her head spun round in the thoughts of where she now sat. She was in the car of a killer. A killer that she'd loved and bedded for over a decade. How? How was this happening? She began shaking all the more as she frantically began grabbing handfuls of pictures and flowers, trying desperately to shove them back into the glove box from whence they came. But it was no use. They kept tumbling back out, taunting her as they fell all over the car, creating a larger mess than when they first appeared. She was nearly hyperventilating at this point, her panicked breaths and flailing arms began sending Hutch into a state of all out horror that only amplified when she heard the footsteps.

"Oh, Ree…"

Regina gasped in terror at Harvey's voice right beside her. Her body went rigid, petrifying in fear as he spoke again, "Oh, Ree…no, no, no, no. What did ya do? Why did ya do that, Ree, why?" He nervously ran a hand through his hair. She kept sitting there, her mouth agape, bottom lip quivering, just staring out the window, too terrified to even look at him at that moment. Her mind just kept playing back the events of the flowers falling into her lap as she whispered a silent prayer inside. A thing she'd never done in her entire existence. The quiet between them was unbearable and it trudged on for a solid, sickening minute of absolute hell on earth.

"Ree?" He let out. She finally found enough courage to turn her head and look up into his eyes. She was terrified. He'd never seen her so scared. "Ree, don't look at me like that."

"Ple…please, just let me go. I won't tell anyone. I won't. Please," tears began streaming down her face as her hands ran down to her stomach. She gently cradled her belly, fearing far more for her daughter than herself.

"Ree?" He spoke again. She wiped at her eyes and tried calming herself.

"What?"

"I'm so sorry." With that last word, a crashing fist came through the open door. It blasted her in the face, breaking her nose and sending her head reeling back into the seat. Hutch jumped back against the Cougar, screaming as she watched her father jump into Ruby, right on top of Regina. His massive six-foot-five frame helplessly pinned her tiny body down. He wrapped his hands tightly round her neck and shoved his knee so hard into her chest Hutch heard her ribs break under the pressure. Regina kicked and writhed. She clawed violently at his hands, but they were like steel vices round her throat. Her face began turning as red as the blood that poured from her nose and dripped down, staining Harvey's white knuckles below. Hutch could do nothing but cower there outside Ruby, watching through the fingers covering her terrified face. She knew there was nothing she could do to stop it, it made it all the more horrifying.

Regina managed to get a finger into his eye. He let go for a moment and she let out a pitiful gasping whimper as she twisted away from him, trying to claw at the driver's side door. It only angered him all the more. He roared out, wrapped a hand round her neck, and began delivering blow after sickening blow to her already battered face.

"Daddy, stop! Just STOP!" Hutch began screaming out. It was ugly and visceral. It was like watching a predator tear apart its prey while it was still alive. Soon, Regina's dainty arms lost their fight. They slipped down and hung motionless while Harvey wrapped his hands round her throat again, squeezing until the skin ripped on his knuckles....it was over. She was gone.

Hutch lowered her hands from her face and watched as her father's face turned from that of an animal to that of a child. He gasped and pulled his hands away. Regina's broken body slumped over into the driver's seat, her beautiful blue eyes stayed open, staring into the nothing. Harvey grabbed her and pulled her up and back over into the passenger seat. Cradling her like a baby.

"Oh god, no. Ree?! Ree?! What did I do?! I god no!" He shook her over and over, as if he were trying to spark life back into her body. He began sobbing, smashing his face into her chest. "Oh Jesus! God no! Why am I like this?! Why?! Come back ta me, Ree?! Come back! Come back! Just come back! I love you!" Hutch had never seen her father in such sorrowful hysterics. It was almost as hard to watch as Regina's murder. He began weeping into the nape of her neck, his shoulders bouncing involuntarily in the agony he brought upon himself.

"I'm so sorry...I'm sorry. I'm sorry," he kept repeating as he rocked her back and forth in his arms. Hutch stood there, weeping along with him for what seemed like an hour. There was so much pain in the air. She could feel it going into her flesh and into the bones beneath. She flinched as her father rose up from the vehicle, still holding Regina's lifeless body in his arms. He walked with a broken gait over to her car and opened the passenger side door. He carefully sat her inside and buckled her upright in the seatbelt. Hutch watched over his shoulder as he gently cleaned her face of all the blood and closed her eyelids. He then pinned a single, green carnation on the breast of her dress. The Cougar soon fired up and Hutch watched as her father backed up and headed down the road, deeper into the mining property. She followed along behind him at a brisk walk as he traversed the bumpy path ahead. He turned right and went up a long incline, deeper into the woods, stopping at the edge of a tree line. Hutch caught up and stood beside the car, it was idling three feet away from a fifty foot sheer wall that dropped right into a deep, blue quarry pool below. The engine cut off and Harvey placed the Cougar in neutral. He rose up out of the car and walked round to the open window of the passenger side. Leaning in, he rested his arms on the sill and began lovingly running his fingers through Regina's hair as he remained in a state of deathly quiet repose. His attention soon drew to her stomach and to the life he'd help create. The same one he now was about to extinguish. He patted her stomach and began trembling all over, his weeping returned.

"I'm so sorry, Marnie…My baby…My sweet baby girl, I'm so, so sorry," with that, he leaned into the window jam and began shoving with all he had. The car lurched forward on the small decline and went on its way. Hutch covered her mouth and stepped away in shock and disgust. She couldn't bear to witness the fall. A tyrannical sound exploded as the car hit the water below, nose first, and was consumed by shades of lonesome sapphire. Her father just stood there for a moment, his face permanently locked into the bowels of melancholy; A sadness beyond any scope Hutch had ever seen consume that man's face.

Within a few minutes, he turned round and walked like the zombie he'd become, back down through the beaten path. Hutch watched him till he disappeared from sight and then she edged herself back to the sheer face of the cliff ahead. She peered over in hesitant horror, witnessing the dance of bubbles on the surface still boiling from where the car had made its journey to the depths below. A few moments later, she fell to her bottom, staring out through the treetops to the forest beyond. Her mind was so numb right then. The terrible events that had just taken place played on a loop over and over inside her head. It was almost too much for one human to take in all at once. Her father was a murderer…many times over. And what hit her almost as hard as seeing the death of Regina was the fact that she had a half-sister, and as far as she knew, she was still at the bottom of that watery pit. Hutch's somber stare across the skyline slowly began to focus on the sun across the way. It burned brightly below the clouds and suddenly consumed everything around her.

A flash of light and a gasping breath later, she was right back to reality, back at the finish line of Leviathan. She quickly jerked her hand away from Regina's and looked around, confused for a moment from the transition, but then it came flooding back once again. She glared at her father.

"You're a monster…" she let out, trying to hold back her tears.

"Pooj…I don't know what she showed ya, but ya can't believe it. It ain't real."

"Did ya send Aunt Cass off the edge of that cliff in her car? Did ya pin a carnation on her too?! Did she sink ta the bottom right on top of her and my dead sister?!" Hutch went into hysterics, pointing at Regina.

"Pooj…I…"

"Why? What did Aunt Cass do?"

"She found out what he was…She was going to turn him in. And you now know what happens to people who find out his dirty, little secrets," Regina spoke for him. They both looked at him with loathing in their hearts. That same fire Hutch saw in her father's eyes when he murdered Regina, rekindled at the moment. He went off.

"Okay! I'm a murderer! A filthy, cold-blooded killer! Is that want ya want ta hear?! All those women…I had to kill them. It was the only way for me to feel alive," he began to calm down, but he trembled as he pointed at Regina, "You. You were different. I sniffed ya out at that race and had my carnation ready for you that night, but…but somethin' happened. You were different. Ya changed me. Ya made me feel alive, Ree….I'm so sorry."

"You keep saying that, Harvey, but I don't think you know what it really means," Regina shook her head.

"All of this…this shit show, McCray McCurse month, almost all of it has been because of what you did," Hutch spoke out. Her father had nothing to say. The redhead turned towards Regina. "And you…you lied ta me. Over and over again. Ya used me ta get back at him. Ya used my aunt's memory ta get your revenge." Hutch shook her head and pointed at her father. "He's worse than you, but you're comin' in a close second." The hurt and disappointment was painted in bitter shades across the redhead's face. Regina felt ashamed beyond comprehension.

"I'm so sorry, Red."

"Are you sure ya know what that really means?"

The brunette looked down. She didn't know what else to say. Hutch shook her head once again and put her hand to her chest. A magnificent light exploded forth as she withdrew the feather from her flesh. She walked over to Regina and bent down.

"Here, I owe ya this. I keep my promises. It's yours now."

The brunette looked up with a pitiful expression. She gently plucked the feather from Hutch's hand and watched her turn and walk away.

"Red?" Regina spoke. Hutch turned around. The brunette went on, "I love you." Hutch just shook her head and turned back around without saying a word. Izzy, Diesel, and Hieronymus were all still standing at the finish line waiting for her.

"Well? What now, girly? We goin' home?" Diesel asked.

"I don't know...maybe."

"It's okay, hun. Even if we don't, we still got each other right?" Izzy said, taking Hutch by the hand. Hutch looked at her little green hand and smiled a bit.

"Yeah, I guess so."

Suddenly, she couldn't feel Izzy's grasp any longer. The demon's hand fell away from hers and they both looked at one another in shock as Hutch's hand began to disappear right before their eyes. The redhead looked to her other hand. It too began to fade away, tracing up her arm under a blue light that burned away like a fuse.

"Diesel, what's happenin' ta her?" Izzy spoke in panic. The yellow demon couldn't speak. He just watched as Hieronymus smiled beside him. Hutch's panic deepened, she spun round to look at Regina as her body was engulfed into nothing, disappearing all the more.

"Oh my god...it can't be," Regina said as she stared with fearing awe. And just like that, Hutch was gone. Not a trace of her remained.

A spiraling force, not unlike the one that had driven her to the pit, engulfed Hutch. Like the whole scenario was being played in reverse, she could feel herself ascending through abstracts of light and then…darkness. A pain returned. Her bones ached along with her head as she gathered the strength to try and open her eyes. All she could hear was a steady beep in the background and the sound of her own whimpering moan as she opened her gaze. Her eyes squinted under a blinding light haloed by a bright white ceiling. Her brow wrinkled in confusion. She tried to move, but it hurt too much. Everything was tight and uncomfortable.

"Jesus…what the hell?" She groaned.

"Hutch?" A familiar voice called out to her. Hutch's heart skipped a beat.

"…Ham?" She slowly found the strength to turn and look to the side. She saw the white sheets and cold walls of a hospital room. And amongst it all, was her brother's thankful and smiling face.

"My god, you're awake," he said. He yelled over his shoulder, "Hey, she's awake!"

"Wha…what? What happened?"

"You don't remember? You were in a hell of an accident. Three semis? Ring any bells? Jesus, Hutch, they thought you were dead when they finally cut through all that steel."

"I…Wha? So…So I'm alive?"

"You sure are," Ham grabbed her hand and squeezed.

"But...but I was dead. I was…I was in…"

"Where? Heaven? Ha! Don't go tellin' me ya had one of those near death experiences? You always said those were bullshit."

"I…never mind," she said as she tried getting up. She clenched her teeth in pain.

"Now, now. Just rest, okay? Hutch you took a beatin'. You're lucky you ain't dead."

"Shit…What's the damage?"

"Well, right arms broke, left legs broke. Several ribs broke. You got some blown discs. Whiplash. Concussion."

"Jesus…So I'm basically hamburger meat that someone taught how to speak?"

Ham couldn't help but laugh a bit.

"Oh, it ain't that bad. They said you're lucky ya didn't get paralyzed."

"Yay, me….How long've I been out?"

"Bout a month."

"Damn…well at least it ain't July anymore."

"I know. McCray McCurse strikes again, I guess."

Hutch sighed,

"I think that's all over with."

"Oh, it is? How ya know?"

"I just got me a feelin'."

There was a moment of silence between them. Hutch laid there and stared at the ceiling for a moment, her body was beaten and broken, but at least she was home and, for that, she was thankful.

"Hutch?" Ham finally broke the silence. She looked at him and he just let it out, "Dad's dead."

The red head turned back to look at the ceiling once more. She sighed.

"I know."

Everything is Kinda Alright

Days passed and then months. Pain was a way of life for quite some time for Hutch. Between breaking her driving restrictions and a slew of fresh charges for racing on the interstate, life wasn't looking so upbeat. But it was life. She was ALIVE and that's all that mattered. The rest she could deal with. Rehab also became a way of life. Not only AA but more importantly her physical rehab. But bones heal. The broken heart she carried with her was another matter entirely. Before long, she was back to her little trailer and living the same life she had before her trip to Hell. And it was okay. She finally got rid of her crutches and was soon back to work at the Gingerbread House. The accident had given her a nice, new limp in her walk. Finally Hank and her had something in common other than their tempers. Speaking of Hank, he was so happy his only sister made it out of the car crash alive, that he went and got Ruby out of the impound for her as a coming home present. The very next night, she drove that car out into the middle of a corn field, doused her in gasoline, and set her ablaze. She told Hank and the police someone had stolen it and tried to look as sad as possible when she did so. Hank suspicioned it was the same kids that drew dicks on the shop truck back in July, but no one was ever caught.

More months past. The winter came and went and so came spring. Anonymous letters arrived at the Dillon county police department and to the regional office of the FBI containing troubling, new tips to the possible whereabouts of Cassandra McCray. Months later a contracted dive team was sent to the back pit of the Starnes surface mines to search on the tip from the letters. A crane retrieved multiple cars from almost two-hundred feet down in the somber depths of the blue pool. A 1970 Chevelle. A 1967 Ford Mustang Fastback, and a 1968 Mercury Cougar. The body of an adult male, later to be identified as Sid Caldwell, Cassandra McCray, and an unidentified infant were among the bodies found in the vehicles. An immediate investigation was launched upon the findings. But Hutch knew nothing would come if it. As badly as she hated her father, even in death, she knew there was simply not enough evidence to convict him in the deaths of the pool or the deaths of the women he'd slain so many years ago. It would literally be her word on trial and she doubted the jury would accept the ramblings of an alcoholic drag racer who was shown Harvey McCray's guilt through a vision a demon had walked her through. Honestly, she wasn't sure even that if the evidence was there she'd even do anything with it. The man was dead and he couldn't pay for his sins anymore than he was now. Besides, she had a sneaking suspicion that Hank was to blame for Sid's death. And as much as she didn't like him, she wasn't going to send her brother to jail over the death of that asshole.

Cassandra was finally given a proper sending away and a burial in the family plot outside Danbridge; a few steps away from Harvey and Henry's final resting places. Hutch couldn't believe the amount of people who showed up to the funeral. Drag racers, bikers, the entire bunch that made up the underground racing circuit, all walks of life, they showed up to pay their final respects to a woman who'd obviously touched more lives than Hutch could've imagined. Hutch went to visit her aunt's grave often. Mostly when she was legally allowed to; when she was driving the shop truck for deliveries and the like. Her trial for her slew of new counts was still months off but it loomed like the creeping black dread it was. She was probably going back to jail no doubt. But what she couldn't figure out was if being in Hell was better than going back to jail. At least in Hell she had three friends to keep her company. Oh, how she missed that band of misfits.

In the beginning of June, Ham handed Hutch a letter that was amongst the shop's mail pile. It had no return address, but there was a handwritten letter inside of it, scrawled in beautiful bubbly letters.

Dear Hutch,

Writing to you to let you know that we're alright. There ain't a day that goes by that we don't think of you and what you did for us. We wanted to visit you, but thought it best to give you some time to process it all. When you're ready, come out west and see us. It's beautiful out here. Lying on the beach beats the hell out of mining firerite,

Love,
Isabelle and Danny

Hutch's heart melted as she put a hand to her mouth and looked at an attached Polaroid picture in the envelope. It was a lanky, bikini clad gal in her early twenties smiling wide amongst a head of gorgeous chestnut brown hair. She was sitting with her butt in the sand of a beautiful beach with a gruff looking middle-aged man beside her in a lawn chair. He held up a beer towards the camera with half a smile crowning his big, beard covered chin. In permanent marker was written *"Another "rough" day in Marina Del Ray"* at the bottom of the photo. The redhead's smile nearly cracked her face as a tear of happiness ran down her cheek. They had made it. Well, two of them had. The letter left her wondering just what ever became of the little, blue demon that had handed her that feather. In the end, she shook her head of it and just simply hoped he was out there somewhere living his dream like Izzy and Diesel. With love, she pinned the picture on her wall, yearning for the day she'd be able to go and visit them. Regina had kept her promise….Regina. Regina Redgrace… the exiled princess of Level 12…Hutch couldn't help but wonder what happened to her. She still thought of her every, single day…and, every night, she danced through her dreams. That little golden-eyed beauty would always be a fire Hutch couldn't put out.

July rolled back round, and with it, came the same old apprehensions among the McCray clan. Everyone seemed to be keeping a quiet bet on who was getting sick, getting killed, or going to jail. Everyone except Hutch, anyway. The very first morning of the month she spent at the graveyard, repeating the

same old actions as the visits before. She stood there, wildflowers
in hand, staring down at Cass's headstone. The first few times
she'd come, she talked away to the stone as if her aunt were there,
but now she was just silent. Maybe she'd run out of things to
say…or maybe there was a part of her that just felt dumb for
talking to a piece of granite. She kneeled down and removed the
old, dried out flowers from before and replaced them with fresh
ones. A huff and sigh rolled from her lips as the pain of her hip and
leg surged while she rose back to her feet…a reminder of the hell
she'd been through nearly one year ago. She put her hand on her
hips, her eyes squinting in the unforgiving glare of the summer
sun. Suddenly, the sound of a vehicle emerged from behind. The
redhead paid it no mind at first, she didn't even bother to turn
around until the pinging of the gravel beneath tires came
uncomfortably close. The car idled down and Hutch's ears tuned
into the clicking of the cams and the rumble of the exhaust.
Something was dreadfully familiar. The engine cut off and she
spun around to see a short brunette climbing out of an ivory
Cougar. Hutch's breath left her and her heart pounded so hard she
felt as if she were going to pass out right then and there. A crooked
smile spread out below huge sunglasses as Regina walked through
the gravel drive. She'd traded in her signature pantsuit for a floppy,
wide brimmed summer hat and a beautiful sundress that swished
along the curves of her body as she traipsed ever-forward to where
Hutch waited in utter disbelief. At first she thought she was seeing
a ghost, a taunting specter from the past, but then the supposed
apparition stopped a pace away and spoke.

"You're a hard girl to track down, you know that?"

Hutch fought off a smile.

"I am?"

"Umm, no. You're still living in a camper in the back of a truck
stop parking lot," she joked.

Hutch blushed and shook her head.

"Where ya been?"

"Oh, ya know, Red…around."

"I thought ya were…I don't know what I thought."

"Dead? In the pit? Or maybe you thought I was just a figment of
your imagination? A spooky ghost." The brunette grinned as she
wriggled her fingers in the air. "Let's just say the pit has a new

furnace master." She then walked on by Hutch and stood there at the edge of the grass. Her eyes panned the McCray family plot, viewing Hutch's grandparents graves, Harvey's and Henry's... and then finally to a small, out of place stone, right beside Cass's grave marker. Regina's smile erased as she read the name on the face of the granite. "Marnie" An uncontrolled wave of sorrow hit her as she fell to her knees and began to weep. Hutch walked up behind her.

"I knew they wouldn't let me claim her body, but I figure she needed ta be remembered."

Regina said nothing. She couldn't. She kept sobbing till her tears ran off her cheeks and pattered down between the curves in her daughter's name. A small tear came as Hutch's lip curled. She rubbed Regina lovingly on the shoulder.

"I'm sorry."

Regina quickly rose up.

"No...I'm sorry for everything I did to you." She took off her sunglasses and began wiping her cheeks. Hutch's eyes widened as she brushed a gentle finger on the brunette's cheek, looking with wonder into her eyes. They were blue.

"Ya...your eyes..."

Regina nodded and sniffled.

"My eyes. I'm human, Red...again. And the grass has never smelled so fresh and the sun has never felt so magnificent on my skin."

"The feather...that's what it does," Hutch thought aloud.

"Yep...That's what the other one did for me years ago. But there's always a little pinch of it left over after the transition..." she spoke as she dug though her dress and then revealed the feather from the pit. It glowed with a weak aura and was nearly translucent, like a delicate piece of holy glass. Hutch eyed it in wonder for a moment and Regina once again spoke. "Yeah, they always have juuuust enough power leftover to...say heal someone." She then pressed the feather into the redhead's hand and watched it disappear into her flesh. Hutch gasped and clenched her teeth as a horrible pain overtook all her joints, radiating with a hum between her ears. She collapsed to her knees into the gravel. The feeling of agony soon melted into normality as Hutch quickly realized every ache in her bones from her injuries were gone.

Whisked away into nothingness. The feeling was so familiar. She felt like a teenager again. She looked up with awe into Regina's eyes. The brunette smiled and placed a loving hand under her chin as she spoke,

"Everything is gonna be okay, toots."

The past came flooding back to Hutch. Tears began streaming down her cheek.

"It was you. You cured my cancer. You were my angel."

"It was me," she grinned as she removed her giant hat.

Hutch leaned forwards and wrapped her arms tightly around the tiny brunette, burying her face into the top of hers. They stayed that way for quite a moment in time till Hutch finally released and stepped back. Regina reached out and squeezed her hand.

"You know when I said I loved you, I meant it."

"Me too…" Hutch smiled.

Regina's beautiful eyes danced as she laughed, chasing off the sorrow from her tear stained cheeks.

"Well, c'mon, Red. Let's go home."

"Where's home?

"Wherever we want, babe. Wherever we want."

THE END?

"Roxy, you knock that off!" Lloyd Romine swatted at his dog in admonishment. The rottweiler slinked off as a man stepped closer through the gate of Riverside; his chrome-mirrored glasses reflected the acres of cars that lie before him.

"Sorry bout that…she usually don't act that way. Old age, I guess," Lloyd smiled a bit.

"Naw, it ain't old age. She's a woman. They're all fussy no matter the species."

Old Lloyd just chuckled at the remark. He spoke,

"So, what can I do for ya today? Lookin' for a part?"

"A whole car, actually."

"Well, rumor is, I gotta few of those hangin' round," Lloyd grinned as he chewed on his cigar.

"So, I heard…Lookin' for a 67' Firebird. Ya gotta animal hidin' round here like that?"

Lloyd's eyebrow rose.

"Buddy, you ain't gonna believe this but I got one in awhile back. Still got er'."

"Perfect."

"Welllll…not so much. She's purty beat up. Someone took the name a little too seriously and actually sat this Firebird on fire. She's purty roasted."

"Even better, I like a gal with some character an' a story." The stranger smiled and pulled of his sunglasses.

Old Lloyd went ghost-white. His mouth twitched at the corner.

"Somethin' wrong?" The man asked.

"I…Jesus…sorry. You are the spittin' image of someone I used ta know. Well, when he was younger. He actually passed away last year. Poor bastard. You might know em'. Name was Harvey McCray."

The man shook his head and placed his sunglasses back on with confidence.

"Harvey McCray?...Hmmm, never heard of em'…now, about that Firebird."

Old Lloyd didn't even answer, his attention was now trapped by another man that came walking up beside the first. There was an odd aura about him, even the dog sensed it.

"Roxy?! Hey! Get back here! Ahhh, hell," the junk-man yelled as he watched his dog run and hide amongst the broken cars. He turned back round, shaking his head. Both the men stood there, stoic, staring at him with a darkness Lloyd could almost feel in his bones. He tried to brush it off.

"How bout you friend? You lookin' for a car too?"

"Maybe…Was mainly along for the ride, but I'm kinda partial to Chevelles, myself," his voice sent a chill up the junk-man's spine.

"That a fact? Well, I might have one kickin' around here somewhere, Misssster?..."

"Caldwell…name's Caldwell."

Made in the USA
Columbia, SC
07 June 2022